Damn! Three long years of razor wire fences, brick walls, steel bars and pork noodle casserole. Three summers where heat exhaustion served as imminent ridicule. The monotony of prison atmosphere allowed three birthdays to sweep by undetected. (Even my 21st birthday that was spent on a prison transient bus). The only day that held substance the past 1,094 days is called, tomorrow.

"Lookout Izzy B," was the phrase I heard as my cellmate, Maserati Rick came trotting up the stairs to our second-floor *penthouse suite*. Maserati Rick made constant allegations that he had connections for anything on the east coast; but ended up being my '*roommate*' for the past ten months for slapping his fourth *baby mama* cousin. Using my best judgment, Rick is around 33 years old but has been on parole for the same case almost two decades. I should have played sleep because I already knew his *ass* is about to come sell me a dream.

"Yooo wake up man. This is your last night in the *bink*," I defiantly tried to cancel out Maserati Rick's animated voice that was projected towards me. His overall approach would leave you with the impression that he was raised by con artists. I can picture him downtown, at the Lexington Market, trying to sell expired metro passes and daycare vouchers.

"Yooo what's good *Sun*," I lethargically tell him.

"Man get your *ass* up. Your about to be back out there with the butt naked smuts, dimes of loud and chicken boxes. Get your *mind right* man, I am trying to make you a millionaire when I get out in a few months."

Knew this fool was going to devise a way to create a dream. He had to be a pimp in his past life. His reference was not easily hidden on his part. Just like everyone else, Maserati Rick wanted me to *hop* back in the *rap game.*

"Ayooo I hear that but fuck that shit. I must get out and take care of my daughter and my *shorty*. By any means and everything else is obsolete," I retort back with a mild temper. When it pertains to me, Rick knows what conversations should be dissipated. But not today!

"Say listen chief, I've been around the block a few times and I know mainstream potential when I hear it. You almost made it before, why not keep pushing?"

There was a moment of silence.

"That's crazy kid," he resumed his second attempt at conquering a conversation starter. I felt the urge to interrupt him before this turned in an hour-long speech.

"Well, shit man life's crazy. That is just how it is. Besides the *rap game* is composed of a bunch of weak *niggas* who do not practice what they spit. I don't want to be surrounded by them anyway."

Apart of me wanted to take back that last part of my statement; while somewhere deep down inside, there is a fire still burning. For what reason, I do not know. But the feeling started to surface once the reality hit me that I am going to be a free man once I wake up. *Yeah*, I had dreams of one day being the greatest rapper alive. But that is all they were, childhood dreams. I must get out and support my family- plus avoid the *knockaz* to prevent coming back here. I missed my opportunity, so what. Just like the rest of the "*hot*" rappers to come out the city, where are they at now?

For the first few days after my release, it is going to be awkward not having to be awoken by Rick brushing his one gold tooth before sunrise. For what it is worth, I am for sure not coming back here. But according to statistics and the recidivism rate, a young black man in my position making that assumption; it would be deemed false. I guess I must figure out where that line of true and false are double-crossed. Before I spend another night in jail, the *narcs* are going to have to shoot it out with me. *Word to my daughter.*

"Kid," Maserati Rick starts off, trying to find the best alternative to get his point across.

"And I don't mean kid in the literal sense," he continues. "But your philosophy and logic on the future is on some kiddie shit. I found no traces of *grown man shit* in your oracle. If you are not going to shoot for the top then you might as well go shoot a cop. At least we will be able to finish this conversation in a few days while you are facing 15 to life. Take some responsibility for your future."

Throughout the couple of seconds where I am mind-fucking myself, the pause between us was filled with the sound of keys jingling in the background. Indicating a CO is on his way around to conduct one of the three normal daily head count times.

"Isaiah Brown, 21217-410. Records indicate that your mark of emancipation and liberation is commenced for the morning," one of the *trusted* officers named Davis projects loud enough for the whole prison wing to hear.

In the next millennium when the soul of Izzy B is resuscitated; it'll also be that rare occasion when he positively interacts with someone yielding a government-issued badge. But recurring loyalty has been demonstrated by Officer Davis with weekly deliveries of cigarettes, weed and an occasional cell phone. With Davis being only two years older than me and from the Cherry Hill projects, he is usually our most reliable source for information about what is going on out there in the city streets.

Once my identity had infected the minds of everyone in my prison facility about what I had done that lead to my three years in confinement; Davis had always tried to degrade his position around me and make it seem like he was one of *us*. It was because he recognized me from one of the City versus Poly homecoming games a few years back. Or maybe because *word* got around Baltimore's inner circle that Mister Popular used to dog out his little sister. My guess would be the latter. Whatever the case, to Davis, in his mind I was labeled as one of Baltimore's elite young niggas.

"So, what are you going to do when you get out Izzy?," Officer Davis nonchalantly asks me. It does not even bother me that he calls me by my street name. *Still, I must ask myself, why the fuck does he care?*

"Shit, there's only one sensible thing to do and that's grind," I begin to tell him. "Damn sure can't apply to become a correctional officer. Niggas respect me too much on the avenue."

Unexpectedly, Rick and Davis begin to laugh like my comment was meant to be a joke. Too bad I was *dead serious*.

A lot of the youth and young adults from East Baltimore would at least recognize me, if they have not witnessed me individually. I have been causing hell from Loch Raven Boulevard to Highlandtown since Tupac was asking the world, *How Do You Want It*. My *born date* was even far from customary since my mother couldn't make it all the way to Johns Hopkins Hospital; thus, giving birth to me at The NorthEast Market. So, you could factually classify me as being an *eastside nigga*.

From the way I surprisingly graduated from Patterson High School to my one and only *mixtape* played on every stereo from Greenmount to Douglas; a lot of people where I am from would call me "*that nigga.*" Well, before I got locked up, that is. Now my future is destined to be filled with either hollow tips, crack vials, a ski mask, or the repetitive motion of clocking in and out of a bullshit Job. Life must have better options. *Oh wait*, I forgot being a correctional officer to get cool with the mediocre dope boys that Baltimore City has to offer. And that is a negative.

"Yooo, you should drop a part two to that *'Eastside Takeover',*" Officer Davis expresses in a semi-serious tone. "Like a *just got home*, still on top of the game and your chick type joint. Niggas are going to feel that for real. There is not anyone else coming out the city except Mister Popular fraud ass. And you know, like I know, he isn't even allowed in the hood anymore."

After I hear Mister Popular' name mentioned, my thoughts were diverted to my *rhymebooks*, the showcase, the Budweiser bottle, book-in and for the past three years being identified by an eight-digit number. Last thing on my mind was to drop another mixtape. I voice my opinion though and made it perfectly clear to not only Maserati Rick, but Officer Davis also.

"Fuck Mister Popular, Fuck Felix Stone and Fuck Supreme Records. Ayooo, I didn't even expect that 'Eastside Takeover' to boom citywide like it did."

Fabrication. I was really anticipating for the mixtape to be jammed nationwide. Or at least the whole DC, Maryland, and Virginia area. Crazy, because one of my main songs ended up on a mixtape that a bunch of Virginia DJ's put together. The recognition caught me by surprise since Baltimore and *DMV* niggas do not mix.

"Say *money*, that mixtape was created over a two-week period. Me and the crew came up on a half-pound of sour diesel and some beats. As a result, 'Eastside Takeover' was made. Nothing more, nothing less. I cannot allow myself to believe that I can make a living and survive off a recreational hobby. Get real *Sun*," I add in to finish getting my point across.

"Well, I don't know if it means anything to you, but if niggas way out Cherry Hill was jamming your shit, you must be *live*," Officer Davis says. "We all thought you were going to be the face of the city, not Mister Popular."

"That's what I been trying to tell *shorty* but he too stubborn. I haven't even heard the mixtape but based off the reactions in here, I know it had to be monumental," Maserati Rick squelched his unsolicited opinion. He does not even attempt to look up while he is speaking. He seems to be looking at some sort of article. Like a cut out of the *Baltimore Sun* newspaper.

As Officer Davis is walking down the *run* to finish his head count, Maserati Rick hands me the article.

"Ayooo, I want you to read this so you can understand what's really going on. It's about to get real tomorrow," he says. As I reluctantly grab the article, I notice the picture of a young-looking black guy. It has two dates under his name symbolizing a birth and death. I come to realize that it is a recently printed obituary.

I was trying to avoid the awareness or rather, the direct cause of why I suddenly got the chills. Possibly because this guy was only three years younger than me. Or maybe because his past existence seems a little too familiar. But I just cannot put my finger on it. *"Oh wait,"* I silently think to myself. This nigga is from my *hood*.

After my memory banks were rummaged, commemoration was achieved. Before I got *jammed up*, I used to see shorty hooping down in the Latrobe Projects. He used to *talk shit* saying he was going to be the next Sam Cassell or Carmelo Anthony. Word *around the way* was that local universities like Towson, Morgan State and Georgetown were feuding over who gets to assign him to their roster. I look over the report to find out the truth about the incident:

"Ronnie Woods, 20, junior at Saint John's University was tragically gunned down in his native East Baltimore neighborhood. Ronnie was actively enrolled at Saint Johns on a basketball scholarship when he briefly returned to Baltimore to witness the birth of his child; subsequently leading to the questionable motive behind his murder. Locals say his death was stemmed from an argument with an

unknown person. Any other valuable information seemed to be forcefully upheld by the witnesses. Police currently have no leads…"

I stop reading right there. That is why I rarely watch the news or read the newspaper. Always something fucked up happening. Crazy because he found a way *out*. Found his route to the top. Got faraway from here. I cannot pinpoint exactly where Saint Johns is at, but I know it is nowhere near Baltimore City.

"Fucked up, isn't it?" Maserati Rick asks me as I hand him back the article.

"Hell yeah, but you know how it is out there," I tell him. I assume this was not the desired reaction he expected. "It is not like this is the first time, someone young with potential was *bodied* before their time. If I would have had a gun on me the night of the showcase, well, let's just say I will be here for a different charge."

Officer Davis is making his way back down the row, towards the stairs, when he stops by our cell again.

"Ayo Izzy, dig this..." Officer Davis begins.

"My relative just opened a studio down Cherry Hill, off Potee Street. If you ever want to get serious and check it out, go down there and ask for Protégé. Tell him Dirty Dee sent you. *Word is bond*, it is a pretty dope set up. You'll like it. You have nothing to lose and everything to gain. I can put you in the *door* for free. All you have to do is come down to the projects and..."

I immediately must interrupt him because I do not speak Gibberish. This nigga cannot expect me, an *eastside nigga*, to randomly show up in some *projects* in South Baltimore. (Knowing that damn near every side of Baltimore beef with each other.)

I can count on my fingers how many times I have been to the Westside and the only thing that separates us is the freeway. I have been to South Baltimore a few times in my life. The main things that strike a memory is going under tunnels and crossing water to get there.

"Yoo lookout Dirty Dee," I say sarcastically. "I don't think there's a good chance of that happening. I am from '*Ova East*.' Nigga like me is going to stand out."

"So, and what's wrong with standing out shorty," Maserati Rick chimes in. I do not believe he is expecting an answer. As I peek out my peripheral, I see this nigga *picking* his nose while still reading this torn up newspaper. "*I don't even think God can bring this fool back down to reality*," I say to myself. It is like he has a syringe filled with life and that is his constant high.

"True that." Officer Davis starts up from where I cut him off.

"I don't think you understand how many *motherfuckers* know who you are out there in the city. It will blow your mind how much love you had out there on the microphone. Besides, why you trying to hide from your past shorty?"

His assumption makes me angry and comical at the same time.

"Who the fuck running from the past?" I say. "If anything, I'm trying embrace the future. I either see me taking over the Luzerne block or have some hoes sell pussy for me off Baltimore Street. I'm going to leave the

16 bars and ad-libs for them radio niggas." I add in with a devilish laugh.

I was really looking forward to hearing some of Maserati Rick's twisted insight. Either something he read from this week's horoscope in the newspaper or something he memorized from the *Five Percenters* his last time in prison. Instead, I watch him casually wipe his boogers on his clothes. Typically, this may be viewed as trifling; but there is no prison etiquette on the clothes. Shit, we get a free pair every day. A thought goes through my mind as I picture myself in a pair of True Religions and Polo boots. A smile is cemented across my face as I think about my release.

"There isn't any reasoning to these new wave *Alley Boyz*. No compromise and no plans for the future," I hear as my concentration is broken. Based on the hoarseness of the voice, that sounds like it has been altered by decades of Newport smoke, I knew it had to be Maserati Rick.

Alley Boyz are what a lot of old school niggas call *young cats* like me on the eastside. A category that fits if you are pumping dope or jacking. I have no problem doing both, but I prefer to stay on the block, jamming all day. Coming up, I was always in the spotlight around my way. So, jacking niggas was always out the question. Unless, of course, they were from another hood then its fair game. I live to see the look on a westside nigga face when he knows he is getting robbed by someone from *Down The Hill*.

As Officer Davis is about to walk away, he stops and back petals as if he must clarify my existence. I began to get suspicious because of his sudden pause until his request surprises me even more.

"Ayooo, I'm not a groupie; I don't want your autograph or nothing. But say, spit that 16 you did on *'Bmore Careful'* and I will be on my way," he says to me. Almost instantly, Maserati Rick adds his *"two cents"* in about how he has been wanting to hear what all the hype was about.

For a moment, I am speechless. Caught totally off guard. For the past ten months, Maserati Rick has never asked me to rap for him. His view on my potential was solely based on word of mouth. My *celly* before him was a Dominican cat on his way to the Feds. So, some young *hoppers* rap dream never piqued his interests.

For the past three years, I have been trying to avoid the inevitable. A subject that I knew was going to arise either in the jail or once I touchdown.

While I was going through the trial process, I thought I was going to get more time than I received; so, announcing my street creditability never crossed my mind. When I was in the waiting room for sentencing, there was a high school kid from the Park Heights Community who swore he knew me. I repeatedly reiterated the fact that he had me mistaken. Him, being from Park Heights, which is one of the largest '*hoods* on the Westside and a 45-minute drive from where I'm from; it was easy to persuade him that he had me mixed up with someone else.

But in the matter of truth, I knew this was not a case of mistaken identity. No matter how humble I tried to come off in order to mask my anger or how disappointed the humiliation caused me three years ago; the truth remains and will always be considered the truth. That everyone who has recognized me since I been in jail, knows me by the same alias.

Izzy B. The rapper. Eastside nigga. One of the hardest flows to ever come out of Baltimore City.

"Oh wait, isn't that shorty who tried to off Mister Popular awhile back?," people would say once they mention my name.

Truthfully, I would rather have the streets remember me for the assault then being some up-and-coming rapper who never made it. I do not know what hurts more; my pride, the constant reminder of who I once was or the headache I have now, trying to decide if I am going to spit this 16 or not.

Whether or not if I have a solid plan for my future, I know that I can shape it starting tomorrow. The two pairs of eyes that are patiently waiting to hear my voice has me thinking of the alternative. Logically or illogically, I still cannot deny the truth.

So, fuck it, what the hell… I will give them what they want. I recall the lyrics, rhythm, and style I possessed three years ago. While I was preparing my delivery, I never noticed there were other inmates listening to our conversation. Apparently, the past 15 minutes with Maserati Rick and Officer Davis has the same substance that other inmates wanted to express to me. But I never allowed them the chance to get that close.

But here we are, the moment they all been waiting for. *Streets always taught me to go hard to finish what you started. So, fuck it. I gave the people what they want. And the result was priceless…*

Chapter 2

The recollection still haunts me like it was yesterday. *Three years ago.* It was a brisk, spring afternoon. The streets had been recovering from a massive blizzard that *hit* back in February. But now with the city clear and ready to make way for summer, every *block* slowly became a sauna. There were strings of murders, robberies, and burglaries from the east to the west. Baltimore Police did not have enough *laws* to patrol the numerous dangerous strips that gave Charm City its nickname. When all you are accustomed to is a rising crime rate, the effects really do not bother you. I still operated how I normally would. *Nothing stopped me from doing me.*

During this time, I lived with my mother in a rowhouse off Broadway. Just walking distance from the Somerset Projects. Once my girlfriend of six years, Sidney, got pregnant with my daughter, Stacy; she moved in with us also. Me and Sidney started *fucking around freshman year at Patterson High and immediately fell in love. The only chick I ever gave my heart to.* She kept it loyal since day one, which is rare when you are always surrounded by these scandalous city *hoes*. I noticed something different, something special about her. She did not carry herself like the normal car-hopping female from Monument Street. So, in return, I fed her my mind and allowed her to ride it out with me. *Felt good to grind it out and have something to come home to.*

Growing up, there was always this singular responsibility in particular that I always blamed myself for. It was my mothers' heroin addiction. Like maybe if I got better grades, mama scars on her arm would go away. Or, if I were home before the streetlights came on, mama would not puke her guts out at night. But once all these attempts failed, I realized it was not me. It was the streets. The streets had a particular hold on her that rehab, probation or a wavering son could not fix. All that mattered was "the fix" for her. Sometimes appliances would come up missing, clothing would come up missing or my mother would come up missing. Luckily for me, my Uncle Lenny lived not too far away off Fayette Street. When I was younger, I would suggest we call the police to find her. But he always told me, "don't worry about it, she'll find her way back home." This always turned out to be true. I always suspected my Uncle Lenny to be shooting smack also, but he never offered any proof. He always kept his bills paid and remained reliable.

After I graduated, my mother made a turn for the worst. There were often times I was called down to the hospital or police station to identify her. During her detox, she would swear *up and down* that she was alright and that we were the ones blowing her situation out of proportion. It was sad, but her circumstance never deferred me from dealing drugs myself. It was not an everyday thing, but when money was needed, *I did what I had to do.*

It was not long before me and my Uncle Lenny got tired of my mothers' shit. Along with the stress of my girlfriend being pregnant, I should not have had to trace my mothers' whereabouts and behavior. So, we ended up placing her in *The Water Shed Rehabilitation Center for Women*. To my surprise, she started to get better.

For the first time, retrospectively speaking, my mother was finally shaking her sickness. Her addiction. We were able to have normal conversations now.

She would stay enrolled in the detox program for at least six months at a time. Once my daughter was born, me and Sidney would visit her on the regular. Sometimes when I am in the area, I would stop by unannounced to *holla* at her. We would casually talk about her plans once she is clean and back in the streets. But talking about her plans never excited her, it was my aspirations that she wanted to hear about.

I precisely remember the day I told her that I wanted to pursue my rap career. It was shortly after my daughter, Stacy, was born. Besides seeing her first grandchild, I have never seen my mothers' face light up the way it did, while I was telling her where my time was dedicated to. I told her I wanted to get the family out of the city. For us to move into a big house in the *county somewhere*. She was part of my motivation. To get my one-and-only mother off these streets. After I told her my goals, she would always push me to do better. She always believed in me and became my number one supporter. That day, she looked me in the eyes and promised that she was going to *get right*. For her granddaughter and for me.

According to my mom, she is going to be present when I accept my *Grammy* and blow up on the *Billboard* charts. Her confidence regarding my talent was always higher than mine.

For the next two years, I noticed my mother was trying her best to keep that promise. *It was hard though when your weakness is exploited every time you step outside*. Nonetheless, whenever she used or felt the urge to use, she would check herself back into The Water Shed. *So, I was proud of her in that aspect.*

-#-

This day, three years ago, it seemed like an average day in East Baltimore. Mother had been at The Water Shed for about four months now, making this trip her fourth visit. Sidney and Stacy were guests to a family cookout in Dundalk. Despite the puzzling awkwardness of Sidney's family having a *shing ding* on a Thursday in late March; the affair did not register as a surprise since her family was renowned for *random seafood brawls*. April Fool's Day meant *Crab Fest*. Rosh Hashanah meant *Shrimp Broiler*. And the Juneteenth was reserved for an all-out *Chesapeake Bay Buffet*.

They loved Maryland snow crabs. Sidney would crave these blue creatures at least three days out of the week.

I would have attended the occasion as well, but the Supreme Records Talent Showcase was less than 24 hours away and this was my *moment of truth*.

Based on the responses that '*Eastside Takeover*' had spawned throughout the streets, I knew without trouble that this was the big break I needed. First place winner would receive a record contract with his label. First place was the only position I will accept, and I was not set on taking any losses. Furthermore, this was the opportunity that me and my mother spoke about two years earlier at The Water Shed. *I could not let her down. I could not let Sidney and Stacy down. I could not let my city down.*

Nothing seemed out of order, in fact, everything was in place as I entered my mother's rowhouse. I walked into the kitchen anticipating finding a pitcher of invisible Kool Aid in the fridge, only to find a bottle of apple juice. *"Baby mama sure know how to make anguished, but got to love her,"* I was thinking to myself. Suddenly, I notice an unknown cool breeze coming through the window. A breeze that I would not have felt this morning. Something was not right.

There was a mini stand that we had positioned by the window to enforce the stability of our air conditioning unit. But for some strange reason, our air conditioning unit was sitting there *disabled*. First thing that came to my mind was that this is a dope fiend move. *Who would have the audacity to break in my shit?*

I had only been gone for a few hours and I know Sidney left before me without returning. I only went downtown to The Galleria to get an outfit for tomorrow's showcase. My plan was to come back and rehearse my new material, so I will perform with ease tomorrow. But now, I have some additional bullshit that I must deal with. 'Some ordinary 'hood shit', I guess.

As a result of my 'Alley Boy' stimulus, I grab the biggest kitchen knife and start canvassing my mother's house. I start upstairs, then to the middle floor and basement to conclude that whoever did this was *long gone. What a surprise*. But what makes this ordeal so strange is that all our expensive belongings were left untouched. Every TV still in place. My laptop was still connected to the speakers in my room. Even the $1200 I recklessly left exposed in my sock drawer was not missing a dollar.

"Man, what the fuck is really good?" I say aloud, not expecting a reply.

As I strategically place the A/C unit back in the window to prevent future break-ins, I try to mentally produce a list of suspects. *Nothing*. What made this situation even more bizarre is that I begin to contemplate that maybe this was an accident.

Could my mother have gotten out of rehab early and did not have her key?

It is also possible that Uncle Lenny needed a spot to hide out. Still with him being older than my mother, majority of the time you will catch him *fucking around* with females my age. He would use them for their government benefits. So, he was bound to piss somebody off sooner or later.

Instead of stressing myself out over the unknown, I decide to get to the bottom of this travesty. I pick up my cell phone and find the contact labeled "Unk Lenny."

It takes a few rings for him to answer, but when he does, I have a strong inclination that he is not trying to lay low. The background noise sounds like he is at a concert and the venue is a compact car.

"Yoo Uncle Lenny, what's up? Are you around?" I say loud enough to overpower his surroundings.

"Yeah, yeah hold up nephew. Let me get to a quieter area," he replies back to me. I wait a few seconds before he returns to the other end of the phone.

"Say my bad Isaiah," he starts up. "I'm out here in Atlantic City getting my gwop up. I done stung these cavemen for almost four large already".

"That's what it is Unk. So, you haven't been in the city all day?" I ask him already knowing the answer.

"No, damn fool," he screams at me without revealing a trace of hostility. "I'm in Atlantic City, not Baltimore City. They opened this new casino I had to check out. I will be back on Sunday. Why, what's up, you alright?" he asks me.

Not wanting to set off any alarms while he is on vacation; I casually end this brief phone call by wishing him good luck and to *holla* at me when he is back in town. With no logical explanation and no leads, like a detective would call an unsolved murder, I labeled this mystery a "cold case."

Without having any second thoughts, I decided to drown this event out with loud beats, weed smoke and rap lyrics. As I walked into my bedroom, I sluggishly placed my outfit that I bought at the Downtown Locker Room next to my closet. I opened the shoebox that usually contains my rhymebooks and *Dro*; thus, grabbing two baggies. Enough to roll three vanilla Dutches. That is, until my attention is displaced by the item not in my shoebox. *My rhymebooks*.

Up until this point, I had been calm about my recent findings at my mother's house. *But now I needed answers*. And now was not soon enough. Sidney is the only person missing out of this equation, so she became the number one suspect on my list to question. Within three seconds, I had contact labeled "Wifey" on my cell phone screen ready to dial.

It took no time for the interrogation to begin.

"Baby, where are you at?" I ask as soon as she answers the phone, not giving her anytime to deliberate an alibi.

"*Duh*, I'm at my sister's house like I told you this morning when she picked me up," Sidney throws back at me.

"Ayo, this isn't a time to get cute. I asked a simple question that deserved a simple answer. So, you haven't been back to the house today?"

"Nigga, what are you tripping for? Are you high or something? I told you that I'm at my sister house and been here all day."

"Oh shit, well have you been in my shoebox? My rhymebooks aren't in there."

To avoid her getting paranoid, I decided not to disclose the suspicions that were subconsciously forming this afternoon at my mother's house. *There would be two outcomes if I told her*. One, she would want to stay on the phone for hours to talk about it. And time is of the essence right now. Then, she would also suggest that her and Stacy stay at her sister house until everything boils over. This is not happening tonight because I have a sudden urgency to get some *pussy* after all of this. Besides, she should know that she's protected when I have these two twin Model 23 Glock 40's under the mattress.

"No," she replies. "You know I don't go in your shit for this exact reason right here. You probably misplaced it or left it at Germ house when you were recording."

I knew she was wrong about both of those accusations. Word is bond; I will lose something bigger like a TV or my uncle's car before I lose one of my precious rhymebooks. That's our *direct flight* out the 'hood. And Germ is like one of my brothers from another mother. He stays across the street in the projects. If I did leave it over there, which I know that I did not, it still would have been in my possession right now.

"Yeah, that diesel be having me *popped*. I probably did leave it over there. Let me hit him up and call you back," I say to get her off the phone. Continuing our conversation would put me at risk of cussing at her. Not anything that is her fault. Just my aggravation and her optimism, right now, are not going to lead to favorable results.

So now I am back to square one. *What the fuck.* I am absolutely, positively sure that someone did not break in my mother's shit for the sole purpose of finding my rhymebooks. And not take anything else. Not even the weed that accompanied my written masterpieces.

The only thing to do at this moment is roll up and tear this bitch apart.

    By the time I finished blunt number one; I had successfully overturned every mattress, dresser drawer and sofa cushion in the house. It only took three puffs off blunt number two to realize it could not have ended up in the basement. Walking back to my room was depressing, but I could not allow this occurrence to deter me from my focus. I had too many people relying on me.

    I was blessed, or extremely lucky to have somewhat of a photographic memory. As I played the instrumental to the track I was set to perform, the lyrics magically appeared in my subconscious. Making it easy to recall to my conscious. "*I can still do this*," I thought. I am not new to this rap shit; I am true to this rap shit. My rhymebooks will pop back up later, but for now, the show must go on. And the show did go on, indeed.

-#-

The next night you had 15 of Baltimore City's, hungriest up-and-coming rappers, all gathered under one roof at the *Paradox* nightclub. A lot of the performing acts had an amateur resemblance since they were not recognizable figures in the Baltimore rap scene. I was pretty much the talk of the showcase due to my lyrical reputation. There was one other person though whose presence commanded just as much attention as mine- and they call him *Mister Popular*.

I grew up with *Mister Popular*, or *Eugene* (I call him by his government name), in East Baltimore. We came up in the same freestyle battles after school since the fifth grade. Ever since I originally met Eugene, nine years earlier, rapping in the Lafayette Projects, he has been in constant competition with me. We both had the same dreams of being the greatest rapper to come out of Baltimore City. If the 'hood was to take a vote, the odds would be in my favor as to who would be elected as the face of Baltimore City.

Meanwhile, Felix Stone and his crew randomly put together the set order of performances. I had spot number 13. Did not bother me though, they are saving the best for last.

Tonight, *Paradox* housed an audience of about 350 people accompanied with five judges who were critiquing our overall talent and stage presence to determine the winner. All the contestants waited backstage until they were individually called to perform. It was set up like a lounge; decked out with couches, a catering service, smoker section… and of course, the competition. "*Damn*," I thought. Another opportunity for Mister Popular to attempt to *jock* my popular style.

Eugene had acquired spot number nine to perform. Out of the eight contestants that blessed the stage before him, it was not evident that you can hear the audiences' applause until Mister Popular performed. *He must have stepped his game up.* Still, this observation did not make me nervous. Just further accelerated my drive to go out there and shine. I had a fresh beat and lyrics that nobody has heard yet. So, performing tonight was going to be a world premiere for the city and myself. Whatever Eugene managed to put together still could not match up to the weakest song I ever wrote. *Yeah, was I wrong about that.*

Once Mister Popular returned backstage, he had this mischievous smirk implanted on his face. Periodically, glancing my direction. Everybody could feel the tension between us. Our energies were forcing everyone else to play on their phones until the final performance. I knew what this night meant for me and Mister Popular. Either do my thing or this rap shit is outdated. *Simple as that.*

How would the 'hood feel if I let Eugene out-do me in something that I've been proclaiming royalty in for almost a decade? I even have a few supporters here this night; so, Felix Stone would have no choice but to accept the fact that I am the face of Baltimore City.

"I'll prove it to him," I was thinking as I smoothly walked the stage once the name "Izzy B" was called. *This is it*. That moment. That opportunity. All the judges were recognizable celebrity faces. Even the announcer was some big shot comedian from New York. Or maybe Los Angeles. So many thoughts were racing through my psyche. *So much power in one room*. The power to make my dreams a reality or a barrel of hopeless possibilities.

The DJ requested my instrumental. Here we go. I am seconds away from accomplishing what some say is unachievable. Minutes away from telling Sidney *to pack up, I did it*. Hours away from the biggest celebration of my life. Days away until the world will know me by "Izzy B." The feeling was liberating.

As soon as the beat drops, I immediately blank out. Transform from human to some unexplainable vessel. I perform with finesse. My delivery on point like certified mail. Hypothetically speaking, even if the judges were not feeling my music then my all-around stage presence would still be ranked remarkably high. But that is out the question. The only motherfuckers who would not feel my music is the *deaf and blind*.

That is until I am 15 seconds away from finishing my set, when I begin to think: *Is everybody here deaf and blind?* Even the announcer seems disoriented as he reminds the audience my name. Everybody looks confused. From the crowd to the judges. By the look on everyone faces, if this were televised live then an unprecedented television commercial would have been occurred. Disgrace was one of the dominant energies hovering through *Paradox* right now. My *nigga senses* started kicking in after processing the cause/effect relationship between a nearly muted hand clap, in addition to the frigid look on Felix Stone's face. *Picture a fully costumed KKK member that was participating in a Martin Luther King Day Parade. My feeling of belonging has vanished.*

Am I in the wrong venue? Did Supreme Records put this together looking for gospel artists?

The only logical thing to do was retreat. As I entered the lounge backstage, my mental state was in a daze. *What was that? What the fuck just happened?* Confusion reigned throughout these enigmatic moments of solving the equation. I check my wardrobe for defects. *Nothing.* The lyrics were not offensive, so it could not be that. "Man, this was an upper cut to the gut," I was thinking to myself.

Just as I was about to evaluate the recent sequence of events, I once again notice Mister Popular eyeing me.

"Say Eugene, you *good money*. What are you looking at?" I say to him not surrendering any idea of sportsmanship.

"Ayo Izzy chill out. Nobody worried about you nigga."

"Yeah, alright well keep your eyes on the prize then not me motherfucker."

"Word up, you sound really sporty right now. We are going to see what's up when we're back on the block."

"Bet bitch," I yell back at him, totally disregarding the fact that Felix Stone is making his way backstage. It already feels like some funny business was going on. Felix Stone is holding a card in his hand as he witnesses our argument. Must be the judge's verdict. My name could not be on it, so this competition is not a factor to me anymore. I struggled to figure out how Mister Popular got a standing ovation, but I, clearly more talented, got silently booed off the stage. Then, it hit me. This conniving motherfucker had to hustle up a lot of money to pay this off. Only sensible explanation.

"Yoo, you young hoppers' settle down."

I have no choice but to respect Felix Stone's authority and power as he demands this. Plus, he had the ability to shed some light on what just happened.

"So, which one of you is the older brother?" he asks for sure losing the *fuck* out of me. Eugene does not look too puzzled though. *Interesting.*

"What do you mean by that?" I ask demandingly.

"Well for starters, you two performing the same exact song just with different beats is something I never seen in my 15 years of artist management. Unfortunately, only one of you can make it. Mister Popular, we need you on stage for your victory speech. Come up with your own material next time Izzy B and I may have a spot for you."

My whole world slows down. Reality is chopped and screwed as I try to process this information. Same song. Different beat. The break-in. It all makes perfect sense now.

This was the type of betrayal even the '*hood* couldn't properly equip you for. My anger would not have climaxed so raw if he would have at least taken a TV or my laptop too. But he did not. *He only took my rhymebooks.* This nigga really risked his life to obtain my most intimate writings. Instead of trying to understand the significance of his actions, I snap. Instead of realizing that people would die trying to get a piece of my reality, I snap. Instead of thinking about my family who is going to need me, regardless of the outcome tonight, I snap.

After seeing Eugene and Felix Stone walking towards the stage, I knew I could not let this go down.

But it was already happening. What could I do? Expose him. Severely injure him. Or, let it go. I damn sure could not let him make it because Sidney and Stacy could have been in the house. This nigga been plotting this for weeks, meaning he has been watching my shorty. Me, trying to expose him, I will sound like a mad man or simply, a hater. That is something I would not allow the streets to add to my resume.

Crazy thing is I was sober on the night of the showcase. I wondered how my reaction would have altered if I had smoked a few 'loud packs' beforehand. *Guess we will never know.*

I instinctively grab the first bottle I find backstage in the lounge. It was a 24-ounce Budweiser bottle. Without second guessing my options, I head straight for the stage where Mister Popular is giving his thanks and dedications.

"Fraud ass nigga," I think to myself. How could he honestly take credit for somebody else's work? Even though we are from the same 'hood, he must've soaked up game from someone who always played on the bench.

Whatever I do, I must make it worthwhile. I mean, come on, he just stole my record deal. He just took the house I was going to buy my mother. He just stole the opportunity for Stacy to grow up in good neighborhoods and go to the best of schools. He just took Sidney's sense of security and financial stability. And with no remorse too. So, I must be sure to show no remorse also.

My palms were so sweaty that I don't know how the beer bottle stayed planted in my hands after the first swing at Mister Popular's head. It broke during the second swing though. I had a debate with myself if I should give him a chance to fight back. But with my adrenaline and the fact that he is in the fetal position, I knew that was *'dead.'* Pretty soon, my size Nike boots joined the fight.

The whole nightclub was flabbergasted. Devastated. I figured they sensed a certain level of deception also because it took security some additional time to intervene. "At least they won't remember me for having questionable lyrics," I thought to myself. With the unscripted commotion, everybody should know *the real*.

I had never got hit with a Taser gun before this night. Shit, I never got hit with a Taser gun and pepper sprayed at the same time before this night. But it is a first time for everything.

As I recuperated and regained stable consciousness, I was in the backseat of a police van facing felony charges.

Chapter 3

Rummaging through the three-year old memory, I could not help but ask myself: was it even worth it? What exactly did I accomplish?

Even if the assault on Eugene never occurred, it was still predestined that a prison cell would one day become my residence. *Mentally.* It would have been a mistake to immediately let me back out in public after the showcase. A mistake that could've potentially cost me, my family and my 'hood more than three years without my presence. Even with my adult responsibilities, my reasoning was like a teenager. *The assault was immature but still righteous in my eyes.*

Even though my sentence/punishment had been completed, I still had another set of consequences to endure and that was witnessing the mayhem caused by the showcase three years prior.

For starters, before my duration of confinement reached 90 days, my mother had already forfeited the deed of our Broadway tenement in exchange for several absent-minded weeks leading her back into The Water Shed. Still to this day, my mother does not know how upset and disappointed I was regarding her decision. *We had been living in that rowhouse off Broadway since I was in the fifth grade.* We rarely missed rent payments when I was out there.

When I had gotten arrested, my mother was still at The Water Shed and Sidney was braiding everybody in the 'hood hair. Even though I considered Sidney incredibly smart and independent, I could not expect her to hold down my mothers' rowhouse for three years. She eventually moved to her sister house and my mother moved herself and our belongings to Uncle Lenny's house.

This is where the drama began.

Uncle Lenny always looked out for my mother as his little sister. After she moved in, he told her everything was free of charge while she gets her life back together. *Yeah, a recovering drug addict with no foreseen responsibilities or duties.* Not good. My incarceration had a lot to do with my mothers' deteriorating mental state. She did not take the news lightly.

Not long after moving in with Uncle Lenny, my mother got heavily involved with a neighborhood crack/heroine dealer named Peanut. Somehow, throughout the course of that relationship, she accrued a substantial amount of debt owed to this nigga.

With no intentions of paying him back, things got ugly between my mother and this drug dealer. Shit got so real, that *ol' dude* was posted up in front of Uncle Lenny's house, on the main strip, with a shotgun waiting for my mother. Once Lenny pulled up and saw Peanut sitting on his stoop, he was furious. This was before he noticed the sawed-off in his lap. Uncle Lenny did not back off though; even after Peanut threatened to kill him if my mother did not pay him back. Come to find out, it was only $220 that she owed. Lenny cautiously gave Peanut the money so he could move around. Lenny was not necessarily fucked up with Peanut because he understood how the streets worked. He was more fucked up with my mother for bringing this type of heat to his spot.

When my mother returned to Uncle Lenny's house a few days later, they got into a heated argument. What transpired from it was that Lenny kicked her out. That was the last time, he, or anyone else heard from my mother.

After I got arrested, me and Sidney's relationship entered rocky grounds also. Not for long though. She was just more upset and disappointed that I would jeopardize our family's' well-being by fucking Mister Popular off.

"What if he would've died," she will say during weekend visits to the prison. At first, she did not write me or visit too often; so, I sort of doubted if her love for me was real. Like maybe her love depended on what I can offer at that present time. Being locked up, you start giving everyone *loyalty checks*. But one thing she never did and that was let me down. After her feelings and emotions were *in the air* regarding my incarceration, we grew stronger as a unit. Pretty soon, I was getting two to three letters a week and visits every Sunday. Her efforts ensured that my locker stayed fat every commissary day. So, in return, I vowed to do by her and Stacy once I got out.

-#-

"The State of Maryland really be on some 'cruddy' shit," I was thinking while being prepped for release. The penal system must be sponsored by Goodwill. They issued me a pair of dark blue corduroys, faded Darth Vader tee shirt, and busted up Champion sneakers. After three years, I could not allow the city to

get their first glimpse of me like this. But fuck it, I must get the hell out of here.

The best amenity I received while walking out of the jailhouse was an all-day metro pass. Did not expire until 3 a.m. Before I got locked up, I rarely had a desire to purchase a day pass. I was always either in the 'hood or within walking distance from where I needed to be. But now, I got the whole city in my fingertips. Still, I was not going to take advantage of it. All I wanted at this point was a spot to crash and a *nice piece of pussy*.

My last year of incarceration, I began getting letters from Uncle Lenny. He promised me a place to lay my head until I reestablished myself. He designed the whole basement for my arrival; and with the assumption that Sidney and Stacy were coming, he took the liberty of making his house "child friendly." I had no choice but to accept his offer (consider its either there, Sidney sister house or the homeless shelter). Plus, it is still on the Eastside, so it did not bother me at all.

As I got off the prison "chain" bus in downtown Baltimore, I took my first breath of freedom. It was empowering. Everything in the city remained the same, but in retrospect, everything changed. I had a new appreciation for the skyline, the harbor and the regulars' who paced the busy streets. It is like I am witnessing Baltimore City for the first time.

As I entered the number 20 metro bus heading towards Highlandtown, I noticed something different about the passengers. The style, clothing and electronics have been altered the past three years. I never expected time to swiftly move past me like this. I also could not expect everything to freeze during my departure. *But damn.* Everybody with a cell phone had a *touch screen joint*. I was still accustomed to pressing buttons. And the hair styles. You can miss me on the pop culture trends, I am a *street nigga*. But I know if times get hard and pressure needs to be applied, I am going to make a killing from these cell phones and oversized headphones. For now, everybody gets a *pass*.

Once the speaker on the bus announced Fayette Street and Montford Avenue, I pulled the string signaling my stop. The crème-colored Toyota Corolla parked in front of my Uncle Lenny's stoop alerted me of one thing. *Comfort.* The knowledge of something familiar. The avenue. The block. Nobody could tell me anything about these East Baltimore streets. This was my comfort zone, not prison.

A twinge of nervousness came over me as I walked to his doorstep. I did not know what to expect. I did not know who to expect. All I had to my name was a stale Newport 100 that a junkie gave me downtown, an all-day metro pass and whatever possessions my mother left here for me. Feeling emasculated, I skulked up Uncle Lenny's three small steps that lead to the entrance of his rowhouse.

Just by knocking on the door, I could already tell who was on the other side. Sounds of a little girl saying "daddy, daddy" made my heart sink. I almost *teared* up when I heard the word "surprise" coming from Sidney and Uncle Lenny. Before I fully entered the house, Stacy had my leg disabled by her tightest grip. I was stunned that she knew exactly who I was and what I stood for. She was only two years old when I got arrested.

Happy could not even explain the emotion I was feeling. For the first time in a while, I felt genuinely wanted, needed, and loved. Like I was a real father.

Walking through the door, my position was quickly revealed and that meant it was all or nothing. Because the same people who relied on my guidance and support three years ago are the same people anticipating my leadership now. Making better choices became my main prerogative. I will be considered insane to reenact my past actions and expect a different result. Ultimately, whatever I decide is a *come up* must be beneficial rather than artificial.

Besides the warm, welcoming, and immensely affectionate kiss from Sidney; something else was requesting my attention. The smell of a chicken box. On my Uncle Lenny's kitchen table, they had food catered from Kennedy's Fried Chicken for my personal enjoyment. Chicken wings, collard greens, lake trout and French fries, topped off with a half and half.

"I made sure we had your favorite here baby," Sidney beams at me with a smile that was caused by my returning presence.

"Thanks love," I reply. "Every chicken joint I passed on the way here made my mouth water. It's like you all were reading my mind."

I did not know where to start. Everything smelled so good and fresh. Instinctively, I grabbed a bottle of hot sauce and Old Bay seasoning. The chicken and fish instantly became drenched with condiments. My taste buds became alive. The past three years I had gotten programmed to the bland and tasteless food of prison. So naturally, I zone out while eating my meal.

When I took a quick *swig* of my half and half, I see that Uncle Lenny is inspecting my current *ratchetified* look.

"What's up, is it the clothes?," I asked him. Before I got locked up, my daily outfits would cost at least two hundred bucks. Compared to now, where my clothes are not worth any more than a throwback bootleg Mobb Deep CD.

"No nephew, you have a fucking tattoo on your face. Where they do that at?", he says.

"Just chill Unk," I pleaded with him. "It's a dollar sign. I didn't get it that big anyway."

"Oh really. So, you got some money?"

"Not yet, but I will once I bounce back."

The whole time you could catch Sidney in the background giggling. Internally, she sided with my uncle's opinion. I remember when she first saw it during one of the jailhouse visits. She started tripping because I am spending her hard-earned money on tattoos. But once she saw the portrait of her and Stacy on my chest, she rationalized her complaints.

"It's actually kind of cute," she says trying to convert his antagonistic views elsewhere.

"Well, I'll have to be the first person to tell you that your bugging Isaiah. Wait until your mother gets to see that shit."

"Where is she at anyway," I ask him.

"Come on, let me show you where you'll be staying," Uncle Lenny replies, totally avoiding my question.

As we walked downstairs to the basement, I expected the worst. *Why didn't he answer me? Where is she? Has he even heard from her since their argument?*

The room Uncle Lenny prepared for me blew past my expectations. I was looking forward to a hot and cluttered living space, infested with roaches and bedbugs. He had to do some major renovations while waiting for my arrival. This is the first time I ever seen carpet in a basement. Stacy has her own bed and play area. He built a wooden closet right outside the room that contains 90% of my clothes and shoes; minus the outfits my mother sold for drugs. Even my laptop and speakers are here and ready for my usage.

"Go ahead and make yourself at home nephew," my uncle says noticing my bewilderment. I cannot help but compare this arrangement to how I was living 24 hours ago.

"Looks like you've put a lot of time and effort into this project. Not to mention money," I say trying to juice information out of him. I must know what I am up against if I am going to be living here.

"Well," he starts up. "Besides the casino and my young broad who work at Mercy Hospital, your uncle been bored Isaiah. Just trying to find my purpose and stay busy."

"Yeah, I feel you Unc. You are getting up there in age. One of the oldest *cats* on the block," I say jokingly. "People probably think you used to run with Peanut King."

"Old? Shit, I'll still whoop your ass up and down Fayette Street."

We laugh for a moment before a combination of awkwardness and reality sets in. Uncle Lenny is the first to realize it though. This is the last place where he saw my drug addicted mother and now here I am. Statistically, this is exactly how *they* view young, black urban youth. Fresh out of prison with kids. No parents and/or a lack of dedicated mentors. No job. No money. No sense of direction. If it was not for Uncle Lenny, I will be out in the streets trying to figure out how to get a fresh pair of socks and boxers to wear tomorrow.

"I'm really glad that you're here, Izzy," Uncle Lenny says. "For real, if you need anything, I got you. You blood, *ya dig*."

"Appreciate it Unk. *That is love*. So, tell me though, I can handle whatever. But is my mother okay," I ask.

He sighs. But it is not the "devastating news" type of sigh, so I am a little relieved. I just expected to be disappointed.

"Yeah nephew, your mother is *good money*. She is a survivor. But to keep it 100, I do not know where she is. The streets are going to talk though, so do not *trip*. We can…"

"What the fuck, then how do you know she's all right? That is your sister, my mother," I say angrily not meaning to cut him off. I felt bad for my outburst. Uncle Lenny has been trying his best to stabilize my mother to sobriety while also looking out for me since I was a shorty. I must cut him some slack. It is not his fault that heroin is now readily available to be purchased by kids barely in junior high school.

"My bad Unk. I was just hoping to see my mother once I got out. You know I got nothing but love for you man."

"You good Izzy. I know how it is," he replies to me.

The stillness surrounding us became so definitive that you could *hear* the city streets really well. People talking while walking up and down the strip. The traffic. The loud brakes of metro buses. You can even hear police sirens blaring in the distance.

Uncle Lenny is standing by the small basement window that gives you a peak of the action that takes place on Fayette Street.

"Come here. Let me show you something Izzy!"

"What's up?"

"Can you take a guess on how long I've been staying in this same house, on this same block, watching the same shit," he asks me.

"Nope. But I always remembered you to be living here."

"Understand, I bought this rowhouse 26 years ago after my accident and never left. I witnessed all these young brothers with their pants sagging to grow up and be murdered in the streets or end up in prison. I see all these girls go from hopscotch to prostitution. It's a sad cycle that's never-ending Isaiah."

Uncle Lenny has never been the philosophical, advice-giving type of person. He is more of a realist. So, hearing him speak like this, I developed a newfound respect for my uncle. I am still left speechless though. I did not know how to respond or where he was going with this speech.

"Yeah, I already know Unk. So, why would you choose to stay around to watch this shit after all these years," I inquire.

"I ask myself the same question everyday nephew. Honestly, it's like I ran out of choices and options a long time ago."

"Stop the madness man, you really got it made compared to other *motherfuckers* around here. I always considered you middle class, living in poverty-stricken neighborhood. Why, I do not know. Never figured it out. Thought it was because you had easy access to four liquor stores on every corner or the chance of being featured on the news at least once a week."

We both got a good laugh out of that. Uncle Lenny found it more amusing though, because deep down, he knew there was some hidden truth behind my statement.

"You know I had career goals when I was your age," he begins to tell me. "I was always fascinated by airplanes. My plan was to go to aviation school to become a pilot.

"So why didn't you," I ask him.

"Well, my excuse was that it was the 80's. That I would not be taken serious as a young, black man from the 'hood. So instead, I spent the next two decades doing nothing."

That is one hell of a story Unk," I tell him.

"For real Izzy, some people are cowards. For what you have went through the past three years, I could never say that *I feel you* because I have never been. But for a while now, I have been feeling mentally incarcerated. Fearing the unknown caused me to settle for the life that my environment offered. You do not want to be my age with regrets. So, my best '*homecoming*' advice to you, man-to-man, is to not be a coward Isaiah."

"All right Uncle Lenny let us cut to the chase. What are you suggesting I do to not become a coward?," I ask giving him my full undivided attention. This must be good. This is a once-in-a-lifetime opportunity to hear my uncle talk about something else other than hoes, malt liquor and if shorty is really a man on the *Jerry Springer Show*.

"That's what you're going to have to figure out for yourself nephew. I am not going to buy you some toothpaste and brush your teeth for you. By the way, I am on a strict schedule. I start my yoga classes next week, so I won't be doing too much babysitting."

"Get the fuck out of here Unk," I say trying not to laugh in his face, even though it is evident by my tone of voice.

"Why are you taking yoga?"

"Listen nephew, I met this bad ass white woman who has her own yoga studio in Towson. She told me to come by to see how flexible she can really get. If shorty is the truth, like I think she is, then I will be breaking up with the registered nurse I have been seeing. I'm telling you shorty look like that Angelina Jolie *broad*," he tries to convince me.

I am now laughing uncontrollably. "Say Unk, I don't think Angelina Jolie is white."

"Well, you know what I mean. I have never been with a white woman, so this is a new experience for me. Have to see what the hype is all about," he explains.

"*Word up*, I can dig it," I reply to him.

"Oh yeah, before I forget. Here take this. Guess it'll motivate you a little more than me."

Uncle Lenny goes into his pocket and pulls out some money. First time I see money in three years. Off the top, I take notice to the crumpled up one- and five-dollar bills.

He does not give me any of his 'chump change' though. Out of all the wrinkled-up bills, he gives me the one that is in crisp mint condition. It has a picture of Benjamin Franklin on the front. It was a hundred-dollar bill.

Neither one of us says anything because the present moment spoke a thousand words.

As Uncle Lenny is walking back upstairs, Sidney and Stacy are on their way down. I am so mesmerized by the significance of what just happened that I barely look their way. *Too caught up in the possibilities.* Caught up in what the hundred-dollar bill symbolizes in America. Wealth. Power. Respect.

It takes 100 one dollar bills just to become equal to the magnificence of this hundred-dollar bill. And some niggas got the nerve to think their *ballin* because they threw 100 ones in the club. But picture having the accessibility to throw 100-hundred-dollar bills and not be hurting for it the next morning. I am not the *'making it rain'* type, but I want to be on that level. Really, I need to be on a higher scale of generating money than that.

Maybe Uncle Lenny was right about using this hundred-dollar bill as a motivator. My first thought was to go buy some hoes, but now I have greater purpose in mind. I am going to sacrifice this hundred-dollar bill to my success, in whatever I choose to do. I am going to use this as my foundation.

In my property that I brought back from prison; I had a Speed Stick deodorant. Meticulously, while caught up in *tunnel vision*, I peel off the stickers while thinking about my plan. There was a blank space on the wall where I found my mark. Using the Speed Stick stickers, I gently taped each corner of the hundred-dollar bill to the wall.

The symbolism is phenomenal when you understand where I came from and where I plan to go. Truth is I do not even have a plan, except a plan to succeed. The same plan I implemented before I got locked up is still in effect. Just following a different route though. But the plan to buy my mother a house in the county is still in effect. The plan that will enable my daughter and future kids to go to the best of schools than I did is still in effect. The plan to take my city over is still in effect. The only thing to do now was figure out the plan.

I am in the same position where Donald Trump and Bill Gates started their journey into financial prosperity. Jay Z and David Banner. Spike Lee and Tyler Perry. Every successful motherfucker in the country had a starting point and it mainly consisted at the bottom. They had a solid plan and dreams. Minus the plan, I have always had a dream. Guess now it is time to wake up and say 'good morning' to the real world. Reality. Fuck the American Dream; I just want my piece of the pie. I do not need a white picket fence or German Shepherd anyway.

I glance over my shoulder to Sidney and Stacy smiling at me. Waiting for me to lead. I most definitely have to *turn up* for my fam, their all I got. Well, not quite.

I still have A *Hundred Dollars and A Dream!*

Chapter 4

Being that I am fresh out, I did not necessarily want to be bouncing around out in public. Not my first day home at least. I had a lot to accomplish, which meant I had more to contemplate. I had to get back in to the 'groove' of freedom and assemble my inner circle back together. Times have changed, so I had to get back into the loop of these East Baltimore streets. And I was going to use Uncle Lenny's basement as my headquarters.

My *baby mama*, Sidney, would be considered a borderline "square." She does not stay too much coordinated with what is going on around the busy avenues and back streets. I cannot rely on her to accurately tell me who got shot and who got *popped*. Who fell off and who is now *on*. Consider that she was not raised on some of the grimiest blocks on the Eastside. It was just that the location of her parent's house required her to go to schools in the 'hood. But still, she understood what and where she came from and fully acknowledged her blackness. Being blind to the streets was never her. Being "stuck up" to the activities of street niggas was never a word to describe her. Besides, she fell in love with a street nigga.

Danielle, which is Sidney's older sister, came to pick up Stacy for a few days, to give us some alone time. I already knew what that meant. She already knew what that meant. After three years, I will finally be deep in Sidney's pussy. Just the thought of picking her up and fucking her against the wall made my dick hard.

Sidney was a yellowbone, who stood about five foot two with sea green eyes. She had a flat stomach (even after our daughter), nice ass and titties with a pretty face to compliment and bring her attributes together. I had the type of female that a lot of these *swagless* bum niggas is killing for. I knew shorty was going to be the truth when we met freshman year, so I quickly "bagged her" and put her under my wing. What is even crazier is that I have only been unfaithful to her three or four times, for which she has forgiven me. When I was younger, I had an oversized ego due to my position in the streets. But that died down as I got older. Now I do not even too much think about fucking another chick. I have a baby with the *baddest bitch* in the 'hood, can't mess that up. When we both reach our full potential, we will be a powerful couple. Russell Simmons and Kimora Lee type shit.

As nightfall started to creep up, me and Sidney were almost at the point of no return. You can tell by the look in our eyes that we wanted to engage in some porno style lovemaking. As we were casually *chopping it up* and smoking the little bit of weed that she had, I decided to make the first move. I could not hold back and control myself any longer.

We started kissing aggressively while she stroked my manhood through my basketball shorts.

"*I'm probably going to get her pregnant tonight*," I said to myself.

While I was in the process of unstrapping her bra and pulling her boy shorts off, she abruptly stops me.

"What's wrong?" I say, breathing heavily. We used to fuck whenever possible before. *Quickie here, quickie there*. The strongest forces could not tear us apart. So, her pausing what was overdue, had me a little worried.

"Nothing baby," she says. "I just want tonight to be fun and special. I have been waiting for this night and saving myself for you for three years. So, I want it to go my way."

"Alright, I dig that. So why are we still talking? Show me what you want me to do," I say trying not to make my frustration evident.

Here I am, after three years of jacking off, my dick taller than a rocket in Houston and she wants to play games. I been in prison; she been out here in the 'free world.' If she wanted to fuck somebody else, she had the freewill to do so. But then again, I would be devastated if she did. She constantly promised me that she has not, and I halfway believe her. So instead of ruining the moment, I surrender to her wishes.

"Just relax Isaiah," she says exposing her Colgate smile that has the ability of raising the hairs on your neck. "I'm going to put this sweet, tight pussy on you in just a second. Do not worry about that. I have a surprise for you, but I need you to go to the liquor store first."

I was hooked up until the liquor store request. She never had been too much of a drinker anyway. Neither of us.

"You want me to go to the liquor store. For what? Lenny got cabinets of liquor and a refrigerator full of beer upstairs'" I explain with a puzzled look on my face.

"No. I want you to go get me a Four Loko," she responds.

"A Four Loko? What is that, like an Arizona Sweet Tea," I ask.

"No, they're like an energy drink with alcohol in them. They're really good and they get you right," she says.

"What the fuck! So, you have been getting drunk off Red Bull while I was on lockdown. I am disappointed in you. Ever heard of the 12-step program? Do you need help?," I say charmingly. That is one thing we could always do and it is enjoy each other's presence. The pressure of the world always seemed to disappear when we were together.

"No silly," she says giggling. "They're going to have me all the way *turned up* if you want to know. Grab two watermelon Four Lokos. One for me and one for you."

"But I don't have any money," I say trying to get her to change her mind. I really did not want to leave. Especially not at a time like this.

"Get some money out of my purse. Their only three dollars a can."

"So, you really want me to go out in the big and bad streets of Baltimore, at night, for a Capri Sun?," I remind her using my last attempt of plea bargaining.

"The only reason their big and bad is because you made them that way. Thought you always said, 'these streets in particular were yours'. What happened, you scared now?" she says still exposing that smile. My dick is still at full attention. I just shake my head. This is how wars were ignited.

"Alright, fuck it, you got me. I'll be right back though," I say while tying up a pair of my old Space Jam Jordan's.

"Good and hurry up. Just go there and come right back."

"You sure have been getting pretty stiff with your demands like you run the show," I say expecting some sarcasm.

"Nigga shut up. You know I like messing with your crazy ass."

While I am preparing for my departure, Sidney ceases my movement for a long, soft kiss by her pretty pink lips. *Consequently, causing me to rise like yeast.* I would not dare go upstairs and walk past my Uncle Lenny like this. She must have been thinking the same thing because without second guess her actions, she commences to pulling my boxers down and putting her tongue ring to work.

I am caught up in a hypnotizing trance while she performs *falatio* on me. Seems like she has gotten better too, do not know how, but whatever. The way she twirled around my balls, back to the head of my dick, all in one swooping motion, had me about to explode. I pulled her long black hair to the side, so I can look in her eyes. A moment after peering into those sea greens,' I could not help myself anymore. I had to nut. And I accidently, or purposely, nutted in the one place she hates. Her mouth.

I give it a minute to digest while she looks up at me in disgust. Before saying anything, I French kiss her to metaphorically say that *I respect her*.

"Ughh you get on my nerves, Isaiah Malik Brown. Lucky, I love you more than life itself."

"I love you too baby," I respond back.

Without trying to waste anymore time, I pull my clothes back on and get the money out of her purse. To my dismay, it looks like she has about $1500 saved up. While putting the money back, I noticed that she has one of those flat phones that all the 'cool kids' on the metro bus had. Figured that she is into these next generation gadgets. I am going straight to the Boost Mobile store.

"I'm going to take your phone with me baby."

"That's fine. And Isaiah…"

"What's up," I curiously ask.

"Come right back," she demands, which is turning me on. I do not say anything, just smile and walk out the door. I am going to have to beat that pussy up tonight to get her mind right. I already know that is what she wants. Just thinking about all the positions that I am going to bend her up in, has me in a daze, almost tripping up the stairs. And just like that, I am back into the streets. *Back to where I am and will reign social supremacy.*

-#-

Doc's Liquor Store is located on the next street over on the Orleans block. I could have easily gone to one of the closer liquor stores, owned by the 'chinks or 'Arabs,' off Fayette street. But Doc's is black-owned and I will rather spend money with my people. Doc's family is *'from the hood and for the hood.'* The 'chinks' will sell a twelve-year-old a 40 ounce if their willing to pay an extra dollar. With this being an all-black neighborhood, the foreigners did not discriminate against their customers' age. But Doc and Mrs. Lynette would not let that shit fly in their spot.

As I was approaching Doc's Liquor Store, I heard the sound of a long-missed pastime. The sounds of ATV crews terrorizing the streets, stopping traffic. It had to be about eight dirt bikes and five 4-wheelers, racing down Orleans Street in a uniformed line. I never personally owned an ATV, but a couple cats in my circle did. So, whenever I needed to make a quick run, I will use they joint.

Relatively speaking, even if I had the opportunity to be anywhere else right now, I would not change a thing. I am probably in the liveliest spot in the country. East Baltimore. An urban slum. I am right in the middle of a million-dollar ghetto. You got helicopters flying around with an ambulance siren blaring in the distance. Every business on the block has its own unique lighting.

Pit Bulls are roaming the alleys, aimlessly. The young 'hoppers are out trying to 'mack every chick walking down the street. Everybody is trying to hustle and sell something. From drugs to bootlegs to cologne to food stamps. I must add myself to the potential financial prosperity that is going around.

    When I entered the liquor store, there were three other people in line, but plenty of people just standing around. Mostly old school winos, gossiping about something that may not even be real. This environment for them was how the barbershop is for the 'brothers. They may just come up for a dollar scratch off or a single bogie and be posted up all day. Doc has his place surrounded by bulletproof glass, so he really did not mind the "scwagglers." Figured they kept him company and entertained him with ghost stories of the 'hood.

"Yoo what's up Doc. Let me get two Loko's, the watermelon joints. Oh, and six Lucy's. they still three for a dollar right," I ask the owner of the liquor store.

"Yeah, sure are. I need to see some identification first young brother."

"Damn Doc, I been living in this neighborhood for 23 years. I just got out 'The Joint' today, so I don't have an ID yet."

He tilts his glasses up to examine me. "Oh yeah, that is you isn't it," he says while ringing up my items. "You Rashida's' little boy. Done grown into a man now. Hope you plan on staying out of trouble."

"Yeah, so how much I owe you," I say trying to avoid a conversation about community politics.

"Don't worry about it. This one, he says. "Enjoy yourself and be careful on those things shorty. Done heard a lot of stories about bad reactions to them bitches."

"Word up."

"Don't mention it youngster," he replies to me.

Before I even left the liquor store, I automatically lit one of the cigarettes I bought. Something about total freewill would do that to you. As I exhaled, my attention was sublimely commanded elsewhere. It was a change of scenery from five minutes ago. *Guess those ambulance sirens were not as far off as I thought.*

-#-

One block away on Milton Avenue, there were two police cars and an ambulance. The area was sanctioned off by yellow tape. I could not help but go be nosy. See what niggas were up to on my uncles' side of the 'hood.

Once I arrived, there was already a crowd of people in the vicinity of the crime. All of them probably from that one block. There were two ladies, crying while talking to police; one of which was elderly. More than likely, a grandmother, mother, sister, auntie, or girlfriend combination.

I could not be accused of *ear hustling*, but the story of what happened seemed to bra floating around the crowd. Word is that this was a carjacking that tragically led to a stabbing. No one knows if the victim is dead or alive. According to a bystander, the victim name is Sammy; so, I could not tell if a male or female was harmed. *I wonder what kind of car is worth almost killing somebody for. You cannot drive it on lockdown or in the grave. I never been robbed before, but I can picture it will be a life-or-death battle between me and the perpetrator.*

"Ayo Izzy." I heard my name called from the midst of the crowd but could not decipher which direction it came from. A few heads turned when my name was called, but nobody spoke up. *Maybe I was tripping.*

"Izzy that is you nigga. What it is," was all I needed to hear to realize this was my childhood partner, Byrd.

I have literally known Byrd my whole life. My mother and his foster mother were bingo hall friends before we could even spell our names. They lived in the Somerset projects, so once we moved off Broadway, I will always walk across the street and catch him on the blacktop. In these project courtyards is where a lot of friendships with everyone in my circle were created.

Me and Byrd were always the 'tightest' though. We got kicked out of middle school together and sent to an alternative program, downtown. This is around the time where he started to exhibit to me that he was a natural born killer. The one day he decided to skip school, was the one day I got jumped by two niggas from Sandtown. But I was always a good brawler, so it was nothing to hold my own. *What messed me up though, was that Byrd came swinging through the alleys like fucking Tarzan.* He had a solid metal pipe in his hand when he approached the two guys. They did not stand a chance. Within a split second, they were both flat-lined. Once I asked him what he was doing in the area; that I thought he was in the 'hood. He would simply respond by saying, "Boss had orders for me to be here." You could never categorize his mischief.

Byrd had to become an adult early because both of his foster parents died when he was 15. Instead of relying on the foster care system, he decided that taking care of himself was going to get him the "results" he craved in life. He started carrying out hits for the Rollin 20 Bloods and Gangster Disciples to survive. Sometimes, he would turn both gangs against each other to maximize his profits. *"They were going to kill each other anyway,"* was his normal explanation.

Byrd had a frightening reputation "around the way," due to his carefree, "shoot 'em up" demeanor. Motherfuckers knew that if Byrd was involved then some damage was going to be done. No mask, no vest he was running in your spot for the loot, kidnapping your kids if you do not get it. I do not understand how he is still alive today with so many likeminded killers walking around Baltimore City. Guess that is why I had so much respect for him. Because he took pride in his reputation even if it meant separating family members forever.

"Ayo what's smacking little nigga," I say to Byrd. He is almost three inches shorter than me, but still in the same weight class. Based on his reputation though, you will think he was some black ass thug with cornrows, a skully and at least six feet tall. Quite the contrary, Byrd was light skinned and capable of being one of those pretty boys dancing in music videos. With us being the same age, he could never get into nightclubs without being ID'ed.

"Damn Duke look at you," he says admiring my new physique and tattoo work. "Three years did you nice sun. I was just thinking about you too Yoo. Word to the Man."

"Nigga get the fuck out of here. You don't even think about yourself too often."

"Nahhh for real duke; why did you do Eugene like that? You should have let me take care of him permanently. God bless the dead," he says while actually closing his eyes and looking towards the clouds. I almost puked up the collard greens I ate earlier.

"Nigga you are tripping. Fuck Eugene, I am going to handle him on my own time. So what's up, what are you doing around here", I ask him.

"Oh yeah Money, I have a spot on the Rose block. I been doing my *thing* for a while now over there," he answers back to me.

"Word, how did you pull that off," I inquire already knowing the answer. "Those 430 Boyz had that block laced up when I got jammed."

"Yeah man. Well one day I was just walking and saw how much of a cash crop that block was. So, I produced a business deal or a proposition, that is what the corporate motherfuckers call it", he pauses and looks around as a dose of paranoia hits him. He pulls me to the side and says, "Look I told them cats like this. Either y'all shed the spot or I am coming over here to shoot this bitch up every day, faithfully. I told them they could not hustle here anymore. That Rose and Baltimore Street was free, just like Rose and Monument Street was free. But Rose and Orleans were off limits. It took about eight days and five murders for them to see it my way. Now it is all love," he says with a straight face.

I laugh a little bit at how serious his expression was. *Same ol' Byrd, still smelling like Doritos and gunpowder residue.*

"Still nothing has changed but the year Izzy," he tells me. "I never had the talk about the birds and the bees, so I was destined to fuck the game raw."

"I'm not mad at you either Money. Look like you have been *eating good*," I said while taking notice to his wardrobe. It was not hard to acknowledge that Byrd "*came up.*" *For real, for real.* Everything about his attire was saying 'cash flow.' No exaggeration, he probably had about $25,000 worth of clothes and accessories on. From his Gucci boots, Gucci pants, Gucci belt buckle, Gucci shirt with the Gucci strapback to match. To his Breitling watch by Bentley on his left wrist. To the two black diamond pinky rings that looked real. I even notice the baby .45, sitting in the back side of his belt buckle. What sets if off though, is that he too has one of those next generation flat phones, hooked on his pants pocket. *"I got to get right"* was the flashing, reoccurring thought going through my head.

"Yeah, I have been doing alright. So, what's up Money, are you hungry or what?," he asks me.

"Nahhh I'm good. *Babygirl* had a chicken box and shit waiting for me."

"Come on Yoo, stop being simple. You back in the streets now. Trying to get some money or what," he says by rephrasing his question.

Without further investigating Byrd's plot to get money, I felt obliged to accept his offer. *I mean, come on now, look at this nigga. I grew up with this cat and now he is running his own block. Pretty confident that Byrd is not going to have me shooting the elderly and chopping fingers off toddlers. It was my first day home. So, in my mind, I am not really harming anybody. Oh yeah, I forgot, Sidney is going to be pretty pissed off that I did not come right back.*

Byrd instructs me to follow him back down to the Rose block, which was nothing but three streets over from where the stabbing took place. Surprisingly, I did not have any suspicions that Byrd committed the crime. It was not his MO to return to the premises so early.

While we walked the short distance to Rose Street, Byrd was yapping off about how Mister Popular isn't allowed in the 'hood. Something about Eugene has a Bentley or a Bugatti but scared to drive it through the city. That the reason he does not have a car is because he is going to New York and robbing Mister Popular for his. That someone is actually keeping track of Mister Populars' whereabouts right now as we speak. Just a whole bunch of bullshit that I do not care about. *Fuck*

Mister Popular. He has a lifelong scar to remember the ass whooping I gave him.

But planning to rob Mister Popular was just the typical Byrd trying to excel past Eastside notoriety. Wanting the world to feel his pain and visually witness his transformation. Transformation from normal to an American Gangster.

Once we got to Byrd's' spot on Rose, I recognized two of the men sitting on the stoop. Just could not put a name that matched their identities. Still, there was not no introducing ourselves. Only a brief head nod. They were not in my cipher before, so chances are they will not be in my cipher now. Growing up in Baltimore City you were trained not to be friendly. From the East to the West, to South Baltimore, everybody has that constant 'mean mug.'

Stepping through the door, I already knew *what time it was.* This is where plots to destroy the community took place. At first, I was skeptical, but after reassuring myself that this was needed in order to enhance my circumstance; I was "ten toes down."

Looking around the spot, I saw guns, guns, and more guns. Guns just irresponsibly lying around. Guns on the stairs. Guns on the couches. Guns on the tables. The screen on the TV was busted but hanging from the demise was a bulletproof vest. Next to the bulletproof vest was a box of bullets and more guns.

As I was mentally inspecting the environment that I just nonverbally agreed to invest more time in, I kept hearing the cries of a baby. It was annoying as shit too. Like someone has not fed this baby in days.

"Say lookout Money, you got kids now or something?," I asked him.

He chuckles and says, "Nahhh Duke. It is this dope fiend baby. I pay her in drugs to test and cook my supply. I let her get high upstairs to be my 24-hour lookout. Plus, she brings in boatloads of customers. Dumb broad probably forgot to feed her baby again. Been thinking about calling Child Services."

"You are wild than a bitch boy," I tell him. "You are fucking that hoe too aren't you?"

"Hell no Money, I would though. She'll probably look good, clean and naked," he says jokingly.

We laugh like we used to as kids growing up in the projects. That is until the obvious hits us. Time to get down to business.

"So, what's good Duke. What are you trying to do?," I ask him.

"Look man, I fuck with you the long way," he begins to tell me. "But I won't contribute to you going back to prison early. So, I will let you decide what you want to do. Open the refrigerator and take what you need, free of charge."

I did not know if I could take his statement seriously. *"Open the fridge." "Take what you need." "Free of charge." What the fuck was supposed to be in the refrigerator? Bottles of water. Salad dressing. Chicken wings.* I told him I was not hungry. Sidney gets food stamps, so my uncles' kitchen was full of groceries.

It was not until I noticed the condition of the refrigerator and saw it was not plugged in. The sole purpose of this refrigerator was not to store food. It was to store drugs.

Curiosity seeped in, which made me not only just open the refrigerator, but I opened the freezer also. That is when I was blown away by the smell and sight of every illicit street drug known to man. There were several pickle jars filled with colorful pills. The freezer alone had nothing but compressed bricks of cocaine and heroin. He had a two-liter bottle filled with a substance that looks like crystal meth. I don't even know anybody in the 'hood who has the desire to fuck with meth. It was my first time seeing it. He also had miscellaneous shit laying around like Xanax pills still in the medication container, PCP *sticks* in a crayon box and an *assload* of mushrooms in a Ziploc bag. That is when I hit the jackpot.

In the cabinets where most people kept their fruits, vegetables, and cheeses; my hands had no choice but to grab two tightly wrapped blocks of weed. The weed was solid purple. This was a rare strand of Kush called *Purple Trainwreck*.

"Yeah Money, I need this. What is the ticket?," I ask him.

"Ayo, I told you that your good Sun. That is damn near two pounds of weed. Even if you smoke some, sell it sack by sack and you will make at least eight large. Easy street," he tells me.

"Already Yoo, that's love. I got you, word to my mother."

Before I got locked up, selling drugs had become essential to my survival throughout numerous time periods in my life. Mostly, when my mother came up short on bills. The remaining funds would be spent on clothes, instrumentals, or duplications of my CDs. I have had short stints of selling ecstasy and crack; but majority of my 'dope boy' credentials come from weed and heroin trafficking,

Chapter 5

I first sold heroin when I was 14 years old, making this my on and off hustle for the next five years. It all started when me and Byrd went to a party off Whitelock in West Baltimore. The shit blew our mind, seeing how much action these young niggas had at getting money. We were so accustomed to weed money that it never crossed our conscious to graduate to narcotics… until then.

Silently, our body language spoke it all. We needed to step our game up, by first, sitting these niggas on the sidelines. Byrd had a .357 snub nose on him and I had a .38 special. We decided that whatever happened, it had to be quick and effective.

One thing we had noticed about these Westside 'cats was that their real flashy. Flamboyant and cocky about their moves. They were hustling on a semi-busy corner right across the street from where the party was taking place. In seclusion, we took notice of their whole operation.

Within an hour, our plan was solid and official. We saw how every car that pulled up, one of the young 'hoppers would dig in the light fixture above this corner store and pull out small vials. There was another youngster on the other side of the store with a chip bag, serving everybody who walked up. Inside the light fixture and empty chip bags; they contained the drug we desired to sell. Heroin.

There was a barrier standing in our way though. It was not necessarily getting away, but at the same time, getting away with the drugs was our biggest problem.

We were on the other side of the city. Bad enough we caught the metro subway over here with two 'straps' on us. Now we wanted to rob a small drug organization on foot. Carry heroin and pistols on the subway back to the eastside. It was a risk that not even the two dumbest motherfuckers would take.

That is when Byrd informed me of a trick he learned from his foster father. How to hotwire a car. As he was running me through the play, he seemed quite sure that the task could be performed. The 14-year-old version of me did not have too much knowledge on cars. I could barely drive accordingly within state regulations and motor vehicle standards. So, Byrd's' sole purpose was to get and drive the car. I had to do the dirty work. Getting the drugs.

We did not have a large time window to get the job done without being noticed. There was a party going on *across the street and even though it was getting later into the night, the flow of traffic was in no way dying down. Our plan to attack had to be undetected and not set off any alarms if we wanted to make it out alive. But playing it safe went 'out the door,' when we saw their supplier come deliver the "re up." Shit. At that point, it was all or nothing.*

Byrd went to startup a Honda Civic that was parked at the end of the next block. In his opinion, Honda's are easier to 'grab' and they normally do not come equipped with intruder alerts. Plus, the streetlights were dimmer at this end of the block. So practically nobody was paying attention to what was going on. Once Byrd flashes the headlights, it will be my turn to make a move.

To be only 14 years old at that time, there was no fear in my heart about the nature of our plan. I was about 30 yards away from the targeted corner store when I noticed the headlights. Moving quickly, but still unsuspiciously, I mentally put together the scenario. I will be on the scene with Byrd pulling up behind me, in less than 60 seconds. So, I had to think precisely.

As I came within ten yards of the store, my hand was on the trigger of my .38 and our target was in clear view. It seems as if whoever is supplying these young niggas came to drop off a much larger chip bag than what they already had. Boldly clarifying my assumptions, I saw one of them separate and distribute the drugs amongst themselves. So far, our target was a three-man crew with their 'connect' still in close range.

I guess it must have been the swift release of my first shot that dazed the crew with terror and froze their ending existence. Not to mention, that first shot was a head shot to one of the youngsters by the entrance. I *only had six shots and had to make every one of them count.*

Without a shadow of a doubt, I knew the kid hustling out of chip bags was armed and getting ready to engage in a shootout with me. Not giving him a chance to react, I fired two rounds in his direction. One of them hitting him and immediately immobilizing his presence. That is when I ran over and took the chip bags and their contents, stuffing everything in my hoody pocket. Now I was to retrieve the bulk of the product.

I must have miscounted these young niggas because as I turned around, there was one kid reaching for his pistol and another one running out of the store prepared to face off. The only sensible thing to do was duck, cover and save my last three bullets for crunchtime. That is when the 'All or Nothing' statement flashed back across my mind. It was either 'get it or get got.' "Fuck I'm running for," I had thought to myself.

One of the young niggas fired seven rounds in my direction, forcing me to dive under a nearby car. Clearly their weapons were more deadly than mine. I saw one of them creeping around my side of the car. In the spur of the moment, I had to stop myself from attempting a leg shot. I am sure I would have wasted a bullet and risked my life if I did. Everything paused though and I was startled by a loud bang. Then, another loud bang. This was the bone chilling sound of shots fired by a .357.

Almost simultaneously after the loud bang, I saw a body drop and heard Byrd yelling "come on nigga." All in the same motion, I rolled over, pistol in hand and ran towards the store. Byrd hopped back in the already running Honda Civic and left my door ajar.

An overcoming stiffness must have come over me because I entered the store, headfirst, not even a slight bit worried about who may be inside.

Once inside, I realized that I had the 'juice' and total control over the situation. The last kid in their crew was giving me eye contact with his hands reaching for the sky. A gesture signaling the idea of surrender. Even the Koreans behind the counter had their hands up and they were protected by four-inch-thick Plexiglas.

I could have let the young kid 'make it.' But he should have known this was a dirty game once he enrolled on the roster. Not thinking twice, point blank, I shot him twice in the stomach. Blood splattered all over the wall and Plexiglas as the Koreans were left 'shell shocked.'

As his body slumped to the ground, I noticed a book bag hidden underneath a milk crate. I opened it up and 'Bingo.' Inside, there were two large chip bags filled with almost ten thousand dollars' worth of heroin already prepared for distribution. I also 'ran' the young kids' pockets and acquired $2230.

I ran out of the store feeling accomplished until I noticed majority of the partygoers were coming my direction. I fired my last shot into the crowd as I hopped in the vehicle with Byrd. We got away safe with the intent to now become young, rich niggas. This was the one and only occasion that I knew for sure somebody was killed by my bullet.

Once we got back to East Baltimore and put the word out about what we had, the dope fiends tried to take us "fast." Primarily because we did not even know exactly what we had. I was not going to ask my mother to explain this part of the game either. Being punished for what I now possessed was the last thing on my mind. I was more hesitant about my mother finding out due to her addiction status and the possibility of her skimming our shit. After we sold all the dope that we earned during the robbery, that was it. No more heroin. That is until we met "Poncho," who became our heroin supplier for the next five years.

Poncho was a Puerto Rican cat who owned a bodega off Eastern Avenue. His bodega was a cover up though for his heroin, cocaine, and marijuana dealings. While I was still in school, Byrd was the one who gained his trust by performing odd jobs for Poncho. Thus, informing him that we are a two-man cipher. Salt and pepper. Ketchup and mustard.

Eventually, Poncho trusted the feedback he received about our character in the 'hood. That we would get the job done. He precisely showed us the 'ins and outs' of cooking, cutting, and jamming heroin. Pretty soon, he was shooting us nine ounces of 'smack' every couple of days. Everything stayed intact and there was never a discrepancy over drugs or payments.

Byrd was always the full-time drug dealer even with the 'hits he was carrying out. My priorities and responsibilities changed overtime. So, there would be moments when I am in the drug game and out the drug game. Byrd would never put Poncho's work in someone else's' hand, so I always had the "green light" to start a "jamming session" whenever money was needed. Just trying to juggle high school, an upcoming rap career, the baddest bitch in the 'hood and selling high end narcotics was tough.

Even after I graduated, it didn't make drug trafficking any easier. Now with my overnight studio *sessions and Sidney getting pregnant, I had started to strive for success that niggas in my circle could not fathom. Not that I thought I was better than them; just I was the first to acknowledge that I had a dream and the first one of us to have a kid. Byrd understood why I had wavering professions, so it was no hard feelings. Plus, Sidney would trip the fuck out whenever word got around that I was "jamming" again. So, it was in my best interests to keep it discreet about where I will randomly appear with two to three thousand dollars at a time.*

Everything crashed down very rapidly though. Poncho went missing for a few weeks which created a drought. We were exasperated once we heard the story on WBAL news. Apparently, Poncho was found at the crest of the Chesapeake Bay with cement blocks tied around his feet. Poncho was dead and we now did not have another heroin supplier. Good thing is that I had saved close to twenty thousand dollars. Naturally, I went back to trying to become the face of Baltimore City while Byrd went back to doing odd jobs, robberies, and "hits" for the highest bidding gang operation.

(Off the top, that was still my nigga. But this is the first time me and Byrd talked business, on this type of level, since I was nineteen years old. Only a couple of months before I went to prison.)

Chapter 6

"Say lookout Sun. Give me something to put this loud in," I tell Byrd.

"Shit just grab one of the Gucci satchels in the kitchen cabinet."

"Damn nigga. Fuck you getting all this Gucci at Duke."

"I robbed the Gucci store," he says as monotonous as possible. Even though his accusation sounded bizarre and unreal, I knew not to question it. I knew there was a deeper degree of truth behind his statement. The only thing that mattered at this point was getting to the money. *Shit, I am trying to go cop my Gucci outfit too.*

As I placed the weed and two Four Lokos into the satchel, I noticed something bulky in another compartment. The bulge poking out said it all. Unzipping the pouch, I found a loaded nine-millimeter with an extra clip. An automatic *dime piece* would be the result of me getting caught with this firearm since I was a convicted felon. *That meant only one thing. Do not get caught.*

"Yoo Money, I guess this is for me too huh," I asked Byrd indicating the *burner* that was left behind.

"Yeah, if you still know what to do with it G."

"Is this bitch dirty Duke?"

"Hell no. None of the *heaters* in my spot has a body on them. If they did then they would not be here. Use them, ditch them. I have an *assload* of pistol plugs.

Even got some grenades upstairs that I got from a nigga out Fort Meade," he explains to me.

"Already Yoo, you still a damn fool I see. So, this is where I can find you?"

"Yeah or hit me on the hip. I got these real estate ventures going on so my whereabouts be fucked sometime Duke," he tells me.

"Real estate?," I asked him.

"You trying to take over another block or something."

A smile comes across his face followed by a light chuckle. "Nahhh Duke. I cannot rob and sell drugs forever. Have to get on some next level shit," he starts up. "I'm about to buy this property across the street from the Popeye's on Broadway. Put a Sonic on that bitch. Let my young goons run that motherfucker."

"Word up. You done came a long way from the Somerset courtyards Duke," I tell him.

"Yeah Sun, I'm motivated by the dollar. I got a Hundred Dollars and A Dream too."

Byrd coming at me like this gave me a better understanding of his viewpoints on life. For the longest, I was always under the impression that Byrd was just a coldhearted killer. Motherfucker with no conscious. But now I understood and had more empathy for him. Byrd was just like everybody else in the 'hood. Trying to make it out with the limited resources he was given. He had no formal guidance. He had an eighth-grade education. He could not rap or play basketball. His "career choice" was based off his environment. I could not be mad at him. At least, he is playing the game of life to win, instead of accepting defeat. Never thought I will say it, but I can learn something from this nigga.

We exchanged numbers and gave our salutations. Byrd kept insisting that if I needed anything to let him know. But with the "tools" that he blessed me with, I could go out and get it on my own. This was a startup. *The come up.* I am a man and was not set on cheating myself out of success this time. Whatever it took.

And with that, I was back out in these East Baltimore streets.

-#-

On my way back to Uncle Lenny's house, I decided to stop by the corner store to grab a few items. First thing on my list were sandwich baggies to aid in the distribution of my new product. When I thought about buying condoms, I thought about how mad Sidney probably is right now. But then again, she will get over it once I step through the door with this skunk ass weed. So instead of buying condoms, I buy four vanilla Dutch cigarillos and leave.

Stepping through the door, I heard loud snores coming from Uncle Lenny. He was passed out on the couch, drunk, watching re-runs of Martin. Without wanting him to notice my new merchandise, I head straight for the basement. *The night was just getting started.*

-#-

Sidney was laying under the covers with her arms folded over her breasts. She had the radio stationed to 92Q and they were playing my favorite. *Baltimore Club Music.* She glanced at me and turned on her side. That is when the investigation began.

"Nigga where have you been? I thought I told you to come right back. That was damn near two hours ago. What the fuck Yooo."

"Baby, just chill. I ran into Byrd and Sun really blessed my game."

"Byrd?" she questions. "*Shoot 'em up, bang bang, Byrd.* What the fuck were you doing with him and where did that Gucci purse come from? Is it real?"

"Look" was the only word I could get out to shut her up. Sidney is wifey, but she be trying to *handle* a nigga sometimes. Nine years in a relationship will do that. I let her play that role though. The tantrums she throws be sexier than a motherfucker anyway.

I watched her eyes light up as I pulled out two pounds of Purple Trainwreck. She did not even pay attention to the Four Lokos or pistol I took out afterwards. While Sidney *ooh'ed* and *ahh'ed* at the exotic weed, I hid the nine-millimeter under my side of the mattress. I took the Dutch's and sandwich bags out and threw the satchel out of sight, preparing to "set up shop."

"Are you going to be selling this?," she asks me.

"Fuck you mean. Hell yeah, I am going to be jamming this. It is a start up to get back on my feet. Might buy a car or something. You trying to sample this shit out," I tell her while passing a Dutch her way.

She did not seem interested in smoking weed at this present moment though. Sidney got from underneath the comforter, stood up and revealed the long tee shirt which came down to her knees. *It was one of my old shirts*. The assumption was automatic that this single article was purposely used as her concealer. *Which was correct.* Just the glimpse of her smooth silky legs gave me an instant erection.

"Hold on babe, I want to show you something," she says while placing the cigar on the nightstand.

That is when Sidney instructively grabs my hand and uses it to elevate the tee shirt. She then turns around so her *gluteus maximus* is facing me and there it was. *A tattoo.* The tattoo said, "Izzy B." The design was amazing and multi-colored. The background had a few music clefs associated with music notes cascading down on my name. There was a microphone wrapped around the whole tattoo giving it this sort of 3-D look. *Too bad, I will be the only person who will ever see this tattoo.* Did I mention she got this "stamp" on her right butt cheek?

I am at a loss for words. I just smile while literally and figuratively kiss her ass. In the blink of an eye, both of our shirts were off. I turn her back around to admire her fully exposed body. We began kissing slowly while my fingers explored her *love pearl*. I knew that this would be a satisfying night for her just by the way she almost exploded by my light touches and gentle kisses.

I laid Sidney back on the bed, so I can tease her just the way she teased me earlier. Thus, removing all my clothing except for my boxers and socks. I was not in the mood to *make love* tonight; "dicking her down" was my main motive.

Taking it slowly became the prerogative. I started with light kisses around her ear, scaling down her neck towards her titties. My hand never stopped playing with her clitoris while the occasional finger or two dipped inside her "*wet tunnel.*" She moaned and squirmed relentlessly underneath my control. In the process of seductively nibbling on her titties, her breathing got heavy and she locked her legs around my back. I knew I had brought her to the first of many orgasms tonight.

I paused to embrace this image. Sidney is the woman who has been *holding it down* for me since day one. You cannot deny the fact that I genuinely love *shorty. Without a doubt.* But tonight though, I am going to fuck her like I hate her.

Temptation crept up and I had to *taste* her. That is, without stopping the "tease show." I began to kiss and lick my way down her stomach and navel heading southbound. Once I became face-to-face with her *juice box*, I was determined to make her orgasm again; before penetration comes in the picture.

With the show in my hands, performance was key. I started fingering her rapidly and spelling out the alphabet with my tongue on her *sensitive button*. I went from A to G, then, suddenly stopped all my movement. My lips traveled to her inner thigh while I stared right in her eyes. The look on Sidney's face was priceless.

After about 15 seconds, my tongue found her clitoris again and I started the alphabet back up. This time finishing from H-Z, while my fingers slowly touched spots that have not been tampered with in three years. But once again, I stopped all pleasure and began kissing her other inner thigh and around her pussy lips.

"Boy stop playing and give me what I want," Sidney cries out with a hint of anxiety.

And after that request, I knew it was time to deliver. My tongue dove straight in and left sensations, not only on her clitoris, but throughout her whole being also. Either my fingers would be repetitively massaging her already swollen clit while my tongue danced around her G spot or it would be reversed. I would switch back and forth, non-stop, over the next fifteen minutes.

After the multiple times, her hips had thrust forward and she would gyrate her pussy against my tongue, I knew she had definitely "got hers." *Now it was time to get me.*

I told her to get up and get in position to ride me. Reverse cowgirl style though. I wanted to see the way that ass looked, bouncing up and down on my dick. Plus, seeing my name imprinted on her butt cheek would make the experience a hundred times better.

Now I was the one laid back on the bed while she directed my *throbbing dick* into her *tropical pussy*. Off the top, I did not just slide right in. It took some maneuvering for her to take *all of me*. I almost went over the edge, hearing her moan out my name and grasp the covers for leverage. *But I held my composure*. I rhythmically pounded away in her pussy to the beats and sounds of Baltimore Club Music.

Over the next two hours, me and Sidney *fucked* in numerous positions sometimes forgetting to catch our breath. Even after the three times I *nutted* in her, my dick still did not go limp in that pussy. I clarified the rumor for her that "fresh out of jail dick" was the truth. During her last orgasm, I was able to "come" with her.

We laid motionless for a while and just enjoyed being wrapped up in each other's sexual warmth. Sidney claimed that she could not move due to sensual and pleasure overload. Eventually we went upstairs to shower together; and in all actuality, that task was truly meant for our difficult cleaning areas to finally have some attention. *It has been three years right.* Afterwards, our attention was focused elsewhere. *We had two pounds of Purple Trainwreck in the basement.*

-#-

After stashing one of the pounds, I kept the other one out to begin the process of manufacturing and delivering. Sidney sat by my side, rolling all four vanilla Dutches. Four hundred and forty-eight grams of weed was going to take forever to sack up, so I told Sidney that I will need her help once she has done. We had to remain aware of how much "loud" was put into each bag. I instructed Sidney to simply "eyeball" an adequate amount after realizing that we did not possess an essential tool when it came to drug distribution. *The scale.*

My main objective for the first half pound was to create clientele. *I was really blessing niggas game. Nothing but dimes were going to be sold. Enough to roll two blunts if you are the truth.* Weight wise, in each bag was around the 1.4-gram mark. After word was to get buzzing about my herbal commodity, taxation would soon follow. That is where the last pound and a half would get distributed. *"Eight large", I thought. Shit if I cannot scratch ten thousand out this shit then I am a pussy.*

Conversation was light, while me and Sidney smoked and drank these nasty ass Four Lokos. It will be a lie though if I said that this quarter of a can did not already have me "wavey."

With 92Q jamming hard on the radio all night, the atmosphere in response spawned an even greater *vibe*. Fayette Street seemed livelier every time I looked out the basement window. It felt like the *Times Square* of Baltimore.

"Hey baby, remember when we used to smoke weed to this joint before you got locked up," Sidney says while heading towards the stereo. I was trying to remember what we used to get high to "back in the day." Most pre-incarceration trivial matters were all a blur to me now.

That is when I saw it. She had a copy of my 'Eastside Takeover' mixtape that I had dropped after graduation. My heart dropped and my face was flushed with humiliation as I watched her place the disk into the CD-ROM. Imaginatively, I wanted to dive across the room and tackle her before she pressed play. *But it was already too late.* She had just unconsciously and indirectly ruined the whole mood of this evening. One thing that I did not want to do on my *first day home* was to put any recognition into the failures of my past.

Sidney went straight to song number two. It was called "*Smoker Section*." Before I got locked up, this was a Baltimore City classic. I used to have Sidney manage my online social media accounts, where you could always locate hundreds of motherfuckers posting links, videos, and comments about the song. Mostly talking about the different strands of weed they were smoking or how awesomely "lifted" they were while listening to my shit. I had even composed a music video for the song which was really a four minute and eight second depiction of my everyday life. Signs that the city was feeling me started to come rapidly. I can recall multiple times when I am walking down the street and cars would pass, listening to this song. Sequentially, smoke would be flowing through the cracked windows.

Now, listening to this song is just a reminder of the past. *A reminder of what I could have been.*

"*Wake and bake every day, nigga you already know it/*

Shorty said hold up, cuz she still, still rolling/

Welcome to the smoker section, everybody come over/

But the fun doesn't end until you leave sober/" is all you hear while Sidney is singing along to my chorus.

She is dancing in front of me and smoking the blunt while trying to initiate the good times that we once shared listening to my creativity. *But it is just not the same.* Masking my anger and humiliation while staying cordial was difficult.

My facial expression was blank as I French Inhaled the exotic *indica sativa*. Sidney has known me too long though because she instantly senses something wrong.

"Damn Izzy, what's up?," she asks me.

"No offense, but I'm really not trying to hear this shit. Can you please put 92Q back on."

"This shit," she looks at me with a sour face of disgust. "You do realize that 'this shit' is you. Right?."

"Exactly" was all that I managed to verbalize before exhaling.

Even though Sidney did not understand my reaction, she still respected my request by taking the CD out of the stereo and placing it back in its natural habitat. *Good.* That is, until she comes and flaunts it in my face.

"You know this is your creation. This is you," she tries to tell me. I believe these Four Lokos had my emotions displaced because I snapped. I never really expressed these types of feelings to Sidney before, so she was still uninformed to my current thoughts.

Taking the CD from her hands, I break it in half. *Straight down the middle.* Leaving her startled and confused as to what I am going to do next.

"That was me. It isn't me anymore," I tell her making sure my eyes never left hers.

"Well then, who are you now?," she asks.

"Honestly, I can't answer that question because I don't even know."

And that is the pure, unadulterated truth. *I do not know who I am anymore. I spent my whole life chasing some rap dream that I never gave myself the opportunity to allow any other talents to manifest. Ever since the fifth grade, I said that I was going to be a rapper. Not a lawyer, doctor, plumber, fireman or scientist. But a rapper. I even served a three-year prison bid for my rap dreams. And that was for what? To get out and hear an abundance of mainstream artists lying on the airwaves. Half these niggas had legal money before breaking into the industry. They did not have to pace the concrete or wear a ski mask like me. But they get paid a million dollars to portray the image of the life that I am living.* Even Mister Popular is living well off being fraudulent and deceptive.

So where does that leave me? 23 years old, starting from the bottom. Maybe the universal energies had favor on my being to have allowed Byrd and me to cross paths again. At least now, I have an "avenue" to make a little money. But Byrd said it best, "*You can't sell drugs forever.*" That he had *A Hundred Dollars And A Dream* too.

I possess the same hundred dollars, but no dream. My dreams were interrupted by reality. I spent the first twenty years of my life stuck in "La La Land." Now I am stuck in this quicksand damned in any direction that I chose to go.

What did I stand for, besides being a black man? How long can I live without a purpose before I am killed or back imprisoned? What kind of role model can I be for Stacy when I do not even know the role I am supposed to play in my own life? All these thoughts lead back to one question; who am I?

Isaiah Malik Brown. Izzy B. Ex-con. Ex-rapper. Someone who is going to have a life full of regrets. I guess instead of trying to shape the future, I should live in the present. Shit, I can live like Uncle Lenny for the next forty years.

After we had finished smoking, Sidney came and sat down next to me. She put her hands on top of mine and brought me in for a kiss.

"No matter who you say you are, don't worry about me Izzy. I'm going to always be by your side" is what Sidney tells me that places an unforgeable smile on my face.

Throughout all the trials and tribulations of my past and what I will face in the future, I am glad to have a down ass chick riding with me. Maybe I should confide in her more. Maybe we should produce a million-dollar idea we can work on together.

Once we started kissing again, I quickly noticed that Sidney never really left that "wet stage." Instead of worrying about the troubles of yesterday or the hassles of tomorrow, we drown out in this moment. *A moment of love.* I planned to make love to her this time and that is what we did for the remainder of the night.

I watched her fall asleep in my arms, but I was not too much tired. Just the sight of the memorialized hundred-dollar bill and an idea of dreaming out my success route; made me scared to go to sleep.

The difference between having a dream and having a hundred dollars is that one is fictional while the other is reality. You cannot pay the bills with a dream. You cannot tell the landlord that I am going to pay you with my dreams. But you can have a dream that makes you capable of paying the bills. What is crazy is that, still when I sleep, my dreams are similar to the ones I had thirteen years ago. *In those project courtyards.*

Chapter 7

A few days later, Danielle had called to let us know that she was bringing Stacy back home. *"Obligations, responsibilities,"* I thought. Even though I could not wait to spend time with my little girl, it was relaxing to just be laid up with Sidney. We had caught each other up in reference to the occurrences' that have taken place during my incarceration.

Sidney seemed really intrigued as I amused her with stories of prison life. Before, it would be quite difficult to keep me interested in her "girlfriend drama." *But now I was all ears*. Compared to jail talk, I would rather hear my girl gossip and complain about her futile problems. Sidney told me about why she now gets her hair done on the Westside, by Mondawmin Mall. Apparently, Sidney and her former hairstylist, "fell out" on some shit called *Facebook*. Throughout the couple of days, we had alone, she showed me how to work Facebook; but it was not my type of "steez." Being a virtual king instead of a visual king was not going to occupy my time.

Furthermore, we talked about the past, present and future. We were both able to pinpoint each other's personal evolution. The Purple Trainwreck we were smoking on enabled us to bring both of our perspectives to light. It was invigorating and enlightening at the same time.

Plus, Sidney got me back on deck with my Jordan's and *True Religion* game. *Wifey material, for real.*

"Say babe, can I use your phone right quick. I have to holler at Byrd," I tell her.

"Damn Izzy, you're going to have to get your own phone. What are you going to do when I am not around or you are at work?," she asks me.

"Shit I'll use a payphone or something."

"Isaiah get the fuck out of here. We are not living in the eighties anymore. Before Stacy gets back, we are going to get you a phone. I'll put you underneath my cell phone contract."

"Uhh its okay baby. Don't worry about it, I will make something happen," is my response that comes out hesitantly. I hate accepting handouts, it feels emasculating.

Getting the two pounds from Byrd and going shopping with Sidney, put me on the borderline of dependency. I should be able to provide for myself. But this is the crippling effect about getting out of prison. Now Sidney wants to buy me a phone. It will feel embarrassing if she drains her funds to get me back equipped for society.

"I hate when you act like that," she informs me.

"Like what?"

"Like I can't do nothing for you," she begins. "I'm your girl, let me take care of you sometimes. Remember for my eighteenth birthday; you took me on a helicopter ride, Red Lobster and we stayed at the Hilton downtown. I know all that shit alone cost more than $1200 and you had the nerve to trip whenever I put more than fifty bucks on your commissary. Get over yourself and this egotistical shit, Izzy. We are a team, dickhead. So, go put some fuckin' clothes on and we out Yoo."

I found her rant hilariously sexy, so my playful smirk could not be hidden.

"Okay Sidney, you got that," I say laughingly. "But after this month, I'm going to make sure our phone bills are paid and that, my friend, is non-negotiable."

"Alright that's fine with me. I just hate when you act like you must carry the weight of the world on your shoulders. You have me to help out with that load," Sidney says as sweet and seductive as possible.

Ironically, the whole time she is massaging my broad muscular shoulders and kissing around my newly pierced earlobes. Ever since I got out, her sex drive has been through the roof. Just the past seven days, we have fucked over thirty times. Expecting to get a "quick pump" in, I start kissing her pretty full lips and pulled her on top of me; prepared to "straddle the beast."

But before any action could be orchestrated, she resumes to the mission at hand.

"Not right now Izzy. We have to hurry up before Danielle and Stacy get here."

"True shit," I tell her.

That is when Sidney promptly puts on a pair of Ralph Lauren sweatpants and crispy, all white Air Force Ones. I was not tripping about her delaying the sexual gratification that we both surely craved. *It was time to get out and get some money anyway.*

The reaction I anticipated from the streets regarding my product was long overdue. Besides White Widow and Catpiss, this is the dankest weed I have ever smoked.

I put on a pair of Nike basketball shorts and took out twenty "sacks." Instinctively, ten went in one pocket while ten went in the other pocket. This is not the first occasion where I have sold weed in front of Sidney. So, like one great mind thinking like the other, she threw some khaki Hollister cargo shorts to put overtop my Nike shorts into my lap. This was my method of concealing drugs since I was fourteen. Whether I was selling weed or heroin.

Putting on my Jordan Six Rings, I felt as if I was existing in my younger days. *Bad bitch, new shoes, and an opportunity to make thousands. If not, millions.*

Before we left, I had Sidney roll up a fat ass blunt. Did not think she could get the job done because I gave her two "sacks" to insert in an original Dutch Master. Damn near three grams of weed to stuff. But to my surprise, she did it. Created a fuckin' *cylinder masterpiece.*

After grabbing the nine-millimeter, flashbacks of the most recent prison lockdown surfaced in my mind. Must have been some sort of intuition. Another thought came across my mind as I placed the pistol back under the mattress.

"Nigga you're going to be on the Eastside, chill out."

-#-

Me and Sidney were going to the Verizon store off Fayette Street and Highland Avenue. Approximately about twelve blocks from my Uncle Lennys' house. We could have easily caught the 20, 22 or 35 express bus that stops five feet from his stoop; but it was a nice day outside, so we decided to walk.

Strolling down Fayette Street you can sense that *niggas* were peeping our style. Probably because whenever they usually saw Sidney, she was by herself or with Stacy; but now she is with me. On top of that, we were polluting the air with this loud ass weed.

"Babe, how do you see us living in five years," Sidney asks me while direly attempting not to cough.

"Shit, I see us living *phat*. Been thinking about acquiring a bullshit trade that gets you *gwop'ed* up though. I see you owning the hair salon that you been dreaming about since I met your *bad ass*."

She smiles. "Ohh Izzy, remember when I used to braid your hair before you had cut it?"

"Hell yeah, that's why I had cut my shit. Every time you would braid my hair, it'll feel like my scalp was bleeding."

"Boy stop playing with me. It's because your scary ass was tender headed," she replies back.

"Or because your ass is heavy handed. To be so small and to have hands so delicate, I've seen them *bitches* do some damage over the years."

"Whatever nigga. But I still don't get it."

"Get what?" I ask.

"I don't get how you can take a trade, that's bullshit and expect to be happy in the long run."

"Hold up Money, how you figure I won't be happy?"

"Because you and I both know what makes you happy Isaiah," she says.

"Word up. So, I guess you have all the answers."

"Not all of them, but some. And I know for sure that the ending equation would not equal you being happy as a fuckin' carpenter or plumber. Get real Yoo," Sidney finishes before she's distracted by me passing the blunt.

"Hmm I can dig it" is my subliminal response that would convey the message that this is not what I want to talk about. One, because it is frivolous. Two, because my attention has become focused elsewhere.

There was a crowd of almost thirty, posted up in front of the Enoch Pratt Public Library. *What they were doing, I did not know.* But from a distance I had already sized them up to be around my age. A chance to get off some of this weed and build my clientele. *"Maybe I should have brought the pistol"* was what my third eye kept badgering me about.

As me and Sidney got closer though, it instantly came evident to me of why all these people were standing, religiously. From the four men in the middle, who took turns "talking." To the head nods of approval and animated "ohhs/ahhs" from the audience. I already know what time it is. These motherfuckers were not standing here for no reason. They were enjoying the lyricism from this freestyle rap cipher.

It never crossed my mind to join, even after Sidney nudged me in the ribcage. I hit her with a "*chill the fuck out*" look though and she got the idea.

"*Got that loud out, loud out*" was the slogan I used to advertise this purple *piff*. People in the crowd became enticed just off the Kush aroma that was still embedded in my clothing. I pulled out a few "sacks" and announced the prices.

"Say lookout Duke, if y'all cop three of these *jiffy's*, I'll let them go for the quarter. All day," I explained to the strangers who were interested in buying.

"For real Yoo. I have forty on me. What will you do for that G?," one of the young hoppers' asked me. He looked at least three years my junior. Probably because he had on a whole Adidas jumpsuit with the snapback to compliment it.

"Shit Sun. Here," I say giving him five baggies while he handed me two twenties. I would not classify that as taking a loss because it is all profit money. *Must produce customers.*

"Damn G, appreciate that for real", the youngster tells me.

"No doubt. Let your crew know I'm on deck."

"Alright man, where are you normally at?"

"I'm up Fayette and Montford. You'll catch me around there posted like a mailbox," I tell him.

"Already. What do they call you?" he asks me.

"Izzy. Izzy B."

I could tell recognition hit him by the way he paused in mid stride. After putting the weed away, he lifted his Ray Ban sunglasses up to thoroughly get a glimpse of me.

"Izzy B? Didn't you drop a mixtape a few years back?," the young hopper says already knowing that he answered his own question. I did not even acknowledge his statement. Too busy trying to "seal the deal" with another potential customer.

"Matter of fact, that is you. You're the one who *beef'ed off* on Mister Popular."

After this accusation that he says loud enough for everyone to hear him; if they were not tuned in before, they were now.

"Ayooo I did cop your *joint* like four years ago. Something about the 'city takeover.' That bitch jam for real," a random bystander adds in his evidence of my existence.

"Yeah, yeah. That is me," I say making no interest of the past.

"Ayooo this nigga the truth y'all. Bless our game with something. I know you have been in the lab lately," one of the hoppers' requests of me.

"Nah man, I'm just trying to get rid of this loud. Niggas just got this shit from Canada for real," I lied with ease to change the subject. With the spotlight now on me, motherfuckers came in flocks to buy out my supply. Additionally, having the name "Izzy B" associated with this product made it an easy sell.

Before I knew it, the pockets on my basketball shorts were empty and my cargo shorts were $170 richer. Instructions were made perfectly clear to text Sidney phone if they needed some more. By that time, I will have my own line as a main contact number.

As me and Sidney began to recover our tracks, someone yelled out my name.

"Hey Izzy B," the young hopper yells.

"What's good shorty?"

"Fuck Mister Popular!"

-#-

Arriving in the Verizon store, I was overwhelmed by how many '*hood niggas* waited in line for these electronics. We did not grow up with this shit, so I did not agree with the need to drastically upgrade now. Half these *cats* had grammar problems but could explain cell phone applications and Bluetooth more confidently than explaining their own cultural heritage. It is crazy to think that motherfuckers are robbing, selling drugs, and killing for the money to buy these phones.

Three years is not too long when you think of the human lifespan, but in reality, a lot has changed in this short amount of time. When I left it was still dope to *bleep, bleep* on your chirp. Now niggas are making whole sex flicks with they shorty off these phones. Average price now for a phone is pushing two hundred dollars. *Somebody car note.*

Standing in line, there was someone in front of us that was bitching about his application not working. *I could not believe my ears.* Nigga said he had an app, which was a digital scale that used to work perfectly fine. Now he claims his phone is defected. I wondered if it was crack or heroin that messed up the screen of his phone. Without waiting for technical support, he went ahead and threw down almost four hundred dollars for the upgraded version of his old phone. *I could not take it anymore.*

"Lookout Sid," I call my baby mother by the name we came up with in high school.

"Let's just hit the market and I'll cop a cheap, throwaway phone. That is all I will need anyway. Ain't about to blow no Benji's for a portable laptop. We got one at the crib," I say with an emerging attitude.

"Isaiah, shut up. Just chill, I am going to show you everything. Promise you'll love it," Sidney tells me.

The only thing I could do was shake my head. Before my opinion was voiced, a salesperson was on her way over and Sidney had stolen the show. *Purposely. To keep me quiet.*

"How may I help you all today," the saleswoman asks.

"Yes, I'm trying to get my boyfriend a phone and put him on my family contract."

"Okay great. Do you know which smartphone you'd like sir?"

"Smart phone," I say sarcastically. "Uhh yeah, it really doesn't matter. I'll get the same joint she has."

While the lady is pulling up Sidney's account information, I decide to overlook a brochure regarding each cell phone plan. Sidney informed me that she pays for the service that offers unlimited talk, text, web, and data usage. That sounds all right if you are going to be on the motherfucker for an unlimited amount of time. *Which I will not.* And for $120 a month, really $240 for both of us; probably will not be paying for that either.

"Babe this is a lot of got damn money just to have an on-the-go calendar and instant weather alerts," I whisper to Sidney.

"Sshh Izzy, it's all worth it. Trust me," she says.

"Uhh excuse me miss. What is the point of having unlimited web and data anyway? Like what is that shit?" I ask the teller.

It is like my question took her off guard. The saleswoman looked at me as if I were from another planet. She was either thinking I am fresh out of prison, based on my appearance; or pulled a bad bitch from the suburbs who put me on this next level shit. *Both opinions were true too.*

"Well," the teller begins. "For starters you will be able to download music, manage bank transactions and keep track of all of your social media accounts. You can surf the net, all day and night, if you like. Have access to applications that range from finding the cheapest gas prices, job offers to even locating the nearest police scanners. Basically, these smart phones will make life easier for you regardless of your status or location in the world."

After hearing her speech, I was moved. By the way, she accurately assumed I will need a police scanner or want to download music. If she could sell these bullshit phones with finesse, I knew she will be a good mule to traffic narcotics. *Maybe I should refer her to Byrd's' spot on Rose Street.*

"Okay so for the new iPhone 6B with full coverage insurance and service to be activated right away… The sales total is $374.28", the sales associate who has been servicing us the whole time tells me. I notice her nametag says Emily. First black chick I have encountered named Emily. She could not be from around here.

"Would you like any accessories to go with your new purchase today sir?"

"Accessories, like what?" I ask.

"Maybe a phone clip, Bluetooth earpiece or screen protectors."

"Fuck it, mine as well go all out. Throw it all in the bag," I tell her.

As Emily is calculating our new total, which comes around the $450 mark, Sidney gets a call on her phone.

It is Danielle and she offers to come pick us up. While Sidney gives her directions to the Highlandtown Plaza, she gives me five one-hundred-dollar bills to pay for my gadgets. I only use three of them though and use my weed earnings to pay for the rest.

    Ever since Sidney gained my trust, she never lost it. That is the reason I can give her majority of my money and not have any negative obligations about it. I always did this in case something happened to me. So, she and Stacy would have something to clutch on. Honestly, I trust Sidney with money over my own mother. When it comes to necessities, Sidney always looks to the future. It will be a waste of time worrying about her fucking off survival money.

    In the process of bagging our items, Emily asks Sidney about where she gets her hair done at. Sidney being friendly, enthusiastically lets Emily know that she does her own hair; but has a stylist on the Westside who does her touch ups.

Apparently, I was right. Emily was not from East Baltimore. She was not from Maryland period. She had just relocated from Pittsburgh and trying to find the go-to spots. They, like most females, exchanged each other's information. Meanwhile, I had cranked up the tool that will possibly assist in my future success.

-#-

Later that night, I had a little alone time while Sidney was upstairs giving Stacy a bath. I let them have their mother-daughter moment while my indulgence was involving two cigarillos. *Planning to take one of these to the "face" and saving the other one for Sidney.* At the same time, trying to configure and decode this smartphone.

Basically, everything was done. Within the first few hours, I had already taken multiple pictures, videos and downloaded a lot of older music that I used to fuck with. It came equipped with a wide array of applications to choose from. Off the top, my first apps were the digital scale, police scanner and Baltimore Metro MTA schedules.

Out of euphoria and slight boredom, I decided to search the internet on my phone. Give it a little *test drive* to check its reliability. Suddenly, the realization comes in about how lucky I am to possess this next generation shit. *This is the future.* Wonder what Maserati Rick would do with this portable, all access connection to the world. *"Hmm,"* I thought. Even though I have not been out a full two weeks yet, it dawned on me that Rick may have had his parole revoked. Hate seeing anybody stuck in "The Belly of the Beast."

I Googled the name Richard York to find pages of criminal investigations. Truth is that Maserati Rick caught a pistol case at thirteen years old and received probation. Not even four months later, he shot a cop and got 15 to life. *That is where that twisted metaphor came from the night before I was released. He gave me the advice that he deserved twenty years prior.*

Maserati Rick ended up accepting a plea bargain for 22 years, but since he was still a minor; parole would see him in five years. He eventually got out on his 21st birthday. According to public records, Rick would only come back to jail for misdemeanor charges ever since he got out. From the DWI he caught in North Carolina, Indecent Exposure in Florida to the domestic violence case he has now.

I clicked on the Maryland Department of Corrections website to see if he had to do any "hard time." Astonishment settled in when it stated that Richard York was set to be released exactly eight weeks and six days from this date. *Damn I was going to have to try and avoid this nigga. He will be pretty fucked up if he knew I was just selling weed and have not accomplished anything besides gaining clientele.*

Next, I type in my name, Isaiah Brown. Stereotypically, I pictured the media to defame my name and label me as a monster. That is not exactly what they did. The Public Records statement says:

"March 16th, 2008- An incident was reported that the ending result was an assault that led to bodily injuries. Based on witness statements, Isaiah Brown, 20, aggressively smacked, Eugene Allen, 20, on the right cheek with a 22-ounce beer bottle. Allen was later taken to the hospital with minor and non-life-threatening injuries. Brown, is now facing second degree assault

charges and is in custody at the Baltimore City jail with a $50,000 bond."

"<u>August 5th, 2008-</u> Isaiah Brown accepts a plea deal for a three-year sentence in relation to the Mid-March assault on Eugene Allen, at an upscale Harborfront nightclub. Based on the nature of the assault, brown will be eligible for parole in March 2010."

"<u>March 16th, 2011-</u> Isaiah Brown is released after serving a three-year sentence for Assault with a deadly weapon. This case has been approved by the governor to be closed and discharged."

To me it seemed like they missed a whole chunk of what really happened that night at Paradox. If they would have mentioned me stomping him to the point of unconsciousness while 400 people watched then I may have gotten a heavier sentence. *So, everything worked to my advantage.*

Sucked that this occasion would follow me to human extinction though. *This is what I will be remembered for.* If I ever had a son and he became a junior, this incident is linked with his name. This is now a part of my legacy.

Which gave me another idea.

Returning to the google website, there was one more person I had to research. *Izzy B.* Typing in my alias name, I was afraid of what I may find. Not too many people knew me by my government name. But presently relevant or not, *Izzy B* is always going to ring bells in Baltimore. So, these findings would give me a clue of how people in my city felt.

The results were monumental. The sight was breathtaking. I could not believe these were so many links where people could get a taste of my reality. From downloadable sites to blogs, even the pilgrims could sense that once upon a time, I was making *noise*. What is even more mind boggling is that I did not even create profiles on all these sites. *These were responses from the streets.*

I could not resist clicking on the website which had a headline that said "#TeamIzzyB." It was a blog, written by an editor for one of the DMV hip hop magazines. Something unimaginable, how this person knew my whole life story and was able to critique it into three well put-together paragraphs. Underneath my biography and discography was the police report from what happened with Mister Popular. Underneath that there were hundreds, if not thousands of comments where motherfuckers took my side. Damn near everybody in the Baltimore/Washington DC area had put the puzzle together of why I did Eugene like that. There was even a video of the whole showcase. The normal comment for the video was "Fuck Mister Popular, #TeamIzzyB."

It was hard to understand how Mister Popular was so successful in the rap game with all these menacing videos on his character. *How could Felix Stone, a multi-millionaire CEO promote a fraud on his label?* The answers to these questions, which I did not know became the exact reason I fell back from the music industry.

Going back to the 'Izzy B' search results, I clicked on a website whose headline plainly said, "Eastside Takeover." This was an indie mixtape database where they keep track of your individual downloads and comments. I had just come into the knowledge that I produced a fuckin' typhoon of a buzz for myself, three years ago. The overall downloads for "Eastside Takeover" were topping the three million mark. *"All for free,"* I questioned myself. It is crazy that three million people took the time out to witness Izzy B. Based off the language on the comments, these motherfuckers were from all over the world too.

I clicked on one of my street anthems entitled "Seven Days." This song alone had over 600,000 downloads and comments posted as recent as last week. *Damn, this shit was still getting play.* The comment this fan posted said: "Hell yeah I still love that hook. Can't wait to hear some new music from Izzy B, fresh out of prison #TeamIzzyB all day and tomorrow."

Too bad, he or anyone else would be hearing any new music from Izzy B. *I retired early.*

A thought crossed my mind though about how I probably missed my chance while I was locked up. If my music was receiving all this glory, then it is highly possible that some music executives were looking to work with me. But after seeing I was incarcerated and what I had done, they labeled me a risk. *A risk that was not worth investing millions of dollars into. I do not like entertaining self-defeating thoughts, but it is true. Obviously, it must be. Because after all this recognition I am witnessing, my residence is still my Uncle Lenny basement.*

But what if? What if they key to my success is embracing the failures of my past? What if the link to my prosperity is stepping outside of my comfort zone, the streets? What if the vision of triumph is to overlook the illusions of a competition? What if everything you have been running from meets you at the finish line?

Then, were you ever running from it at all or simply hoping it would not reappear?

You cannot ride the wave of life forever, not expecting to fall off. But once you do, there is only three options: either drown into the pressures of the world anticipating your descent to rock bottom. Or, conform to the currents of the ocean and have your identity swept away. Or get back on your surfboard and try again.

Suddenly, I catch myself listening to "Seven Days" and reminiscing over the memory of that recording session. Suddenly, I catch myself thinking about the countless performances where people in the crowd were throwing up their "sevens" with me. Suddenly, I catch myself rapping the lyrics aloud:

"I got seven days, seven ways of getting money/

I got seven days, seven ways of getting money/

I got seven days, seven ways of getting money/

Got to do whatever it takes got to keep the paper coming/"

Suddenly, I think about what these lyrics really mean to me. Suddenly I think about what I am going to do to keep the paper coming after these two pounds of weed are gone. Suddenly, I think about the promise I made to my mother. Sidney and Stacy. Suddenly, I think about how you must get back on your surfboard and try again if you are ever going to accomplish anything. Suddenly, I think about this *Hundred Dollars And A Dream!*

Chapter 8

"Izzy wake your motherfuckin' ass up."

This must be a nightmare. Had to drink too much Cîroc last night at the harbor. I was kicking it with some of my old partners from Somerset Projects. Good times though, good times.

"Izzy, I know you're not still sleep. I am about to take my belt off on your ass" is all I needed to hear for consciousness to settle in. I was pretty much awake, and this was not a dream. This was the voice of Uncle Lenny, standing in the doorway with a newspaper. Looks like the classified section of the Baltimore Sun.

"What's smackin' Unk, you alright?" I asked him wiping the sleep crystals out of my eyes.

"I ought to punch the shit out of you. Why does my basement smell like a skunk?"

I look around to see what he was seeing. *Searching for an explanation.* But the condition and contents of the room spoke it all. There was about $900, in all types of bills, sitting in an open shoebox. There were empty, cut-up baggies where weed once filled that space, covering multiple areas in the room. Not to mention, the countless cigarillo wrappers and abundance of new clothes, with no known resources of how I am getting money.

Every day for the past three weeks, I always came in the house with something new. If it was not clothes, then, it was some type of exotic food or electronic gadget. My Uncle Lenny was not stupid by far. I wonder where Sidney was at to help cover for me.

"I don't know Uncle Lenny. You know the city be running late sometimes picking up the garbage," I say to buy a little time to get my shit together. *Really, I am trying to pull a fast one.* But he does not budge at all.

"Nigga what the fuck did you say to me? Do I look *green* to you? I have been pimpin' hoes and slamming Cadillac doors before you were a fragment of anyone's imagination. Don't insult my intelligence," he tells me while I hear footsteps creeping downstairs. *Now they want to come to my rescue.*

"My bad Unk, I'm tripping. Had a long night."

"Damn right you are tripping. Your about to ruin a good thing by going back to prison. Leave your shorty and little girl behind while you do what, a *nickel* this time. She is not going to ride with you when you are in the *bink* for another five years. Somebody else going to be playing daddy to your daughter and knocking your dime piece off. That is what you want, right?"

I do not think he knew Sidney and Stacy were behind him until they gained entrance into the basement bedroom also.

"Uncle Lenny, Isaiah isn't going back to prison; and even if he did, I'll hold him down for five, ten, twenty years. Doesn't matter," Sidney says taking my defense.

"That shit sound good right now. If you *cut* so much for my nephew, then why aren't you pushing him to do better? Get a job, accomplish something, be something. Instead of following these ignorant niggas in the streets."

"I already did, we talk about that all the time. I told Izzy about how my homegirl, Emily, says that there is an abundance of job offers at Mondawmin Mall right now. He said he was going up there today and applying. Right Isaiah?"

I had no idea what the fuck she was talking about. Liked the way she stood up for me though. I simply agreed to Sidney's' statement, expecting some closure to this argument.

"Yeah alright, well here's some job openings I circled for you in today's paper. Most of them offer training too," Uncle Lenny says while handing me the newspaper. *I wonder why he never circled these jobs for himself in two decades.*

"And" he continues. "You better not be selling drugs in my house unless I'm getting a sixty percent cut. You do not know what type of business I have going on upstairs. Going to make my spot *hot* after I been living here for 25 motherfuckin' years", he just continues to ramble on, leaving the room. Me and Sidney could not stop laughing because we knew he was not serious about getting a sixty percent cut. He was solid and firm about selling drugs in his house though. *Even if it is just weed.*

"So, what's up with this Mondawmin shit," I ask Sidney. "You never told me anything about that."

"Because I just found out. Emily told me last night that a lot of stores are looking for help. You know summertime is coming up."

"Word, I'm going to check it out later in the week," I tell her.

"No Izzy just go up there today and fill out a couple of applications. It won't hurt you at all."

"Damn babe, I'm going to make that happen. Just chill," I say while glancing at my phone for the first time today. There were already six text messages where motherfuckers were trying to buy some weed.

"I have to attend to a few sells first though."

"Whatever Isaiah, do what you want. You heard what Uncle Lenny said. Walking around here with drugs and guns every day. You're going to be fucked up if another nigga is tapping this ass, while you do five to ten," she says releasing that Colgate smile. I was in no way amused. In fact, I was more fucked up that she will even let that thought cross her mind. Giving "my" pussy up to some lame nigga.

"Ayo don't fucking play with me like that. I look like a hoe ass nigga to you."

"Okay Izzy. You sold that stiff shit to the streets, but I do not buy it. I been with you too long. So, what are you going to do?" she asks me.

"Damn Sidney, okay. I am going to get dressed and go up there. Watch your mouth though, talking about letting someone else fuck. That is my one-way ticket back to prison. Because I am going to have to kill him, then whoop your ass. For real Yoo."

"Your right baby, I'm sorry. I should not have taken it that far. You know I am only yours, forever and always," she says while leaving a lip gloss print on my cheek.

"Hurry up and go shower. Me and Stacy already took one, we just have to put some clothes on."

"So, where all y'all going," I ask hoping she did not want to tag along.

"Uhh to the mall with you. I have to stop by Reisterstown Road Plaza anyway to get this piece for Emily hair."

"No, it's okay baby, I'm going to take this trip solo."

"Bullshit Isaiah, I'm not letting you go to the Westside alone. You always go over there tripping. Getting jumped and calling the whole Broadway over there with military weapons. I would not be surprised if you robbed or killed someone over there. That's all you used to talk about."

"Sidney, I don't need you babysitting me," I tell her. "Beefing with them Westside niggas was my younger days. I am going over there with a vision and I am going to make that happen. Y'all go out and do your thing. We will meet back up later, do something together as a family. Maybe go out to eat on the waterfront."

I knew that will put butterflies in her stomach and get her off my case.

"Alright Isaiah, I'll just have Emily take us to The Plaza. She has a car. Answer your phone anytime I call so I know you are okay. Anticipate a text message later with the address of where to meet us. I heard about this crab shack off Boston Street we can check out."

"That's a bet baby," I say letting my lips feel the sensation from her lips. Even allowing my tongue to do a little exploring.

As we were all getting ready to split separate ways, me and Stacy had a brief bonding moment. I asked her what kind of toys she wanted me to buy at the mall. She got excited and started talking about Dora

The Explorer, Little Mermaid and SpongeBob. She also told me bring her back a pack of Skittles and Slim Jim. Before I got locked up, Stacy could barely put together sentences. Now with her holding full conversations with me, it made a brother feel proud of my co-creation. *Something to live for.*

Sidney and Stacy left first, five minutes later was my departure. I threw on a pair of 501 Levi's and Diamond Supply tee shirt. Trying to pull off a more casual look. After peering through my phone, I now had eight customers expecting weed. Totaling 16 "sacks" to be sold, $140 to be made after the deals I had cut. I told everyone to meet me somewhere off Fayette Street, which is where I will be walking towards the subway station.

I have never been this bold before. *Going to the Westside, unarmed.* But I was going for a different reason though. *So, it did not bother me at all.* Although I have not been to the opposite side of Expressway 83 since my teenage days. Consider that I have not been to West Baltimore, without a pistol since I hopped off the stoop. Take it even further, this is my first time in West Baltimore, unarmed, since I started selling heroin. Almost ten years ago, after what happened off Whitelock. So today is a milestone to the city takeover.

-#-

I had cut three blocks up to Monument Street, walking towards the Johns Hopkins Hospital subway station. All the weed that was supposed to be sold was gone before I even hit the Jefferson block. So now this sunny, spring day was for my leisure.

"I should have brought more weed," was what my inner self kept telling me. With everybody lounging around the strip malls and Northeast Market, I could have gotten rid of a whole quarter pound. My neighborhood was so big and diverse that a million-dollar corner could form daily. Plans to come back and set up shop were put into effect.

The idea of getting a Half & Half from the market were sporadic. These beverages could not be avoided. A Half & Half has been my favorite drink since I was a shorty. Half tea, half lemonade with a lemon peel in that bitch. Something about the syrup and formula makes these the desirable non-alcoholic drink in the 'hood.

Standing in line, something unorthodox appeared in my line of sight. It was a youngster, probably still in junior high school. He had a shirt with a picture of Mister Popular on it. What made the picture so serene though, was that his face is crossed out. I could not believe that people were walking around East

Baltimore, with X'ed out images of Eugene. Especially *young cats* because Eugene's' deception happened when they were still in the sandbox. Guess the movement was bigger than I thought.

    Arriving at the subway station, I bought a day pass and walked down numerous levels to the underground platform. Before me and Sidney stated fucking around tough, the subway was where me and my crew would go to pull bitches. Johns Hopkins was the last stop on the metro line too, ending in East Baltimore. So naturally, all the shorties coming "Down the Hill" will eventually come through here.

    Once the train came, I sat down and put some music on. For some odd reason, the night my phone was originally bought, I had downloaded 'Eastside Takeover.' This became my choice of tune whenever I was alone. Would rather listen to a real nigga then some scripted niggas. *Crazy because this real nigga was me.*

The train pulled off announcing its next stop, Shot Tower. Then, Charles Center. Lexington Market. State Center. Upton/Avenue Market. Penn/North. Finally, Mondawmin. The heart and social center of West Baltimore.

Chapter 9

Riding the escalators back to the street level took a little extra time that was not anticipated. But the slow elevation allowed me to get a preview of the locals that frequented this area. The atmosphere did not even feel the same as East Baltimore. They dressed differently over here. The wind blew differently over here. The smell was even different over here.

You will get a rather good view of downtown once you finally reach the top. *"Damn,"* I thought. It has been a while since interest overwhelmed me into coming "Ova West." "Up The Hill". I do not even remember *Mondawmin* looking so fresh and active.

In the five years that have passed since I last visited Mondawmin Mall, the city must have done some major renovations to this urban shopping center.

My current scenery was epic. The same way hundreds of people congregated in busy spots, "Down the Hill," was synonymous to the activities of *cats*, "Up the Hill." Walking thru the Mondawmin parking lot, you had Jehovah witnesses trying to get the "lost" to convert. You had an older guy, sitting on the ground with a mini table, enticing others to play *Three Card Marley*. I knew better though. I will rather give my twenty dollars to a bum than to partake in a mystery fraud. The radio station, 92Q, was even out here. I could tell by the decals on their van but could not figure out why they were here. *Right now.*

Entering Mondawmin Mall, I could have easily forgot my reasoning for coming here. There were so many *bad bitches*. Niggas in *The Game* who looked like money. Little homies skipping school trying to hide out from mall security. If there was a shopping mall in East Baltimore, then this is what it will look like.

    Without attempting, I had already convinced myself there was not a job that will hire me up here. All the workers looked like *square* ass niggas. Or at least, not like me. Figured they would not hire ex-cons with an assault record. My plan was to put more effort into the jobs that my uncle checked out for me. They will probably be more reluctant at giving work to felons. *I at least had to put in one application though*. If I was not going to try for myself, I had to try for Stacy and Sidney.

    The 'Help Wanted' sign in front of *Foot Locker* seemed like the best option for me. I walked in and asked for the hiring manager. It was a middle-aged *cat*, whose nametag said "Scooby" and he had a mouth full of gold. Maybe these establishments do hire street niggas.

Sitting down at the *Popeyes*, I realized that this was my first time ever filling out a job application. 23 years old, with the only thing on my resume is a plummeting rap career. 23 years old with no prior work history. 23 years old with no special skills, qualifications or achievements that this application is asking for.

Name. Address. Contact info. Education history, I did graduate. All the standard generalized questions took no brain power to jot down. Work history, none. For the desired schedule chart, I put anytime, for any day; really hoping I did not have to work anytime, any day. I never joined the military. Negotiable seemed like the most appropriate answer for my desired hourly wage. For someone who never applied for a job before,

I was doing well. Until the last question, before I put my signature and date.

Have you ever been convicted of a felony?

I sat motionless, froze in time, trying to decide what to circle. Should I lie and say, no! Or, maybe just a simple, yes! I even contemplated just putting "I'm the one who gave Mister Popular that permanent scar." I deserved a chance to explain the situation though. Just putting "yes, for assault" would probably get my application trashed right next to the outdated receipts. So instead, I logically put "Discuss in Interview." *Cannot go wrong with that.*

I walked back into Foot Locker and gave Scooby my application. He began to look it over and to my amazement, he seemed somewhat interested in my persona. *"What the fuck,"* I thought. They may have enough trust to enroll me onto their payroll and have access to all the new releases. *Hope a nigga get a discount.*

"Everything looks good to me Mister Brown. So I have a question and no worries, your answer will not affect your employment eligibility. But you've never had a job before," he asks me.

"Nahhh Duke, this would be my first time if y'all did provide the opportunity," I tell him not offering any corporate manners.

"That's cool shorty. So, you have reliable transportation?"

"Yeah, the buses and subway."

"Word up, is this address close by here? I'm not too familiar with street names."

"No not really," I explain. "I'm from Ova East. *Down The Hill*. But still, on the metro it will take about 30 minutes to get over here. So, it's really nothing."

"I can dig it. So, what is there to discuss about your felony? You on parole Yoo?," he inquires.

"Look man, this is the real. I just did a three-year bid for assault. I flat timed my sentence, so I'm not on any parole restrictions."

"*Oh yeah.* Say shorty, we kind of strict on assault charges due to the rising gang and drug violence. We don't promote those activities on our premises."

"Nah Duke, it's nothing like that. I, uhh. I *smashed the gas* on Mister Popular a while back."

Scooby stares at me with disbelief. Like what I just claimed was impossible. He does not know that I grew up with Eugene. *Before the Bugatti and BET nominations.*

"Whoa, what you mean? Smash the gas? You lost me shorty."

"Peep game, I fucked Mister Popular off a little over three years ago. That is why he has that scar on his right cheek, which he screams it is a war wound," I attempt to go ahead and give him the real. *He still does not believe me.*

"What? Why did you do that?" he asks me.

"We came up in the same ciphers before puberty even hit us. Mister Popular was always jealous of me though, because lyrically, I was considered the truth. So, one day, this motherfucker breaks in my house and steals my rhymebooks. We ended up performing the same song at Felix Stones' showcase that got him signed and me shunned with embarrassment. I really did not think about an alternative. I just snapped and beat his ass. *Now here we are.*"

Scooby looks at me with wide eyes.

"Damn Sun, that's crazy. Can't believe your right here applying to work under my command," he tells me.

"Yeah, I can't believe it either."

"Nah for real Yoo, I heard about that. I am not from Bmore, I am from DC. My brothers are on that promotion shit tough down there. *Word is bond and bond is life*, niggas was just talking about that. They call you like Eazy Bee or something right?"

"Izzy B."

"Yeah Sun, you got mad love out DC, for real. Okay so this is what I'm going to do for you," he begins. "Going to put a star on your application. All my recommendations on new hires must go through the general manager and he's on vacation for another week. I am going to make sure he grabs your joint and I am going to tell him about you. That's the best I can do Money."

"Already, I appreciate that Duke."

"Word up, real recognize real. I salute," he says motioning towards me for a handshake.

I felt empowered hearing him describe my street prowess. Like my actions were justified by the streets.

Before leaving out of Foot Locker, I stop to check out the fitted caps. That is when I heard Scooby calling my name before I am given the opportunity to think of my next move.

"Ayo Izzy," he yells out not even acknowledging the many customers and his managerial position.

"What's popping slime?"

"Fuck Mister Popular!"

-#-

Feeling as if the key to Baltimore City was in my hands, I left Mondawmin with something with which I did not arrive. *Possibility of employment.* The missing links to my success; desire, determination, and dedication. This "Fuck Mister Popular" campaign has me intrigued also. Especially when I am the "ghost author" to the movement.

But that is the problem. Everybody screaming this shit and do not even know exactly why. Like Byrd, I believed that my pain should be felt by the masses. Whenever I am in the streets, people should already know that I am Izzy B, exposer of Mister Popular. That I am Izzy B and I don't tolerate unauthenticity. If I claim to be the face of the city, then my presence should be a recognizable figure on every block. *From the East to the West.* Looking at these 92Q vans, they should be bombarding me for an interview right now. Instead, their camera crew were focused into the crowd by the metro hub. *Wonder what the occasion was.*

I have never been starstruck before since I always considered myself a *ghetto superstar* anyway. So, seeing some of Baltimore's' well-known DJ's and on-air personalities did not faze me. But the reasoning for their appearance did catch my attention.

This was the second time since I got out that I saw a large crowd surrounding a freestyle rap cipher. Plus, with the fact that 92Q was here, I had to check these niggas out. Size up their lyrical capacity. *Maybe this was a sign.*

I remember freestyling for 15 minutes straight in front of crowds this magnitude. A lot of the videos are still online to this day. From ciphers Downtown, Patterson Park, Lexington Market, and numerous different housing projects; motherfuckers had the chance to witness my glory days. I knew without trouble that I will lyrically slaughter these dudes too. Punch line after punch line, you will hear no nursery rhymes from me. On the freestyle tip, I will make niggas *tap out* and choose new career goals. I ride the beat better than North Avenue car hoppers.

Something drove me to the core of this cipher. If it was not arrogance, then it was these "*spittaz*" amateur rhymes. No matter the amount of avoidance that I applied, rapping was always going to be a part of my essence. It was like riding a bike. Playing basketball.

Making Kool Aid. Getting pussy. It was a fixed behavior that could not be forgotten.

But just like rapping, I had other habits that could not be dismissed as well.

Floating thru the air was a stench of some *loud* ass weed. Along with the aroma, was a young nigga who was trying to market something. As he got closer, that *something* became illuminated. He had Sour Apple Diesel for sell.

"Got these dimes of diesel out" was his repetitive sales pitch that attracted people. I knew if I had some Trainwreck on me then my shit would override his product. I must admit, my intentions were pure at first. Until…

"Ayo what that shit look like Duke," I ask him to get a glimpse. He meticulously pulls out small jars which clarified my assumption. *That this was some loud ass Dro.*

"What's a *zone* running for?"

"I'm down the block wit' it. Shoot me $220 and I got you", he tells me.

"Bet. Let me get two dimes for now. What is your *math*? Going to hit you up in like an hour for the zone," I tell him already mentally putting together a few scenarios.

I whip out my money to pay for the twenty. Really, it was a diversion to temporarily build trust and to see the full potential of my scheme. I purposely pay with a fifty so I can get change. Shit was better than I expected. This nigga had a wad of cash, exceeding the three-thousand-dollar mark.

"Niggas got these pills out too Sun."

Could not believe he was still trying to advertise his drugs when I was now plotting to rob him. I told him that I will check my cash flow and let him know something. I put on a friendly front towards him to antagonize his defense. He would have put a wall up if he knew that I was from Ova East. So that was the information that I strategically left out.

He gave me his number and we parted ways.

Before I got to the escalators to the subway, I pick up the phone to call Byrd.

It is ringing… Ringing… Ringing…

"Yerppp," Byrd answers the phone in our normal 'hood greeting.

"Ayo what you got going on Duke," I asked him.

"Shit Sun, just getting this money. What it smell like?"

"Say I have a liq."

"Where you at?," he says sounding confused.

"I'm Ova West, by Mondawmin."

"Fuck you doing over there? Never mind that, is this shit legit Yoo?," he inquires.

"Yeah man, I already peeped the play."

"So, what do you want me to do?"

"Meet me at the Hopkins Metro in thirty minutes. Come ready," I tell him.

"Say no more."

Byrd hangs up the phone, solidifying our future. Anytime there was a window open to jack a Westside nigga, Byrd was down. Byrd is originally from West Baltimore. He lived there as a toddler. His parents were from the McCullough Projects and that is also where they were murdered. Just a case of mistaken identity and wrong place, wrong time. Walking in front of a dice game, they were both shot dead in front of young Byrd. So ever since, any young hopper from West Baltimore was on his hit list.

There was no hidden pain behind my deeds though. Just greed and the pursuit of money. Sidney was going to be mad about this one but fuck it. This was a terrific opportunity to *bounce back*. She will understand. *"Shit,"* I thought.

This is like Whitelock all over again.

Chapter 10

Adrenaline was rushing the whole ride back to Hopkins. The sweat glands in my hands were working overtime. Performing profusely as anxiety and nervousness took over. Doing robberies was the least of my worries, even facing the inevitable of what may happen to the target. It was just my first month out, after serving a trey and I am already knocking niggas off. This had to be done though. Somebody must die uncomfortably so someone can live comfortably. Or, at least that is what I told myself to make the transgression more justifiable.

-#-

Luigi's Pizza Parlor, off Broadway, has always been a trademark destination throughout my life. A lot of first times have occurred in that humid, fly infested environment. I took Sidney to Luigi's on our first date, nine years ago. Me and Byrd sold our first batch of heroin in the alley, behind Luigi's. We ate a lot of pizza that autumn. I sold my first copy of 'Eastside Takeover' in front of Luigi's. *Within ten minutes of coming up the metro escalators, I had already sold four copies.* From fights, mackin' bitches, drug deals, dice games, freestyle ciphers to simply just standing around; Luigi's has always been the place to meet whenever you got off the subway.

So, without saying a word, Byrd already knew where I will be waiting.

It must have been our project chemistry. Not even sitting in Luigi's for a full 180 seconds, I see the loosely fitting Baltimore Oriole baseball cap, walking through the Broadway and Monument intersection. The only nigga I know who buys twenty supplements of the same hat. The same color. The original joint too. Always a size too big and flipped backwards, facing the right side.

Byrd walks into the parlor with a childish smirk on his face. Like you just talked your mother into letting you eat milk and cookies after bedtime. I did not even have to ask about the supplies that were in his multi-purpose book bag. I will just let time reveal and unravel that answer.

"What's smacking Duke?" he asks me. We greet each other in our 'hood secret societal handshake.

"Peep game Sun," I begin. "Done caught another nigga slippin' Ova West. Same formula and execution.

Look the nigga has a couple bands, weed and pills on him. He left himself too vulnerable. That's how I know I got him."

"Word, do you think it's worth it though? We are not kids anymore robbing to buy Jordan's. Shit you have a kid now. I can shoot you some bread or *work*. That is nothing. I just don't want you to get caught up on some petty shit."

Byrd's' response catches me off guard. I am 23 and still trying to hit *liqs* for less than five thousand. It will have me closer to the million-dollar range though. But what if he is right? Am I just wasting my time or creating my rites of passage into manhood? Becoming self-sufficient.

I did not know anything about my intended target. If he had a family or his reasons for hustling. But I could not let that influence my decision because the same heartless feeling I have towards him is the same heartless feeling others' have towards my hustle. Take the situation with Mister Popular for instance. Byrd knows, just like I know that there is no love on these streets. For anything. Love and the feelings surrounding love get you killed, not bullets.

With much love to the Creator, I could not show any love to the creation. Unless they were family, or my *day one* cipher and this west side hustler was neither.

"Fuck that nigga man. It is an easy win. You know I would not formulate a plot that will get us jammed up or popped. I just need you to ride with' me Duke."

"Say you my man's Yoo. Known you since *knee high*. Not going to let you do this alone. I just do not want you to freeze up when shit hit the fan. That's all." Byrd tells me.

I laugh. "Nigga when have you ever known me to freeze up during a mission?"

"Motherfucker, them niggas on Whitelock had you hiding underneath a compact *joint*. If I did not save the day, we would've been smoked."

"We were fourteen years old, Money. Have to cut me some slack on that. It was always easy to talk about catching a body until it's time for the job to be done," I explained to him.

"Well let us not make any excuses today. We are going to go there, get that and get back. I put my business on hold, thinking we had to assassinate the alpha and omega for at least fifty large."

"You crazy Duke. A come up is a come up."

"Yeah alright. Let's grab some wheels," Byrd instructs as we leave the pizza parlor.

-#-

Crescent City Apartments sat two blocks away, behind Luigi's Pizza Parlor. This complex was diverse and multiracial compared to the rest of East Baltimore. It was a home, away from home for many doctors and students who visited Johns Hopkins Hospital and University campus regularly.

Meaning, they more than likely were not knowledgeable to the frequent car thefts that circumference their living area. Translating that into our language- these cars were indirectly prepared to be stolen.

Byrd found a Nissan Altima with the windows cracked. He gave me the formality to watch out while he performs his signature act. Every childhood duo had their own "call." Ours was "*sqwale*." That was used to say either look out, come on, police officers or to pinpoint each other's location. So, once I heard the engine start and Byrd yell "sqwale," I already knew what time it was. *No turning back.*

Chapter 11

Sometimes I wondered what type of life did my sperm donor live. Has he ever been to prison? If so, after his sentence expired, did he ride around in stolen cars brandishing firearms? Did he have a 'no matter what' attitude when it came to taking care of himself and his family? Did he have dreams and accomplish them, or did he simply succumb to the repetitive cycle of miseducation? Shit, was the nigga even still breathing?

I do not have too many fluent memories involving my biological father. In fact, I do not have any memories or at least a picture to affiliate our genetic association. Every time I asked my mother about him, the story was the same. That he was a "middleman drug dealer" from Richmond who was pursuing a boxing career foundered in a larger city like Baltimore and DC. Uncle Lenny swore he was 'the truth' when it came to his skill set with the gloves. But a drug deal went sour and my father was shot. Thus, pushing him away from the boxing ring and more into the streets.

Being a semi-country boy, the Baltimore drug scene, fascinated the shit out of him. My mother, a Baltimore native, introduced him to all the power players she knew. That is when the money started rolling in and soon after, she became pregnant with me.

According to rumors, my father had promised my mother that he was just getting in "the game" to stack up and move around. That he wanted to save up enough money to move us to a nicer neighborhood in the suburbs. He wanted to give me a fair chance at life without the privilege of being exposed to the shit he was witnessing in the late eighties. From the stories, he carried a reputation of being a decent person. Like a motherfucker with morals.

But all his dreams and aspirations erupted very quickly or ended tragically, if you ask my mother. She said I was eight months old when she last saw him.

My father and a neighborhood hustler named Crum had become drug trafficking dummies, transporting "work" to Philadelphia, twice a week. Everything was all good and the money was even better. Especially in the late eighties. But this one trip, something had to go wrong. Because after this one trip, everyone lost full contact with my father. According to Uncle Lenny, after the strange disappearance, my mother was never the same.

So that makes me think. What kind of father did I want to be with Stacy? How can I teach her about valuing her purity and self-worth, when you have these trifling bitches running around, sucking dick for a Xanax pill? How can I tell her to follow her dreams when I gave up on mine? How can I be a good role model without being a hypocrite?

The first 23 years of my existence, I was led into a destructive lifestyle. From shit others taught me, shit the streets taught me, but mostly the shit I taught myself. Because of my mothers' extensive drug addiction, I in so many ways had to raise myself. If it was not for Uncle Lenny, I would've either been serving an L or got bodied a long time ago. But Uncle Lenny was not always there. So, the solo walks through the 'hood, seeing people sell drugs had programmed the idea in my head that this was a normal part of life.

Picture this is all you see, consistently, from a shorty on up.

Picture saying your prayers, as a youngin' and having your thoughts interrupted by gunshots. You start to think that if God cannot even save the innocent babies from stray bullets then who can? And the older you get, the more you stop giving a fuck. Why, because the art of destruction has become a normality in your cipher. Destruction is what you think. Destruction is what you see. Destruction is what you speak.

Growing up as a young 'Alley Boy,' we were taught to practice the meaning behind every famous 'hood quote that has been quoted in every ghetto across America.

"Don't get high off your own supply." "Trust no bitch." "Fuck these niggas, get your money." "Cash

rules everything around me." "Fuck the police." "Either sell the crack rock or have a wicked jump shot." "Shoot first, ask questions later."

Seems like every young 'hopper across Baltimore City, from the East to the West had taken these sayings to heart. Because that is all we know. That is all I know. Destruction.

So how can I keep this destruction away from Stacy when my departure is the antidote? Did I think that robbing and selling drugs would enable me to be a better father? Or was it my own selfish desires that caused me to risk even being called a father? Am I right for supporting my family in this manner or wrong for never giving myself a shot at anything else? How can I stop destroying when the destructive thoughts are still destroying me?

"This is my last robbery, doesn't matter the situation," I silently tell myself. There must be a better way. I deserve to see Stacy graduate. I deserve to be successful. My family deserves to have my freedom preserved. Even after the prison sentence and I am still living uncivilized. Byrd was right, this shit is not worth it. Maybe I should just take my Hundred Dollars and pursue a Dream. The Dream of all Dreams.

I wanted out, for real. Out of the car and out living the real life. But what is the real life and aren't I already existing in it? What if this was all that life had to offer me? I could be wrong though and if I were, I was prepared to die for the truth.

Before I could even say anything or act upon my thoughts, I notice that we were riding down North Avenue. West Baltimore.

"Lookout Izzy, get ready, its dinnertime Sun," Byrd announces to me.

-#-

The phone was ringing... Ringing... Ringing...

"Shit Yoo, this nigga isn't answering," I tell Byrd.

"Give it a minute, then call the motherfucker back. We are already over here."

Just as Byrd was finishing his statement, my phone was now buzzing. It was Sidney. All type of red flags appeared in my mind. It was too late to negotiate and converse. The plan was in motion. Regret touched my heart as I pressed the ignore button.

"Who was that Duke," Byrd asks me.

"Shit, just Sidney."

"Oh. Cannot believe her siddity ass still fuck with you. Got something good boy."

"Yeah, she isn't going anywhere," I tell him.

"Word, anytime you got something good, you got to hold on and don't let that go. Luckily, I'm not a lovey dovey type nigga or I'll have Rocsi from 106 on the team."

"Man get the fuck out of here. I never heard you talk about having a girlfriend before. Well, besides Mary Jane and Nina..."

Our conversation was interrupted by my phone ringing again. This time it was not Sidney. It was the hustler we were plotting to rob.

Ring... Ring... I let my phone buzz for a second before answering.

"Ayooo what it is?"

""Yeah, this Matlock huh," he asked me. I gave him an imaginary name when we first met. Disclosing my identity might have been detrimental to the task at hand. So, the name I chose was based off my surroundings. There was a mattress and locksmith company sitting side by side, close by where we met earlier.

"Fasho, you still trying to do that?"

"Yeah, where you at Yoo?"

"I'm Ova West right now Duke. North and Madison. You 'round here," I ask him, already quite sure he is in the area.

"Already, you think you can meet me off Penn and Fulton in ten minutes. I'm about to grab that right now."

"Alright, that's a bet. I'm going to pull up over there shortly," I tell him.

"That's cool. Just get out and meet me up the alley from the barbershop."

"Alright Duke."

-#-

I precisely explain the details of our phone call to Byrd. He says he knows a little about the Penn & Fulton intersection. Enough to know that discreetly pulling off a robbery would be difficult to do in the daytime. Especially when you factor in gunshots. But we were already in progress, so it was all or nothing. *And I was not too fond on taking a loss.* Even if it was not financial, this trip was time consuming. I could have found a come up on another block in the city. Although our plan was negative, this was still a part of my productivity for the day. *So, in a twisted mindset of a way, this had to be done.*

Riding down Pennsylvania Avenue, I quickly assessed the difficulty level of this mission. If this shit was a videogame, it will be labeled as advanced. I could have easily estimated that at least one hundred people encompassed these two city blocks. There were several businesses that lined Pennsylvania Avenue. From liquor stores to barbershops to a record store to even a New York Fried Chicken joint sitting at the main corner of Penn & Fulton. *We knew our plan had to be modified.*

At the intersection, there was a Baltimore Police camera above the streetlight that would blink blue every few seconds. Whether or not if it worked was unknown.

That is when it hit us. The element that would make this damn near impossible. Another major factor that would send us back to the East Side, empty handed.

-#-

There was a uniformed police officer making patrolled rounds, on foot, at this intersection. *And I thought the streets of East Baltimore were rough.* These niggas over here must have made the block hot recently. The only thing that would work to our advantage is the overcrowding of people.

Me and Byrd looked at the horizon silently. Probably thinking the same thing. *Like how the fuck can we pull this off in such a small-time window?* The potential outcomes were devastating and had the power to change lives forever.

We would either get arrested for robbery and attempted murder. If so, for these charges, I am holding court in the streets. Or this hustler could have allies who come to his aid. If so, once again, I am holding judgement on the streets. Or everything could go as planned. We get what we came to get and move around. Too bad, the first two options seem more logical than the latter.

I look for wisdom from Byrd because this has been his profession and a part of his survival for nearly a decade.

"So, what're you thinking about this one?," I asked him. Byrd says absolutely nothing though. He never once takes his eyes off the streets. I did not even see him blink. He mentally inspects the junkies and dope fiends roaming around. He takes notice of the actions and behaviors of the young niggas in the area. Seeing which stores they go into and how long they were in there. Seeing how many people are with *them* when they group up. His focus is on the police officer though.

That is when I realized that Byrd was not just my partner in crime. He was my consultant when it came to business deals in the streets.

My phone began to ring… Ring… Ring…

"Yoo," I answer to the contact labeled 'Get Got.'

"Say where you at Money."

"I'm on the avenue right now. You ready?," I ask him.

"Yeah Yoo. It is a side street right next to the liquor store. I'm walking down that bitch right now."

"Alright here I come. You about to see me."

Byrd makes one more circle around the block before dropping me off. He still does not say anything, but points to the multipurpose book bag. Inside, I find loose money ranging from ones to fifties. A bar of Dial soap and a box of Arm & Hammer baking soda. A ripped-up metro bus schedule for routes 20 and 22. Underneath all the miscellaneous shit though were two Smith & Wesson caliber .45 pistols. I instinctively go to grab one until Byrd releases a sudden urgency.

"Nah don't fuck with them Sun. Let me see the bag," Byrd instructs while reaching for the military inspired travel bag. Byrd unzips a pouch and pulls my fate out. It blew my mind once he handed it to me. It was a fucking Swiss army knife.

"What you expect me to do with this Yoo."

"Shit. What do you mean? You already know what the clock read. Its quiet time, Money," he tells me.

Chapter 12

Getting out of the car, it seemed as if every pair of eyes that could see was looking my direction. I got caught up in a trance as if my past, present and future flashed through my subconscious. I saw images of me with my mother at the National Aquarium before her sickness enslaved her. I saw clips of my future. Could not tell what was going on though. It looked like either cell bars, a grave or lit up platform. It might have been a stage. *Wait, it was a stage.* So, at this stage in my present, I had to strategically make it out of this shit. *Damn, what did I get myself into?*

-#-

The multiple vehicles created a slight traffic jam. This must be interpreted as a benefit.

I walked across the street as a normal pedestrian would. Contemplating, I took one more glance behind me to see Byrd preparing to drive off. *What the fuck.* This had to be a part of his ulterior motive that he forgot to inform me about. *Or was I just fooling myself?* I have known Byrd since I was a shorty, so did I think that he will leave me stranded to save his own ass?

It was already too late in the grand scheme of things to retreat. Doing so would impeccably put my life in danger. Instead, I stand tall and conform to guerilla mode.

Within ten seconds the hustler comes into plain view. We are both walking towards each other, down this side street. To my disbelief, he was alone and this street was pretty much deserted. Most of the rowhouses were boarded up. The only sign of human activity was sounds coming from Pennsylvania Avenue and a basketball goal that sat lonely on the curb. It looks like this street has not been habitable in years.

"Ayooo over here," the hustler signals to the stoop of an abandoned rowhouse. (To the naked eye someone would think that it was a cat hiding underneath the trash by the stairs. But up close, you will know it was a fat ass rat. The type that you find on the roof of your car in the morning. *A family of them bitches.*

"What it look like Duke?," I politely demand as I approached the stoop.

"Here check this out man. I hooked it up for you too. Ain't going to find no love like that anywhere else on some diesel."

Remorse hit me because I knew I was about to 'serve' this nigga and he had no idea. *Motherfucker was right too.* He showed mad love with this package. I requested an ounce of diesel, which was 28 grams; but from the looks of it, I was holding at least 34 grams. Shit was loud too.

"Yeah, I'm feeling that. Do you have change?," I ask him while personally handing over three-one-hundred-dollar bills. He gives me the weed while continuing to break my change. His rubberband stacks were still valid. This *move* was legitimized. Now my part had to be done.

I knew this cat was not a petty hustler from the moment we initiated business. Indeed, maybe a little friendly but about his money all the same. Just as I envisioned, he was *packing*. I could see the pistol print through his hoody pocket. I was always told *'don't bring a knife to a gun fight.'* So to reign superiority over this situation was going to be a challenge.

As we were "finalizing" the transaction though, I froze. *Damn it.* I could not let him get away, had to stall time to take what is mine.

"What's up, do you still have those pills?"

"Oh, for sure, check me out," he says while reaching back into his pocket. *Game time.* It is over; all I had to do was make these next ten seconds' count.

But there were so many unanswered questions though. Like, where the fuck did Byrd go? After I *handle him*, where was I going to duck off? This hustler has one of the next generation flat phones, so it is possible for the laws to trace his murder back to me. Overall, after getting the supplies, I had to make sure to get his phone. That is one of the main objectives also. Break that bitch and throw it in the Chesapeake Bay or something.

I took my stance. Made it possessive, but still nonchalant as he advertises his colorful Ecstasy pills. Once I saw that one hand was occupied with drugs, my mind said, "the time is now." *All or nothing. Checkmate.*

We stood within two feet of each other. Give or take, it will be four seconds for his free hand to grab the pistol and for the trigger to be pulled. My knife was already prepared for battle. So, within that same four seconds, I had action at disempowering him with terminal stab wounds. Our posture, demeanor, energy, even the birds flying around let me know that it was *now or never.*

He did not see it coming. Within that split second, my knife had penetrated his clothing and was saying "hello" to his intestinal region. I exerted more force to disable him. *But I was too late.* Something about a life-or-death situation will make your reflexes work more profoundly.

The hustler managed to get his pistol free. Thank God I still had full activity of my limbs. So, it was nothing to grab his arm and point the pistol away from me. Three gunshots rang out and temporarily deafened the both of us. (Meanwhile, my knife never fully exiting his body. This was the worst way to kill somebody. The blood, gore and being face-to-face with your victim was sickening.)

Within that four seconds I spoke of, I had delivered the "pokes" that said it all. Watching his eyes widen, as his irrevocable death became imminent, said it all. After his hand went limp and the pistol fell to the ground, said it all. After seeing my whole outfit covered in blood and bodily remains, said it all.

With limited time to spare, I quickly ran his pockets and took the belongings. My expectations were clarified as I took the money, remainder of the weed and bottle of pills he had. I wiped the blood off my knife with his shirt, folded it up and placed it in my back pocket. Just as I was grabbing his phone though, terror shook through my whole being.

Chapter 13

"*Stop put your hands up,*" was the voice I heard echoing down Pennsylvania Avenue. I turned my head to see that a police officer was cautiously standing about 30 feet away with his gun drawn directly at me. He must have heard the pistol discharge.

"*Slowly get down to the ground or I'll be forced to shoot.*"

My mind became cluttered with all types of thoughts. *Where the fuck was Byrd? Was I ready to go back to prison for a murder rap, after only being out for a month?* Surely Sydney would leave me for this stunt. I had to think of an escape route. Quick. Or else, I will be going to prison for life or I would also be facing my death in the next five minutes.

-#-

The officer must have thought I was a lunatic when he saw the smile come across my face. If only he could see the scene taking place behind him.

"*Ghostriding*" up Pennsylvania Avenue was a fearless, lawless, and tactless individual that the streets christened and respected as simply, Byrd. His actions today were congruent with his actions from a decade ago. Present-Day Byrd currently had his arm dangling out the window aiming at the sky. Instantly, he shoots multiple rounds which was the leading factor in distracting the police officer.

"Sqwale" was all I needed to hear.

The time allotted that I had to react was limited-so, I had to make sure that every second was worthwhile. Especially when my escape route became illuminated once the police officer turned to respond to Byrd's' defiance. In the blink of an eye, I ran full speed up the side alley street, opposite from where the police officer was located.

"*Stop*" was the fading command I heard as me and the police officers' distance barrier increased. Before I was able to "*bend the corner*" though, the police officer shot two rounds in my general direction. This sort of scared the shit out of me because personally, I did not put this man's life in jeopardy for him to shoot at me. *Damn, I almost died twice in five minutes.*

This will be a pretty interesting story to tell once I get back to the 'hood. *Just got to make it back first.*

-#-

After I made it to the top of the street, police sirens could be heard throughout the whole vicinity. I did not know whether they were chasing Byrd or looking for me. *Hell, on this side of town, they could be on the hunt for someone else.* Once I saw the "Ghetto Bird" though, it was imperative to stay low. Their suspects were currently in the same five block radius as me.

While deciding which direction to scurry, I see the maroon Nissan Altima zooming directly towards me. It was Byrd. I quickly slide over the hood and hop in the passenger seat, all in one sequential motion. The car did not even come to a complete stop. Tires skidded as we *burned* the scene with high hopes and beliefs that our presence was undetectable.

"Damn Money, what the fuck happened?," Byrd yells as he is swerving uncontrollably to get back to the Eastside.

"*Say* Duke, the little nigga almost popped me," I tell him. "But I toughened up though. I don't know where the fuck that cop had came from though. Yoo just popped up out the *wood works*."

"Word up. After I heard gunshots, that cop went running to the alley like he was Captain Save-A-Nigga. Knew it was time to make a power move."

"Hell yeah, appreciate that Sun. Motherfucker almost had me boxed in."

"Ayooo I already knew your ass would freeze up. I halfway expected that," Byrd says laughingly. "So, you get what you were looking for?"

"Shit check it out."

As anxiety subsided, I began to explicitly relay the events of my recent unplanned homicide. While venting, I began to empty my pants and hoody pockets of all contents. The *Diesel* aroma is what caught Byrd's attention so rapidly. *Soon as I opened the bag type shit.* After everything dies down later, this was going to the *face*. But first, let us count the currency that I *hit* for.

I had a thick ass wad of cash. I can tell it is mostly tens, twenties, and hundreds as I began to separate it. Once everything was accounted for, it was clear that we had acquired $3360. *Free money.* I evenly distributed the 'dough' in two stacks of $1680.

"Lookout Byrd, this is for you Sun."

"Nah keep that Yoo. Buy your shorty something nice," he tells me.

"You sure Duke?," I ask him. "You're entitled to the jackpot too. You are the one who saved the day. Know I can't do *the game* like that."

"Yeah man, take my little niece to Disneyland. Know she would like that shit. We did not have our desires filled growing up. Do something nice while you can G."

"That's a bet Money. That is love for real. Know that I got you no matter…"

"Aww shit," Byrd says while interrupting my speech. I did not have to observe my surroundings to peep that something was not right. I never really saw Byrd panic before, until now. This motherfucker solemnly wears a seat belt, until now. By the awkward silence and immediate pressure, one thing popped in mind. *We have not truly got away.*

"What up Duke?," I ask Byrd already realizing the worst.

"Don't look back Sun," he tells me. "The *red and blues* are trying to pull us over."

Chapter 14

Sometimes greed will get the best of us. Turning you into a savage that is almost willing to do whatever for the dollar bill. I was just now starting to realize how trivial the hunger for monetary gain was. Money and everything linked to money was just an illusion.

So now here I am. About to go to prison over an illusion. Excluding a handful, majority of people in prison are there due to money-related incidents. *I was better off robbing a bank if I was going to get locked up anyway.*

"Aye Izzy peep game," Byrd says boldly without slowing the car down a notch.

"I'm not going to jail, so this is what I'm going to need you to do."

Preparing for a shootout, I instinctively started cocking the pistols back. *It was only one police officer behind us and if this one cop jeopardized our getaway then this one cop might not make it home.* But according to Byrd, that would have just made matters worse. Shit though, what was worse than a murder, aggravated assault on a public servant, robbery, and grand theft auto? Hopefully, *they* sympathize with our situation and give us a light *quarter*. I will be home in 15 years.

"Nahhh Sun. Wipe the pistols and knife off thoroughly. Do not leave any prints. Anything you touched in this car, wipe it off. Throw the bag out the window. Dispose of any evidence. Were about to take a detour. Call Lor Jeff in Somerset."

"Alright. But fuck do you want me to call Jeff for?" I asked him.

Lor Jeff is one of our *day one* childhood friends that we grew up with off Broadway. He did not live like us though. Still to this day his grandparents were disciplining him with the infamous '*go pick your own switch off that tree*' line. So, Jeff never really was a participant in some of our hardcore street missions. But still our homeboy, nonetheless.

"Tell that nigga to let everyone on the *block* know it's about to get hot. We are coming through and straight to his spot," Byrd declares.

Now it was slightly starting to make sense. Lor Jeff lived in the heart, the middle of Somerset projects, where it is bound to be dozens of people wandering around. We would indefinitely blend in with the crowd. If we made it back "Down The Hill," that is.

-#-

I trusted Byrd more than what the word trust symbolizes. He never let me down or sold me out even if it risked his own survival. So, I regarded his plan as our only way to freedom and a deferred prison bid.

"Burgundy sedan stop the car NOW and throw your keys out of the window" is what a voice from the police cruiser says from a loudspeaker. *Of course, we did not comply.* We were on one of the busiest strips in Baltimore. It was not anywhere to pull over anyway; so, we just kept riding the speed limit back 'Ova East.'

By the time we crossed over expressway 83, half of Baltimore City Police were behind us with two helicopters riding overhead. At this point, the doubts started to surface in my mind. *Even if the alleys off Broadway were dead end traps, how the fuck would we get away from these choppers*?

Attempting to alleviate the police chase, I roll down the window with the book bag in my hand. *"This shit is a sight to remember,"* I think to myself while aiming for the right peace officer to "attack." My goal was to create some sort of interference or diversion that would indeed delay their goal. *Locking up young, dumb niggas.* These two fully loaded pistols sustained just the right amount of weight I needed to inflict the damage that needs to be done. All I had to do was aim.

I felt like an outlaw, hanging out the window with fifteen police cars at my tail. Like a young *Tupac Shakur* or *Bobby Seale*. *OJ Simpson* or *"Bull" Hairston*. *John Dillinger* or *Wayne Perry*. The only difference is that I was not going to die or get arrested for the cause.

(Well, not right now). The ambition to get ahead and succeed drove me to this current affair. Getting caught up would mean that everything I stood for, stands in vanity. So, there was only one thing to do. *One potential outcome out of this.*

BOOM! The sound of tires skidding, and a sight of a police cruisers' windshield spoke volumes. The other police cars simultaneously swerved around the disabled vehicles to avoid another accident. This diversion enabled the distance gap between us and the police to widen. *Good.* Right now, we needed every extra yard. It will be extremely beneficial once we hit the "Concrete Jungle."

"Hell yeah, fuck the po-po," Byrd laughs devilishly. What I hope he realizes is that this was another charge if we get caught up. Another five years on top of the already 15-year sentence that I had predicted and that is not including the possibility of paying restitution.

-#-

Turning right onto Broadway, off of North Avenue would be considered the final stretch. Twenty blocks give-or-take and we will be on the courtyards.

"Aye call Jeff and let him know ten minutes," Byrd tells me.

"Alright. Hold up."

The phone was ringing… ringing… ringing.

"Ayo, I know this isn't you two stupid motherfuckers on the news," was Jeff's way of replacing the word *hello*.

"Damn, I didn't think we were that major."

"Yeah man, y'all niggas *hot* bro. it's a helicopter following your every move. *Damn, now they are trying to accuse y'all of being suspects of murder.* I do not know how you expect to just waltz up in this bitch like your Mister Rogers or some shit. You going to get the whole projects quarantined."

"Nigga will you shut the fuck up and listen," I scream. "Look, we going to ditch the cops a few blocks away from the projects. We going to hop out and lose the choppers in the alleys. Have the block cover us until we hit your building. Tell everyone we have a hundred dollars apiece for their full cooperation. Old ladies and all…"

-#-

I hung up. That last part, the bribery, really had just rambunctiously been blurted out. I knew the 'hood would look out for me and Byrd just off the strength of the love we've dispersed throughout the years. From school clothes and supplies for the little homies to helping pay medical bills for the elderly; even if we made our 'hood *dirty*, we still put in the *work* to keep it semi clean. So, in return, we could always call Somerset Projects, our safe haven.

Silence floods our vehicle again. Fear of the unknown and unspoken generated goosebumps that quickly covered my body: That is when my phone rings again. *It is Sidney.*

To not answer the phone certainly did cross my mind but I owed it to her (as my girlfriend and mother of my daughter) to explain the situation. *It was just her response I dreaded.* But who knows, this could be our last conversation ever. So, I sluggishly press the "ACCEPT" button.

"Hello?," I lethargically answered the phone. Sure, she could interpret that something was wrong by my tone of voice.

"Baby, what's up? Where are you?" she pauses. "And why does it sound like there's a bunch of police sirens in the background? You know someone got bodied by Mondawmin a few minutes ago and now they are on a high-speed chase right around the corner too. I'm watching it on the news now."

Oh, the irony of all her questions. Out of everything she could be doing in the world right now, she was watching my dumb ass on the TV. Probably has Stacy sitting right next to her, laughing. Little do they know is that their source of entertainment is supposed to be their representative. The one who is supposed to keep their best interests in mind, so we can prosper.

All I could do was shake my head.

"Baby" was all I could muster to verbalize. "Look I don't know how to tell you this. But I really fucked up this time. I really did. But the motherfuckers you're watching on TV is…."

Chapter 15

"It's me and Byrd!"

I hear her gasp in exasperation. It must be from the element of surprise. All I hear was muffled sounds as if she were moving throughout the house.

"Wait, wait, wait! Do you mean to tell me that the reason you pushed us to the side earlier, was so you can go kill someone? What the fuck is wrong with you Isaiah? You are joking right nigga?"

"Sidney, look, I'm really sorry. I do not know what I was thinking. I didn't intend for shit to turn out like this…"

"You… Did not intend… For shit to turn out like this," she says sarcastically. "Duh Isaiah. If you do not intend to go back to fucking prison, then you don't intend to go out and kill someone. Its common sense. I can't believe you right now."

"Fuck Sidney, what do you want me to say? Shit, I saw a come up and took it."

"See that's your problem, Isaiah. You always talking about some come up. *Fuck a come up*. What do we need to come up for? We were perfectly fine this morning. This morning we were in a position where the only thing we could do is succeed. Now look at you… I am really disappointed in you Izzy. Hope you're proud of yourself."

In the most, mathematically, and logically explanation, I knew she was right. *Byrd was right too.*

That this shit was petty and was not worth it. But there is a cause-and-effect relationship to everything. So, this is what it took for me to understand it.

"Baby, I tripped out alright. Just trying to give Stacy everything I did not have growing up. Promise this was not my intentions earlier. Just some shit went down in the process and now here we are."

"I don't get it Isaiah," she starts up. "How are you going to give Stacy what you didn't have growing up? You did not have a father, now she is not because you're robbing her of that opportunity. This morning, she had a family and support system. Something you did not have. So, tell me, what were you trying to accomplish with this?"

"Alright Sidney, your right, okay. Look I do not have much time. So, what's up? Are you still going to ride with me? *Forever and always*?," I ask her.

"Isaiah, you're fucking crazy," Sidney tells me. "Of course, I'm going to always be there for you. I know the fun, loving, less devious side of you. I know you can do better than this, that is why I am so fucked up with you right now. And uhh, where do you and Byrd plan to go? That helicopter is following you like a hawk."

"Shit we about to ditch the whip and burn to Somerset. Figure out the next move."

"Okay, so what do you want me to do?"

"What do you mean by that?"

"Well, I'm guessing you're going to Somerset to lay low and find an escape. Do you want me to meet you over there and help figure out how you will get away? I'll use Uncle Lenny car since he's asleep."

At that moment, I knew Sidney was the truth. Bonnie Parker did not have shit on my girl. I started to think that I may get away. *Swear I am done this time. Going to find a different path to the top. I am going to marry this girl. Word is bond.*

"Yeah, as a matter of fact, do that. I need you to meet us at Lor Jeff spot ASAP. He stays in building seven, apartment J. Tell him I sent you and bring me a set of clothes please."

"Alright baby, I got you. I'm going to see you there."

"Thanks Sidney, for real. I love you with all my heart Yoo, want you to know that," I express to her.

"Don't try to get all sentimental now Izzy. I have to hurry up. Love you too and be safe. See you soon."

-#-

Johns Hopkins Hospital/University was one of the most prestigious medical districts in the world. Motherfuckers like Ben Carson performed the head splitting surgery on the two twins who were born joined together: right here at this hospital. For all I know, they have a cure for AIDS and cancer inside this facility. So, in the back of my mind, I knew it will be *hell* trying to cross through their premises. From the hundreds of people that flocked the area to the fact that Johns Hopkins has their own personal security team- this final section before we hit Somerset would prove to be the climax of our getaway."

-#-

And just as I expected, it was. Maybe if we did not drive so recklessly down Broadway, they would not have thrown the tire spikes at us. Those damn pedestrians were just casually crossing the street like it was not a high-profile police chase going on. *Fucking imbeciles.* Good thing is that we saw them lay the spikes out in advance. It gave us a few extra seconds to deliberate before we hit the impact.

"Izzy hop out first, we have to split up. Going to take care of these coppers and meet you at Lor Jeff shit," Byrd breathlessly tells me.

"What? Hell no. We in this shit together Money."

"Izzy get the fuck out. GO!"

Chapter 16

Pop. Pop. Pop. Pop.

All I see is smoke surrounding the car, as I am forcibly pushed out the door by Byrd. It fucked me up when I stood to take "flight," only to realize that Byrd was not behind me. I did not even hear him get out of the car. Taking one glance back, I saw our getaway vehicle, immobile, on the middle of Broadway. From the looks of it, there were four police officers chasing me on foot. (They did not stand a chance though). One of the helicopters stood hovering over our stolen car while the other one got into position to follow me. What I did not see though was what Byrd had going on or any tricks he had up his sleeve. I hope he did not plan to take this case for me. *This was my 'liq,' my idea.* I should be back there awaiting my punishment. But it was already too late. Running full speed, I had made it at least two football fields away from the hop out site. *Straight into the checkerboard blocks of East Baltimore.*

Cutting through an empty lot, I was able to "dip" into an alley towards Lafayette. While the chase on foot temporarily subsided, the helicopters and police cars were still in heavy pursuit. This still allowed me to have a moment to catch my breath. I used this time to alleviate the dead weight in my pockets.

I threw the "Westside Hustler" phone into a sewage drain and said 'fuck it' about the bulky container of Ecstasy pills. It was not even absolute that I will be free in five minutes. So, I left the pills up for grabs. *Finders, keepers.* The only thing that remained in my pockets was my phone, money, and diesel I "hit" for. If I did get away, I was entitled to clear my mind with this fruity *piff*.

Bark, bark. Fuck. I did not incorporate these bitches into my mind about the chase. But here they are.

At the end of the alley behind me, a cop stops and opens his back door. Hungrily and vicious, these two German Shepard's came running out, prepared to devour. *Fuck, this is it.* I ran like my life depended on it, but knew eventually, it was not going to be enough. These highly trained, poorly fed police dogs were planning to take chunks out of my ass.

I ran and ran and ran. From alley to alley. Exposing myself on busy streets to get these fucking dogs hit by a car or something. But they would not budge. Personally, I did not do anything wrong to these dogs for them to disrespect me like this. I wished I had a pack of bologna to present as a peace offering.

Luckily for me, a climbable fence appeared about ten yards away. It was the fence that would grant me access into Lafayette Projects. The housing projects right next to Somerset. *If only I can make it.*

These dogs were literally at my tail, bridging the gap after every step. The police cars could not keep up with me and the chopper became hidden momentarily. *If I could just lose the mutts, I can win my freedom.*

Zigzagging through this alley, I am knocking over garbage bins trying to gain control of the situation. Anything to stop these dogs from moving forward, even for a just a second. But just as I figured, these bitches were gangsters. It did not matter though because I made it. Two more steps with a hop and I would have cleared the fence.

"Ahh shit," I yell out as one of the dogs bites my pants leg roughly causing his teeth to scrape my flesh. But he did not have a full grasp, so I still had action.

Hanging loosely from this fence, I began to kick the shit out of the police dogs to break his grip. Good thing I wore Timberlands today. The last kick sent the dog wimping away and me, face first over the fence. I landed on my elbow and it felt like my shit was broke. There I was, curled up on the ground, for what seemed like an hour. That is, until I heard a loud "stop" running in the direction from where I just came from.

Injured, but still motivated, I got up and ran into the Lafayette courtyards. God must have had favor on me. According to the ideology of divine time, the universal forces must need me to escape. There must be a greater plan for me. Especially after witnessing this blessing. It could not be just a chance of fate.

While running, I notice a well maintenance mountain bike laying in my intended get away route. *"This shit is mine, all day,"* I think to myself. There were people out as I claimed the bike as my property. But still, they acted like everything I was doing was righteous. Really, the attention was barely on me. Everyone just continued with their normal affairs. *Hear no evil. See no evil. Speak no evil.* Code of the streets.

I did not waste any time cranking up the gears on this bike and heading straight towards Somerset. It has been several years since my feet embraced some bicycle pedals, but it took no thought as to how this motherfucker functions. No time for test drives or fancy shit, my future was at stake.

Honestly, I predicted another roadblock or at least some additional debris before making it to Somerset. Besides dipping through alleys to lose the chopper, the ride was smooth. Even the police sirens following me died down. *Weird.*

Shit, even if the police officers did decide to come through the projects, they will have a hard time identifying me. Niggas was outside deep, waiting for action or any opportunity to put up some resistance. Soon as I pulled up, all you could hear was "Damn Izzy what happened?" … Felt embarrassing that I had to go through these extreme measures to escape the police. I felt guilty that Byrd got caught up and I did not.

I ditched the bike by a dumpster and ran straight to Lor Jeff's building. All the questions Jeff was going to ask me, raced through my mind. The main one was going to be about Byrd's whereabouts. Without any doubt, I knew Jeff could be trusted with the storyline of what just happened. But still, I felt skeptical about releasing every single detail. *Some things are better left untold.*

-#-

Knock... Knock... Knock...

Jeff hesitantly opened the door with the chain still locked in its deadbolt. You could tell his grandparents are not there because it was quiet, dark and had a regular smell seeping through the door. If they were there, the blinds would be open with candles complimenting the aura of their apartment. A deep smell of southern fried chicken would have pleased your nostrils and *The Price Is Right* would be on the television. *But it was not.* Just a serene silence.

"Who that there," Lor Jeff asks from the other side of the door. He did not even attempt to look through the crevice that would have provided him with an answer.

"It's me motherfucker, stop playing."

"Aww shit Izzy, come on man."

Stepping through the door, you could tell Jeff was paranoid and he did not even do anything wrong. Off the top, his grandparents' apartment was pitch black, which was not normal. Instead of Jeff's usual "college boy" attire, he was 'blacked out.' *Which also was not normal.* What set it off though was his peculiar nervousness like the National Guard was after us. *"It's just Baltimore Police,"* I thought to myself. While I was making myself at home, Jeff was busy looking up and down the hallway. For what, I did not know.

"Yoo nigga. Sit the fuck down and act normal. Everything is going to be all right B," I tell him.

"True shit. I'm lost though Money," he begins. "How are you sitting on my couch while Byrd is still on a high-speed chase, damn near in Delaware? I have a few classes left at BCCC, so I am by far unconscious sort to speak. What the fucks up?"

Delaware? Lor Jeff must be tripping. Our car got popped up Hopkins, less than fifteen minutes ago. Byrd was not here with me because he decided not to run. Either he got caught up or chose his own destiny. Right?

Lor Jeff's' accusation caught me by surprise, but the demanding knock at the door broke both of our concentration. The thought of me being followed, metamorphosed a panic attack. I did not know what to say, where to hide or what to do. I was taken so off guard that changing clothes did not even cross my mind (so I would not at least fit the description). Someone in the courtyards ratted me out. Motherfuckers could not take the heat.

"Fuck dude, I'm about to go to prison with you motherfuckers," Jeff starts crying out.

"*Sshh*, just chill out Yoo. See who it is."

"Chill out… I am aiding a fugitive right now. I am accessory to this shit too. I can handle a 5-10 though. Just tell me, is it true about the whole not dropping the soap thing… because everyone drops the soap in the shower, right?," Jeff keeps blabbering on.

"Nigga," I say getting annoyed. "I'm about to fade to black in this closet. Let me know whether it's good or not."

"Alright. Alright. Cool."

-#-

Stepping into this closet, it felt like I was time traveling back to the sixties. I met my grandmother a few times before she passed; those times I cannot even remember. So, I never had too much contact with *old people.* This motherfucker smelled like all types of Bengay and cheap fabric softener. Better than the smells of Baltimore City Jail holding cell that I experienced a little over three years ago. *That is for sure.*

"Got damn, who is this?" Lor Jeff asks himself.

"What's up?"

"Man, this bad ass yellowbone at the door. Damn Duke you have to see this, she righteous. She has a little girl with her. Wouldn't mind playing step daddy."

Before anything could click in my mind, Jeff had already recanted his observations. By the way he said, *"Aww shit my bad Sun,"* I knew who was at the door. It was not Byrd. It was not the police or National Guard. It for damn sure was not a bad bitch that he or I knew from Somerset. At least not knocking on his door. But in fact, it was Sidney and Stacy.

"Man watch back, you are tripping."

"Ayooo tell Sidney to take that old ass picture of her off Facebook from high school. Nigga couldn't even recognize her."

Soon as I opened the door, Stacy came and jumped into my arms. If only she knew the extent of the emergency, I was in. Come to think about it, this is the first time I allowed Stacy to enter the projects with me. I let her into this environment to aid the plot of me escaping a life sentence. This was not one of my proud moments as a father.

"Daddy, daddy."

"What's up princess?"

"Nothing. There are a lot of airplanes flying around outside," she tells me.

Damn. Hated to prey on the innocence of my daughter. She looked up to me in such a highly esteemed "light." Wonder how it would affect her if she knew her father was a murderer. *A thief.* Someone who has and will continue to destroy his community. She probably wouldn't look at me as the same 'cat who bakes cinnamon rolls and watches her favorite cartoons. *Something had to give.*

After politely telling Stacy to go sit down, I reach in for a kiss from Sidney. But clearly, she was not having that.

"Nah nigga. You got every street blazing for your bullshit. Hurry up and put these clothes on. We about to bounce," Sidney tells me while handing over a shopping bag.

"Hell no. We are going to chill for a minute and let things die down. You trying to get me the chair or something. Fuck I look like showing my face so soon?"

"*Ahh*, so your man enough to take a life; but when shit get real, your pussy ass curled up in a closet. Let me find out Mister Brown," Sidney expresses so sternly. *Obviously, she is angry.*

"Check that nigga man," Lor Jeff started cheerleading from the side. He is always going to be a sucker for pretty women.

"Say Jeff, make some Kool Aid alright. Slide back and relax, for real," I tell him.

"Yeah, my bad. I tripped out, I tripped out," he responds.

"And Sidney, fuck wrong with you? Common sense would tell you to lay low if the cops outside looking for you. Just chill, I got this. Everybody making this shit harder than it has to be."

"For your information Isaiah, I stole your uncles' car to come save your ass. So, to me, it looks like the ball is in my court. All you have to do is change clothes and walk outside with Stacy in your arms. Go straight to the car and ride out. *Simple.* If you are going to do the crime, at least see the shit to the end."

"Man, that shit isn't about to work."

"Actually, it might Izzy. That is a decent plan, unless you have an alternative," Jeff chimes in again.

"Aye Jeff, how that Kool Aid coming along? We are thirsty."

"Yeah, I'm on it," he says.

"So, what's it going to be Isaiah? You do not have long to make up your mind. I do not want Uncle Lenny to wake up and see his car gone. If he calls the police, you are not the only one fucked. It is going to work trust me. I watch plenty of Law & Order and Criminal Minds to know the hind points that cops overlook," Sidney says smilingly and so assured.

Wow, so she really wanted me to base my freedom off some fictional TV show? *If that were the case, I wouldn't even had made it this far.* You know in all the movies; the bad guys never prevail. Does not matter the storyline, at some point in time, karma comes around and the "terrorists" either get caught up or *fucked off.* As of right now, karma was working in my favor (totally dislocating my whole idea of the word). But still, one mistake and I will end up just like the characters playing negative roles on TV. *Either caught up or fucked off.*

Trusting Sidney's women intuition, I grab the Foot Locker bag containing my new wardrobe. It consisted of my all-black Chuck Taylors, Jordan sweatpants and plain black muscle tee. A complete difference from the denim outfit I wore this morning. She even brought my Oakland Athletics fitted cap.

"See now you don't even look like the guy on Channel 13, running from the police ten minutes ago", Sidney says after observing my nonchalant demeanor.

"Here, take this basketball with you. Make it look more legit," Lor Jeff adds in. The whole time, Stacy was peering over the couch listening to our whole conversation. She did not even possess an oblivion look on her face. It was as if she knew what was going on. *God, how I hope she did not.*

After changing clothes, I knew it was time to make my move. *All or nothing.* The events that take place over the next five minutes would dictate my physical freedom. Mind as well go ahead and get it out the way. Figure out the verdict of my future.

"Ayooo we out shorty," I tell Jeff. "I'm going to hit your phone later on and let you know what's up. We have to discover a way to bond Byrd out of jail."

"Uhh baby, I don't think your little friend is going to jail. Last I saw, he was still evading the police and he was not on foot. Either he going to get away or die trying," Sidney tries to explain to me.

But this was a concept that is hard to grasp. I just could not understand Sidney and Jeff's' accountability for what happened not even an hour ago. I did not think their reports were accurate. They had to be witnessing re-runs of the police chase. But if I am wrong then Byrd must be labeled as a mastermind manipulator of any disturbance in his circumference.

What could've Byrd meant when he said to 'split up and he'll handle the coppers'? Did he have an ulterior motive that was determined by my one-sided insomnia? Was I dealing with an eccentric person with supreme foresight? Like he saw all of this happening on the car ride "Ova West". Come to think about it, our conversation at Luigi's is speaking volumes now.

-#-

My heartbeat was thumping heavier and heavier as we got closer to the exit of Lor Jeff's building. The sunlight peeking through the door kept getting interrupted by birds or a helicopter. I was not close enough to decipher the difference yet. One thing I knew for certain was out there though were… Police!

The scene outside was a manhunt. Police were questioning Somerset residents. They had their German Sheppard's on leashes, sniffing for clues. The helicopter was scanning the area, looking for culprits. *Oh wait, the offender they were looking for was me.*

Marked paranoia crept in, but I kept my suspiciousness down to the lowest minimum allowed. With Sidney by my side and Stacy in my arms, I began to dribble the basketball with my freehand. *To make everything look normal.* Like this was the regularity of my schedule. I was surprised at how calm Sidney was. Too calm if you ask me. When there are fifty police officers and multiple dogs surrounding you, there should not be a serene ignorance about yourself. Especially walking through the projects. Her strange, outward manner caused one of the officers to come question us.

"Hey, can I talk to you all for a second?" the police officer says walking towards us.

"What's up?," I had asked with my hat brim low. At this moment, a doctor could diagnose me with a severe case of anxiety; but I still held my composure though.

"We are looking for a murder suspect that was last seen in this vicinity less than eight minutes ago. How long have you been out here?"

"We actually just left the house for the first time today," I tell him. This officer was black and by the look in his eyes, he must've known *the real*. He never took his eyes off my face and physique. It was as if Sidney and Stacy were not even with me. Everyone on the courtyards were subliminally looking in our direction.

"So, you live in this building Sir?" he asks me.

"Yes Sir. With my roommate."

"Can I see some identification?"

Fuck, that's when I realized my wallet and everything I "hit for" was still in my denim outfit- back at Lor Jeff grandparents' house. I did not even have my phone with me. My mind must have been in such a jumbled trance that I forgot to transfer my belongings over. This could not be a good sign. Everything goes downhill from here.

"Damn, you know what, I left it back at the house. I can give you my name so you can look it up."

"Yeah Sir, just stay right here for me. Can you put the child down for me please", he exclaims to me. Meanwhile, three other officers are heading our way. *Fuck, this is it.* I could tell by the code that the cop sends to dispatch.

"Brown to dispatch. Neighboring officers, my 20 is in front of building seven, Somerset Homes. Need additional assistance. I have the potential suspect in custody from the disturbance earlier. Over."

"10-4."

What? Suspect? How the fuck did he just assume I am the suspect? He did not even truly have me in custody yet. There were no "silver bracelets" on my wrist. I am seriously thinking about taking off running right now. But that would have equated my guilty judgement. Besides, the projects were too thick with police for my thought to turn into action. I just had to ride it out.

"Is everything okay officer?" I asked him.

"Yes. We just have to take you in for questioning if you do not mind. Is this your sister or something?" he says pointing towards Stacy.

"No, this is my fiancé and daughter. They just came to pick me up."

"That's fine. They can come too; it won't be long."

"Where are we going," I inquire expecting a different answer from what I already knew.

"Downtown. To headquarters," he responds. I already know what this meant, and it was opposite from his assumption. When he said it would not take long, that actually meant it will be a great duration before I see sunlight again. This would consist of "them" giving me a cigarette and my last soda pop. The process of "them" questioning me and twisting my words around to concede a conviction.

All I could do was look at Sidney and her eyes told it all. She tried hard to hold back her tears. It took strength to watch your first love go to prison for life. It was selfish of me to torment this girl with my street endeavors throughout the years. Everything she stood by my side for. But this was the end, she knew it and I knew it. The day she would have no choice but to move on without me. *Due to my own stupidity.*

And I could not blame her, she deserved better. Sidney was worthy of being with someone responsible, who she could at least count on. In a sensible way, I am that dude. "By any means," like Malcolm X would say. Just that my "any means" was not conservative and derived from negativity. Instead of being helpful, I was helpless.

POW. POW. POW. POW. POW.

Everything the police officer had said went out the window when this sound caught me off guard. I grabbed Stacy and hit the ground. Sidney and the other officers followed suit.

This could not be a random act of violence. Not with all the commotion and publicity going on in Somerset. It had to be a profane motherfucker to let off a couple rounds in the presence of oppression. Nonetheless after all the trouble that I am immersed in, this had to be the gateway to longevity. *Maybe, just maybe, there was a way.*

Even though my hearing was deafened due to the multiple occasion of gunshots today, I knew freedom when I heard it.

"*Ahh* fuck. This is going to be a long day," the black cop says running in the direction of an immediate threat. That is when I look up and the sun is shining directly in my face. Feeling a little disoriented, I thought there was an angel smiling down at me. More than likely, I was just tripping. The mystery of recent events caused my thoughts and emotions to become extemporaneous.

"Let's ride out before he comes back," I tell Sidney. She does not say anything, just nods her head. The tears started to downpour from her eyes. It was uncontrollable now. If everyone in the projects were not looking at me, I will probably have shed a tear also.

Without knowing the true origin of the gunshots, I knew it was my 'hood, looking out for me. There was no other logical explanation. Real recognize real.

Chapter 17

The car ride back to Uncle Lenny's house was reserved. Just the occasional snivel from Sidney broke the taciturn silence. After every police officer we passed, another tear would fall down her cheek.

"For what it is worth, I'm sorry to have put you through all of this baby. I really appreciate you though for not leaving my side," I began to expound to her.

But her eyes never leaving the road was an understatement of a blank response. What did she honestly expect from me? She knew exactly what she was getting herself into nine years ago by messing with a 'street nigga.' *Yes, it is true, I fell in love with shorty too.* But I cannot allow pussy to discourage me from getting money. Especially when I am the main provider for our "tribe." *Fuck, I got away. Cool. Great.* So, I do not see what the big ordeal is. In my opinion, my actions are justified. Chaotic, but still reasonable in their own essence. So, her unwarranted anger should not be placed all on me, but on the system as well. *Anybody else but me.* Maybe this life is not what she wanted.

-#-

Fayette Street was clear and luminous as we pulled up. Everybody was active and handling business like they normally would on a Tuesday afternoon. It seemed as if everyone was trying to make a power move. *Everyone except for Uncle Lenny.*

Uncle Lenny was sitting on the stoop, drinking a 40 ounce of King Cobra, and smoking a Virginia Slim cigarette. *The epitome of a washed-up slug.* I knew he would not mind us using his car without his permission. If I were alone, he'd kick my ass. But since I was with Sidney, I get a pass. Crazy that I lacked confidence with my own flesh and blood. I understood though. I would not trust me alone with a vehicle either. Maybe a while before you see me again. I am a metro subway type of nigga until I can afford my own chauffeur.

"Lookout Unk, you know only fiends drink the *cobra*," I say jokingly trying to omit the details of my day.

"Yeah, whatever motherfucker. Where y'all been?" Uncle Lenny asks after seeing Sidney empathetically make her way into the house. Her stern attitude was transparent.

"Nahhh baby had just picked me up from Hopkins. I didn't feel like walking, the streets hot for some reason."

"How come your not wearing the same clothes you were wearing this morning little nigga?," he asks as a cloud of smoke exits his nostrils. I could not believe how observant he was. Escaped the judicial courts to enter Uncle Lenny's skepticism remarks. I should just brush his questions off as being a drunken stupor. Besides, he is just asking for the sake of conversation starter… Right?

"Oh, I had these clothes on underneath my outfit earlier," I tell him making my way into the house. "Went balling down Somerset after I left Mondawmin."

Something about Uncle Lenny's posture right now is extremely unusual. Off the top, him drinking King

Cobra is queer. Normally, if he was not drinking white wine, it will be an inexpensive Vodka he'll sip on. So, him consuming this cheap malt beverage should have been an indication of something wrong.

Following me into the house, I notice Uncle Lenny had the TV set on in the living room. *Which also was rare.* He is always complaining about bills. So anytime we were not using the TV or lights, we were instructed to shut them off. But sometimes his mood swings were unpredictable and mercurial. Guess it was a symptom of menopause (or whatever older guys go through).

But it was not the fact of his TV set on that caught my attention. Not even the realization that Sidney and Stacy were sitting on the couch, witnessing the horrid images being displayed. But once Uncle Lenny joined the viewing "party," I knew it was certain. I knew the voices of WBAL news spoke truth. The reality of my existence and savage etiquette were in the hands of the city for their own disposal.

"We are coming to you live, from Pennsylvania Avenue in West Baltimore, where a brutal murder turned into a high-speed pursuit ending in the questionable suicide of the suspected offender…"

What the fuck? Hell no, this could not be true.

"Officer Ezekiel Brown, recently transferred from the Philadelphia Police Department was the official on duty when the said slaying took place."

"Yes, I was on post at the Pennsylvania and Fulton intersection where a slew of bullets wreaked havoc on the community. Once I approached the scene, I noticed a young African American male standing over the deceased with a knife. Attempting to take the perpetrator into custody, another series of

gunshots rang out behind me. This tragedy was premediated and the missing suspect is highly dangerous. The missing suspect is not actually from this West Baltimore neighborhood."

"*Damn,*" this same cop who witnessed my actions on the Westside, was the same cop who questioned me down Somerset. So, in all actuality, he knew my face and where I was from. Glad I did not have my ID on me.

"Thank you, Officer Brown."

"*The police chase ended on the Broadway and Fayette Street intersection, where officers threw tire spikes in an attempt to immobilize the culprits. After which, one suspect got away while the other, somehow managed to seize a police cruiser.*"

Oh, so that's why Lor Jeff and Sidney remained steadfast on the fact that Byrd never got caught up.

How did he acquire a police car, unarmed? *I would never know.*

"Thus, allowing the pursuance to continue statewide. Officers followed the suspect across the Francis Scott Key Bridge, where the corrupt forced himself into the Chesapeake Bay with the vehicle. Once the vehicle was retrieved, it was found empty, but officials promise the city that this man has indeed perished. Baltimore City Police are offering a $50,000 reward for the whereabouts of the aggressor who escaped on the Eastside of the city. Any additional information, you will be compensated graciously. Now here's Rebecca Stevenson with the weather…"

-#-

Damn man, I did not know what to think. Fatigue, plus the lack of air flow to my brain caused me to get lightheaded. *Shit, what did I do?* My nigga Byrd died because I *bailed out* on him once shit started to stink. Now some overachieved retiree from Philly knows my face and where I can be found. It would not be long before I am on *America's Most Wanted*. I am going to have to stay out of Somerset for a while now.

I wondered how this would affect my name in the streets. *"Ayooo that nigga Izzy a mark Duke. He let Byrd go down to save his own ass.* Or *"Stay away from Izzy. The cops have him labeled 'shoot on sight'".* I know people would be saying, *"I don't know how Izzy pulled that bad ass yella bitch and he's a crash dummy."*

Still, no matter how flagrantly I violated the laws of righteousness and society, Sidney remained devoted to our union. But I knew since she did not say anything on the vague car ride home that she was saving a mouthful to be said in private. Uncle Lenny, on the other hand, was not going to allow any of his thoughts to be projected in secrecy. His vagary ideas were the worst and that is exactly what his opinions represented.

"You know what's funny nephew?" Uncle Lenny breaks the silence to ask me. "The same motherfucker that got away, he was wearing the same outfit you wore this morning. What is crazier is that he was in the same area as you. See where I'm going with this?"

Damn, even though his insinuations could just be coincidental, I knew Uncle Lenny was not 'green' and that he had already put together the similarities. *That his nephew was a stone-cold killer.*

"No, I don't. So, what are you trying to say Unc?"

"I'm trying to say that you need to get the fuck out of my house. You are a lost cause Isaiah. I give you the resources to get on your feet, but you want to live like a savage. So, if you want to remain uncivilized, then go live with the uncivilized."

"Unk, your tripping man!," I began to plead. "Everything is all good. Got damn, just relax. I don't even see how you can be mad at me for trying to provide for my family."

After that declaration, the tears started to flow in excessive amounts down Sidney's cheek.

"I don't have the luxury of living off insurance checks, casinos and other women. I must get up and get it. You know what, give me a second," I tell Uncle Lenny heading towards the basement.

I did not mean to verbally assault Uncle Lenny's character. Sometimes when the truth is already known and visible, it does not need to be reiterated. It has just been a long day and after my escape, I needed time to think things through. But instead, once again, my survival is being tested. This time by my own flesh and blood. It seems like everything has been going downhill since I left Foot Locker earlier.

Reaching my living quarters, I proceed to the stash in my Jordan shoebox. This is where I have been storing majority of my day's earnings since I came *home*. Mostly accumulated and assorted into stacks of $500. The leftover amounts always go to Sidney in case of an emergency and I am not around- meaning I'm either dead or in jail.

I carefully inspect that there is $950 in the stash. *Guess that is acceptable for not even being out of prison for six weeks yet.* Not to mention, that Sidney has around a 'G Stack' in her possession; and I had *three large* tucked away at Lor Jeff spot (I have to tell that nigga to bring my loot). So, pitching Uncle Lenny my earned profits to keep him quiet would not necessarily hurt me. *I was going to keep a hundred-dollar bill though, just for good measures.*

"Lookout Uncle Lenny, this is for you," I say handing over the $850 while returning upstairs. The look on his face was discomfort. He really did not want to take the money from me because it could mean he's taking money away from his niece.

"What's this for Isaiah?" he asks me.

"For rent. Prostitutes. Liquor. Whatever it does not matter, but I am going to pay you for the room downstairs. So, the way I see it, this is worth about three months of rent. Agreed?"

"Come on Izzy, if I didn't charge your mother for rent, then why would I charge you? But at the same time, I need to teach you some sort of responsibility and personal accountability as a man. So in fact, this is me. I need a new electric barbeque grill anyway. But these are the rules little nigga," he pauses to consider his rambunctious perception as a mentor. *I had a feeling this was about to be entertaining.*

"Alright number one, you have to get a job if you're going to continue living underneath my roof. I do not know how you got this money or what really happened today, but that is the past. If you want to live here in the future, then you must get a J-O-B. *Or your ass is out.* And whatever dumb shit your doing- selling drugs, robbing, *what the fuck* ever. It must stop now! *Or your ass is out.* Your shorties can stay, but you will have to go. Like I just told your motherfuckin' ass this morning, I do not want any type of heat at my house. Agreed?"

"Damn Uncle Lenny. Alright, I got you."

"Okay motherfucker and if you get a job and show some type of concern for your seed and future; I might give you this punk ass $850 back", he tells me.

I could not help but laugh. Probably the first amusement I had all day.

"That's a fairly good incentive Uncle Lenny. Might get hired at Foot Locker too, by the way," I assuredly explain.

"Yeah okay, we'll see. In the meantime, stay in the fucking house. You need to lay low, off the radar."

"True shit."

"And don't let me catch your ass in my car again. Bought it with my insurance check, casino visits and sexual endeavors with multiple women," he says changing the TV station to *Family Guy*. The malt liquor was catching up with him.

Off the radar. To me, that cliché can have various meanings. When most people hear it, they automatically think about staying out of the line of sight. Plainly spoken, *off the radar* sounds like being taken off the scene for a period. Just off *the radar* for three years, unwillingly. So to knowingly vacant the scene for a while did not sit too well with me. *Besides, was not my dream still in effect to not only take over my city, but the world also?* To become a household name. To be commonly talked about like *Newport's*, the *Bible* or *Crisco* peanut oil. *How could I accomplish that while being off the radar?*

But everybody was right. I fucked up, again. Now my predicament had the possibility of taking me off the radar- *permanently.* So, in all truth, I did need to stay off the radar until shit died down. *And since we are talking about truth; honestly, I did not "come up" today.* What is

$3000 when your best friend dies in the process? What is $3000 when you cannot flip or spend it? Why, because you must stay off the radar.

This was not my desired result I expected plotting on the Metro earlier. But what did I think was going to happen? That stepping on another man toes, who is in the same position as me (just trying to come up) was going to help my dreams and goals manifest. *Bullshit.* Now I am in a harsher position than being in the cell block with Maserati Rick. *Not physically, but mentally.* In prison, my motivation and devotion to succeed was more enthusiastic. I must get back to that mind state before I become extinct in these streets.

So, I have to ask myself, what is next? Continue banking on these weed sales and robberies to support my family. Then what? End up back in prison or killed at the hands of another man. Put Sidney and Stacy through torrential sorrow because of my departure. Institutionally or fatally. Or am I going to construct another path that will enable my most far-fetched dreams to come true. I must develop a vision- ability to see the end. Maybe to get to where I want to be, I must avoid short cuts and inner doubt. Anything that is worth having is worth working towards.

Which makes me think. Why is it so easy to fail, but so hard to succeed? There are millions of people out there wondering the same thing. Failure represents deficiency while success defines completion. Most street dreams lack honorable success because at some point in time, it is going to come to an end, and you'll be labeled a 'failure'. So, in return, I must reverse my inadequacies to compliment the goals I want to accomplish. My dreams, desires, and aspirations.

From this day forward, that is what I am going to focus on. My inadequacies living up to my expectations. Allowing karma to bring me good fortune. If I expect success, then I must become fluent with proficiency. If I expect stability, then I must build a foundation fixed upon growth. If I expect greatness, then I must embrace affliction because that is the condition that causes us to reach for it.

So now I am back to square one. Getting out of my mental prison. Back to the same funky ass hundred-dollar bill and motivating imagination that they call "dreams." Years ago, I was successful at making my dreams come true. It should not be anything different now. It was only one thing to do. *It was so obvious. Logical and reasonable at the same time. The epiphany was clear and felt like a smack in the face. There was not any more time to waste.*

Chapter 18

Counter production ruled my next few days. Just merely bonding with my family and/or *serving* weed out of Uncle Lenny's alley. *Whatever you want to call it.* Still, this time was needed as assurance that Sidney's opinions were indeed supported and to further assist Stacy with fundamental building blocks of her future. If I was going to start trending towards success, then I will have to start with my foundation. *My family.*

Sidney was going to make sure of that too. She would not want me to be out of her reach. The only thing on her mind was cuddling, fucking, and talking. Every time someone would call for weed, her pouts and discomforting looks would form. I will have to candidly remind her that I am only going to the alley for less than a minute. Her remarks would be "hurry up" or "be safe." To a high degree of honesty, I appreciated her concern. It presents the idea that my other half has an intuition that is not all the way illuminated in my eyes. But still, selling this weed was practically safe. This was how our needs were being met until something better came along the way.

Ring… Ring… Ring…

"Ayo," I respond seeing it was Lor Jeff calling.

"What up Izzy, you alright?"

"Yeah, slow motion man. How shit look around the way?" I ask him.

"Everything clear Duke. Stop hiding out like a pussy. Do you want your shit or not?"

Lor Jeff was book smart; but not too much common sense regarding the streets resided in him. So Lor Jeff thinking Somerset was clear did not actually mean it was clear for me.

"Uhh yeah about that... Bring it over my uncle house, I got you Sun," I tell him.

"Alright. Oh yeah, you know that was Scooter and Germ who had gotten the cops off your tail. They said that they want their $100 on credit but will settle for a quarter of loud. Everybody in the 'hood know you got that piff right now."

I chuckled. "Fasho Money, that's going to be ready when you get here. Be safe Yoo."

"Be safe? What the fuck you on Duke? This my 'hood too..."

I hang up before giving him the chance to finish his studious rant. Why did I tell him to 'be safe' though? Maybe because recently, that has been Sidney's way of indicating that she is worried about me. Or simply because walking around East Baltimore is a risk in its own quality. *Especially with three racks on you.* Then, add on the stress that I am a contributing factor to Byrd dying- I guess it was justifiable to tell Lor Jeff to 'be safe.' I did not want anything happening to my little nigga. That would destroy my conscious.

"Izzy, who was that?," Sidney takes the role of an inquirer. It will be a while until I can get her off my case and trust me wholeheartedly again.

"Damn baby, it was Jeff. He is about to bring my clothes and shit. Why what's up?"

"Oh, you're going to leave?"

"I didn't plan on it. Is there something on your mind, Sid? You been acting normal lately. Thought we talked about what happened the other day? I told you I was not going to fuck up like that again. I'm not trying to lose you and Stacy; you two are all I got," I explain to her.

"Yeah, I know that you wouldn't intentionally leave us and you do what you do to maintain. It's just…"

"Just what?"

"You don't know what it was like while you were in prison Isaiah. The cold and lonely nights where I longed for your touch. The birthdays and holidays that we anticipated your presence. I stayed down for you and did not fuck around for the whole three years. 1085 days, remember? I can put Stacy's life on that. I just expected different from you. I did not think that you were going to go to prison and come out worse than you were going in. I am really scared baby. Scared I'm going to lose you to the streets or the system."

Damn, I had no choice but to feel complete empathy for her feelings. This whole time I thought I had my priorities aligned and dignified; but in reality, my queen was suffering. I allowed my most essential piece in winning this "game of life" become cluttered with anxiety(bishops), distrust(knights) and a negative, impetuous view of me(rooks).

In the game of chess, the king is the main target; but the queen is most powerful and plays an apprehensive position. There are a lot of *cats* in the game who say they can take the streets (game board) over, without a queen. It is possible, but still skillfully challenging. *What I have now is rare.* A queen whose main purpose is to purposely defend my purpose. *I cannot believe I took that for granted.* All she wanted to do was clear out our path of bullshit/negativity (pawns), so we can excel (administer a checkmate) and sleep better at night- with a victory at this "game of life." All she wanted to do was demonstrate loyalty.

"Baby get dressed," I smoothly tell Sidney. "I am going to make a run, but once I get back, we're going out. I have a surprise for you!"

"Izzy, what the fuck are you talking about? Last time you said, *'we are going out,'* you had to dodge a life sentence."

"Sidney just trust me. You deserve this. You love me, right?"

"Yes Isaiah, you know that I love you but don't use my loyalty to your advantage nigga. You be having me worried sometime. Yooo never mind all that, what do you have up your sleeve anyway?" she asks me.

"Let's just say I'm going to let your mind wander."

-#-

Waiting on the stoop for Lor Jeff to arrive, I took notice of my surroundings. *These living conditions were fucked up.* Things I would not normally question became the peer of my examination. *Like why does Stacy have to come outside and play on a sidewalk, infiltrated by syringes and cigar 'guts'? Did I feel comfortable with her growing up with the children of the smuts that I grew up with?* It is never the children fault, but the cycle of ignorance that floods my neighborhood will never be recycled. Guess that is why I am fucked up, my mother fucked up and majority of everyone around here is fucked up.

Which makes me think about why it is so easy to fail, but so hard to succeed? When your cipher is encompassed by failure, it is easier to conclude that your weaknesses outweigh your strengths. Therefore, coming up short is expected and stagnation is satisfactory. Also, with the image of success at a deficit, it almost seems imaginary that you will ever accomplish anything. So, when a promising opportunity does arise, motherfuckers approach it with moderate attempts. Making the success-to-failure ratio greatly unbalanced.

-#-

"Izzy," I hear no other voice but Lor Jeff yell my name as he hits the corner. This nigga was really carrying a small duffle bag too, making everybody on the street suspicious of what is inside.

"Yoo what's smacking Duke?" Lor Jeff reaches out for a handshake with this youthful grin on his face. He acts as if he does not have a care in the world. *I wonder what it is like to live with no responsibilities or aspirations.*

"Yoo Sun, fuck you got a duffle bag for?"

"How else was I supposed to bring your shit? Here," he says handing over the smelly luggage. "I'm going to need this bag back too before Grams and them start tripping."

"Alright all my shit better be in here too," I tell him.

"Guess this isn't a good time to tell you that I wore your jeans and Tim's to the club last weekend."

"Nigga you out of control man. The 'Hop Out Boyz' didn't hit you while you walked over here?" I casually ask him while looking through the duffle bag. It was not just my clothes in here either. There were some loose hangars, biblical pamphlets and a dusty ass bowtie that looked like Martin Luther King owned it.

"Nah... But speaking of the 'Hop Out Boyz,' you heard from Byrd yet?" Lor Jeff asks me. The 'Hop Out Boyz' were police in unmarked vehicles, who will hop out on you at any given time, if they sense your engaging in criminal activity. So, the chances of you encountering the 'Hop Out Boyz' in East Baltimore was not just a freak accident. *But running into Byrd would be.*

"Man, shit fucked up Duke. I heard on the news that his car went overboard in the The Bay. He was trying to getaway. Like that shit be haunting me at night too especially since its technically my fault Yoo."

"So, you actually believe that shit?"

"Hell yeah, it was my liq. I produced the plan. Nigga had asked me too if it was going to be worth it in the end. Now I'm on the run and he dead…" I tell him.

"Say Money, something isn't right. They said the cops recovered his vehicle and he was not inside. I think the nigga still out here."

"Bullshit."

"Ayooo Tupac, I think that nigga is definitely dead. He got shot four times, in two different altercations within a year time span. Even though he is dropping albums talking about flat screen phones and a black president, I still washed my hands with that shit. But Byrd on the other hand, he could have survived. All the nigga had to do was swim," Lor Jeff tries to persuade me.

"Yeah, alright and since when did Byrd know how to swim? Hell, when did any of us know how to swim?"

"Shit Duke, when your life is on the line, you'll do some remarkable things," he tells me.

This nigga could not be serious. Even if Byrd did manage an escape into the Chesapeake by deflecting the vehicle overboard; he still would have gotten swept away by the currents in The Bay. *At least that was my opinion.* Even though Byrd was like David Copperfield in life-or-death situations, the thought of him walking away from this was illogical. As much as I hate to say it, that is just a part of the game. *This shit dirty Yoo. You win some then you lose some and vice versa. Fucked up that my partner, my accomplice in taking the 'hood over got lost in these streets due to my carelessness.*

While me and Lor Jeff were wrapping up our informal rendezvous, some lady walks up like she was looking for a "*hit.*" I do not even sell crack, but the urgent look on her face told me to go inside and cut a piece of candle wax. She probably would have taken it too. *Lucky this is my 'hood.*

"Hey y'all, is Leonard around?" she asks me. *What!* Uncle Lenny be fucking with 'smokers' now. *This was a first to my knowledge.*

"No, he went out Towson."

"Oh, and who are you again?"

"Who am I, who are you?" I snarled at her. "Lenny's my uncle, I'm his nephew."

"True, my bad shorty. So, you must be Rashida little boy?"

"Uhh yeah, that's my mother. How do you know her?"

"Your mom is a good person. She was my mentor at The Water Shed. She talked about you a lot. You should see her. She's doing great now and told me to tell Leonard to stop by," this random woman tells me.

"Hmm, alright. Appreciate you Ma. Lenny will be back in an hour or so if you still needed him. Just slide back through."

"That's cool shorty. Stay out of trouble."

"Yoo Izzy, I'm out too. Hit the hip later Sun," Lor Jeff tells me.

I forgot he was still sitting on the stoop with me. Finding out my mothers' whereabouts had my mind sidetracked. Throughout the past six weeks of turmoil, I have not even thought about finding my mother. *Maybe because I thought she would have been embarrassed of me.* Still, I could not allow those feelings to harbor and become displayed. *This was my one and only mother.* Just as I have forgiven her in the past, I know she has forgiven me for leaving her and going to prison. Remaining frank, I still had butterflies in my stomach just thinking about going to see her. It has exceeded well past three years since I last seen my mother. Even though she was not the perfect mother throughout my childhood, she was still the number one lady in my cipher. *I did not know exactly what I was going to say to her, but I knew what had to be done.*

Chapter 19

The Water Shed Rehabilitation Center for Women. Majority of the female population here are African American. I always hated coming because this is where these lady's downfall became exploited. I know rehab was rendered as a good purpose, but I see it as a way for the *straight laced* to place these addicts in a negative light. Even though The Water Shed has helped my mother, I always wished she did not have to resort to these measures in an attempt to get "clean".

To me, drug addiction is all in your mind. If you genuinely wanted to get "clean," then that is what'll happen. The rehab centers and anonymous meetings were set up for motivation because everybody could use a helping hand. *But I wasn't motivation enough for my mother to escape her sickness?* (But a heroin addiction is like no other. It'll claim your body as its own and have you depending on the next 'hit like you depend on your next breath).

I remember as a child witnessing the horrific looks on my mothers' face when it was time for her "fix." Seeing her cold sweats, her restlessness and walking in on her shivering on the bathroom floor created combined years of permanent mental scars. Then, after however she 'came up,' her disappearance was always expected. Throughout those early years, I had to fend for myself (with the support of Uncle Lenny). Just the thought of me turning my back on Stacy for a sedative substance made the unresolved anger in my soul surface. So, for what you could possibly lose and you are still willing to take the risk then heroin had to be a bad motherfucker.

Putting my feelings aside, I knew The Water Shed was my mothers' only shot at full recovery. They had the appropriate therapeutics to combat her opiate usage and truthfully, this is the only facility that never gave up on her.

"I'm here to visit Rasheeda Douglas," I politely announce to the receptionist at The Water Shed.

"Absolutely sir and I would have no problem granting you access to spending time with your loved ones, but unfortunately visitation is strictly designated only for the weekend sir," she tells me.

"Please I haven't seen my mother in over three years. I just want to check on her. Ten minutes is all I need."

"What's your name?"

"Isaiah Brown."

"Okay, let me see if I can get you a special clearance sir" was her response. Just by her contemplating giving me a clearance, I already knew that it could be accomplished if the right strings are pulled.

Seconds felt like hours as the time weighed in on me. Becoming my own antagonist, I thought she had declined the special visit. Or maybe she had checked out and we just missed each other.

"Mister Brown can you follow me please?" a security guard comes out of nowhere and requests of me. *Confusion clouded my mind.* Was this some sort of set up that stemmed all the way back to the random lady on Uncle Lenny's stoop? It could not have been coincidental that she appeared at the same time as Lor Jeff. *Damn, this nigga must have caught heat and folded.* Or maybe I was just paranoid. I could not decipher that as a fact or opinion, just yet. But I was already here so the sensible thing to do is "ride the wave."

The security officer escorted me through a series of hallways- passing by different lounges, fitness centers and classrooms. To be a borderline mental hospital, the atmosphere was comfortable. I can see why my mother chose this facility as an alternative to being on the streets. It carried a laid-back aura to it, but still gave you the choice of personal accountability.

The suspicions that I was being taken to an interrogation room filled with detectives quickly passed as I was led into a beautiful garden. I have never seen flowers or trees of this radiance out in the city streets.

Whoever designed this décor had to be some French motherfucker, 'geeked up' on Acid or Ecstasy. *On some Paul Cezanne shit.*

Throughout me admiring this interior, that is when I see her. *My mother.* She was sitting on a bench, in the non-smoking section. Last time I visited her here, we sat in the smoking lounge, destroying our lungs with the pollution of Newport chemicals. I would 'short' her down on one and she would 'short' me down on the next one. This was probably the designated area for my special clearance. *I could not even smoke a cigarette with my own mother.*

Words were not even said between us. We were the only ones in this secluded garden, but for a slight moment, it was as if we were by ourselves individually. Frozen in space, I notice a tear form in the crevice of my mothers' eye.

"Hey mama."

"Hey son," was what my mother said while wiping her eyes. We embraced each other with a long, overdue hug. Afterwards, we both sat down on the bench and stared straight ahead. It is like one of those times when you have so much to say but the words will not accumulate in your mind. I start off by stating the obvious.

"Ma, you look really good. How have you been?" I ask her.

"Child, your mom has been surviving, that's all that matters. *Jesus Christ* hasn't given up on me, so I haven't given up on myself either. I'm so sorry Isaiah that I didn't take the liberty in contacting you while you were in jail," my mother starts to tear up even more while talking.

"Just at that time, I foolishly allowed this sickness to overwhelm me. But I am better now baby, I can promise my life on that. I have never felt this good and optimistic in almost 25 years. I am sick and tired of being sick and tired, so I am taking my life back with the strength of Jesus in my spirit. I want you to know from the bottom of my heart that I'll always believe in you and won't give up on you son."

"Thanks mama, I love you. I really needed to hear that. So, when are you getting out of this place?"

"Soon enough Isaiah. Soon as the Lord is ready for me to be out there. You are staying out of trouble?" she asks me. I do not really know how to come at my mother because this is foreign hearing her talk about God and that faith shit. Nonetheless, her ironic question leaves me at a loss of words. *Could she have seen the news report last week?*

"Ahh mama, you know how it is out there. Just trying to get it," I tell her.

"Get what?"

"Get paid! I just spent three years in prison. Three years away from my family and the streets. What else am I supposed to do besides *catch up and catch in?* I cannot get left behind and end up raising Stacy in Uncle Lenny basement."

"Hmm, so how do you plan on getting paid? I must be getting old because I just do not understand Isaiah. What do you need to *catch up* with when you were in a league of your own before you got locked up?"

"What do you mean by that mama?" I ask her.

"Izzy B, you are not stupid. You never paid attention to the reactions you got in the neighborhood?

How do y'all young folk say it…? You were pretty turnt up."

I could not help but laugh. Whenever my mother called me by my alias, it was always just "Izzy." *She never added the "B."* And yes, my creditability in the 'hood back then was superior. *But we are talking about three years ago.* I do not even rap anymore. Being lyrically inclined is not going to get you a house in the county. Especially when you are authentic with it.

"Yeah, mama you are right, those days were breathtakingly awesome. I wish I could get another chance at those moments, but I cannot. The only thing to do now was push forward and figure out how I'm going to make a meal for tomorrow."

"So, I guess expecting another mixtape from you is a waste of time? The Grammy's and 40-city tours really were just an illusion too then? Isaiah, I was addicted to crack for 21 years and heroin for 19 years… But I never gave up the battle. It took me this long to finally overcome this shit, but I did. And you are really giving up your dreams because of a prison sentence? Lord forgive my language, but that's weak as fuck."

"Dang Ma, you are taking it the wrong way. I'm just giving myself an opportunity to accomplish something new."

"Yeah Isaiah, but in life you have to create opportunities to accomplish something great. If you give up on your God-given talents, then what is next? You going to give up your bullshit nine to five, your family… Yourself! What if Noah gave up building the ark? What if Spike Lee gave up on his vision? What if Michael Jordan gave up basketball because he got injured? We have a black president who did not give up his campaign despite the invasion of racial slurs and opposition that I can imagine was tremendously discouraging. #DreamBIG! Isaiah because one day you're not going to be able to dream at all."

"Times up Miss Douglas," a security guard comes in and points at the clock. *Damn, they were serious about only having a ten-minute special visit.*

"I feel you Ma. I am going to keep that in mind. Make sure your out for Stacy sixth birthday. Plan on doing it big."

"Alright baby. Make plans to bring my granddaughter and daughter-in-law up here soon. How's that living arrangement going with Lenny?" she asks me.

"Everything is all good. You know Unk be tripping sometimes when he drunk. Pretty soon me and Sidney are going to end up taking care of him," I jokingly tell her.

"Yeah, my big brother always has been and still is a damn fool. Once you cop the big house in the 'burbs, he still going to be in the 'hood. That's his natural habitat."

We laugh for a moment and that is when I am suddenly taken aback by the childhood memories with my mother. From bus rides to the Patapsco Flea Market to go to school shopping to when we used to go to The Inner Harbor to feed the Orioles. *To when she first introduced me to Hip Hop.*

(The song that sparked my interest was "The Message" by *Grandmaster Flash & The Furious Five*. At the time, she showed me the lyrics in a pacifying mindset to give me an example of how a song was composed. I have been hooked ever since. Guess in a way, my mother, my earth is partially the reason music became my first love.)

I truly respected my mother's judgment. Regardless of the past, I had mad respect for her strength in overcoming the addictive struggle that spawned 20 years ago. Having a family of my own now, I could not fault her mistakes because I am making the same ones and learning from them now. My mother never gave up and she is always reaped the benefits of having a reflating and impulsive nature.

In order to be upset about her former parenting skills, I would have to think about how Stacy feels about mine. I will never understand what my mother was going through 20 years ago. *Guess the sketch of being a single parent living in a drug infested city broke her down to the core.*

I am only glad to know it's all over now!

"I love you Mama."

"I love you too Isaiah. Do not forget what I told you. If you do not plan to succeed, then you're already made a plan to fail."

"I got you Ma. Real talk," I tell her while reaching for a hug.

"Isaiah, let me ask you a question."

"What's up mama?"

"Do you pray?," she asks me.

"No, not really."

"Whether it makes a difference to you or not, God is listening. You should try and talk to Him."

Chapter 20

Maybe my mother was right. Or the detox recovery process had her a little bit delusional. How was I supposed to talk to this mystery God and where was He at?

Growing up, me and my mother never went to church. So as a result, prayer was never instinctive to me as it was in others. You will be lucky if I said 'bless you' after you sneezed. I did not believe in ostentatious victories and believing in religion has never crossed my mind.

It was hard to believe that God existed when you grew up in Baltimore City. The horrendous shit you will see on a daily basis would make you think; who would create these types of conditions for His people? I remember at the Fourth Of July Parade a few years back, 22 people died.

(All downtown, within a nine-block radius- in two-to-five-minute intervals). Infants got hit by stray bullets. An out of towner got his throat split by a broken glass bottle. There were neighborhood *block* riots on every corner. *Shit* got so real that the only way for the BPD to contain population density was by arresting everybody standing around for loitering. *Me and my crew included but the charges were later dropped.*

Even in the city jail you had people calling on God looking for a time reduction. But their prayers were never answered and the system still screwed them.

During my sentencing process, I exclusively can recall overhearing the deliberation about a man who was given 25 years for protecting his family. He was drinking a beer when a crackhead broke in his house, wielding a baseball bat. Instinctively he got his gun and shot the man . Crazy thing is that the 'basehead' did not even die or acquire any criminal charges. But the family-oriented person was convicted of intoxicated assault and unlawful possession of a firearm because the pistol was not registered. I even saw the guy paperwork, so I knew he was not bullshitting when he told the story.

So now who was protecting his family from the same crackhead while he serves a *quarter* in 'The Pen'? Why didn't God or the justice system stand up for this man's rights? Is God biased with His blessings?

The most clichéd thing to do in prison is find a religion. Usually, whichever was the most widely recognized and practiced in your cell block. Whether it was Christianity, Nation of Islam, Five Percenter, Rastafarian, or Taoism; more than likely you will start seeking guidance from some outside source. *My viewpoints on authenticity and sincerity were the barrier on why I did not take that route though while incarcerated.* Even when the DA first offered ten years, I did not cry or plea bargain with my "higher power." I just rode it out until something better came along.

The reason I never prayed was because it would not change anything. You got some people in the 'hood who pray to get out of debt; but end up filing for bankruptcy the very next year. You got people who lie and use God's name in vain, but never get struck by lightning or anything. That is the reason all of my knowledge, wisdom and understanding is obtained from experience. *Real world experience in these streets.*

-#-

Foot Locker was moderately crowded when I walked in. There were mostly teenagers that came to prepare for summer by purchasing miscellaneous items such as socks and snapbacks. Being that The Galleria was in the heart of downtown Baltimore it was also where most of the young population migrated in the afternoon. So as a result, there were two security guards and mystery shoppers floating through this athletic store. With a pocket full of money, I was not even worried about the suspicions that I would be stealing. *Hell, I was getting tempted to buy a whole wall of Jordan's just to prove a point.* But I had a greater purpose in mind for the money in my possession.

Behind the check-out counter was an eye catching, caramel complected female who looked *dumb* familiar to me. Just the dyed-blonde hair that she was *sporting* threw me off. But still it was something about her that kept creating a loop in my consciousness. It was not until I saw the nametag that said 'Rhonda' (which made everything perfectly clear). This was my late-night creep when Sidney and I used to argue back in high school. Rhonda was adamant about breaking our relationship up too. When Sidney found out (she had to visually witness the infidelity). That is when Sidney gave me an ultimatum- by choosing to stay with her or give up our family by being with Rhonda. Figure the obvious does not need to be explained.

Ever since the ass-whooping Sidney gave Rhonda, she had not been in the public's eye much. But still, I had to re-live the memory anytime Sidney thought I was or would cheat on her. Even though I am a flirt, I learned my lesson. Juggling my personal and family issues was problematic enough. Adding a sideline "dip" would create unnecessary drama. Even before Sidney came into the picture, my motto has always been "*Fuck Hoes Get Money*"! Since I had Sidney by my side now, I undoubtedly lived by those words.

"Oh my gosh Izzy, look at you boy. Think you all grown and shit," Rhonda says with an ear-to-ear smile on her face. *Knew what she wanted but she was not going to get it.*

"Yoo what's up shorty? I need the four's in every size starting at 8", I say with a light chuckle to alleviate the awkwardness. "No, I'm just playing. How have you been?"

"I'm good, just working. Staying out the way. Where is your girl Sidney?"

"At home with our daughter."

"Damn nigga, it's been that long? You have a whole kid now. That is what's up though. Hope she take after the mother and not your ugly ass," Rhonda tells me clearly trying to start something that is not going to get finished.

"Yeah alright, but if I offered you the dick right now, you'll address me like a drill sergeant. YES SIR!," I say activating my flawless charm. I love Sidney and would not fuck her over; but sometimes I needed my ego stroked by outside sources.

"Boy go on. What are you doing up here anyway?"

"Looking for the manager. Think his name is Darius. I have a job interview."

"Hell no. if you start working up here then I'm quitting," she tells me.

"Well then go ahead and put in your two weeks' notice. I'm not going to give you any discounts either when you come up here."

"Whatever nigga. I thought you were some big-time rapper," Rhonda makes her assumption unblemished.

"Who told you that?"

"I heard your lor mixtape awhile back. Niggas have not seen you in a hot minute, thought you was in New York doing it big. Eugene all over the airwaves like Baltimore is his city. Figured you were out *'putting on'* too."

"Yeah, something like that," I tell her. "Going to let that nigga get his shine on for the time being. Eventually, his ass is exposed. I do not even want the Bentley. I just want the truth to be known."

"Yeah, yeah alright. Hold up, let me get the manager."

"Hurry up shorty before I make that ass do what it does."

Rhonda clumsily looks back and smiles before walking away. Not even appalled at my latter statement either, but rather the part about me wanting the truth to be known is actually puzzling. *What was the truth?* That Mister Popular got signed off the lyrics in my composition book? That Mister Popular lied about the origin of the scar on his face (he says he got jumped and received a 'buck fifty'). My eternal truth is that when people ask who the hottest rapper in Baltimore City is, they should say 'Izzy B.'

But the truth of the matter is that I quit. I forfeited the desire to achieve my childhood dreams. Why? I could not even truthfully answer that question. Was it because of the crowds' reaction at the showcase? Or, maybe because of the way that Felix Stone trumped Eugene as the sole proprietor of my own lyrics. Was Eugene more of a fit for the image of Supreme Records?

After getting arrested, I lost all knowledge of the truth in reference to my lyrical abilities. Throughout all the years of developing my sound, you will think that I was one-of-a-kind. An original royal flush in the music game. But I was not. All it took was for a nigga to steal my rhymebooks and duplicate my sound to win him a meal ticket while I won a ticket to the prison cafeteria. Still, I am having mixed emotions about the past three years. *Was the turnout of the showcase a justifiable reason to lose all hope for my future? Was the assault on Eugene even worth the trouble of a felony conviction?*

Truthfully, I feel like I dry wasted three years of my life trying to prove something that was never verified. Yeah, motherfuckers' sense that Eugene was founded off deception; but where does that leave me? Mister Popular is still on top while I am filling out applications for Foot Locker. Truthfully, Mister Popular won by pulling my mental card. Truthfully, I have become the sucker in this situation. *Not for long though.*

"Ahh so you must be the infamous Izzy B?" some square ass black guy says after appearing from the back room.

"Uhh yeah that's me. How would you know?," I asked him not realizing this is the hiring manager that I came to see.

"Well after Scooby gave me the *heads up* about you, I decided to do a little research of my own. Your music videos were, Uhh… Let's just say very intriguing. I like your style though. Darrius Montgomery by the way…"

"Yoo what's up man? Nice to meet you," I tell him with my right hand extended out accepting his interaction request.

"The pleasure is all mine. Follow me this way Izzy so we can discuss your application."

For the second time today, here I was. Following a stranger down a hallway to my unforeseen fate.

Is this what I really wanted? Taking instructions from an individual who is taking orders from an even larger corporation. Even if I did not see it, everybody else saw me as someone capable of projecting their ideas into success. I think it is time for me to start putting myself in a higher esteemed light. It is time for me to start believing in myself again. It is time for me to become a champion. Not the other way around where I am constantly degrading my own mind.

"Hey Mister Montgomery, I don't want to waste your time. But I'm actually having second thoughts about this position."

"Hmm and they say that great minds think alike."

"What do you mean by that?," I ask him.

"Man, I don't want this job to be a deterrent from you accomplishing something great. I am not the biggest hip-hop fan, but I can see you have massive potential. I just do not think you should be wasting it here with us. Go out and take over the world. It's waiting for you."

"Yeah, I guess your right huh?," I tell him analyzing the deeper meaning behind his statement.

"Yoo do you know anything about the Liberty Heights area?"

"I don't really hang out over there, but I know where it is. Why, what's up?"

"Because I have somebody that I would like you to meet. I believe he will be extremely beneficial in your future prosperity. A friend of mine just bought a house in that area and remodeled the whole property into multiple recording studios and video production labs. He is legit, I went to Penn State with him over a decade ago. He gave up everything to remain a prominent figure in the music industry. It is paid off very well for him. His name might sound familiar; he goes by Domination X."

"*Word up*, you know him?" I asked the well-connected manager. "Isn't he the *cat* who produced a lot of noteworthy tracks for '*The Empire*' and *Bria Monae*?"

"We are definitely talking about the same exact guy," he tells me.

"Yeah, so how do you figure that he'll want to work with me anyway? I'm not even in the same caliber as some of the artists that he's worked with."

"Look Izzy, I know it may seem like I'm just a manager at an urban shoe store, but I'm also an entrepreneur before anything. Everything that I have touched has been gold. I have lucrative investments in every area of life. So, my consultant advice is bonded and respected," Darius tries to convince me.

"So long story short, based off your word, Domination X would be willing to work with me?", I curiously asked him. *This was too good to be true.*

"Off the top that's guaranteed. But there's one thing in particular that we're going to need from you."

"What's that?" I ask.

Shit, I did not have anything to offer beside time and talent. I can bet my "bottom dollar" that Domination X is charging anywhere from $1500 to $10,000 for an exclusive track; and that is just for one beat. Even after selling the rest of my weed, I will enough cash to buy two or three beats. But that will be selfish of me to do. I have a family that needs me.

"Izzy, do you understand the relationship between having faith and assessing a risk?"

"Uhh yeah, I do from a secular standpoint. But I am quite sure you're going to explain it anyway, right?"

He chuckles. "To have good faith is believing in something, without a shadow of a doubt about the risk of being wrong. Even if proven wrong, your faith is so solid that the risk of it slithering away is relatively slim. The same is true in religions, marriages, and business. To be honest with you Izzy, you're a risk."

"Lookout Darius, with all due respect you don't have to bullshit with me. Let us not beat around the bush. What do you need me to do?" I ask with a hint of aggression.

"I need you to put the same amount of faith in yourself that I put into the unknown not captivating me. You will suffer from the lack of progression when you live a life scared of productive risks. Digg what I'm saying Chief?"

"Overstood," I tell him.

"Ohh yeah but the main thing I'm requesting from you Izzy… Is that you stay out of jail?"

Chapter 21

What the fuck just happened?

The correlation between oceans and mountains was the compatible comparison between my expectations of returning to Foot Locker and what did occur! Or could I have mishandled the information that Darius Montgomery had relayed during our interview session? Could Darius have been so intimidated by my presence that he rendered me a dream to replace the job interview? *But what if it was all true?* On a scale of one through ten, how enthusiastic should I be about this opportunity?

Just wait on a phone call. This nigga really told me to wait on a fucking phone call. As if I was supposed to continue living in Uncle Lenny's basement until this *phone call* is made. Then you have my mother who is all religious now. She will probably say, "be patient and pray for this phone call." I could not tell the landlord that I'll complete the down payment once I get this mystery *phone call*. I could not continue to prolong Stacy's college funds for a possible measly phone call. *It just was not going to happen.*

Approaching the Galleria exit, an assortment of gaudy objects stole my awareness. Swear that the advertisements/marketing schemes were genius. Even the location of this Marketplace was brilliant. But in reality, what caught my attention was a jewelry store with numerous sales and clearance signs out front.

'Coming up,' I was a semi-jewelry type of nigga. Big ass bulky chains and watches was not my *stealo*. Just something normal that will project wealth but keep me off the radar. Like some gold nugget earrings with the pinky ring to complement its essence. At the present moment, I had on some gold-plated diamond hoop earrings (the size of Michael Jordan's) and an iced out white diamond G-Shock. So at least I did not look like a meager window shopper walking into the jewelry store.

"Hey my friend. How are you doing today buddy?" the Middle Eastern salesman quickly confided in my consumerism.

"Yeah, I'm just checking you out man."

"Oh, I see. Nice watch. Where did you get that piece?" he asks me.

"This motherfucker old. I got it as a gift way back."

I most definitely just lied. I bought these two weeks after I got out, at a similar jewelry store off Howard

Street by the Lexington Market. For all I know, he could have been working with the FEDS trying to accumulate profiles on all of Baltimore's' "made" niggas. I am technically still supposed to be out of the limelight.

"Ahh, you look bling bling enough anyway. But what about your girlfriend's buddy? They deserve some lovey dovey too *ehh*," he still tries to persuade me into purchasing the tangible.

Damn, I should have never came in here without plans on being bargained.

"Nah Yoo, my girl has enough jewelry. Besides, she is not into all of this shit. You know, your status being known by the precious stones and crystals you rock. Feel me?"

"What? I do not get it. Are you sure she's woman?" he says. A lot of pressure eased off my consciousness after the mirthfulness of his oblivion.

"Yeah Ock, you are crazy. She better be a woman after having my child," I explain to him.

"Well, me still don't get it. Why no shower her with finer things in life? You *are ballin,' shot callin'* right?"

I laugh hysterically now. "Shit I don't know man. I really don't think that a fucking necklace could convey the message of how much I really love and care about her."

"No buddy. Who said anything about necklace?" he says in a tone that would make you think that his favorite soccer team just lost the World Cup.

"Alright Duke, what do you have in mind? Help me, help you."

"Well, you say you love girlfriend right?" he asks me.

"Yeah, no doubt."

"Okay then its only one thing to do."

"What, go and tell her?"

"No, no, no my friend. You marry her. Get down on knee, kiss her feet and give ring. Its right thing to do." I could not decode him as being honest or just a dope ass salesman. Fuck would I get married for anyway though?

"Yeah man, you done took off on me in a whole private jet. Marriage is way out of my league right now," I tell him.

"Heavens no, I'm on my eighth marriage now and I love them all. Marriage is like this ring, see. It has no start, no end, no end, no start. Can you tell me where this ring starts buddy? No. Bet you wanted to marry girlfriend before you even knew who she was. This just strengthens the ship, Uhh or relations. You know, the Boom Boom Pow."

"Ayooo you are tripping. Even if it was true, I'm still too young to get married."

"Ahh you crazy kid. If it is there, it's there. Love has no age," he clarified to me.

-#-

Departing back into the luminosity of downtown Baltimore, I had this inscrutable feeling about what just happened in the jewelry store. Could the Arabian salesman have been right? Was it time to start thinking about someone else's' interests other than myself? Marriage was a title and if not handled properly, it can cause your life to rapidly combust. *Shit, your savings account too.* Come to think about it, I cannot even name five people who are happily married. It is just not common to find people where I'm from committed to anything else besides crime and depression.

Instead of heading directly back to the Eastside, I rationally decide to go hang out at The Inner Harbor. Somewhere I can do a deep evaluation of my conscience and values. It was a sunny spring day, and I figured the calm breeze of the Chesapeake Bay would be soothing to the soul.

Birds were flying, tourists were shopping, and the locals were lingering around restlessly. I guess you can say that I was temporary minding my own business until the radiance of this crowd drew me closer. The presumptuous gathering of the audience struck an intimate and familiar fiber in my being. *The timing was exactly right.* I heard the beat that will separate amateur lyricists from the champions. I heard the rhythmical 'body beat' coming from an individual in the center of a freestyle rap cipher.

It started as an elementary, infatuated desire to hear these "cats" express themselves lyrically. Intrusion was never my intuitive decision. But after the novelties of curiosity that everyone articulated towards my talent; I knew today was the day to make my move. *I have been quiet for too long.* If God did exist, then he created me to be a lyrical 'hood oracle. Moreover, who could I hurt by spitting a brief "16"? *I knew it would not be a repeat of the Supreme Records showcase.*

Why? Because when I freestyle, it is straight '*off the dome.*' Could never be duplicated nor replicated.

Finessing my way to the core of the cipher, I could already sense multiple eyes monitoring my behavior. It is like the pheromones of my species produced a phenomenal feeling of incongruity between myself and the bystanders. *They knew the truth when they see it.* There were four lyricists taking turns 'spitting' to the beat made of mouth movements, claps, and other harmonious sounds. I positioned myself two people away from the guy already on the mic. *Gives me enough time to compose my mind.* After the welcoming expressions from the other lyricists, I knew I was in. *I knew I had to shine.* This was similar to life and death. Jumping into a foreign cipher with no actual skills on the mic could terminally damage your cerebral to the point where you will settle for flipping burgers throughout your existence. *Shit is that critical.* But I had nothing to worry about; just like how muscles have memory, the art of rapping never diminishes. It is only waiting for you to exercise it again.

One person away until I am expected to demolish. My palms start to perspire. Some of these 'cats' had a little content with their flow which was inspiring. Gave me more of a reason to "turn up" and outshine them. I could tell the baton was being prepared to be passed to me. The contestant was running out of juice. I couldn't decide on an appropriate opener, so I decided just to "go in" ...

"See, this is a preview of how my presence is prevalent/

Turn you into a pretzel if you come to my residence/

Prior to the prison sentence, yeah, y'all were irrelevant/

So, you think that you're the truth, well Yoo think I need evidence/

And the principles of pistol play is crowning the shooter/

Its body bags in the game and my flow a recruiter/

Yoo I spit in Godspeed but y'all praying for Cuba/

Bro, these niggas are not real, y'all should be praying for tutors/

Yeah, I been at my prime while y'all was playing the tuba/

Better go tie your shoes or take a trip with the scubas/

Stash the dope in the couch like I was one of the movers…

Or get one in your mouth like them bitches from Hooter's/

Somerset on my back they do not like the position/

Got me pressing for perfect but I still made the transition/

From cocking them hammers back, empty clips in a kitchen/

Leaving the projects, crack residue on my dishes/

I am in a portal full of quarters, left the dimes for my bitches/

Until Byrd said, "Let's get it" so I had to get with it/

Niggas wonder why there is an O on my fitted/

That is for every 15th that we got acquitted/

Pussy… Play the prince, get your face in paper print/

Yeah… That's the price I propel dominance/

Uhh… They persecute to persevere the petty promises/

My providence is proof to prosper is astonishing/"

-#-

Damn, what did I just do? I did not even 'spit' the intended 16 bars. My "24" was punctual and right on time. I could tell by the crowds' reaction during and after my performance. My energetic word choice was the boost everyone needed to 'turn up.' Still, I could not tell who was more stunned, me or them. *Did I always go this hard?* Or, have the calamities of the past three years enrapture the lyrical beast that resided inside? Whatever the case, I think some additional investigation was needed.

Walking away from the cipher was not easy. I did not realize a bunch of young niggas came to hear me rap.

"Ayooo where are you going B," someone from the crowd yells out as I create my departure.

"I have to burn off Duke. What's up?" I yell aimlessly. Two females who were listening asked if I was freestyling while a couple of other 'cats wanted me to rap again. Even the emcees stopped rapping to see if I was going to "go back in."

"Nah I can't give y'all too much just yet. Word is bond though, anticipate a mixtape," I pridefully boast.

"When does that 'joint drop Yoo?" someone asks as if I knowingly had a release date. *Hell, he asked like this mixtape wasn't just an erratic decision, but an actual palpable object.* Now what?

"Soon Money. I'm going to give the streets what they want." My confidence has been fully restored.

Maybe I was tripping for throwing this rap shit away. I still had action at being the face of Baltimore City.

"Ayooo what are we supposed to call you?" a dread-headed youngster shouts as I walk away.

Before leaving the scene, I turn around and all eyes are on me; that is when I propelled my moniker, "Izzy B" with a demeanor so convicting that Christopher Wallace was preparing for this mixtape also.

Chapter 22

Blue Point Crab House, off Aliceanna Street in Fells Point always has been Sidney's favorite spot to devour some seafood creatures. After leaving downtown, I had texted her and gave fleeting instructions to catch a cab over there. I was en route via the 19-metro bus.

This section of Fells Point was predominantly housed by people of Caribbean descent and, affluent Caucasians who could afford house boats and yachts positioned on the bay. This was not far away from the neighborhood where Sidney was raised in. To be still considered East Baltimore, I did not regularly travel down here. Except, to go to Blue Point with *babygirl*.

Arriving on the locale, I instantly notice Sidney and Stacy settled on a picnic table, outside the restaurant. Stacy saw me first. My baby mama was playing on her touchscreen phone (probably about to cuss me out for being late). I was trying to scare them, but Stacy ruined the surprise.

"What's up *Princess*?" I address to my daughter, giving her a kiss on the forehead.

"Hey daddy. Guess what I learned today?"

"And what's that princess?" I ask while giving her mother a "wet one" on the lips.

"That people who go to college make a billion dollars," she tells me. *Her childhood innocence always brightens my day.*

"Hmm word. So, what are you going to do?" I ask Stacy.

"Well, my teacher says I can go to college now; but I want to go to the aquarium first."

I would not trade this moment for a gold doubloon.

"Don't worry princess, we will go to the aquarium. Matter of fact were going to go this weekend- you definitely deserve it. But when you get to college, what are you going to do though?" I ask her.

"I want to sing like Alicia Keys but rap like you daddy."

"Hey, I thought you wanted to be a doctor?" Sidney chimes in.

"Uhh I changed my mind mommy," Stacy mischievously says while drinking the chocolate milk that was pre-ordered before I got here.

That is live. Hopefully, Stacy gets my genes when it comes to having an ear for music. I would always want her to explore her options though. But the way she is always running around, screaming, and talking, you'll think that she was preparing her personality for the business. A young Whitney Houston in training. Maybe I should enroll her in some type of singing lessons or church choir. Oh wait, I will have to go to church for that right?

"So how did the interview go baby?" Sidney asks after ordering her normal nine ounces of butter garlic shrimp and pound of Dungeness crabs.

"Let's just say it was different. Matter of fact, I just had different expectations walking in. Did I tell you that I seen my mother today?" I ask realizing that I did not fill her in on the improbable events of today. This was going to be an interesting conversation.

"What the Fu-... ", Sidney starts up before noticing that Stacy was studying our dialogue. We do not like to cuss in front of her. "How come you didn't tell me? I want to see Mama Rah too. What all did you do today Izzy? Since you're all full of surprises today."

"Alright look... Long story short, I got word that my mother was at The Water Shed from one of her roommates.' She is doing really well. Better than I have ever saw her. She will be out for Stacy birthday. But I must tell you about this crazy ass... Uhh, interview. And the cipher I was in."

"Whoa, whoa, whoa pause. Rewind. You hopped in a cipher today?" Sidney asks me. "Oh my gosh, I hate you. You never want me to mob with you anymore." *When we were teenagers, Sidney's pussy used to get wet watching me freestyle in front of fifty motherfuckers. Whether she believes it or not, my evidence is carved into our history.*

I chuckle. "See that's the reason you can't ride with me now baby. Because when we are spending time together, you think that we are *mobbing*. You sound like one of those county girls taking a selfie."

"*Whatever* Isaiah. Bet no county girl can put it on you like me though."

"Alright you win," I tell her.

"Yeah nigga, thought so. Anyway, what made you all of a sudden start rapping again? Aren't you the one who shunned me out for listening to one of your old songs?"

"Uhh, well you see what happened was…"

Like two peas in a pod, we somehow simultaneously bust out laughing together. Something about love will enable you to finish each other's sentences and/or know what your opposite is thinking.

Ring... Ring... Ring...

"Hold up right quick baby."

She scowls at me. "*Ughh* tell them to call you back. This was supposed to be our time."

"Man, just chill out. Let me see what's up," I tell her.

"Okay well what are you ordering? Since you are too busy to tell the waitress what you want. So much for family time."

Before answering the phone, I tell her to order me the seafood platter. For almost a hundred dollars, this comprised of a 12-ounce lobster tail, filet mignon, two dozen baby scallops, and a half-pound of heavily seasoned horseshow crabs and a slab of freshwater salmon. Figure I could do a little splurging after recognizing the number on my caller ID.

"Hello."

"Yoo Izzy, this is Darius again. Are you free to talk?"

"Yeah Yoo, what's up?" I tell him.

"Look Young, I'm a man of my word. Just got done talking to Domination X and he wants to meet you. Tonight! You ready?"

"Hell yeah! Where are y'all going to be at?" I ask him.

"Can you be on the Westside, off Liberty Heights let's say around 9:00 P.M.?"

"That's a bet. Just text me the address and I'll be there."

"Cool. I'm shooting that to you now and I will holler at you in a minute then," he expounds to me.

"Alright bet. We are about to create magic man. See you soon. Peace."

Hanging up the phone, I see both Sidney and Stacy, wide eyed; ready to begin the interrogation process. I presume that Stacy is going to acquire this regimen from her mother. *We should have a son; at least these beautiful angels would have a leveled playing field. Or simply another male to cross-examine. Everybody knows my heart grows feeble for these two ladies.*

"So, should we just grab a to-go box since obviously you have something more important to tend to," Sidney sarcastically scowls.

"Ayooo don't play with me," I tell Sidney with a hint of irritation that was clearly perceptible.

"You know nothing is more important to me than you and Stacy. Nothing in this world could withstand the magnitude of value that you both bring to my life. *Nothing!*"

"Yeah whatever. Well, I can't tell *Mister Nomad*. Help me out here because I may have your previous statement misconstrued. But aren't attentive actions supposed to follow up with your allegations?"

"Well, if you stop *tripping* and give me a chance to explain…"

"Alright Isaiah, I'm listening. I am always listening. You just don't communicate with me anymore," she retorts at me.

To a certain degree, I could empathize with her on that. Ever since I got out, I have been on this mission that involves restoring my broken pride. And on a more premier level of selfishness, I was denying her of something so simple- a phone call. If I was going to rob a bank, she will just want me to call first. If I was going to break into The White House, she will just want a phone call first. If I hit the lottery, before I call anyone down Somerset, she just wants to hold precedence on who gets notified. Maybe, just maybe, I could fulfill that effortless request for her.

"Lookout *Sidd*, distance isn't even a conceivable option for us. I can admit that I have been on an *egocentric excursion* lately; mad at the world and myself. Nothing you have done though. Your perfect baby and I absolutely appreciate your patience with me. But say, today is the day … I'm about to bounce back!"

"Isaiah, what are you talking about?" she asks me.

"Peep game, you know the interview I went on today, right?"

"Yes."

"Well, the manager denied me the job but offered an even better opportunity. He's some big-time entrepreneur and wants to invest in me. My music in particular," I explain to my possible future wife.

"Oh my God Izzy, why have you been delaying on telling me…" she says with intentions on stealing the mic. *Could not let her though.*

"Hold on baby. There's more," I continue. "So, this 'cat is connected with that super producer Domination X. Guess old' buddy heard about my style and now, he wants to work with me. They want me to meet him at his studio out Liberty Heights tonight."

"What time?" Sidney inquires.

"Nine."

"Okay well you still have a few hours. Let us finish eating and I'll give you money to catch a cab over there."

The latter part of her statement carried a perplexing feeling even seconds after the words were spoken. She was planning to give me money as if some mysterious opinion veraciously aligned itself with her intuition that I was a *broke nigga*.

"Huh, so you're going to give me money?" I ask with a drolly tone accompanied by a screw face.

"I don't know Isaiah, but don't look at me like that. I'm just so happy for you. Cannot wait to hear what you record. I'm sorry for blowing up on you earlier too baby."

All I could do was smile as me and Sidney fastened our gaze on each other. Stacy covered her eyes so she would not have to witness me pull her mother close for a long, sultry kiss.

"You know I love you right?"

"*Mhmm* well start acting like it then," she says while pulling me in for another kiss.

"Oh yeah Isaiah and what's up with this shocking surprise you kept talking about earlier?" Sidney asks me.

Damn, I had forgot about what I truly had in mind this morning. All the windows that have *opened*, due to the chancy occurrences today have changed my course of direction. But still, I should have followed through with my original plan. To purchase what some may call imponderable. Shakespeare would have defined it as my opportunity to embosom my sincere intentions.

"Uhh… Don't worry about it, nothing major," I try to convince her.

"No Izzy come on. Tell me."

"Sid baby just drop it. Look the food is coming."

She smacks her lips. "Didn't you just say, not even two minutes ago that you'll start communicating with me better?"

"Alright, you really want to know?"

"Yes dork, spit it out."

"Well, *Uhh*, you see, *umm*…." I tentatively screech because the fear of my words not being processed clearly outweighed the confidence that I was doing the right thing. The butterflies in my stomach created a merger with the nervousness that just settled in my pride. *I never wanted to repeat these words ever again, to anybody else.*

"I just wanted to tell you that I, Uhh. You know it's like…"

"Baby are you going to tell me or what? I'm trying to start eating."

"Ayooo look, I wanted to ask you to marry me," I assertively chant. She got quiet. The whole restaurant got quiet. Shit, the whole city got quiet. You could have heard gunshots going off 30 miles away in DC. It was as if existence stood motionless to see the outcome.

"So, are you asking me or telling me that you wanted to ask me?"

"I was telling you the surprise. That is what I wanted to ask you," I say with an unsteadiness in my voice.

"Okay well I'm waiting for you to ask me," Sidney says allowing our emotional energy to silently become intertwined together. *For certain, the unthinkable has happened.*

Chapter 23

Getting off at the Rogers Avenue Station, I could still hear Sidney's' final words echoing through my head. *"Izzy, please be careful over there." "Call me so I won't have to worry about you." "And don't go over there bullshitting with the mic. Shut it down."*

The weight on my shoulders was beyond implausible. Mainly because this meeting was not convoked on my terms. There was no time for preparation or deliberation. But that's how million-dollar opportunities transpire sometimes.

Besides, this is what I wanted, right? I proclaimed to be the truth; so, this was my time to 'turn up.' I declared lyrical supremacy a decade ago so now is the moment to solidify my protest.

I picked up my phone to inform Darius Montgomery that I was in the area and to be expecting me soon.

Ring… Ring… Ring…

"Yoo Izzy. What's up man? You didn't get lost, did you?"

"Of course not D, this is my city. I'm at the metro subway stop around the corner," I respond not heeding the nickname I unconsciously just gave him.

"Oh alright. Are you talking about the one off Rogers and what's that, Uhh…?"

"Wabash Avenue," I quickly interject.

"Yeah, that's it."

"*Fasho*. I'm at that intersection right now."

"Word up. Just chill right there. We'll come pick you up."

"You sure Yoo," I asked him.

"I could walk and be down there in about ten minutes."

"Dude don't sweat it. We need you just as much as you need us. We are business partners now. Relax. We'll see you in *five*."

Darius Montgomery hangs up the phone before I could even give my salutation. I was left speechless anyway. Speechless at the title of our association. Speechless at his necessity claim. If I blow up with the assistance of these individuals, I will feel indebted for their support. So, in all actuality, I was left speechless trying to figure out who was in greater need. *The dope boy or the connect. The consumer or the franchise. The rapper or the label.*

Deep contemplation had to forcibly be detached by my own voice for my consciousness to reawaken. Bizarre thing is that I did not even say anything. A *black on black*, Cadillac MTS pulls up beside me bumping '*Eastside Takeover.*' It was Darius Montgomery and Domination X. *And a takeover did occur.* Confusion took over my thoughts as to how the fuck did, they acquire this mixtape, three years later.

"Izzy let's ride chief," Darius Montgomery signals for me to hop in the back seat. It was a two-door coupe and Domination X was driving. Darius gives me a welcoming handshake and puts the seat up so I can get in.

"Yoo Izzy B, nice to finally meet you man. Your name has buzzed past my ears throughout the times. They call me Domination X when I am in the limelight. Just call me Dom though," the mega producer tells me.

"Damn Sun, I can't believe that I'm in the presence of the production mastermind behind all of the current street anthems that's playing on the radio right now. Shit, you have worked with *K-Mack*, *Two Pimpin'* and *Justified*. All platinum selling artists. Word is bond, I'm trying to go diamond though," I tell Dom not allowing my slight nervousness to surface. Wouldn't anybody be nervous in my shoes? Especially when 12 hours ago, your future success was fueled solely off marijuana sells and luck. Now I have two millionaire motherfuckers wanting to invest their time and money. There were no other thoughts to be projected besides determination.

Dom releases a smirk, lacking humility.

"Yeah Izzy. I've been hearing *'X through your ears' pretty* often lately. It seems like the artists I work with just cannot manage to dodge the mainstream rotation. I hope you don't make a difference."

Damn, talk about confidence to the third power. In his position, you had a reason to be overconfident though. The epic *'X through your ears'* greeting can be heard on a minimum of twice an hour on the radio. He had to use some ultramodern software to produce the distinctive sounds that his beats possess. Anytime one of his tracks are played, you could literally feel the beat twinkle down your spine towards your heels. Hopefully, whatever we record tonight can have the same unfathomable effect on the hip hop community. As a local artist whose been given the chance to work with

Domination X, I had a lot to prove and even more to lose. *It was either go hard or go home.*

"So, I am trying to understand the urgency, Dom. What is on the agenda for tonight?," I curiously asked the prideful producer.

"Hmm good question," he says.

"I bet you didn't know that I skipped going to the 4/20 festival in Denver just to meet up with you Izzy. I did my research on you before I even knew that this day would come. How else did you think I recovered your moderately promoted mixtape?"

"Word up. So where is this meeting going to leave me… let us say, tomorrow evening?"

"Another good question," Domination X tells me. "This is what I'm going to do for you, free of charge. I am going to put the same production behind you that has gotten artists sold out shows at the *Staples Center, Madison Square Garden, Reliant Stadium,* and the *Mercedes Benz Superdome.* But it's up to you to actually make it to the venue."

"So, you're putting me in the studio?"

"Yes. But understand the extent of our relationship is relying on your performance tonight. And tonight only."

"Alright bet. That is all I need to know," I tell him. *Shit, I am going to make not attending a festival that is based off of lawless weed smoking worth it. I will be there next year maybe I should go ahead and make my reservations.*

-#-

Entering Domination X' house, it wouldn't remind you of a place of residence but rather more a student lounge at a HBCU university. The whole ground level was renovated to resemble a receptionist working area. Walls were torn down and replaced with multiple expensive couches and loveseats. A few pool tables. Flat screens and even two vending machines sat diagonally from each other. *I would throw an album release pre-party here; my guess is that its capacity can top one hundred*. What caught my attention though was the three separate alarm systems we had to go through. Cannot forget about the intense decibel levels of what sounded like dinosaurs in the backyard.

"Damn. My brother probably forgot to come feed these mutts today," Dom says.

"Hell yeah. Them *motherfucker's* sound hungry Yoo," I exclaim.

"Yeah man, they could probably eat a human right now. We make at least $50,000 a year alone on our Pit Bull, Rottweiler, and Boxer kennels. This is just one of the locations where we breed dogs. This was my original hustle that got me on my feet."

"For real. That is what's up Yoo," I tell him. "Ambition got you paid. The vision got you rich."

"True shit, all it took was a *Hundred Dollars And A Dream!*".

"You know what's crazy Duke? You are not the first person to recite that to me. Lately, I been thinking about what that really means to me," I explain with an inventive mindset.

"You know what… I have an idea shorty, let us hit the lab."

Walking upstairs was even more fascinating than the domestic marvels that I saw downstairs. There were platinum plaques lining the walls with the artists Domination X has worked with. I pictured my debut album fixated in an empty space with the *Diamond* achievement award next to it. I even pictured my actual album cover, *Grammy* speech and *Good Morning America* interview.

Upstairs, there were only two massive rooms. One was labeled 'Lyrical Cavern' and the other was labeled 'Spittaz Den'. Domination X told me to choose my destiny. I cautiously chose 'Spittaz Den'. The name matched my current mood to "*go in*." To destroy a beat and not leave any leftovers. To embrace this milestone opportunity that will ultimately make me the face of Baltimore City. Permanently!

Chapter 24

"Alright, check it out *Young*," Domination X begins.

"I've been working on this new street anthem that will feature some of the hottest artists in the game right now. *Hundred Dollars & A Dream!* is not just a slogan; it is a way of life. That is the name of the song and, the feeling behind it. After hearing your story, I believe this will be a positive momentum changer for you. Think about the times when you were down to your last dollar. Think about the times when you could not afford your daughters' Enfamil. Think about the times when candles replaced lights and syrup sandwiches were considered a five-star meal."

"So, this is the come up, the million-dollar plot," I say highly intrigued at his idea. "Lookout Dom, real talk, I've never been outside of these Baltimore City limits. I have never owned a vehicle nor had a job. But I always had a *dream*. My mother is a recovering heroin addict and I live in the basement of an East Baltimore slum. This *dream* is what wakes me up every day wanting to push harder. If I am not mistaken, Martin Luther King made a historical speech about his *dream*. He wanted to end social segregation so every race could use the same bathrooms and go to the same schools. My *dream* is similar to his in a sense that I want to use the same bathrooms as *cats* on the Forbes list and send my daughter to their descendants' school. What is crazy though, is that ever since around 5:00PM earlier; I stopped dreaming. I'm trying to make this rap shit a reality *Yooo*."

Domination X and Darius Montgomery look at each other in amazement. I had simplified my reality in an understandable format for them. It was me getting 23 years of pain, poverty, and fear off my shoulders; to make way for a lifetime of progression, satisfaction, and success. *I was ready.* Ready to showcase to the world where effort and motivation could lead you.

"Well, I guess nothing else needs to be said huh?," Domination X says while loading up his high-speed computerized equipment. He had to be using the newest upgrade to FL Studio when I heard the beat. *The bitch was monumental.* You had to have an Armageddon type flow to even bless this track. My whole body became covered with goose bumps listening to the instrumental.

"What's this for?," I asked after Domination X tries to hand me a pen and pad.

"So, you can write your verse. You have 16 bars on it", he says looking confused at my question.

I believed that these two gentlemen could sense the energy protruding from my being because after I said, "I'm good," they didn't even question it. Some things just must come from the heart. This will make up for the marriage proposal I backed out of earlier.

"Is it alright if I smoke in here?"

"Yeah, do your thing. Let me know when you're ready," Dom tells me.

"Alright. Just give me fifteen minutes and I'm going in."

"Take your time. We got all night shorty."

"Word just keep the beat looping for me. I'm trying to break records tonight," I say with a passion deeper the depths of the Pacific Ocean. These niggas might know something, but they do not know my full capabilities. I have never unleashed my purest form of rap. This is almost four years after 'Eastside Takeover,' and I have clearly evolved.

Exactly 26 minutes has elapsed, and I just finished my second blunt of *Purple Trainwreck*. After smelling how loud this shit was, Domination X and Darius Montgomery decided to infiltrate their lungs with me. Dom escorted me to the recording booth that sat adjacent to "Spittaz Den."

This studio was ten times more elegant than Germ' in Somerset Projects. Besides Germs' studio and the one I used to go to in Waverly, Domination X had the most professional set up. Even though my prior two studios both were possessed with engineers who considered their expertise to be in mixing and mastering; there was still something about my current setting that radiated advancement. Attaining victory by overcoming defeat.

"Ayooo Dom, turn me up in the headphones and press record. I am not too big on promises, I am about action. You're not going to regret this, *word to my mother.*"

And just like that, he pressed record. Domination X told me that he will endow me with the first verse if I do not leave any room for competition. Meaning I must become paramount with the artists already dominating the airwaves. But to me, they pose no threat towards my 16.

Before today, I was my own barrier. I created constraints on myself based off the lack of courage that girded 23 years of my existence. But everything happens for a reason, so it was all a part of the synopsis.

After dropping my colossal introduction to "*Hundred Dollars and a Dream!*," a wave of memories abruptly challenged my concentration. Like the thought of living in that tenement off Broadway, which was constantly infected with bedbugs and fleas. Or the childhood Christmases where the homeless shelter would donate me and my mother their leftover food so we could have a complete meal. And those winters… Shit, I do not remember a time where I did not sleep with three layers of clothing because the heat got turned off. Even as a teenager, having to rob or sell drugs to prolong the onset of becoming famished.

Now it all made sense of how a positive can manifest out of a negative. That everything which has happened in my life brought me to this present moment.

The misfortunate place of my upbringing created a fire inside that would not die. The same fire that will grant me access to a better life. The prison sentence was not done in vain, but used to sustain the fire for this moment. *My moment.* The moment the world would finally hear the pain of Isaiah Malik Brown. *Izzy B.*

I am going in…

"Look I used to have fantasies of six figure salaries/

Move more pounds than calories, hallucinating causalities'/

Then came the tragedy, I stagnated casually/

To get a hundred bands, mail a finger to the majesty/

They say this white tee is luxury then why the fuck I am still broke/

Sprinting to the projects for Pyrex and ghost dope/

The preacher said, 'hold ya head and keep hope…

Do not let go of your dreams and let them fade in the smoke/

But… Hell yeah, I did just that/

Got used to the gunshots, seen my mother on crack/

Everybody I grew up with want me to rap/

But I see more fiends daily, so I decided to trap…/

Peze… and wonder if these obstacles are optional/

Distress is in my optical, success is all subliminal/

My failures are identical with stains at the pinnacle/

I try to be original, oppressed but still lyrical/

How far do the lyrics go, I saw where my lyrics go/?

The whole world felt me from small ears to tentacles/

I never had a Bentley Coupe, stole a few hoopties/

Come to think about it, I never been to the movies/

No attention to the groupies, my pockets getting thicker/

No admission for these haters to stand in my picture/

Hold up, I have a call, Destiny I will be with you/

Got a Hundred Dollars and A Dream... trying to get richer/

Nigga/"

-#-

Deep stillness enveloped the space between me and these two industry tycoons. If you asked me, I would give two thumbs up to revamp this verse. It went over the 16-bar mark, plus I would not call this my most vigorous creation. *I could've gone harder.* But judging by Domination X" speechless expression, he thought otherwise.

"Ayooo hold up shorty. What the fuck… Do you even remember anything that you just said?," Dom asks me through the microphone in his section.

"Nahhh, not really Money. That was straight off the dome."

"See I told you X," Darius Montgomery chimes in. "This young brother is going to be headlined as the next *Rock N' Roll Hall of Fame* inductee."

I snicker at his assumption. "Shit, I don't know about all of that. So, what's up…? Are y'all digging the verse?"

"Like it, man. I love that shit. You earned the introductory verse, Izzy B. Perfect way to pop this *bitch* off," Dom tells me. "Listen Young, if time isn't an issue then I'll like to check out your vocals on a few of my other tracks."

"Alright let's ride," I tell him.

Over the next few hours, we eventually polished the *'Hundred Dollars & A Dream'* verse and collaborated ideas on some of Domination X' inclusive material. I thought back to the faith/risk analogy that Darius Montgomery addressed to me earlier. No persuasive actions were necessary because these two *cats'* rendered enough faith in me to even risk the possibility of having their name slandered just for allying with me.

Along with my family and the city, I now had Domination X and Darius Montgomery relying on my talent. *Observing my leadership. Watching me exterminate the lack of confidence that previously occupied my being.*

As we finished my new single called "*Primetime,*" I noticed that the sun was starting to peak in the horizon. Give or take, I'd been in Domination X' studio for about eight hours; lyrically composing my life story and the progression was remarkable. Besides '*Primetime,*' we also recorded another track called '*Casanova*' and '*These Niggas.*' Me and my new ensemble produced the idea for me to conceive a revival mixtape. The title of it was going to be called '*Just Made Parole.*'

(Shit after the outcome of Supreme Records showcase and everybody preconceived notions, the title was perfect. It is the element of surprise that will break three years of curiosity down. My way of giving the city what has been long overdue).

"So, when is the next time I can come dominate your studio?," I quizzically ask Domination X.

"I am not going to lead you astray Young, but my schedule is pretty packed for the next two weeks. I have a few conferences I am required to attend and I am wrapping up the production on *Noonie* new album. I am going to shop your songs around with my network and get "Hundred Dollars & A Dream" ready in the meantime, in between time. I am going to hit your cell as soon as I hit BWI airport. I've been itching to ask you a question though Izzy."

"What's good?," I inquire.

"What's the beef between you and Mister Popular?," he asks.

"Has it reoccurred since your release or has it subsided? I understand you both grew up in the same neighborhood. I just do not want to go to war with Felix Stone over something that is deeper than rap. I'm only here for the music Izzy; *nothing more, nothing less.*"

"Lookout Dom, our disputes never turned violent until the night of my arrest. Even though we came up as lyrical rivals, I never had thoughts of *getting at* the nigga until March 16, 2008. Long story short, our statuses are supposed to be reversed. He stole my rhymebooks and used them against me in the showcase that night. As a result, he got signed while I got fingerprinted. It may seem juvenile now, but at the time, I felt justified."

"Word up, I can dig it. So how would you respond if you had to accept awards, under the same roof as *Popular*? If you have not noticed, Mister Popular has become a force to be reckon with. This feud can either become lucrative or deadly."

"Yeah, I feel you on that," I tell him. "Let's look at history though Duke. Jay Z versus Nas. 50 Cent versus Ja Rule. Biggie versus Tupac. Regardless of the problems these niggas had with each other, it always came back to the music. So, let's stick with that. *The music*. If it is one thing that I know about time is that what's real will become unraveled prior to its prevalence. So why waste my time exposing Eugene, when either himself or the streets would do it anyway?"

"So, is this *dream* about hip-hop or is it gassed up on revenge?"

I thought intently before answering.

"Say, I still remember those frigid nights back on C block. The atmosphere was never peaceful, so interpreting your daydreams was never easy. *But I still saw six figure salaries.* I used to think that if you possess $10,000 in the 'hood, then, you're rich. But shit, eventually I ended up back broke- in the projects with ghost dope. Throughout all the turbulence, I do not know how my dreams never ended up in smoke. Guess it was the promise I made to my mother, *baby moms* and shit... I told the whole Broadway section that I was going to find us a route through the obstacles we called life. Figuratively speaking, I'm the *Young Voice Of The Ghetto*. Of Baltimore City. From the 'cats in the slums off Dolphin Street to Pulaski to Edison, I'm the lyrical passageway that helps my people temporarily escape hopelessness. After they see someone who comes from the same concrete jungle where most young niggas do not expect to see 25; it will promote a clique of dream chasers to simply *#DreamBIG*. You see Domination X; I am the face of Baltimore City. If I was down to my last hundred dollars, my vision will still be active. So, to answer your question, this shit is bigger than Mister Popular. It is bigger than fame and fortune. It is about giving back. It is about giving the world a piece of my reality through Izzy B. But most importantly, it is about me giving back to my first true love. The one who deserves my time, dedication, and expertise. Hip-Hop."

"I saw something tonight Izzy that I haven't seen in a while ", Domination X explains. "What you did in my studio was breathtaking. It was as if you crystallized desire and injected it into your veins. I feel honored to have had witnessed your hunger. You are yearning for success. Your inclination to make something out of yourself. You have my word Young that I am willing to put the same amount of effort that you are going to dish out towards your success. If you are trying to reach the top then, ride with me. We will get there."

"Alright, then you have my word Dom. This is it. This is where dreams come true."

"Just give me two weeks Izzy. Two weeks and I will be back in Bmore. That is when we can go full focus in the studio. I just need you to produce ideas for *'Just Made Parole.'* Do not worry about money, promotion, or distribution. I got that. Just focus on the music Izzy. This is for Hip-Hop."

"For Hip-Hop," I eagerly exclaim.

"To Hip-Hop," Darius Montgomery follows suit in an approving manner. As we embrace each other 's departure with handshakes, Darius offers me a ride home. Just two more weeks of living in East Baltimore until I am pursuing the dream of all dreams. Two more weeks until *destiny* shows up and shows out. Two weeks of doing nothing but writing music. *What could go wrong?*

Chapter 25

Memorial Day Weekend. I knew the city was going to be a firecracker as soon as the meteorologist announced that the temperature would be a comfortable 88°. I had been *feeling myself* lately especially after the studio session with Domination X a few days ago. Four songs had already been conceived mentally and written for my homecoming mixtape. (One of which, I am going to use Sydney's' vocals for the ad-libs). I wish *"Just Made Parole"* were already pressed up though, so I could dispense them out at the festivities this weekend. From the parades being held downtown to barbecues in the project courtyards; it was clearly overstood that the streets would be flocking with hip-hop heads.

While sitting on Uncle Lenny's stoop, I noticed how Fayette Street looked like a ghetto music video. You had a posse of toddlers that were playing in a mini splash pool that was set up on *the block*. In the background of their rendezvous, there were lingering dope fiends. But what was demanding my attention were the half-dressed *bitches* in two-piece bikinis. I had to be careful not to allow my eyes to loiter because Sydney would be back any second from picking Stacy up from school.

"Sqwale"

My mind quickly became lost in bewilderment as to where this familiar axiom came from. Drowned out in a stupendous daze, the illogical suddenly became logical.

If I was lacking rhyme or reason, then I could protest that what I was physically seeing still could be a fallacious image. But there was no mistaken this shit. I had to blink twice just to make sure my eyes were not playing tricks on me. But after a brief deliberation, reality sunk in and facts became obvious. That I was staring in the face of a true American Gangster. And it was not Frank Lucas or Billy Ray Maddox.

"Ayooo Izzy, what's smacking' Duke? Told you that I would've had to save the day once again," Byrd expresses in a felicitous tone, as if he isn't perceived to be dead.

Nobody had put together a funeral for him (he had no family), so the streets wrote him off as another soldier gone. Everybody from Somerset put candles outside of Luigi's Pizza Parlor and posted pictures outside of his frequented visited establishments; but that is about it. I always poured out a shot of every bottle that I popped for him. *Liquor had become my vice to forget about the events of that day where I lost my best friend.* And here the nigga was standing right in front of me.

"Damn bitch, you act like you've seen a ghost or something. It's me Money," Byrd says leaving no trace of hostility or ill will.

"Nigga, what the Fuck are you doing here? What the fuck happened? The whole East Baltimore think you drowned in the currents of Chesapeake Bay. I even went on the Rose Block last week and the cash crop had ceased. Niggas act like they could not get money without you. How the fuck are you even here man?

How do I even know I'm not talking to a ghost or snitch?"

"Money, you serious? After all the bodies I caught for you! All the ones that I will still catch for you or your *shorties*. Remember Whitelock? Cold Spring? Sandtown? I cannot believe that you would come at me like this Duke. You know it's love."

Damn, for him to know the dirt that we were supposed to bury over our graves, I know he was not a ghost or a snitch. This was Byrd, my day one nigga. I was just dumbfounded at seeing him, after the whole 'hood thought he tragically departed. Repentance was needed over my previous statement that was stimulated by confusion. You just do not regularly see the deceased appear in your cipher.

"Yeah, Sun I'm wrong," I tell my partner. "You have my most revering apology. But Yoo, for real, for real... How did you make it out of that shit? If you simply glance at any newspaper or watch daytime news, the reporters are so assured that you didn't make it out alive."

"Nigga you actually thought that I'll let the *knockaz* get me. You know better than that. I am the judge, jury and bailiff when it comes to my physical freedom."

"Ayooo Money, I didn't know what to believe! Especially after hearing you hijacked a police car."

Byrd unleashes that roguish smirk. "Yeah, I definitely have to add that to my list of illicit achievements. But come on now Sun, I thought common sense was presumed to be common. You didn't know that I was right behind you when you jumped out of the *stolo*?"

"Fuck you mean? All I saw was *mad* smoke everywhere when I hopped out and *paced* the concrete. By the time I thought it was safe to turn around, there were four cops chasing me- but no Byrd. Off the top, I was pretty fucked up if you got jammed for my liq."

"Say Money, chill and be still. That made the perfect getaway. I used you as a decoy to make my grand escape in a police cruiser. They always make a nigga ride in the backseat. It was about time we take over and start running shit."

"Hold on!," I express in a puzzling tone. "What the fuck? How could you have even gotten that accomplished? Even with me as a decoy, you do realize that half of BPD were chasing us; ready to *bust our melon* for the slightest move. Something is not adding up."

"Got damn Yoo, I thought what's already understood doesn't need to be explained. I do not want you trying this shit out on your own Izzy. But check it out…" Byrd begins.

"Once our car hit the impact of the tire spikes, it created a thick cloud of black smoke. Remember? When I pushed you out of the car, I was right behind you the whole time. Then, somehow, I managed to crawl up underneath a police car that became smothered by that thick cloud of black smoke. The laws were so adamant about apprehending one of us, that you are running off had deflected their attention for just the right amount of time. I ended up rolling out that bitch, straight into the open doors of a police cruiser. You want to know what is even more crazy than a motherfucker… They already had someone cuffed in the backseat. He is the one who drove into The Bay, not me. I used my first opportunity to hop out and let him out the backseat and told him that he is on his own. Some smoker who I could tell was battling withdrawal symptoms. Guess I had utilized both of you niggas for my getaway."

Now it all made sense. Byrd distracting the laws on Pennsylvania Avenue. His instructions for me to throw the book bag of weapons out of the window. Leading to him, taking the whole 'hood back by his unforeseen appearance. A jacket of idiocy could never be worn by Byrd. He possessed a distinguishable amount of coherence when it came to versatility in these streets. Off the top, I would have frozen up and got smoked. Either by a bullet or the electric chair. No if 's, and 's or but's about it.

"Ayooo *my nigga*, I never told you this… But you really are the *truth*! I do not know how you did it, but you did it! Glad to have you back on the block with me," I tell Byrd as we execute our mysterious handshake. "There is a lot I have to fill you in on too. Your boy is about to take the crown. "

"True shit, I can dig it. You still got some loud left? And what crown are you talking about nigga? I have to be skeptical when it comes to your ideas now. You're bound to have me piloting a charter jet for $10,000 next time."

We laugh for a moment before I retort an answer. "Nahhh for real Yoo, I'm back in the rap game. No whammy's this time…"

"About motherfuckin' time nigga," Byrd cuts me off before I finish talking. "Look you put in work and did your dirt out here in these streets. But you do not belong out here in the streets; *hell, neither do I*. Your comfort zone is in that booth Duke, nowhere else. If I had what you have, God himself couldn't coerce me back into the streets. "

"I *smell* you on that. You heard of Domination X, right? The nigga is about produce and fund my new mixtape. "

"That's live, Izzy. Real talk, I am behind you 1000% on whatever. I can be your hype man, hit man or personal driver. When you *get on*, I just want two things from you. Nothing more, nothing less. "

"You know your *good money* with me Sun. What is on your receipt?," I ask.

"Well for all my troubles, I think it's an understatement that you have to hook me up with one of these hood rat industry *joints*. Preferably Nikki, Kiesha or Pinky."

I laugh hysterically. "Alright, done! What's your second request?"

"You know I don't like to be classified as a gangster, thug, hoodlum or mobster. Throughout my various professions, only one word comes to mind. *Capitalist*."

"I spent that brief recess attaining my auction and dealers license. I am about to start buying cars from the auction and tripling my original purchase. After I finish the rest of this paperwork, I will own that abandoned lot over by Douglas. That is where my car lot and my *Sonic Drive-In* restaurant will both be located. All I'm asking for is your stamp of approval, Izzy."

"*Fasho, Fasho*! Fucking with me, you are going to have Lamborghinis and Bentleys sitting on the lot. *Word to my mother*."

"Ayo Money, so where were you heading anyway?," I ask anticipating making a move. Speaking about *the come up* gave me an industrious feeling. Like I had the world in my palms and the chances of my hand breaking were zero to none.

"Shit I was about to drop these *onions* off in the projects. Are you trying to ride?," Byrd asks already knowing the answer.

"Yeah, yeah. Let me go grab the rest of this loud. I have a couple of ounces left and can probably move them on Broadway. "

Within that split-second of me entering Uncle Lenny 's house, I noticed Sidney and Stacy approaching the stoop. Stacy seemed apathetic when it came to the concern of Byrd's presence. But Sidney, on the other hand, did not look too thrilled at the sight of seeing Byrd. Even after the realization that he was still alive.

"Uncle Byrdie! Why do you always have on the same hat?," Stacy innocently asks him.

"Because Señorita, I don't want anybody to know what my hair looks like. Did your father tell you that he's taking you to Disney World?"

"Excuse me... Daddy, no way! Is he telling the truth?," Stacy inquires with an expression as if she had just found out that ponies actually do exist.

"Yes princess but only if you're good in school then we'll go this summer. I am going to talk to you about it later though. Let us go inside and get cleaned up for supper. "

"*Yayyy*" was the echoing response that you heard from my little angel. Guess Byrd was going to remain adamant about me taking Stacy to *Disney World*. Now it was inevitable since she knows. Even though me and Byrd did not really have the best childhood growing up; his constant vexing was suspicious. He did not necessarily have a hidden agenda, but underneath the veil of his street endeavors- he deep down really wanted to go to Disney World himself. I could not blame him if the unspoken was true. Shit, that's every child's dream to see Mickey Mouse and Universal Studio. *Even as a child in the 'hood, who chances of actually going were relatively slim.*

"Ayooo what's *poppin'* Sidney?," Byrd addresses to the mother of Stacy.

"Hey Byrd." She says before cutting her eyes back to me.

"Umm Isaiah, I need to talk to you for second. "

"Alright here I come. Lookout Byrd, I am about to go grab that and come back out. Let me see what Baby is talking about. Give me a minute."

"You good Sun." Byrd sarcastically taunts. "I am going to hit Doc's and cop a few bogies anyway."

"Already. Come right back… Matter of fact, buy a three pack of green leaf Garcia Vegas, so we can smoke something."

"Done. But peep game Izzy..."

Byrd says before I step foot in the house.

"What's *Smackin'*?"

"Don't forget to be a man," he whispers before walking off.

"Fuck you nigga," I yell walking through the door.

Once inside, I bolted downstairs to collect my *loudpacks*. Sidney 's petition to speak with me privately could only be about one thing. The one thing I truthfully did not want to discuss right now. Either now or later, the topic was going to resurface in somebody's conversation, once were seen together. But like asking, *why is it 24 hours in a day?* Some things just are not meant to be illuminated. Shit, the secret to Byrd being here has not even been fully explicated to me yet. Only thing that mattered is that he is here now, and any auxiliary explanations were obsolete.

"Told you that your little friend didn't die," Sidney says converging with me at the top of the stairs.

"Yeah, I know. Swear the past 10 minutes have been *larger than life*. Crazy, isn't it? Wait until I tell you how he had managed to getaway. You'll forever look at Byrd differently after this."

"Hmmm. So, you are about to leave, aren't you?"

"For a little while. About to go down to the projects and get rid of the rest of my weed. I will not be gone that long. Why, what's up? "

"Figures…"Sidney pouts revealing her disagreement. "Don't you think you should just chill and get ready for the studio? I hate to say this babe, but I don't trust you niggas together. Y'all be *tripping* on some ill shit sometimes."

"Man, Siddd fall back with that shit. You know we not on that *tip*, especially in our own neighborhood."

"You know what, fuck it Isaiah. Guess I am wrong for not wanting you to screw up a good opportunity. I am sorry. I won't say I told you so."

"So, what are you trying to say?," I asked sort of regretting the tantrum I just exhibited.

"Nothing. Don't worry about it. "

"Come on baby, don't act like that. Speak your mind. That's what you told me. "

"I already said what I had to say about the situation Isaiah ", Sidney begins. "I just don't feel comfortable with you two together, after y'all made headlines of every tabloid in the city, not even a month ago. Does not sound like the brightest idea ever, now does it? But on another note, I wanted to see if you want to take Stacy to watch the fireworks tonight. I already got permission from Uncle Lenny to use his car once he gets back."

"Baby relax and trust your man alright," I tell Sidney while bridging the gap for a little intimacy.

"I'm this close to having my dreams become a reality. I would not fuck this up for us. Look, this is how it is going to play out. I'm going to run down to Somerset really quick and come back. By the time I get here, Uncle Lenny should be here also, and we can burn off. Where are they doing a firework show at anyway?"

"In Columbia. At Merriweather Post Pavilion," she responds.

"Columbia? Like Howard County?"

"*Umm, duhh* nigga. Like on the other side of Route 40. Really, we can take Orleans Street straight through and be there in 45 minutes."

"Damn Yoo, that's far as fuck. I never even been out there before. What if we get lost and end up in the words of West Virginia?", I humorously reply.

"Izzy, you *are bugging.* I know where to go, I have been out there before," Sidney explains.

"What the fuck? Since when have you been hanging out in Howard County?"

"Babe, you need to settle down. I am not you; I am not scared to leave outside the city limits," Sidney counters my assertion.

"Hmm, you have a point there."

"Yeah Nigga! So, it is Wifey, one, and Isaiah, zero…," she says reaching in for an overly desirable and lustful kiss. Until she pulls back…

"And you better not fuck me over. You said you are going to be here and we are going to go together- so you need to stick by your word. Swear you are going to pay if you're not here. Talking about all types of pussy restrictions…"

"Damn Sidney, I got you. We are already locked in! That is the *move* for tonight. Where did that outburst come from anyway?"

"Because Izzy, me and Stacy always get put on the *bench*. Usually for nothing too. Like so you can roll up or watch repeats of *That's 70's Show*. I am not going to play with you tonight Isaiah. You better be here."

"Alright baby, you have my word. Happy?" I say planting my hands on her hips, making sure she could feel the girth of my full erection. Something about resolving our disputes always made me crave for her *tropical juice box* to engulf my solid eight.

Once that dick was pressed up against her pussy, I could tell by her heavy breathing that she was on *fire*. She tried to wistfully squirm out of my grasp, until our mouths/tongues started to *attack each other*. I was prepared to take her against the wall, but our daughter was restlessly active in the next room. I took Sidney by the hand and lead her into the bathroom. *What happens next, could be left to the figment of one's own imagination.*

Chapter 26

While me and Byrd were en route to Somerset Homes, I let him listen to the quality of music that Domination X and I had generated. Besides my investing entourage and Sidney, he would be the first to criticize my work. The first person regarded as an outside *listening party* to witness my fresh style. *Izzy B, almost 4 years later.*

Byrd could most definitely be labeled as sovereign when it came to understanding the needs of the *streets*. So, having him judge my refined workmanship was parallel to privileges. I trusted his shrewdness and ability to be astute in reference to street politics. This movement started in the streets and is going to end being pierced into the summits of success; and I'm taking my *main man's* with me.

"Say lookout Izzy, do you know the definition of valor?," Byrd asks as we are walking up East Baltimore Street.

"Nahhh Money. Enlighten me."

"Being valorous means that you represent courage. Bravery. That your bold enough to remain firm in the face of adversity. We have been indirectly assaulted with hardships our whole life. Look at this shit," he says with his arms pointing towards the neighborhood. "This will be the range of our legacies unless one of us stands up to break the chain."

"Yeah, Sun that's true," I explained.

"I am prepared to take poverty hostage in exchange for our most fruitful goals to be attained. The only way this ransom could be paid off is if the blemishes of our existence become obstructed by our most remote concoctions being fulfilled. Real rap Money, it's about this *Hundred Dollars & A Dream!*"

"Ayooo Izzy, that's fine and dandy. I am feeling the movement. *I dig your vision.* But above all, this is where we currently stand!"

"Below the poverty level, in the streets of East Baltimore. You got the power to change that though, Sun. The *rock* is in your court, you got the juice. Just promise me one thing…"

"What's up Duke?"

"That you make this *dream* come true for yourself and your *shorties.* For your mother! For these pubescent motherfuckers, running around admiring the *dopeman* instead of the high school graduate. For all of our brothers on *lock* who is never coming home. Then maybe, just maybe, these niggas will start taking pride in the gift of life."

"Lookout Izzy, fuck Eugene! You are the only chance Baltimore city has at producing an honorable motherfucker from the streets. And, for me I guess, just always remember I told you to fuck the game raw…"

"Ayooo that's a given; it's already done!"

-#-

Somerset was at risk of combustion as me and Byrd arrived on the scene. Hands-down, an audience of eyes had us under heavy surveillance. Vigilance was not the word to describe these residents. Confusion would put more emphasis on the situation. I could not tell whether it was me or them- who was more perplexed at Byrd's immortality.

Our *day one* nigga named Kannon was the first to address the issue. Kannon is one of the most *animated* motherfuckers you are ever meet. *In third grade he accepted the fact that he was cross-eyed and ever since then, there was not a conversation with him that neglected comedic effect.* You never knew when to take him seriously.

"Aww hell no! Which one of Satan's angels did you make a deal with this time?," Kannon humorously asks Byrd.

"I thought for certain your body got cremated by sharks or an octopus nigga."

"*Hell yeah Kannon.* Nigga you owe me $20 and an eight-piece chicken box. Told you that he didn't die," Lor Jeff added in the conversation.

"Man, fuck y'all," Byrd says as we all greeted each other in handshakes.

"I just went into hibernation for a minute. Ayooo Jeff, you owe me four pieces of those chicken wings too and dip them *bitches* in ketchup."

"Nahhh Duke bet off. I had my fingers crossed."

"More like you had your eyes crossed. Nigga I am going to get my chicken box. You have until tonight to produce the money or we're making the news next," Lor Jeff tells Kannon non-aggressively. None of us believed his rant so it was easily written off as a parody.

"Money? Y'all are tripping. What I want to know is whose idea was it to have me a candlelit ceremony anyway?," Byrd curiously asks. Without answering the question, Kannon and Lor Jeff both look in my direction, solidifying the uncertainty.

"Damn Sun, say it isn't so. It's like that now?"

"Nigga, What the fuck did you expect me to think?," I exclaimed voicing my opinion. "Any sane person would have thought the same thing. That you went off the deep end, *literally*. I thought the shit was righteous, considering how you were perceived to have gone out like a soldier."

"Yeah Izzy. What's been going on with you lately?" Kannon asks in an implicative tone, changing the subject.

"Uhh same ol' shit, trying to come up. Why do you sound so belligerent about my whereabouts, *Money*? What's up?"

"Belligerent?", Kannon says. "Are you still studying *Webster Dictionary* in your spare time Izzy? Man stop playing with me. I heard about what you did at The Harbor last week."

I found his accusation to be flutteringly puzzling. The last time I was at The Harbor was indeed last week and that is when I broke up the freestyle rap cipher. *He could not be talking about that though*. And the time before that was when we were all together; the day before I *bodied* that Westside hustler. Maybe he had gotten the gossip misconstrued.

"Damn Izzy spit it out. What happened?", Lor Jeff adds into our *now* intriguing conversation.

"Ayooo this nigga is tripping; I don't know what he's talking about *for real*. You know Kannon be in a constant stupor off them dummy pills anyway," I throw back at my day one crew.

"Bitch you better not be cheating on my goddaughter' mother. That, my friend, will be the day that I had to serve you in the gloves", Byrd says.

"Man, you know none of you niggas can stand in the paint with me. Kannon, your first if you do not stop torturing us with this *so-called information*. Fuck it, expose me…"

"Black Man, your name was buzzing all over Twitter. It was a trending topic last week. I kept seeing #WhoseIzzyB, so I decided to eavesdrop on the topic. Word around, is that you destroyed some lames in a cipher to the point where they did not even want to rap anymore. Allegedly it was a big crowd too. Once I heard the matching description *shits* from every motherfucker, I knew it had to be only one *motherfucker*. You…"

"Izzy, I thought you stopped rapping because Eugene *dropped you off* in the showcase?," Lor Jeff asks.

"Nahhh Yoo, my manz is working with Domination X now!," Byrd counters in my defense. "Pretty soon, Mister Popular is going to be selling *Lucy's* out Edmonson somewhere."

"Doubt it", Kannon immediately intercepts not to actually *throw salt in my game* though.

"Even if you are better than him, how do you plan on dethroning a chart-topping artist? I think it'll be in your best interests to collaborate with him until you get your weight up…"

"Fuck no and be labeled a fraud, just like him. That's a negative!"

"Going to strip the title from Eugene. The title for who is the representative of Baltimore City. '*Down The Hill*,' especially."

"Alright, well I hope you're stocked with *mad* ammunition. Matter of fact, 'spit something.' It has been a while anyway. Let *us* be the judge on if Izzy B still has what it takes. *If he's still that pyromaniac…*" was Kannon's last words before Byrd cut him off with the answer that would satisfy everyone's curiosity.

"Nigga it's nothing! Get at these boys Izzy. Let them know what the real is," Byrd says egging me on.

"Ayooo *people*, come listen. Izzy motherfuckin' B is about to drop some exclusive shit," Lor Jeff announces to the whole Somerset courtyards.

I could not help but bask in the moment. My 'hood accredited the lyricism I owned as a meritorious gift.

Congregations of people that I have known my whole life started to assemble a massive cipher around me. These are the same people who initially heard 'Eastside Takeover' before any other 'hood in Baltimore. These are also the same people who witnessed, me and Mr. Popular battle it out every day after school. Yet, these are still the same people supporting Izzy B not only as a brand, but a real nigga as well!

To *deliver* was the only pragmatic thing to do after the platonic love that I have received. Deliver to the people who halfway gave a damn about me. This movement. Izzy B…

"Look, I'm smoking nothing but sour diesel/

Bad bitch call me Mandingo/

This dope clique, dope whip, hell yeah, it is all illegal/

Hell yeah I'm State Prop and I Ain't talking 'bout Beanie Siegel/

But I'll Roc-A-Fella wit' this Desert Eagle and send his head to his fucking people/

Yeah, I have a cold demeanor, from a cold city, got a gold Beamer/

It's cold gray, the G code is always find Catalina/

From Baltimore to Argentina, the duck off, my auntie cleaners/

And next time, I am going Fed so I Ain't worried about misdemeanors/

And I Ain't worried about who the meanest, who got popped or seeing Jesus/

Got my mind on my money and I grind for my money, outside of that can suck my penis/

Cubana has to be a genius; her head game was egregious/

And I am too greedy, I ate fajitas and paid with VISAs/

That codeine, promethazine, got yall leaning like the Tower of Piza/

Need a pound of ice, pound a smack, starting off with whatever cheapest/

Pants pocket, they be the deepest, to carry all these dead peoples/

Just me and my two-seater, this 40 Glock and white beater/

Let's ride..."

-#-

"Yeah, yeah. That is my motherfuckin' nigga Izzy B y'all. Don't give them too much man, they know what it is", Byrd chants in a boisterous manner. The whole Somerset turned into an uproarious, chaotic scene. Just knowing that I am the source for this commotion was exalting.

"Ayeee Sun, that was nice. Real talk," Lor Jeff says after giving me dap for my outstanding performance. Leave it to Kannon though, to incite a riot on the spot…

"When I say Izzy, y'all say B," he instructs the crowd to cite. Putting up no resistance, everyone follows in unison. But just like the deviant spirit that Kannon is, he could not stop there. Apparently, the mood was too conventional for him; so, making matters more unorthodox was the message he wanted to convey.

"Now when I say fuck, y'all say Popular. *Fuck*…"

-#-

While I was captivated at the entrancing spectacle *back at Somerset*, I had received a call from one of my neighborhood "*Kush Heads.*"

He was a pupil at Morgan State University. Normally, if you wanted to cop 14 g or less, I would make you come to me. But this *cat*, specifically, never bought anything under an ounce. Today made no distinction as he ordered 42 g of *loud*. Approximately, $385 after the offer I bestowed.

After we agreed to meet at Northeast Market, I told Byrd to tag along with me. Truthfully, I did not want to get blindsided by the unknown. My mind was still fastened by the prodigious event that just happened. Remaining humble was going to going to be hard after the mini concert I just had. Moreover, at the revelation that my confidence has been fully restored. The embarrassment of my incarceration has strategically subsided. And Baltimore City will once again be mine to dominate. My mother was right about us having a limited number of limitless opportunities to accomplish remarkable things in life. I was not prepared to *fuck* this one up.

As me and Byrd approached the Monument Street corridor, we kept noticing an outlandish new model Yukon Denali, roaming the back streets. It wasn't uncommon to see abnormal vehicles riding *'Down The Hill'*. (Despite the condition of my neighborhood, it was still a busy hub, due to Johns Hopkins Hospital/University Campus). Just the repeated pestering of the Denali, made us hesitant. On top of that, the motherfucker was white on white. *Cocaine complected.*

Eventually, we just marked it off as a dope boy who finally got some money and decided to ensue the stereotype of a typical low-level drug dealer. Purchasing a whip that is going to get repossessed in the wintertime. Unless he got loot. *Doubt it though.* Who gets lost in these checkerboard blocks of East Baltimore?

Ring… Ring… Ring…

"Say lookout Buc, meet me on the other side of the market. You'll probably smell me before you see me," I tell one of my big spenders.

Pernicious as it sounds, I did not even realize my pockets were empty until I reached for my *loud packs*. It was very unlikely for me to leave the house without any money too. I was in such a rush to avoid a confrontation with Sydney that hitting my shoebox for some cash did not even cross my mind. Fuck it though, I had damn near $400 about to touch my palms and that is more than enough to get me through the next few hours.

"Ayooo that shit smell faultless My Duke," Buc says advancing my way with a smile on his face. Generously, I let him tap the blunt me and Byrd were smoking on. *Least I could do for refilling my finances.*

"Yeah, yeah Sun. I'm really running low on the 'piff . Got about a HP left. Look Money, shoot me 2 bands for the last 8 ounces and *they all you*" was the offer I presented to Buc. No swindling was involved in this deal either. Anything was better than nothing. From my point of view, it was all profit since I will be back in the studio with Domination X next weekend. So, any supplementary money I made off the weed was basically to sustain my family. Until this rap shit jumps off, that is.

"Ayeee that's love man. Check me out," Buc begins to explain. "I have parties popping off for the next two days. So, let's just say that I will be coming to get everything that you are sitting on it tomorrow night. Hold it off for me and I will *toss* you something extra. Word is bond."

"Alright then I got you. Say no more. What's up with these parties though… You are throwing them in the 'hood?"

"Shit, I better not. Hey Yoo, I never told you… I am a club promoter. Go back and forth from Baltimore to DC, every weekend. If I do not touch *six bands* in those two days, then I'm a pussy."

"Oh, for real," I say fully engaged in our discussion. I have never been to college, but I had enterprising entrepreneurship skills. I was in no way deaf to the sounds of a come up.

"Damn I must be in the wrong business. How did you make that happen? We might be able to collab on some next level shit in the future."

"Fasho. I already heard about your mixtape from a couple of years ago. Just did not know whether it was you or not. Come check me out. I will be at the Dubai tonight and Lux Lounge in DC, tomorrow."

"Word, I am the one and only Izzy B," I boastfully tell him. "So, what's up… You own these clubs or something?"

"Own them exclusively, no… I guess you can say I partially own them on the weekends though. President of DroBoy Entertainment. Me and my team have contracts with certain clubs. Let's say I paid $1,400 to rent out a club that has a capacity of 800 people. Off the muscle, it is $10 to show your face at my spot. Take away the security and DJ fees, everything else is profit. You sell loud, so I'm quite sure you're good with numbers to know niggas are not playing with breadcrumbs."

"That's righteous Sun. Got to respect your hustle."

"You already know my Duke. Say, I have an idea of how we can both get paid and tactfully benefit in the end."

"Just say the word," I exclaimed prospectively.

"Do you still rap?" he asks me.

"As long as the sky is undoubtedly black, then, you can throw it in the bag about me dwelling in the booth."

"Ayooo I like that Izzy. Well, drop some *new shit* and I will put you on stage. Put your face on my flyers. Advertise your music to my 30,000 + Twitter, Facebook, and Instagram followers. It's a solution where everyone benefits."

"Shit I'm already two steps ahead of you Buc. But peep game, you are not just selling me a dream, are you? I do not mean to sound ludicrous, but my luck has never been this good. Shit look at where I'm from and how we met," I tell him.

"Where do you think I am from Izzy? I am from Greenmount and 33rd. Raised in Murphy Homes, but I do not keep my mind on the status of Murphy Homes. These auspicious opportunities came because I wanted something different than I already had. Shit, you probably have more than me growing up because I never sold dope. So, I am used to being flat broke. You do not have to be in the streets to be a street nigga. I am never going to forget where I came from, but my mind is always planning on where I am trying to go.

"Ayooo that's a lie. Being cunningly self-made. I'm glad to see my generation finally starting to break free from the grips of tyranny."

"Hell yeah man. Look Izzy, the decision is totally yours and the move is completely legit," Buc begins. "Do your research on me Duke. All my events get hosted by 92Q. You can expect to work with the most well-known industry figures from the DMV. Mingle with the *baddest* bitches in the area. Plus, have your music played nightly. I am going to pay you for blessing my stage. Matter of fact, if you have some new music already, email it to me, so I can put them in rotation tonight."

"Word up. Real recognize real and I recognize you. Look forward to us *poppin' bottles* together in the future," I tell him while we exchange email addresses.

Throughout the chat, between me and Buc, I never once noticed that Byrd's attention was diverted elsewhere. Once I saw the direction of his observation though I suddenly became alert with caution also. Not because of fear, but more of prudence or sound judgment.

I had to show discretion at this disguising scene. It was not exactly out of the ordinary, but by judging Byrd's reaction, I had to activate my nimblest self. Maybe we were just paranoid, but better safe than sorry. I am not even a Taurus, but I had a complex against dissimilar situations. Before any unfavorable repercussions could happen, the most rational thing to do was investigate. Investigate why this white-on-white, cocaine complected Yukon Denali was now parked across the street from us.

Chapter 27

The Northeast Market has three entrances that were stoutly situated on Monument Street or Jefferson Street in the back. This historic establishment, constructed in the late 1800s, served as a flea market for everyone in the area. Cheap jewelry, and printed T-shirts, throw away phones, candles and marijuana paraphernalia could all be bought at this marketplace. But the modernized design of Northeast Market was to supply food to the community.

You could either purchase a chicken box or whole chicken. Fish sticks or a live fish. This is where you buy majority of your meat in bulk. *(Beef, poultry, seafood).* You are not going to find a *Wal-Mart* in Baltimore City and grocery stores were just as limited. So, in return; *Lexington Market, Cross Street* Market, *Avenue Market, Northeast Market* and *Caton Avenue Market* were some of the go-to spots growing up.

(Ironically, I was born in the Northeast market, so guess that is where my love for Exquisite food came from).

But if you ever want to know what the neighborhood is like then, watch the crowds that formulate in the posterior of these emporiums. Jefferson Street sat behind Northeast Market and emerging from every street corner off Jefferson, were police cameras to monitor crime. In the back parking lot of Northeast Market is where you will see fights, muggings, and police brutality. I can even recall a time when I saw someone shot over a game of tops. So, seeing the Yukon Denali, accompanied by a legion of people, became just the spark me and Byrd needed to do some further probing.

After I gave Buc a *real nigga salute*, me and Byrd began walking across the street towards the parking lot. Yet, as we got within 30 feet of the premises, the *cocaine complected* Denali sped off.

"Fuck Yooo. Who is this nigga? Hey, are you strapped Izzy? I don't like the looks of this shit," Byrd says allowing his suspicions to remain barren.

"Nahhh Duke. Figured I could not be caught *slipping* today. I have not even been on the block tough lately. What do you have in mind", I asked starting to condemn myself for not staying with Sydney.

"I can't really say at this point Money. But let's see what this crowd is talking about. Hopefully, we can get some answers from them," Byrd tells me while checking the condition on his Smith & Wesson, caliber *deuce-five*(.25).

It was undeniable that the nature of this crowd became perceptible to me before Byrd. He was searching for deception; I was on the lookout for reality. It would be an invalid statement if someone said that me and Byrd combined, could not virtually overcome any hindrance in the streets. Together we were like *Loudpacks* and *Dutches*. Sugar and *Kool-Aid*. I was the more introverted one and Byrd, was rather extroverted. The perfect alliance when it came to street durability.

Without saying a word, Byrd gave me the approving gesture to make my move. Lately, I have been feeling *mad* comfortable about commandeering the spotlight again. Impounding my way back to the prominent days of *'Eastside Takeover'*. If I could get drunk off the thoughts of a promising future, then I would have had cirrhosis of the liver already. After straddling a pessimistic fence for so long, I must have tumbled into a pool of optimism- and this whole evolution happening within a week.

There were sonorous sounds coming from the core of this *'hood* assembly. These had to be the coldest spittaz that *Down Tha Hill* had to offer. I recognize the lyricists from neighborhood ciphers throughout the years. Some of them had skills but chose to employ their time elsewhere.

One of the rapper's name was *4-Way*. 4-Way was old school, probably around 32 years old; but he still rapped his ass off, nonetheless. Four-way used to be considered the most superlative lyricist that Broadway claimed as its offspring. That is, until me and Mister Popular '*hopped off the stoop.*'

As soon as 4-way saw the passion in my eyes, *he already knew what time it was*. Consider that he has not heard me spit since my teenage days; this could be taken as a chronicle moment for him as well.

After 4-Way reserved my spot in the cipher, I noticed that Byrd had walked away erratically. More than likely, to dissipate the headache that Yukon Denali grieved him. But I had another purpose in my mind. To eradicate the illusion that is Izzy B fell off. To exterminate the myths about *dreams* only come to the *dreamers*. To let the world know I am back and do not plan to thrive anywhere else, but the top…

"Ayooo I ain't on the bottom no more, fuck it's missionary/

Automatic, pragmatic, like what the fucks a visionary/

Had to wake up and smell the coffee, by the dictionary/

Niggas living fairy tales, waiting on the tooth fairy/

These niggas real scary... October 31st... So now I am here to kill the game, pour the liquor, buy the Hearst/

Feel like I am going to hell every time I step in church/

Cuz for my product, they are selling pussy for a Gucci purse/

Tried to teach independence but the shit ain't work/

So, for what the minds worth, I am back to the chalkboard/

You want a penny for your thoughts, I am thinking mines worth more/

Trying to achieve greatness, they trying to settle the score/

Thank you for the makeshift, the substitute was expedient/

Kush and Absolut were the erotic ingredients/

Now my success finally experiencing my experiment/

I was expected to fail until the top came speeding in/"

-#-

The ovation was majestic. Even if someone detested my character, you still could not show rebellion against the fact that I had talent. Even though it is called 'freestyling,' sometimes I feel like the material I have been putting out there should be paid for.

But that is where the issue of talent comes back into play. My natural aptitude for rap began in the neighborhood ciphers. Before the *pen & pad* came into the picture. Before exclusive instrumentals were bought to broadcast this talent to the masses. Before the pursuit of monetary gain was imagined; this is where it started.

In school, I never played sports. But producing maximum *word play* became a recreational activity for me. From studying the dictionary and thesaurus to incorporating educational lessons in my raps; I have tried it all to be considered supreme in my neighborhood ciphers. *16's* and *24's* was my homework. Remaking the hottest songs out to fondle my liking was an extra credit assignment. As a result, you have the lyrical monster that I am today.

One person I have always respected and looked up to in the cipher was *Cassidy*. Being that he's from the East Coast, excess lyricism was always expected, and Cassidy never fail to deliver. *Crazy because the way I used to look up to him is the way these shorties are looking up to me.* To remain intrepidly bonafide to exercise with this talent, on demand.

As I ejected myself from the cipher, looking for Byrd; I was left confounded by what seemed like a mythical creature. I suppose that the two golds, smiling in harmony at my public display was an aristocratic sign from the heavens. Many could argue that this was an appointed time for his wisdom. Take away the foresight, only one question came to mine: what the *fuck* was

Maserati Rick doing in my neighborhood, at one of the most eminently spots to catch a freestyle rap cipher?

"Ayooo, now that's what I am talking about shorty. Looks like you got your *mojo* back. I was worried about you getting out. *Word is bond young hopper.* But I see you are attacking the top spot with aggression," my old cellmate says while lighting up a Newport 100.

"Yeah whatever you want to call it, old school. What you are doing around here anyway?" I ask.

"Look Izzy, I'm just a black man, trying to make it on the black market. Every day is Black Friday for me. From Blackjack to *black magic*, I cannot be denied. But I heard they put me on every Blacklist from Rikers to the Black Sea. So, my number one vow on my Blackboard was to find you and turn you into a millionaire. *Diggg* what I'm saying Black."

Blah, blah, blah is all I heard. But if a confession was needed, I honestly miss this nigga. Homage would have to be paid to him because some of his "hood morals" that he taught me are still attached to my daily living today.

"*Word up*. So, what is on the agenda, Black? And how do you know that I have not acquired a six-figure salary already?" I asked Maserati Rick.

"Because that "*Hundred Dollars & A Dream*" track you did with Domination X has not been released yet. You have action after that though if you stay dedicated to the task at hand. It's about consistency, *young hopper.*"

"Wait a minute, wait a minute… What the fuck? How do you know about Domination X?"

"You thought it was a game, youngster. Nothing really moves on that I-95 Corridor, without me knowing it. *Connected to the connect*. Associated with the association and I network with the network. They don't call me Maserati Rick for nothing," he says pointing towards a *Maserati* Ghibli S parked on the curb.

"*Oh yeah* that's you?" I begin. "Guess you been playing stupid this whole time huh. You must have known who I was as soon as someone said that you would be cellmates with Izzy B."

"At the time, I never had the privilege to hear your music. But the name, Izzy B had hummed past my ears before our initial meeting. I enjoyed those 10 months *shorty*. Knowing that my job had been fulfilled."

"Your job?" I asked puzzled at his statement.

"Yes, young brother, my job! You think that I wanted to hear your conniption fits about your past and upcoming future. Like the shit was for my own mental stability. Hell no! Your protesting made my ears bleed. But no matter the objection, I knew one thing... That you had *mad* potential. So yes, it was my job to keep you on focus. To get you to examine your other options, which there were none. I'm glad to see that you've grown and are obsessed with progression."

"So basically, you conned me back into the *rap game*?"

"However, you want to slice the cake at night shorty. Least you did not get out and shoot a cop," Maserati Rick says using the excerpts from our last discussion. *Shit, somehow, he was able to track my whereabouts, I wondered if he knew about the body, I caught a few weeks ago.*

"Alright well since we're past the deceptive stages, are you going to honestly tell me how to *cop* one of these joints," I express gesturing towards his automobile that had a *removable top*. I never had a vehicle or driver's license; but once I do, I needed to cop a whip of this magnitude and 'hood appeal.

"Ayooo shorty, that needs to be the least of your worries. Right now, you need to figure out how you are going to get whatever new tracks that you already recorded over to Felix Stone. Don't want to sound shallow, but this is your time to surpass that counterfeit motherfucker that you used to cry about."

"And how do you suppose I get my demo over to Felix Stone?" I inquire caught between shock and disbelief at his idea. "You do realize that he's a CEO of a multimillion-dollar company. He will probably look at us in an imperious light. I respect myself too much to let some *cornball* belittle my craft."

"See shorty, you have to stop allowing your emotions to dictate your moves and start thinking with your mind. You are smarter than that. Look, I have a prestigious influence over Supreme Records main overseers. I could go sit in at their press conferences and Felix won't say a word."

"So, you got it like that huh?" I asked.

"Yeah young hopper. Just like that," Maserati Rick responds.

"This is what you're going to do. Supreme Records occupies the whole 12th floor of King County offices, in Brooklyn. It is off Jay Street, pretty close to Fulton Avenue. Your best bet is to go up there and shoot your shot. Only two things can happen: You will either be accepted or rejected… But all-around respected!"

"That is *live*, I may go catch a cab down there later on. But hey, I do not think Fulton goes down to Brooklyn. You are sure that you were at the right press conference?"

"*Motherfucker*, my knowledge is authorized. How would you know where Fulton goes, if you never been to Brooklyn before?" Maserati Rick asks with a trace of intolerance at my skepticism.

"Yeah, you're right. I do not go to South Baltimore that often, but this is still *my* city. Fulton Avenue goes through Sandtown, *Ova West*. The 909 boys run them blocks Yoo", I say ostentatiously while beating on my chest.

There was not too much you could tell me about Baltimore City. Even if it was not my typical hang out, there were no sides of the city that you will miss me on. Just by naming a main strip, I could tell you the bus lines, neighborhood crews, schools, *'hoe strolls'* and "get money" spots that govern the area. Especially Fulton Avenue because me and Byrd used to put in *work* in the Gilmor Homes a while back. *So, I am not saying that Maserati Rick exaggerated with his declaration; but I know for certain that Fulton doesn't meet up with any J streets. Matter of fact, there is no J Street in the 410(Baltimore).*

"You see Izzy, I'm going to need you to step outside of your cramped up, microscopic box… That is the only way I could put you on some International shit," Maserati Rick explains in a tranquil matter. "I once lost a $5,000 bet that East Saint Louis was not in Chicago. I was so hooked on the reality that I just left East Saint Louis, the city that I brushed off the fact, how it was also a neighborhood on the south side of Chicago. Lookout Izzy, I am not talking about the Brooklyn in Baltimore. Felix operates out of Brooklyn, New York. The Big Apple. Take the A Train from 42nd Street Port Authority. You won't miss the office building."

"Ohh shit Rick, my bad. *I tripped out*. But how do you expect me to get to New York City? I do not drive. I can give you gas money to take me up there."

Maserati Rick lets out a laugh that attracts attention. Really it was along the lines of a pig's snort intertwined with the shriek of a Billy goat. Honestly, I could not detect the amusement in my manifesto. I was impeccably serious.

"What's so funny?" I demandingly asked.

"You, *young hopper*. I gave you the jewels now it is up to you to flaunt the *motherfuckers*. Anything in life that is worth having is worth working towards. Stop looking for the shortcuts or alternatives. *Here is one way to the top and that is by your devotion to creating better opportunities.* Frankly stated, those who are broke decided to be broke- those in prison, decided to be in prison. This is your moment Izzy, *time to get your shine on.*"

"I feel that Yoo… So how am I supposed to contact you when it's all said and done?"

"I will contact you when it's all said and done Izzy! Do not rack your brain with frivolous shit. It is *4th quarter*, you're *down by 2, 10 seconds left,* and the *ball is in your hand*. What are you going to do? Answer that next time we meet."

"Ayooo Izzy, come on. Check this shit," was the outwitted voice of Byrd that I also overheard. He was coming from Monument Street with the face of urgency. What is crazy is that when I turned back around to get Maserati Rick my farewell, he was *gone with the wind*. So was his Maserati. Weird!

Chapter 28

I do not know what was inaner; chasing around an inconspicuous vehicle to reveal its habitants or risking prison time for the intangible. Here I am, weeks away from being inaugurated into the *Billboard Top 40* and I'm still stuck on this 'hood shit. I cannot go International when my mind has not been displaced from Fayette Street. So, I am going to take the first step. I am going to New York.

Once I met back up with Byrd, he was dynamically pleased to report his findings. That is when I suddenly realized, he was desperately unyielding in regard to the Denali. Another thought became clear; that this was going to be a long day.

-#-

The cocaine complected, Yukon Denali, became visible as me and Byrd walked across Monument Street. We decided to post up at *Kennedy Fried Chicken* and watch its movement. Well, really it was Byrd's decision. I just could not leave my boy with *naked eyes* out here in these streets, so I tagged along. *Damn fool I was*!

"Ayooo, so what's the *word* Money?" I asked Byrd itching for him to abandon the mission.

"Say Izzy you know I never lied to you. But I am almost 100% positive that there are major moves and even bigger *gwop* is being transferred right underneath our noses. *Look!* Look at that dread headed motherfucker coming out of *Shoe City* right there."

As I unskillfully rechanneled my posture to "*Peeping Tom*" status, I actually see a lot. The type of shit you should not see broad daylight, in the middle of the hood. If I did not have my big break with Domination X at stake then, I will probably opt for some additional scrutiny. So, in an unexplainable way, Byrd's inspection could be absolved.

Within 30 seconds of being observant, there was a peculiar transaction that took place. A Lexus LX 570 pulls up behind the parked Yukon and two Asians got out with dual *E'Mio m*edium Scritto leather briefcases. That is when one of the deadhead's had gave the foreigners both shopping bags with shoe boxes in them. In return, the Asians handed over their briefcases.

I am in no way naïve to what just happened. I will be deemed ignorant if I thought a fashion purchase just took place and a receipt was received. *I just spectated an illegal business deal, so what?* This is East Baltimore; illegal shit happens here every minute. I must admit though, these motherfuckers were really *gutsy*. As soon as the Lexus pulls off, an Audi A7 fills the *void* and the same ritual is performed.

"Alright Byrd. So, their making *moves* out of the Shoe City... Now what?"

"Now is the fun part Izzy. Let these motherfuckers know that they are vying for their existence. *That I want a piece of the pie or there is no pie. That if they want to live, then I have to eat and if I don't eat then nobody lives.*"

"Ayooo come on now Sun; doesn't that sound kind of unreasonable. We don't even know who's calling the *shots* over their *plays*."

"If I'm not mistaken Izzy, the Africans run this spot," Byrd says.

"So, what's the plan? Just run into their place of business, making demands. That is a one-way ticket to the city morgue and for our bodies to be unidentifiable," I explain.

"Nahhh Money. We are going to let the streets, be the streets."

Sometimes it was difficult to interpret Byrd's austere behavior as being abstractly realistic. He's got a hundred-man army by himself. And to my understanding, you are not going to win every war. Byrd's been fighting this fight for so long, that I get scared the smallest mistake will be overlooked by him. And that will be the mistake that cost him everything. This whole plan seemed like a mistake. As his partner, I felt obligated to get him to go another route. Fucking with the Africans was not going to get him the desired outcome he wanted.

Just as I was going to inform Byrd of the opposition, he signals for a scroungy dope fiend to join our entity. It looked as if he was fresh off the needle, the way his eyes kept rolling back to his brain; but *you cannot take everything at face value.* I was still amazed that he was mobile enough to walk, yet alone play his position in the hood.

"Ayooo, pay attention. Are you trying to make some money or what?" Byrd asked the stranger.

"Uhh, yeah. Sure! I guess so, maybe...," the dope fiend responds while waning off. If Byrd expected to get some answers then he had better hurry up before this addict's body locked up. Then, he will be unresponsive for hours. *I knew the symptoms from my mother.*

"Have you ever seen that *truck* before?" Byrd asks brandishing a $100 bill in his face.

"*Yeah, yeah. Now, earlier. All the time youngster!*"

"Look I'm not about to keep playing with you, *my guy*. Whose truck is that for the last time?" Byrd inquires flashing another piece of currency which had Benjamin Franklin's imprint on it.

"It's African Dee truck. He run the Glover *block*. Best dope in town. Crazy motherfucker though."

After hearing that name, I already knew what was on Byrd's mind. African Dee, long ago paid his subscription to live in the depths of Hell. Only other *nigga* I know that is our age, who put in as much *work* as Byrd.

African Dee was a descendant of a hungry, ruthless mob of Nigerians that infiltrated parts of East Baltimore, back in the 1990's. But once the eldest members of his tribe began to get popped or deported, he took over the family business- which included racketeering, prostitution, firearms/explosives smuggling and heroin trafficking.

There was one, singular era where the *Eastside* can testify that Byrd developed a *strong*, intimate attraction for a woman- *and this era also created the personal vendetta Byrd had against African Dee.*

Tonya was the victim and she was from the Latrobe Homes. One night during our juvenile years, we had *double-dated* to a party in Somerset. MDMA had just became the major trend that served as an aphrodisiac for inner city youth. My *partner*, Weezy Wayne was an MDMA dealer but he was not an MDMA dealer. It was not ironic that he always just seemed to have MDMA at the right time *except* this catastrophic day in particular. Discretion should have been used before trusting an outsider like African Dee. *But it was not.*

We had bought six pure, MDMA capsules to be taken amongst me, Byrd, Sidney, and Tonya. The only reason, me and Sidney had not consumed our portion yet was because we had gotten into a quarrel over some pictures on BlackPlanet. So, I spent majority of the party trying to get back on her good side. Byrd had already made it understood that he was not ingesting his until after the party. Restlessly, Tonya divided, secured then recklessly poured her 1.5 grams of MDMA underneath her tongue as the passageway to her blood stream. *Normal practice on a normal night.*

Apparently, Tonya was not the only person who consumed narcotics that were distributed from African Dee that night; because halfway through the party, *people* started to blackout. This toxic batch of MDMA that African Dee was *serving* came with distinguishable signs that were not limited to death. For some, their mental equilibrium has not balanced to this present day. Tragically, Tanya was one of the deceased.

Deaths caused by African Dee's bad batch were so widespread that it made WBAL news. Once families started to question African Dee about his accessible products; his response only came equipped with a smile and his conclusion saying *maybe it was for the better.* For that comment alone, African Dee was permanently placed on Byrd's *hit list*. Byrd just never had the opportunity to follow through, until now.

The fervency in Byrd's eyes exalted his stubbornness on the unspoken option of backing down and allowing his chance for vengeance to disseminate. This was almost as good as finding his birth parents killer.

I did not know how to respond to Byrd's incessant stammering. Every other word was *fuck* or *I got to get this nigga.* His mind was fluctuating between what he could do and what he wanted to do. Eventually, I knew his actions were transparently going to show what he was going to try to do.

"Fuck man, I should have known. I don't know why I couldn't see this shit from a mile away."

"What are you talking about Duke?," I asked Byrd.

"Ayooo I have only been *off the scene* for a week or two and that's all it took for Rose Street to *dry up*. I thought it was because money wasn't circulating in the 'hood, but really it's because these niggas *jammin'* two blocks away. No negotiation. This shit ends today!"

"Lookout Byrd don't be so quick to get irascible about shit like this. It happens. Sometimes you have to lick your wounds and take your losses."

"Losses? Izzy nigga, the day I take a loss is the day that I lose my life. These niggas disturbing my cash flow like they are invincible. Ain't nothing safe *'Down The Hill'*", Byrd expresses in an enraged manner. I knew shit was about to get real by the way his palms voluntarily crashed into his temple.

"Ayooo Money, I can't fabricate this shit like it's a good idea," I tell Byrd with a gallon of regret.

"I honestly believe it's a death wish if you go by yourself. So, whatever you plan to do, don't plan on counting me out."

"Appreciate the offer Sun, but this is a solo mission. I would not be able to live with myself if something happened to you or *this* fucked up your rap dream. I have been annihilating street gangs since I was a shorty. I can handle myself."

"And nigga? In the same light, I will be fucked up if something happened to you when I could have had your back. You always saved the day before Sun, now it is my turn. What is the deal Yoo!," I tell Byrd while initiating our neighborhood handshake.

"Are you sure that you want to do this Izzy? There's no turning back once you squeeze that trigger."

"Ayooo, say no more. It's already done. So, what's the *move*?"

"Alright. Well shit, let's hit the Rose *block* and strap up first," Byrd instructs in an admiral way. Guess the *warning before destruction* has been came. Probably when Maserati Rick asked me what I would do in that fourth-quarter scenario. I incontestably knew that this was not a part of the regulated game plan. But still, I have seen some Super Bowls won after players took matters into their own hands. The ball's in my court with 10 seconds left. I must be the one that graces my team into championship status. *This is how Street Legends are made*!

Chapter 29

Byrd's spot on Rose Street looked like Hurricane Andrew just stopped by for a visit. *From the exterior to the interior.* Stepping into the rowhouse that has not had neighbors in years, you could still hear that annoying ass baby crying. The mother was *dope sick* on the stairs, using a University of Maryland hoodie as a blanket. The child who appeared to be almost a year old was strapped into a car seat, that was originally manufactured for a newborn. It is was a sad sight to see, but all around, typical in this type of setting. Pertinently speaking, I have witnessed worse conditions, growing up across the street from Somerset.

"Ayooo, so what are you going to do with *her* after you move on from this block?," I asked Byrd.

"Don't judge me Money. But I fucked her the other day. She really has a nice body and *pretty* pussy. Just these streets have her in a death grip," Byrd says describing the high yellow mixed breed. "She got turned out by her baby father and her baby father ended up getting *whacked* over a gram of tar. Basically, the average debauchery around here. Been thinking about helping the smut out. Getting clean and shit."

"Fuck no nigga. Let me find out you are falling in love with your clientele. Guess she's going to be the one to turn you out and I'm going to be the one to smoke you over a twenty."

"Nigga please! I am the one who taught you how to load a chopper. You would merely just be haunting niggas in their dreams if it weren't for me. Besides, she might be loyal. Bitch hasn't set me up yet, after all the promising opportunities that have arose."

"Whatever Yoo and what about the kid?," I ask.

"Shit I'll probably take care of it or give him to you. Let you playhouse with the motherfucker."

"Yeah alright. Stacy would smother that baby after hearing him scream for so long. Ayooo what new toys do you have anyway?," I questioned Byrd to check out his new artillery.

"Aww shit. Come on, check me out," Byrd says instructing me to follow him upstairs. His dope fiend *'girlfriend'* did not even budge during our conversation, her baby crying nor Byrd kicking her on the side as we walked upstairs. I wondered if she was still alive. I hope that sour smell was not coming from her and if it was, I don't know how Byrd fucked this girl. Knowing Byrd, he did not even make her get in the shower either.

Entering the last, windowless room in the hallway, I was shocked at Byrd's assortment of military hardware. His armory contained more lethal weapons than a brigade of Marines. From automatics to pistols, shotguns to muskets- Byrd possessed it all. You would think he was making ABM's (Anti-Ballistic Missiles) in this *motherfucker*. The idea had just dawned on me about how he was able to acquire this fortress of *deadly instruments*. You had to have a plug at Forte Meade or some shit.

"Peep game Duke. Not that it really matters, but when the fuck did you join the Army? Wait a minute nigga, is that a grenade?," I capriciously express.

Byrd laughs. "Nahhh Sun, I never joined the army. Just robbed some veterans from the Army."

"What nigga? That is bullshit. Do you mean to tell me that some military minded motherfuckers, let you walk out they shit with a musket? Do not take this the wrong way Money. You *bad*, but you ain't that *bad*," I fractiously tell Byrd.

"Say Izzy, you know that every *jackboyz'* motto is- *take what you want and keep what you need*. It just so happens that none of my robberies ever produced frivolous outcomes and today isn't going to be an exception," Byrd says throwing an old school Tec Twenty-Two (.22) in my direction. He had an exact replica in his hand.

It never hit me about how *real* our plot was until he passed me an extra clip. The clip alone held 32 rounds;

so, add in another chance at anarchy and you had potential extinction for whoever was at the end of the barrel. Not to mention that there were hollow points collaborating with each bullet.

If I could weigh out the sacrifice I was making compared to the narrow-mindedness of my deeds, I would then realize that I am a selfish motherfucker. No matter the amount of compunction that I felt about breaking my word to Sidney, I knew regardless that the burden of this responsibility was still going to haunt me. I owed a substantial deposit of extra duty to both parties. But, to what extent?

Who did I owe a higher grade of responsibility towards? *My past or my future*. My family or my comrades, the streets. It is because of the depravity of my past which has depleted and exhausted my moral compass. But throughout everything that I have been through, I couldn't continue to use the streets as an excuse. Why, because I now know better and have an opportunity to do better.

At the same time though, I felt liable to Byrd for his selfless acts in the past. He could have left me for *dead* on Whitelock, but he did not. He could have left me stranded on Pennsylvania Avenue, but he did not. He could have let me starve once I got out, but he did not. *So, should a pledge of loyalty become non-existent in a situation like this?*

Let us not forget about Sidney, who has and still does display absolute loyalty to me. Who has remained sincere since day one. She never broke her commitment to our relationship, and I could always count on her to stay devoted to the cause. She was supportive throughout my incarceration when nobody else was there. *Not even Byrd.* Sidney was my life partner and the one I was coming home to fuck every night. She represented my family life, my last name, and my legacy. Still, there were no type of contingency where her love should be taken for granted. So, should not I still stand by the contract of dependency, which involved my presence being present.

It felt like I been here numerous times. Like this was a graduation of déjà vu. Humility and righteousness were expected, but my mind was subjected to the confines of self-exaltation. This was the <u>Primrose</u> <u>Path-</u> a course of action that seems easy but can easily be led into disaster. Ultimately, I was not hitting this *liq* for backup money. The reason was far more barbaric. It was a combination that comprised of bragging rights, helping Byrd get his block back and *simply because I could do it.* Retrospection would tell you that we could do it and get away with it. What made this mission any different than all our other robberies we've committed?

I could go shut the Africans down and still be back to take the family to Columbia.

"Ayooo Duke! When we get in the *spot*, I got you and you got me. Everybody else would be considered a target and must be taken out if the assignment calls for it. We are not dealing with the regular street niggas. These are some *Zulu* and *Tutsi* motherfuckers", Byrd says adding emphasis on the task.

"Ayeee we good, Money. I have seen *Shottas*. We going to get that and come back with that."

"I think they were Jamaicans in Shottas though," Byrd explains.

"Same motherfuckers. Look, we can talk about the movie once we get back. I am trying to see if this Tec is really the truth or not. Heard these *hoes* don't Jam."

"Nigga look at the aesthetics of this *bitch*. I chose this tool to get the job done because that's exactly what they're going to do."

"Alright! So, what are we waiting for then?," I asked Byrd.

"You're right, let's ride out!"

-#-

Glover Street was only two blocks away from Rose, so essentially our time window was short to counter all conflicting estimations. We had to accurately calculate the African tribe, runners, and bystanders. We could not misinterpret any factor that laid on the Glover block. A simple false step or slip-up could be the catastrophe that cost us our lives. I did not plan to die tonight. The Baltimore Police or city coroner would not be knocking on Uncle Lenny's door tonight. Stacy and Sidney would be traumatized.

"So, what's the plan Yoo? We're not about to just hit Glover and *make it rain* with shell casings?"

"Yeah I know Money. Honestly, I don't have a precise plan. But one thing I know about planning an attack on the unexpected is that you have a better chance of catching them *slipping*. We just have to get close enough to peep their whole operation while staying undetected. That is it… That is exactly how we're going to do it. Hey, toss me a hundred-dollar bill," Byrd requests while trying to conceal his Tech. It was going to be hard for him to sneak around the back streets with this big ass gun. Byrd was only 5 foot five, 135 pounds.

"What do you have in mind?," I asked while digging in my pocket. "And I don't have a straight *Benji*. I have change though."

"Perfect. Shoot it and follow my lead."

As we approached Luzerne Street (which was the block before Glover), I began to notice an increase in the defective obstacles that stood in our way. For starters, this area was jittery with dope fiends. More than we had originally anticipated, and they were all coming from Grover Street. It is like you were forbidden to enter that block unless you were a "*zombie*," looking for your fixed.

Any seasonal robber would not hit that strip unless they wanted their chances at discovery to intensify. Me and Byrd had to refine our method of action because up until now, I thought our scheme began by busting down the front door. Debilitating the adversary.

Compulsive thing about Byrd though is that he reacts to street circumstances with a scientific procedure called a hypothesis. If I respond like this, then these results should go as followed. These postulating ideas are what fueled Byrd's survival ever since he watched his parents murdered right in front of him. Guess that is another reason I'm comfortable taking penitentiary chances with him. Mainly because of the charismatic style he uses to get the job done.

In a startling instant, Byrd whistles for one of the dope fiends to come and converse with us. Without saying a word, I knew exactly the route that our plan had veered. The same way we figured out that African Dee ran Glover was the same way we would gain access to Glover.

"Ayooo what's up with all that traffic around the corner?," Byrd asked the withering junkie.

"Good dope, man. The best dope God has blessed us with in a while."

"Yeah. Let's say I gave you $100. Would you be able to map out everyone inside the spot?"

"Uhh, I don't know youngster. I am just a *smoker*. I don't really pay close attention to detail," he says.

"Look, what if I offered you an ounce of *crack*? Would you be able to pay enough attention to who's carrying out orders on the inside?"

The dope fiend eyes lit up. "Re… Really? I could do that. *Yeah, yeah*. Trust me when I tell you that I can do that."

"Alright, well this $100 should get you close enough to scope out the scene. We will be waiting in this alley. Oh yeah and if you are not back in ten minutes, I'm going to find you and shoot you in the dick a hundred times," Byrd warns the dope fiend by exposing his *street sweeper*.

"Oh Lord Jesus. Don't worry, I'll be back three minutes early," he says while running off.

"You think that he is going to come back?," I asked Byrd laughing at his insolent threat.

"*Fuckin' right*, wouldn't you? What sounds more promising- an ounce of crack or 100 puncture holes in your dickhead?"

"Ouch. I do not even want to picture some shit like that. I would rather you shoot me in the head 100 times", I squeamishly exclaim.

"Exactly. So how do you think that smoker feels as he's high off his ass then hears that promise?"

"Shit, that motherfucker is probably going to come back with a blueprint of the whole *block*."

We laughed comically like there is no tomorrow. Laughed because we could not openly say that we'll be able to laugh tonight. Laughed because we dreaded the information that we were predisposed to receive. Laughed because we were not kids, robbing to buy Jordan's anymore. Laughed because preferably we wanted to get the last laugh tonight. Laughed because the cocaine, complected Yukon Denali just turned onto Glover Street. Laughed because the dope fiend was already on his way back and it was already too late to turn back around.

-#-

"Okay, okay so this is what I saw. I'm not the smartest man in the world, but you know a full-blown infirmary when you see one," our informant begins. "I'm surprised that they even let me in. It is like when the free clinic gave out $50 food stamp vouchers for everyone to get fresh needles and condoms. It's fucking bananas over there…"

"Ayooo, I never did ask you about no venereal diseases. What the fuck is going on over there?," Byrd says.

"Oh yeah, right. Well, I don't want to get in your business, but I hope you're not planning on doing what I think you're going to do," the dope fiend boldly opined his thoughts. This was all that needed to be said to damn near push Byrd over the edge. My relentless best friend, known as Byrd, shoved the man closer into the alley and was prepared to banish him from society forever. Once I saw Byrd release his Tec and point it towards the smokers' chest; something had to be said or our layout will become mutilated.

"Lookout Duke. Chill and see what the nigga has to say first. If he ain't talking about *nothing* then put one in his thinking cap," I hastily tell Byrd.

"Nahhh man. Fuck that nigga. How do we know that he did not go over there and tell those dread-headed motherfuckers what's going on? I know not to trust anyone, especially a smoker. I tripped out on this one, so I have to *plug him with the lead*."

"Please, please. I am telling you I wouldn't do that. Just trust me, please. I have grandkids on the way," the smoker tries to verbally defend his life.

"Nigga shut up. Do you want to live or not?," I asked the sick addict after kicking him in the stomach. I felt compelled to apply some *direct pressure* because he used that spurious excuse.

You are not too worried about being acquainted with your grandchildren when you are out here smoking crack. But suddenly, I felt like I needed that same kick to the stomach. I am not worried about assisting my family or dropping multi-platinum albums when I'm planning to execute an African Mafia. An incredibly sad, but sagacious realization. Too bad, it was too late.

"Alright motherfucker. Talk!," Byrd demanded.

"Look, this is what I bought and it's a lot more in there. The *main guy* had just pulled up," the smoker says while showing the heroin and crack he had acquired.

"But this is the brilliant part fellas... They carried briefcases and boxes of diapers into the house but there were no fucking diapers in the box though. I had gotten close enough to see them dump wads and wads of cash onto the floor. *At least a quarter million.* I have 20/20 vision and money; well, I love money. Who doesn't?"

"Bingo! So how many people were in the house?," I unanimously asked the smoker without a speck of disbelief. Today was Friday and the end of the month, so they were probably accumulating their combined profits.

"This is when I tell you the bad part. I really tried though but I do not want to give you the wrong head count and it spoils your plan. I couldn't see everyone."

"Well, what the fuck happened to your 20/20 vision, *Mister I Love Money?* All it's going to take is for me to pull this trigger and so many slugs will hit your dick that all of your future generations will feel this steel," Byrd threatens.

"Look, look, look...," the dope fiend begins.

"I had gotten inside information a while back that they do all of their cooking, cutting, and packaging in the basement. Just a lot of naked women, wired up on cocaine. You do not have to necessarily worry about them. The basement door, leading to the outside is cemented away. So, the only way out for them is through the house and I heard they keep that door dead bolted as well. As far as the main level, I could see about eight people, including the ones who just arrived in the truck."

"Weapons? Did you see any guns? Kids? Dogs? Lookouts? Anything that could stand in our way?," I asked him.

"Izzy nigga fuck the kids. Check it out," Byrd says forcing me to focus my attention on the Yukon riding down Orleans Street (away from the Glover block).

"Now is our chance. Which house is it?"

"It's the seventh rowhouse, *down this alley.* Besides my ounce of *hard,* don't you think I am entitled to some of your winnings? I mean, I did give you the scoop on...", was all the smoker could get out before Byrd pulls his Deuce five (.25) out of his back pocket and positions it point-blank range at our snitch's genitals. I did not believe Byrd was that ferocious until I heard two fading crackles. He had the gun so close to his pelvic bone that you could not hear the full vehemence of the firearm.

"Damn, nigga. What the fuck?"

"Chill Izzy. We could not allow his presence to come back and agitate us in the future. Throw that garbage bin over top of him and let's ride."

Chapter 30

Tigerish. Stone-hearted. Savage. Sadistic. Abominable. Blood-thirsty. Uncivilized. Malicious. Venomous. Rancorous. Assassin. I was thinking of all of the adjectives that partially embodied the full figure of a *ruthless motherfucker*. Guess it was a little too late to venerate any respect for our impending victims. I just found it difficult to grasp how Byrd could effortlessly pull a trigger with no remorse. It was even harder to digest that I ended up in prison before him. I can count how many *bodies* I have caught with one hand. It will take both hands of every *Kardashian* sister to determine his body count. *Maybe even more.*

Walking down this alley- you could hear babies crying, families talking, dogs barking and overall, the soundtrack of East Baltimore. Nothing distinctive though that would alert our targets. It just seemed like another day in the 'hood for these impoverished tenants. But for me and Byrd, we were just trying to survive another day in the hood. *There is a big difference.*

Most people around here just settled for these conditions as if any other option were inaccessible. I despised the thought of being broke. Held the idea of being late on bills in a scornfully manner. Withdrew the involvement of indigent people from my cipher. Guess it was difficult to become complacent with the fact that I was not born with a "silver spoon" in my mouth. Ironically, if I did not go after the money with aggression then the hunger pains would disturb me at night. This ideology was the prime influential motif of how me and Byrd became congruous before puberty hit. *It was for the pursuit of happiness and happiness through the dollar bill.*

I retained a real *eyesore* as we came within proximity of African Dee's Spot. I had to make sure this was the right rowhouse before we prudently abandoned the mission. *One. Two. Three. Four. Five. Six. Seven.* Fuck, this was the seventh rowhouse and it was dubiously perceptive that we would not be gaining entrance through the back door. Everything was boarded up. All entry points on the ground level and second floor were all strategically boarded up. Even in a moment of dexterity, unless you were *Spider-Man*, there was no way to discreetly raid African Dee's citadel.

"Damn, Money. So, what the fuck are we supposed to do now?," I asked my confidante.

"Shit, it's only one thing to do. Devise a route *inside* through the front door."

"Man, it's like *Dawn of the Dead* out there. He has the whole block under safekeeping. We are *out of bounds* already. Don't you think it's time to repress our plan until we do more research?"

"*Nah, nah, nah* Izzy! I have a theory. Follow me," Byrd says walking towards the sixth rowhouse. It was clearly abandoned. If some dope fiends didn't already claim this dilapidated building, then the roaches and rats did.

Me and Byrd hopped the fence and disappeared through the absent door of this dwelling. Just as I suspected, the territory was governed by stray cats, cigarette butts and an unearthly smell. *I hope we would not have to stay here long because it felt like my nose hairs were burning off.*

"Now what?," I asked as we stood by the front window that was also on the border of being truant.

"Just watch Izzy. I have been operating *blocks* long enough to know when the fog is settling in. You see if the result is money being made then the cause is currency rotation. But to save time, we are just going to identify that stimulus as a term that some people call *traffic*. They go hand-in-hand."

"So, with that being said... Don't you think that even an illiterate motherfucker would know that only a dimwit would run out there, *naked* face and extirpate their neighborhood? We both reside just a few streets over. It wouldn't be hard for one of them niggas to identify us later."

"Oh yeah, that reminds me. Put this on," Byrd says while handing me a gray bandana. Byrd allowed his philosophy to remain vague on his reasoning behind coming equipped with bandanas that were gray of all colors. Niggas *'Ova West'* were more inclined to identify themselves with the color *gray,* while camouflage became the standard if your address was east of *Shot Tower.* In Baltimore, every 'hood adopted its own unique color for when its *reppin' time.*

"We from the Westside now?," I asked Byrd.

"Shit, we are today! *Say you see him right there?* He has to be a lookout," Byrd informs me about the thug across the street. He was sitting on the stoop of another abandoned rowhouse. We were in the middle of a drug-infested battlefield where majority of every visible structure was deserted.

"As soon as we hop out Izzy, that's your target. Abduct his life quick and watch my back. I am going to make sure we get inside. Be prepared to let that Tec *loose*. Remember, I got you and you got me. Everybody else is closed casket."

"Wait, so that's the plan? Byrd, *real talk*... My mind has been involuntarily projecting red flags ever since we learned that African Dee was running this *shit*. There are certain rules that we must abide by in these streets and it feels like we're breaking a big one. Let us at least precisely map this shit out. Or go grab your bulletproof vests!"

"No time Izzy. If you watch my back then we won't need any vests. We are going to be in and out before anyone could even question the *upset*. Gone in 60 Seconds, my Duke. Come on," Byrd breathlessly chants.

"Ayooo, my nigga. Hold up. *Fuck*…"

Chapter 31

Byrd crashes out the front door like a madman and starts heading to the neighbors *establishment*. African Dee's Distribution Center. Off natural instinct, the noise that we caused automatically coerced everyone to glance in our direction. *Great, another defect in our spontaneous scheme. So far, so good.*

As soon as my left foot inched out of sixth rowhouse, I impulsively shoot three rounds at the "lookout." You would think that my marksmanship was premeditated by the way I silenced his life so swiftly. Without a dose of modesty, another thug storms out of the *lookout spot* waving a Heckler & Koch

93 automatic assault rifle. Unfortunately for him, I was two steps ahead of the defense. *Niggas talk about 'holding down the fort' in training camp, but this is the big leagues baby.* No preliminary could be overlooked. But at least I put him out of his painful misery as courteous as possible. An *easy* seven shots exploded in his main bodily systems. Think all of them hit too.

That is when I heard it.

Boom. Boom. Pop. Boom. Pop. Pop. Pop. Pop. Pop. Pop. Pop. Pop. Pop. Pop. Pop, Pop, Pop, Pop.

It sounded like the climaxed moments when popcorn is popping in the microwave. Hopefully, that is the shots coming from Byrd's Tec.

This was impasse because I could not desert my homeboy in the middle of a revolution. At the same time, I could be eligible for a "dome shot" if I proceed through African Dee's door. It was a lose-lose situation, so after I made sure the outside was clear, it was time to invent my destiny.

"Please. No, do not shoot me. I'll tell you where everything is at" was the female voice I heard coming from African Dee spot. As I peeked in the door, there were five bodies deteriorating on the floor and none of them were Byrd. In fact, he was in charge standing over the last presuming survivor.

"Nigga it's me," I had to yell at Byrd after he points his Tec towards me. I was a nanosecond away from being Byrd's seventh immolation for the day. He was on an avaricious roll to finally end the feud between himself and African Dee. The only way this strife would discontinue is by first, Byrd ending

African Dee's cash flow by taking it all. Last and most importantly, Byrd would have to end African Dee's life.

"Shit Izzy, you better say something next time. Here, keep this *smut* down while I bag up all this *cheddar cheese*", Byrd says pointing towards the floor covered in rubber band stacks of money. *I have never seen this much dough at one time.* It was well over $100,000. *It must be a twist in this plot because shit was never this easy.*

"Damn Duke. You going to just say my name like that?," I asked after realizing he put my alias in the air. That could only mean one thing; Byrd wasn't going to let this survivor *make it* in the end.

"Fuck that hoe nigga. I was going to tie her ass up anyway. She is probably burning, so I'm going to let her burn up for real, for real," Byrd says flickering a lighter he found on the floor.

"Please. I promise I will not tell anybody. I will suck your dick. I will do whatever you want me to. *Fuck Little Dee.*"

"Shut up bitch."

Pop. Pop. Pop.

Byrd's death toll for the past 10 minutes has just reached eight; mine was still at two. After all these gunshots and murders, you would think BPD would be on the scene. But in all rationality, these maleficent acts that we have just committed are probably taking place in other parts of the city right now. So, I guess it's just our luck that police decided to patrol those areas and not ours. I hoped that the killing spree was done now so we can go split up the cash. There were still other obligations that I had to fulfill. All the thoughts poured through my mind about what Sidney would say when I walk through the door with an easy $50,000.

"Izzy, real talk. I am sorry that I got you involved with this shit. You are not no killer Duke. You have a good heart. You are going to be something big in life. Don't turn into no *cutthroat* like me Sun," Byrd nonsensically tells me.

"Ayooo this isn't a time to get to delicate nigga. We have to get the fuck up out of here," I say while helping Byrd stuff the last bit of money into a Shoe City shopping bag.

"For real Yoo. Don't pick up the *ratchet* again unless you have to protect your shorties."

"All right. Done. You ready?," I hastily asked.

"*Yeah, come on. Watch my back*," was the last thing he said before running out into the clear view of Glover Street. Motherfucker did not even check if there were any lucid hostilities. Byrd's egotistical conduct towards life finally caught up with him. The numerous high-risk robberies that he is executed made him feel like this was just a normal, facile *job*. As if no matter his performance, he was still unconsciously superior to his opponents.

I could not diagnose the telltale sign that shit just got superbly real for me. That my existence is now solely based off my personal course of action. I literally had split seconds to put together a getaway plan.

After I saw the shopping bags, filled with money, hit the surface it was verified that shit was legit. The *foreign accents* I heard outside made me feel like I could not escape my own death. This was haphazardly grotesque because I had a million-dollar assurance of success this morning. *Now my life clock was ticking, and the batteries would soon die.*

Boom. Boom. Click, click. Boom. Boom.

Those were not the sounds of Byrd's Tec. His weapon just slid across the floor to me after his body slammed on the ground. Byrd's movement was not even flinching. A fragment of his ribcage was hanging from his physique. After the cold look in his eyes turned dark, it was for certain. There were no reset buttons to this shit. So, Jeff should have just taken the $20 and bought the eight-piece chicken box. *Why?* Absolutely, Byrd just died.

Boom. Boom. Click, click. Boom. Boom.

And from the looks of things, I was next.

Chapter 32

I have always known sawed-off shotguns to be rather good and powerful. Especially when you had three of them, robustly aiming to change your reality. The exoneration of these weapons was spectacular. Take my circumstance out of the picture, it was impressive to see these buck shots start to regenerate the outside wall that separated me from the shooters. Using all apprehension, I was 60 seconds away from being penetrated by life-altering bullets. It did not matter if I continued laying on the floor with both Tec's and if I took the same road that Byrd did too.

The shit was unforgettable.

Boom. Boom. Click, click. Boom. Boom. Click, click. Boom. Boom.

"Fuck," I yelled underneath my breath as the thunderous roars of shotgun slugs never ceased to take a break. I started to see sunlight peak through parts of the wall that have been getting plastered. Even the couch I was lying next to you had smoke temporarily protruding from a *Bible*.

My chances at getting away were forsakenly slim. *The only tolerable option was using my body weight against the back door hoping I will be able to produce just enough force to unclasp the screws that held my blockhead together.*

Shit, I was only a hundred and sixty pounds though. If I didn't make it after the first charge, then I would be "swiss cheese." My other substitution was either waiting for them to run out of bullets or think that I was already dead. *Good luck with that.*

Boom. Boom. Click, click. Boom. Boom. Click, click. Boom. Boom.

Now for certain, a section of African Dee's building blocks just lost traction. You could fit a shoe in the chunk of concrete that was disrespected. They were willing to tear up this structure to tear up my structure. The difference is that it will be easier to emasculate my framework than this brick rowhouse.

Boom. Boom. Click, click, click, click, click.

Oh shit, this was my chance.

The *rescue boats* have arrived. If I am not mistaken, they are all in the process of reloading. I was equipped with dual old-school Tec (.22) with an extra clip. (Byrd had the other clip in his pocket, but he was positioned in their line of sight). Still, it would not take 32 shots to expel a nigga. All it took was the right one.

I quickly conformed to the actions of *James Bond*. I gripped both Tec's and spiraled towards the outside wall. There were two striking points. You had a window and the door, in which Byrd laid stagnant in front of. The door was off limits, so my best offense was to start an assault through the window.

As I adjusted my back against the outside wall, there was a strange dialect being spoken. The window was only a couple of inches away, but I could clearly see the cocaine complected, Yukon Denali.

African Dee was out there.

Just as I was in position to start my slaughter, someone came creeping downstairs. You could simply assess the fact that he did not know that I was installed against the wall. He might be the assailant who killed Byrd. Probably shot him in the back, a coward's way of survival in these streets.

Pop. Pop. Pop. Pop. Pop. Pop.

Being assiduous was now ancient because slaying the unwelcome visitor became a priority. Seeing him roll down the stairs was an announcement that an ambush was onset. *Call me a dumbass to still be standing by the window.* The unwarranted problem that I was trying to dissolve now became a realization that I could not avoid.

Boom. Boom. Click, click. Boom, boom. Bang. Bang. Bang. Click, click. Boom. Boom.

Simultaneously, bullets came in the same concurrence as raindrops. *Snowflakes.* The weatherman could have said that the forecast on

Glover Street was gunpowder and he would have been accurate. Feeling the blood ooze down my face, I could not tell if I've been shot or not. All I could tell you was how the ground felt as my vision got murky.

Sounds became rumpled underneath the deafening gunshots. Time became torpid at the expense of my own bloodshed. I was negligent at the civil unrest that was taking place outside- mainly because I thought I was already dead. Looking over at Byrd, I wondered if life flashed before his eyes.

As I was patiently waited for that segment, assurance came in the form of a vibration. *Assurance that I still was alive.* As I regained consciousness, I find out that the blood I am tasting is coming from a gash on my face.

Probably caused from glass on the window. The vibrations and music that I was hearing came from my cell phone. It was ringing and Sidney wanted me to be the recipient. Inexplicably spoken, my *"Hundred Dollars & A Dream"* verse was the ringtone. Sidney sure knew when to call at infectious times.

It would be disenfranchising to answer the phone because that would make my vulnerability levels skyrocket. But at this momentous point, I found it relevant to look at my screensaver. Not allowing my barrel to dispel from the front door, I gaze at the photograph of me, Stacy, and Sidney. *Something sparked called ambivalence.* The ambition to persevere versus me giving up and simply succumbing to the elements of the rising Baltimore City murder rate. I have witnessed nine murders today (one of which was my best friend) and if I didn't want to become number ten then something had to be done.

Its fourth quarter, I am down by two with 10 seconds left and the ball is in my hand. *Thinking unreservedly, I was going to die anyway*. I would not be Izzy B if I didn't go out with a bang. This was for Tonya and Byrd- both killed indirectly by the greed of African Dee.

After wiping the blood out of my eyes and sliding my phone back into the holster, it was *crunch time*. A tense and crucial moment, where in 10 seconds I will be either dead or alive. That spacious honesty alone became the source of annexed adrenaline. There was only one way out and that was by becoming diplomatically adroit. *Demonstrating the street intelligence that Broadway bred.*

Bang. Bang. Click, click. Bang. Bang. Boom. Boom. Click, click. Boom. Boom.

Bullets continued to ricochet throughout the house. But one thing I know, two things for sure- their *repetitious acts* would not last much longer. There was a time and place for everything. There was a time to kill and a time to heal. A time to shoot and a time to reload. A time to hide and a time to seek. A time to hunt and a time to be hunted.

Boom. Boom. Click, click. Boom. Boom. Click, click. Click, click, click.

"Bingo."

I rose out of seclusion so rapidly that I did not even give the five men standing outside the window any chance to register with the *fear factor receptors* in my brain. They were more spooked than me since my emergence sporadically occurred. Yet alone their weapons weren't aimed at me, but my dual Tec's were trained on them.

Pop, pop, pop. Pop, pop, pop, pop, pop, pop. Pop. Pop. Pop, pop, pop, pop, pop, pop.

I heartlessly exhausted a whole clip on the Africans without blinking an eye. Primarily, filing three of African Dee's men with more holes than an *Early Wind* instrument. The remainder of my ammunition went on the Yukon Denali. Thus, realizing that at least two more perpetrator's haven't entered a state of dormancy yet. *My mission has not quite been fulfilled yet.*

Getting out of dodge from the windows' display was the best judgment call I have made today. Gave me enough time to secure another cartridge and extend my lifespan. The Africans were not giving up without a fight though.

Boom. Boom. Click, click. Boom. Boom. Click, click. Boom. Boom. Click, click.

While developing my exit plan, an interesting discovery was made that there was only one person outside aiming to kill me. I was able to get a glimpse of the dramatics outside through the mutilated bricks that once sustained this threshold.

The other two motherfuckers were busy trying to rejuvenate their firearms. It was possible that their pistols got *jammed*. Whatever the case, this was my liberation period. *The ball was back in my hands except now the score was even. Five seconds left. Checkmate. Touchdown. Game time.*

Without thinking twice, I sprinted out the front door with both Tec's as my leverage. I would be a fabricator if I said *withdrawal* did not almost subdue me. Anybody in my position would unashamedly say that they would have dominated their foe. *It is easier said than done.* Picture being surrounded by 12 dead bodies during a bright sunny day on a gravelly back street in East Baltimore- and your only chance of survival is by terminating the remaining participants. Unless you were born with a humanitarian error (like Byrd), then this was not going to be an easy task. But sometimes in life, someone must die for someone to live. There was only one thing to do!

Pop, pop, pop, pop, pop, pop. Pop, pop, pop, pop, pop, pop. Pop, pop, pop, pop, pop, pop.

The residual Africans began to cascade on the asphalt as I made my way back into the sixth rowhouse.

There was no cessation or letting up from my lethal inception. I made it. Even though the police sirens in the distance grew louder, I still made it. *I am still alive*!

That was the only bearable thought going through my mind as I ran back to Uncle Lenny's house. The admissibility of my past 10 minutes of pantomiming acts was the mental encounter that I never wanted to re-live. The treacherous mechanisms that just rendered the dissolution of 17 lives would be the reason Baltimore makes murder capital this year.

As I created my divergence from Glover Street, a tear of remorse rolled down my cheek. I should have discarded the idea of robbing African Dee from the start. Maybe Byrd would have eliminated any remnants of the idea, too. But instead, my agreement caused his aggression to heighten. *Was this a part of the treaty about when being REAL goes wrong?*

What was being real? Realizing everybody ain't loyal. I thought I was being loyal by conforming to Byrd's impetuses until the shit backfired. Now I feel even more fraud because I could have been a better friend. Even though it was remarkably possible that he would have hit the *liq* by himself, there was still room for reconsideration… *Didn't I owe Byrd a little more persuasion into doing the right thing?*

What was being loyal? Staying true and faithful to the cause. Ever since elementary, me and Byrd had an earnest desire to get rich. We started off jacking niggas for their lunch money. To jacking the low-level weed *salesman* for superficial means. To jacking lucrative, yet folly, drug dealers for their earnings. Up until now, where we were grown and had the option to do better. It just did not seem like shit was supposed to end like this.

While I stashed the Tec's and cleaned up at Byrd's spot on Rose, I thought about the undertaking discussion we had earlier. Byrd made he promised him that I will make this dream happen for all of us. *For the fam, the 'hood and the city*. The projected path was unequivocal. The sentiment over what just happened clearly justified this *dream*. I now inconsolably, had to *fuck the game raw*!

Chapter 33

Shit seemed overly odd as I walked into Uncle Lenny's house. Excluding my current condition, everything was substantively desolate. The dynamic atmosphere that I just left an hour ago has died. All the lights and TVs were turned off. It was as if a Desert Storm had swept through and dropped off feelings of abandonment. I knew Sidney and Stacy did not forsake me. There had to be a deeper truth to this mystery.

Walking downstairs, I heard the sniveling revelation. Anxiety hovered over my being as I defiantly open the door. *What exactly was I walking into? What could be the cause of Sidney's mourning?*

I had made it back before Uncle Lenny even arrived, so she couldn't be tripping about our firework plans. Maybe it was the rampant gunfire that just devastated our neighborhood. Without any inducing facts, she could have thought I became a casualty. In her mind, anytime that I was with the infamous Byrd then there was a chance I would not return home at night. That would explain her phone call earlier… Right?

"Damn baby. What's up? What is wrong?," I asked stampeding into our executive cellar.

"Izzy. Where were you? We called you… We needed you and you were not there for us", Sidney manages to get out before her tears became uncontrollable. Stacy broke free from her mother's solacing grip once she saw me.

"Daddy" was the only word I heard before Stacy ended up in my arms and her head on my shoulder.

"Hey sugar booger. Sidney, what is going on? Why are you crying? Look at me…"

"Isaiah… Uncle Lenny…"

"What… What happened?," I said while sitting down next to Sidney. Now we were all in arms reach, able to extract each other's body warmth. We were sitting so close together that if everything got silenced, I will be able to hear their heartbeats. Something exorbitant had to happen for her to display this severe lamentation.

"Baby… Uncle Lenny came home drunk and he… He tried to rape me…"

All cognizance went out the window as Sidney replayed her story. I could not believe my ears, but knew she wasn't lying. I have been around for some of Uncle Lenny's incoherent stupors to know that he can get outrageously flagrant, sometimes. Betrayal would undervalue the feelings that I felt. Of all the people who I thought would ever cross me, never once suspected that it would be family. *Blood.* Uncle Lenny at that.

"It was horrible Isaiah," Sidney continues. "I kept pushing him off me. But he would not stop trying to grab and kiss me. I slapped him after he ripped my shirt. Then, he got aggressive. The only thing that stopped him was Stacy running into the room. I was so scared…"

"Damn baby, I'm so sorry I wasn't here for y'all. Promise I will not let anyone hurt y'all again. You and Stacy are my life Yoo," I tell Sidney empathizing in her pain. I kissed both of them on their forehead, condemning the thought that I will one day have to let go. *These are my shorties*. Fucking with them is like fucking with me. I could not release all of my anger at Uncle Lenny without being angry with myself though. I left them to go *parlay* in the streets.

"Lookout babe, go ahead and pack a bag. *We are about to burn off*. We're not staying here with this nigga anymore," I tell Sidney while giving her an amiable caress on the shoulder. It was hard trying to refrain from cussing in front of Stacy. There were so many vulgar terms that I could express towards Uncle Lenny right now. Luckily for me, he wasn't here anymore or I'll be catching my second felony assault case.

"Okay Isaiah. But where are we going to go?"

"I don't know yet but far from here though. We have a lot of money saved up on your little checking account thing. I figure we can go to a hotel until we sort everything out."

"Ayooo that's fine and all," Sidney says. "But let's really think about this. We can always go to my sister house. Oh yeah and Emily has two extra rooms in her duplex. She lives up by North and Washington. Izzy, what happened to your face?"

"Oh, it's nothing. We were just slap boxing in the projects," I told her lacking the ability of persuasion. After the recent discovery, it had slipped my mind about what I was running from.

"Slap boxing? Nigga you are buggin.' See how deep that scar is," Sidney says while grabbing my jaw and tilting my head for a better view.

"Please Isaiah, don't make this day any worse by lying to me!"

"Alright Sidney, you got me. We had gotten jumped walking through Lafayette. *But it is all good.* Hit your friend up and see *what is smackin.'* Tell her to rent us those rooms."

"Hold on, hold on Izzy! My intuition is telling me that the whole truth has not been disclosed. If you so-called got jumped, why did you change clothes? And where were you when these trigger-happy niggas *hit the block up*? Huh!"

Just as I was formulating an adequate comeback, Stacy picked up the remote and turned the TV on. Maybe this moment was inexorably ordained. It did not matter how cunning I was when the imminent subject couldn't be deviated. Apparently unplanned, the channel was set on FOX. *WBAL News* was playing on FOX. Simultaneously, the WBAL newscasters were gathered on Glover Street. (It must be mortifying for

Stacy to affirm her fathers' nuisance behavior once again via the television screen.)

"*We are coming to you live from East Baltimore, where residents are calling this the <u>Memorial Day Massacre</u>. Police are still stumbling upon more bodies, but as of right now, there are at least 14 homicides under investigation.*"

Turn it off. Turn it off. Turn it off.

"*City officials have made the assertion that this was a violent drug transaction gone bad. DEA and the ATF have attained over twenty automatic assault weapons, including the ones that were used in today's warfare. Also, 115 pounds of heroin and cocaine were seized, along with almost two million dollars in cash were found at this Glover Street home.*"

Two million dollars? What the fuck? I must go back!

"Locals are relieved that this drug reservoir has been relinquished but are still skeptical if this is an indication that the crime rate will drop also. Many believe it is the authorities' responsibility to end drug trafficking rings, not the citizens themselves. The Baltimore Police commissioner has planned to increase their presence in this shaken up community, to decrease crime. Juvenile curfews are going to be imposed and random frisking will be done to suspicious figures. Among the identified slain of this unruly occurrence goes as followed…"

Damn, please do not show their pictures.

"David Omontizro… Maria Anne Lopez… Priscilla Haskell… D'Angelo Tisdale… And business owner, Le'Trell Martin."

Byrd had a state issue ID on him? Crazy, because after almost two decades of knowing him, I just figured out his real name.

"*Police are asking for the help of this East Baltimore neighborhood to identify any surviving shooters from this massacre. The Baltimore Police tip hotline number will be posted on numerous intersections around Johns Hopkins…*"

"Daddy did you see Uncle Byrdie on TV?," Stacy innocently asks as I withdrew the remote from her hands. I was so appalled at the news report that I had let them watch it too. *Terrible, terrible mistake.*

"You know what Isaiah; I'm done with you. I cannot do this anymore. It is like I'm dragging myself down, trying to lift you up. You don't appreciate the fact that you have a good woman, willing to stand by your side through whatever."

"Whoa baby, just chill. Do not try to overanalyze this shit. Let me explain first…"

"No, fuck that Izzy. There's nothing to explain," Sidney screams.

"Baby, can we please not argue and cuss in front of Stacy?"

"*Oh yeah right*. So, it's more righteous for her to witness your good deeds on the evening news?"

"Look Sid, everything just went sour ultra-fast. I lost my best friend; I'm not trying to lose you too."

"Isaiah you don't genuinely care if I stay or leave. Then, you are lying to me now. What part of the game is this? Nigga you changed and I can't be with the new *you.*"

"Sidney, I'm not perfect. I do *fuck up* sometimes, but my love for you has not been altered. I'm still the same Isaiah that you fell in love within high school."

"No, you're not. The old Izzy cherished me and would not lie to me about anything. We talked about everything, no holdbacks. The old Izzy would not place me third or fourth to anything. Man, I'm tired of the competition."

"Competition… Who are you competing with?," I asked.

"I'm tired of being in constant competition with the *streets.*"

Damn, so that is the simplistic complication of it all. Being in a relationship is a consolidated connection that is meant to unify and strengthen both parties. Specifically, me and Sidney formed a relationship based off loyalty. Before true love was ever evident, loyalty was present. You could love somebody but have a moral compass that's lacking- therefore the degree of loyalty you can exhibit is low. But if you show the utmost level of loyalty towards someone, then the only thing that can manifest is love.

So where did that leave my relationship with Stacy's mother?

Was Sidney's loyalty, a feeling of obligation because of my declaration of love? She made it her responsibility to remain loyal throughout my three years of incarceration. There were a million other things she could have done, but instead she chose to *ride it out* with me. That is loyalty! During the beginning of our relationship, her parents did not approve of me. Instead of solemnizing her family's wishes, she stayed with me. Izzy B. That is loyalty! Somehow, someway, we made it this far off her loyalty and my love.

But where did my loyalty reside? Where was my devotion to the cause? Did I take Sidney for granted?

Did I just want to be recognized as 'Izzy has a *bad bitch* by his side'?

It is possible that she settled for my lack of commitment and I got comfortable with her cohesive support. Our unconditional love was transparent, but somewhere along the line, a boundary was crossed. That frontier was explored earlier today when I left my family for some excitement.

"So, you don't have anything to say now Isaiah?," Sidney bids as I replayed the series of events that have led us here. I was conscience-stricken with sorrow at my pettiness. Not just from today, but from all the times I pushed Sidney away for some small-minded task.

"Uhm yeah babe. I do not think there's a perfect combination of words that could express my apology- but I want you to know that I'm terribly sorry for hurting you. I do not deserve you Sidney. It took a great deal of courage to stay with me this long and I am always going to honor you for that. For everything. For real Yoo, I love you…"

"Cut the *Shakespeare* shit Isaiah and get to the point!"

"So, what do you want me to say, Sidney?," I contentiously snapped.

"Say that you're ready for this family! That your ready to make something out of yourself! Say that you are going to stop this immature shit in the streets! Say that you are going to start looking out for our best interests and not just what Isaiah wants! Say something...," Sidney retorts before the heartbroken tears began to fall.

"Baby come here Yoo," I tried to tell Sidney while having my request accompanied with a hug. It is true that I get weak in the knees having to see my *true love* cry. *Especially when it is my fault.*

"No Isaiah! Get off me," Sidney rejects.

"Damn, what's up?"

"You say that me and Stacy are your life. That you do not want you to lose us, right? Prove it!"

"How do you expect me to prove that right this second?," I answer before giving myself any time to consider another response.

"You know what Isaiah? I am done wasting tears on you. You're never going to get it," Sidney says wiping her face.

"If you don't know how to prove it by now then I guess it's too late for us."

"Wait, wait, wait Sidney. Just chill. Give me a chance!"

"I can't keep giving you chances Izzy. You want me to *let you make it* until you end up with a headstone or acquire another D.O.C identifier. I cannot do that again. I cannot do this anymore Isaiah. I am going to my sister's house. Whenever you are ready for something real, you know where to find us. My *insides* are sweltering but I don't know what else to do."

"Sidney, what are you talking about?"

"It's up to you, whether or not, we get back together. But right now, I am thinking for myself and Stacy- and based on your *movement*, I think its best that I end this relationship!"

Chapter 34

Sidney and Stacy were gone! Byrd was gone! Uncle Lenny had treacherous ways and my mother was not rigid enough to handle society. Not to mention, I had less than $500 on me after paying for the West Baltimore motel room in which I was staying.

I was a mess, a lost cause. Someone violated my family while I almost booked funeral service reservations. *Now they are gone.* Technically, I will not have anywhere to live after next week. This opaque, domino effect started the day I got out. Or maybe even earlier… Like at the Supreme Records talent showcase.

Shit, I was probably doomed in the womb!

This was the prime of my life with no respite in sight. Disappointment after disappointment, from others and myself was starting to take a toll on my clairvoyant approach of *living*. Does not matter my perception on balance regarding my *survival instincts* when the revolving door always channels me backward into a destructive position.

What is the philosophy behind resuscitation when the sufferer doesn't want to be revived? Who in their right mind would overlook success to find a benefit from defeat? Was my existence so condemned that the submission to failure became a swarming reality that I accepted? Did I become infected with the *contagious disease* called hopelessness? Was my suppressed life even worth living? Why did I just take the safety off my Glock 23? What was stopping me from pulling the trigger directed towards my heart?

Nobody surrounded me either, which meant nobody could reverse my decision of life or death. Before I performed the irrecoverable, I wanted to get one last look at my *cipher*. Life, or an utter disaster is what I called it.

After seeing the deteriorated motel room (which only cost $175 a week), it made suicide seem rather delightful. There were a few particles laying around such as an ironing board, my two duffel bags, a decayed chair, and a body size mirror.

I eased onto the putrid chair to await my faith and possibly diffuse the thoughts that were swirling through my mind. *Like how receptive certain individuals would be after receiving the news that Izzy B committed suicide?* Domination X and Darius Montgomery. Kannon and Lor Jeff. Sidney and Stacy. Strangely, I was overly convinced that this was for the better. *Why?*

Think even the sightless could see that destruction was the end-product to whatever I touched. That was the comforting reassurance which would make *this* even easier.

My *Glock Model 23* pistol was ready to shoot as I "cocked the hammer back". *I am sorry Byrd. I am sorry Mama. I am sorry Sidney. Stacy! Swear that despite my shortcomings, I have always tried to be an emulated version of success.* "Changes" by *Tupac* had randomly played in my mind because of the direct translation this moment had with his infamous first verse.

Just before I carried out my dishonorable suicide, the lights in the motel room began to flicker on and off. The annoying flash probably meant that the light bulbs were about to die. *What a coincidence!* Suddenly, everything went dark. I sat my pistol on the dresser to find a solution to this problem when the fidgety lights *jumped* back on. That is when the suffocating image made me retract any prior conclusions that I had made earlier.

What I saw in the body sized mirror was a depleted man with stainless dreams. Beneath the potent scars of yesteryear was an honorary drive for success. Every wound that I saw was a time to celebrate growth and development. Every blemish was a mental representation of an imperfection becoming complete. Every flawless defect was a reminder that I was still someone capable of exploiting greatness. This was me; Izzy B and I deserved a chance. *My existence alone meant that I had earned the right to suitably go after my aspirations!*

It was my choice to exercise that right though. I could eagerly continue to live with fear, anger, and embarrassment. Or I could overcome this struggle and ambitiously obtain the value of hard work. It was easier to accept destitution when every dilemma you encounter counters progression. It was easier to not risk vanishing in the uncertainty of life's puzzle than to risk the humiliation of not making it to the end. But I was ready to be humiliated. Mortified. Chastised. Whatever it took to bear the fruits of success, triumph, and prosperity. *My Hundred Dollars & A Dream!*

    Scoldingly, my Glock 23 was innocuously placed further from my custody. Off intuition, I grabbed the demos that I had made with Domination X and inserted them into my *Jordan* knapsack. My wallet only contained $229, but I was determined to make this my last night living under the poverty line. After packing my phone charger, hygiene necessities and pre-rolled Duchess- it was time to make a move!

    There is only one thing to do…

Chapter 35

Shit, if I would have known that New York City was in the backyard of Baltimore; then this could have become my second home a long time ago. For only a 3-hour bus ride and round-trip admission totaling $68- no architect could design this empirical feeling that I was currently experiencing.

Veracity struck me as I arrived at the 42nd Street Port Authority in Manhattan. Even though the stipulations were not necessarily favorable, this was still a remarkable moment for me. They say that there is a *first time for everything*- well, this was the first time that I've ever been outside of the Baltimore City limits.

Besides going to prison, my first nomadic excursion was *to the city so nice that they had to name it twice*. New York, New York! It took 23 years for me to finally step outside of my comfort zone. My *restrictive virginity* has finally been broken.

Growing up, me and Sidney garrulously fantasized about running rampant through the streets of New York. *Sucks that this was not the shared experience we always dreamed of.* It took every fiber of my being to not call Sidney and 'spill my heart out' about our altercation yesterday. My family was the supreme motive behind me being in New York right now. My motivation to execute an even bigger play. *This was for us.* (My versatility in the multiple, apologetic SMS messages had to have a heavy effect on her nevertheless.)

Stepping outside of the bus station, I did not know which way to go. Everything was so industrious and energetic. *Nobody* stopped moving. On the surface, New York City reminded me of an expansive, more massive version of Baltimore. One of the notable differences is that I see multiple ethnicities here versus Baltimore's demographics of being 80% African American. This could either be a pro or con towards getting my mission accomplished.

I now had to snap into guerilla mode because I did not know what to expect from the unexpected. I was in a foreign land, miles away from relief with only $161 to my name. Strategically getting to Downtown Brooklyn was my core objective. From the realistic depictions that you see on TV, I figured the Brooklyn Bridge had to be crossed. *Wait, Maserati Rick told me about the A train!*

I walked across the street to purchase two chili cheese coney's because the *munchies* were trying to kick my ass. Coincidentally, right by this hot dog stand was an underground subway station where hundreds of people gathered. Before making my descent under sea level, I took notice to the signs with different colors, letters and numbers. *Joyriding on the New York City public transit lines was not a part of the itinerary.*

With an anonymous way of defending myself, I needed *time* to be on my side. That would enhance the chances of my prerogative being conquered and decrease the chances of me being featured in *The New York Times*. Timing! Plus, with the Baltimore Orioles fitted cap I was wearing; niggas could probably smell that I was an immigrant.

Upon finishing my meal, I saw someone who looked like they would genuinely assist me.

"Ayooo you! Think I could *scream* at you for a second?"

"Yeah. *What's poppin' slime*?," the stranger says confirming that he was a street nigga like myself.

"Yoo man, I'm trying to get to Downtown Brooklyn. Jay Street."

"Already Sun. You must not have been informed but you're talking to the *Mister Five Boroughs* himself!," my vibrant tour guide fictitiously expresses. *I am under the impression that he grew up in Yonkers or New Jersey.*

"Yoo understand. *Times Square* is two blocks that way. Stevie Wonder would even recognize where he was. You are going to see *mad* people, *mad* bitches, and *mad* lights. It should not be hard to notice people walking down a flight of stairs that leads you underground. You only need to focus on the yellow platform with the letters N, R and W written by the *shits*," he says pointing towards the direction of my future transportation.

"Alright. Appreciate that my Duke."

"Don't sweat it chief. Yoo, where are you from anyway?," he asked me.

"Baltimore City!"

"Baltimore? Didn't y'all have an HBO series there a while back? Think it was called, uhh…"

"The Wire."

"Yeah, yeah. That motherfucker was the *truth*. Y'all really *getting it in* like that down there?"

"No doubt. It is actually 10 times worse than that TV show though. That was just a glimpse," I told the stranger not adding any hype on Baltimore street life.

"Word up, I can dig it. I am not trying to get in your *mix*. But Yoo, it is not every day that young niggas like us randomly hop off a Greyhound bus in Times Square. Take it a step further, Sun you really 'lost in the sauce' out here like you do not care about living. *What's poppin'?*"

"You good Money. I'm here to see Felix Stone!"

Whatever preoccupation engrossed this stranger prior to us meeting suddenly became second place to my unknown intentions. He became absorbed in the mystery of my adventure. More than likely, he viewed me as a passionate scrub. *A starving artist.* Someone who traveled from Baltimore to New York engulfed by a mild stench of urine; possessing a *lonely* Jordan knapsack. The mystified look on his face revealed that his insides were bursting with laughter at the cause of my crusade. The simple, unaccompanied goal of speaking with Felix Stone.

I intended for my scheme to prosper despite me overlooking limousine and chauffeur reservations. I was in one of the most exotic conurbation areas on the globe and never even intended on utilizing one of the 14,000 taxicabs that seemed to be stalking me. After that blundering fact had subsided, I understood why I deserved the label as a 'starving artist.'

"Wait a minute, Sun. Are you talking about the Felix Stone? CEO of Supreme Records, Felix Stone?"

"Yeah! We're talking about the same motherfucker," I respond.

"Whoa, I have got to hear this. I knew you *Bmore* niggas were crazy, but I swear you're the *illest* Sun. Word up! So, what, you're just going to storm in his office and demand a record deal?," the stranger inquires.

"I am one of the *'livest'* ones from Bedford-Stuyvesant and I'm not even *gully* enough to do that!"

"Ayo Duke. I am going to break this shit down, short and sweet for you. Quite sure that you have heard of Mister Popular before, right?"

"Hell yeah cousin, who hasn't… *'Mr. Pocket Full Of Money For The Strippers'*… That is my shit man!," he says after reciting one of Eugene's corny slogans.

"True. Well, I grew up with the nigga. I'm talking ABC's, 123's type shit. We have always been *microphone* rivals. Basically, he stole my material and presented it to Felix Stone- so in other words, our roles should be reversed. That nigga is a fraud Yoo…"

"Hey Yoo, watch your mouth! Look Sun, I am sorry that I even asked in the first place. I cannot take this shit! I just left my bitch for using TiVo and recording *General Hospital*," the stranger says trying to make a mockery out of my suspicious claim.

"You think this shit is a game, Duke?"

"Yoo Sun. This is New York City! There is over a million people walking around here with the same story. Somebody please get this brother on *Snapchat*", he screams hysterically with laughter.

"Alright. You're going to know the real, sooner or later," I say with a prideful stride towards Times Square. If I would've brought my forty (.40) with me then he would've been at danger for getting pistol-whipped in a dark alley. Primarily because he tried to generate his stand-up comedian career off an issue that's deeper than rap. But compared to an actual starving artist, my ego was not even affected by his slanderous remarks. Mainly, because that was expected. I would have reacted the same way in his shoes. Plus, I have always heard that New Yorkers were ten times ruder than natives from any other city. So, I took his

bluntly proportionate comments as a 'Welcome to New York City' gift.

"Yoo Sun. Kick back," the stranger yells as I increased the span between us.

"What up, Money? Look, I didn't start talking shit about the Yankees, so don't come at me with no bullshit!"

"Damn cousin, chill. Get out of your feelings. So, you consider yourself to be a lyrical specialist, right? That Mister popular is your novice. Well, run that shit!"

"So, you want me to spit something for you?," I asked highly delighted at his proposition.

"Yeah. But do not do it for me, do it for Baldimore!," he says while mocking my accent.

"Do it for New York City. This is the birthplace for rap and hip-hop. I do not know how y'all do it in Baldimore, but this is where you figure out if you really got something. Right here Sun!"

"Alright. That is a bet. Don't mind if I do," I humbly respond while turning my Baltimore Oriole fitted to the back. This was the step before being drafted into the freestyle cipher segment of the BET Hip Hop Awards. I had to infallibly shine. Perform like the freestyle veteran that I was. I came up here as Baltimore's rap scene representative. The only way to

turn these motherfuckers into believers was by my avidity in word choice. I had to convert Manhattan with Brooklyn proceeding as my final combat zone. Felix Stone, here I come…

"Look I have been grinding to the top and I'm not looking down/

I am not even afraid of heights, I'm breaking through perimeters, similes… these bars are filled with so many subliminals/

The messages, the resume, portfolio, these niggas cornholio/

I am like Don Julio, Don Juan in his prime/

When he had a vision to get it, there was no intervention/

Just pray to the Lord for a little supervision/

The mission to get richer, no medicine, so we sicker/

All these pounds that I'm moving and my bitch getting thicker/

Now niggas start the focus, and they ears start to hustle in/

In my city, we call it jammin'/

But still, we are trying to double it, triple it, quadruple it/

Check my stats, records, CD sales and analysis/

The capital is Annapolis, I am smoking Minneapolis/

These lame niggas antagonist, to me, beef is smaller than some maggot shit/

The game is on some faggot shit, no disrespect but did I turn into the Exorcist/

Biggie, Pac, and Jimi all together through some magnet shit/

Here you can have this shit, I do not think you want this shit/

I have been plotting so long that I done turned into a plot and shit/

Took the roof off the drop, now the drop really dropping shit/

So, when I say that I'm the best… Silence, they ain't saying shit/"

-#-

Jaws dropped. People were in awe. Reverence was not just received from the random stranger that I have been talking to- but there was a large crowd that now enclosed me. Observing my surroundings, I saw multiple cell phones videotaping my every move. The habitual comment that I heard was either, "Oh my God, is he a rapper?" or "Let's get his autograph." You would have thought that TMZ was around after seeing the migration of people flocking from every direction. All I can think of was lyrical approval. *I am ready for the world*!

"Sun, my bad. On my baby sister's, uncle daughter's best friend, you are the wave. And I fuck with her more than my own mother," the stranger who denied me earlier had proclaimed.

"Ayooo Duke. I fucks' with you. Just always render enough faith that real always prevails over deceit."

"Hey rap guy! Can we get a picture with you?," was the request of a group of *snowbunnies* as they approached me. The benefits of talent.

"What's your name?"

"Izzy B."

"Oh my God. Oh, my fucking God. Are you serious right now? I have some of your songs on my iPod from like, ten years ago," she says over exaggerating the time period.

"Can I have your autograph too?"

"Yeah I got you shorty", I told her with the same smile still lingering from when the cameras were flashing.

"Can you sign my titty?," a member of the same entourage had requested of me. Damn, I wonder what Sidney would say to *shorty* if she was here? Maybe this was why she wanted to start 'mobbin' with me again, like the old days. She was my better half- the intuitive, better judgment half.

"Where are y'all from?," I asked with the omnipresent smirk still visible.

"Columbus, Ohio."

"Ohio... They *are jamming* my shit out there?"

"Uhh, duh. The internet. I do not remember you having all the tattoos in your pictures though. But I could tell that you were Izzy B though by your 'rap flow.' *Fucking A!* Give me a shout out on your next mixtape," the white girl says while giving me a hug and letting her camera phone go wild.

"Sun you're on the internet?," my original tour guide asks.

"Yeah, just go Google is Izzy B. I'm working on another mixtape right now too."

"Bet that cousin. I am going to make sure the whole Brooklyn is jamming your shit. From Canarsie to Crown Heights to Brownsville. Your shit is verified in the borough. You got my pass Sun," the stranger tells me.

"Already Yoo. I'm going to hold you to that," I say while noticing that the N- train was scheduled to arrive in 30 seconds.

"Hey *cousin*? You are going to probably need this," was the final gracious utterance I heard before depressing underneath the New York City streets. My new Brooklyn connect had humbly gave me his MTA day pass to ride the subway.

Was this a good sign? Could I produce the same audio stimulation in Felix Stone that enabled me to arouse this crowd? Would I be able to display my street influence upon his staff in this pressured whim? Is my business proposal encouraging enough to strike a sympathetic chord?

True, I did not even devise a plan of getting into the offices of Supreme Records. True, the odds were inevitably against me. But still true, I had nothing to lose and so much more to prove. That was the essence of success- being able to choose if the results given are sufficient to your taste.

Success is a state of mind. Sort of like a work at your own pace type of thing. You do not have to be a millionaire to be considered successful. Your accomplishments and achievements are based upon your own individual thoughts on success. Someone can sell *Lucy's* their whole life and set their standard on moving 15 cartons a week. If this is properly executed and achieved, then they're successful.

I had a different idea of success that involved street notoriety, lyrical distinction, familiarity with wealth and close acquaintance with overcoming the struggle. Maybe these regulations were not typical for a nigga in my position. But once again, the driving principle in my success is to keep in mind that I have nothing to lose and everything to prove!

Chapter 36

Kings County Offices. A towering skyscraper that served as the home office for various thriving businesses. All the companies that marketed their affairs in this establishment had reputable names. *NuVision Wireless. ActivAte Snacks. Stakk N' Hunt Clothing Line. Supreme Records.*

No research would have to be done to know that gaining entrance to the 12th floor is a unique solicitation. Security reigned dominion over every doorway, elevator, and stairwell. ID cards were an essential and going through metal detectors was a requirement. Maybe, just maybe, I took this trip in vain. How the fuck was I supposed to surpass this major barrier while remaining incognito?

Standing outside of the office building, I thought of every route possible. Conceived every detour and meandered every consequence. Still with no avail, I remained in the same spot. Outside of the office building. Until enlightenment came in the form of a woman making routine deliveries.

"Hey lookout *Ma*? Aren't you delivering those submarines to Mister Stone, right?," I asked the cute dispatcher.

"No papi. These gyros are going to Live It Up Pharmaceuticals. 22nd floor", the Spanish mistress tells me. She had to be one of those ever-popular Puerto Rican chicks that New York City repeatedly breeds. Got me thinking about *Jennifer Lopez* mixed with *Lumidee*.

"You sure? I could have sworn my boss just ordered a *roast beef joint*. You from '*Mauricio Diner*?,'" I asked after peeping the name of her employer on her shirt. Could not help but notice her plump breasts jutting through her attire. *Stay on task Izzy.*

"Si. Hold up, I'll call and double-check."

"You know what, don't worry about it *Ma*. Would you get in trouble if I just pay for these right here?"

"No papi. They love me at the job," she smilingly says.

"Word. So, what do I owe you?"

"$8.64."

While I was counting the remnants of my cash, the feelings of discretion dawned on me. If this last-minute experiment did not work, then I'll be left in New York City with only $162. Truly, I will only be left with $150 because I just gave this petite cosigner $12 for these gyros. It was exhaustively random that I was left with a $50 bill and that intimate Benjamin Franklin- that had the corners partially missing from Speed Stick deodorant stickers.

One of the last two pieces of United States currency that I sustained was the hundred-dollar bill that Uncle Lenny gave me my first day out of prison. How is that for irony?

"You know something *daddy*? I've been working at 'Mauricio for almost four years and this is my first time seeing you. I would have remembered a handsome *cara* like yourself," the Puerto Rican entrant confides in me. The *jig* was up!

"I'm not even going to lie to you *shorty*. I just took an overnight trip here from Baltimore," I say revealing my true intentions to her. Me and Felix Stone had a controversial disagreement about three years ago, that ended with my theory being undiscovered. I'm here to give him a brief idea of why he should reconsider my talent," I tell her while exposing one of my demo CD's.

"Damn papi, that's live. Tu hombre, for real."

"Yeah, I have to go hard or go home. Isn't that how y'all do it in Brooklyn?," I say after getting a brush up on my second language. Good thing I took Spanish 1 and 2 in high school or she would have lost me, verbatim.

"True, that's the *wave*. Hey, I have an edea. I'm going to get you into his office."

"For real? Think you can pull that off?"

"Si Amor. Everybody knows me in this building and if they don't, then, they would like to know me," she says rather seductively.

"You just have to follow my lead, si."

"Alright mami. Let's right then."

This Boricua woman grabs my hand and guides me into the front entrance of the building labeled, King County Offices. I had to distract some of the whimsy fantasies that crossed my mind or the zipper area on my *501's* would begin to rise. I had to think about success, chicken boxes, baseball, anything. Damn, why did she have to touch my hand? *Pussy might just rule the world.*

"I have a delivery for the 12th floor and I have to hurry", the seductress yells as we approached the ID scanners. Nervousness controlled my receptors as the population of security guards increased. Still, I was confident that this young lady could get me through; otherwise, she would not have offered.

"All right. Ma'am, ma'am. We just have to call 12 and verify this. If you don't mind, could you step to the side please?," the security guard had requested.

"No, Papi. Didn't you just hear me say I have to hurry? There is a whole borough out there that's craving my goodies," she says alluringly. After she whipped her hair to the side and placed her free hand on her hip, I could literally see drool start to dribble down their chins. *It's official, pussy did run the world!*

"Okay and who are you?," one of the guards addresses his concern towards me.

"He's with me papi. I'm training him, capiesce."

"Alright. You kids have 5 minutes to be back down here or I'm sending the SWAT team to you… Understood?"

"Si amor, deal. Come mi panocha while you're at it," my consultant says while we were being escorted to the elevator. I wonder what the guard would have said if he knew that she just told him to "eat her pussy."

-#-

Arriving on the 12th floor, it just felt like I was under surveillance. There were two 'electronic spies' on the elevator and many more of their *relatives* in the Supreme Records lobby. The cameras weren't an object of my attention anymore though once I saw the two 6' defenders, safeguarding my intended destination.

I looked to Rosalyn for support. (I learned her name in the elevator). What is funny, is that her tranquility almost seemed surreal. It is like this wasn't her first *rodeo* on getting unsigned acts into the office of Felix Stone.

"Mi amor. His office is down the hall to the left. Este solo after this," Rosalyn whispers to me. *Guess this was not a world premiere for her.* Still, I could not quite grasp what she had up her sleeve on how exactly I was supposed to get past these two linebackers. The only thing I was cocksure sure about is that Felix Stone conducted business, down the hall to the left.

"How may I help you?," one of the security personnel asks Roslyn after she advances past me.

"Yeah papi. I have these gyros for Mister Stone."

"You're on the wrong floor, ma'am. No sandwiches were ordered here. Try the…"

"Oh daddy, why is it so hot in here?," Rosalyn says while enticingly proceeding to take her shirt off. I was completely convinced that she was a stripper at nighttime.

"Ma'am! Your shirt, you have to keep your shirt on in the building," the security guard stammers.

"Calmate papi. I wasn't going to get enculado for you anyway."

During Rosalyn' striptease for the guards, I was able to covertly slither past their post. Something about a *bad bitch* would change a nigga. Make you forget your job, name, and what year it is. If everything goes as planned, then, I owe Rosalyn *big time* for even wasting her time with me. She through all this trouble with the sole conviction that lyrically, I was the truth. At least I had gave her one of my demos in the elevator before our valediction.

Down the hall to the left, there were many unmarked offices. There were also platinum plaques suspending from the wall. One of which was Mister Popular's debut album entitled "Kush Talk." If I would have had permission to be on these premises, then, I will probably rip this motherfucker down. Just the sight of his album cover almost sent me into an extravagant rampage.

I was already in prison when Eugene dropped "Kush Talk." Still to this day, I remained unyielding that the success of his album was fueled off three main factors. *First*, he was the first rapper out of Baltimore to obtain some sort of fame- so motherfuckers wanted to see what the hype was about. *Second*, your destined to go platinum when you have Felix Stone funding your project. *Finally*, four out of the 13 songs from his album were originally derived from my rhymebooks. *And all four were multi-platinum radio hits.*

I can only imagine the immensity of sales that my first album would have brought.

The last door in this hallway had a commendable name imprinted in solid gold- seated in eye view. The name said, "F. Stone." Underneath that name said, "Chief Executive Officer." On the other side of this door, lies the man who denied me rights to my own music. Also, on the other side of this door, lies the man who could turn my negative situation into a positive. All I had to do was get him to hear me out. What was I waiting for…?

Bursting into Felix Stone office left a queasy sensation after the initial deed has settled. Looking at his panoramic view of Lower Manhattan, I realized that I never been up this high before. Does not matter if a whole ounce of *loud* just got put in the air- I still have never been this high. You could see the New York City skyline. Brooklyn Bridge. Boats floating in the river. Some housing projects in the distance. Then, you saw him, the man of the hour. Felix Stone.

"Hey Kanye. Let me give you a call right back. Something just came up," the plutocrat says before hanging up the phone. Instantly, I froze. This is one millionaire who just got done talking to another millionaire. I did not fit the occasion.

"You want to know a secret, *young hopper*? I have really been expecting you."

"So, you have been expecting me to come find you?," I asked him.

"Ever since I got word of your release, I was expecting to hear your sad story again. Pretty sure my pals at the NYPD would love to enhance this break-in to a felony. I do not know how the prison system works in Maryland, but I could ensure that you will have a sexually deprived celly in Attica with no standards," Felix Stone recites while snobbishly laughing.

"But I will do you a favor this time *buster*. I'm going to press this button for security, and they are going to rough you up before you head back to your little basement."

"Whoa just pause on the button for one second Mister Stone," I say while underhandedly placing my demo on his desk.

"You think I'm going to come all the way up here and risk being put on my ass for nothing. I just need a moment of your time sir, that's all."

"Well, your one second is up. So, if you're done, I'll gladly be pushing my button now."

"Look out, Mister Stone. I apologize for my actions that night of the showcase. I just blanked out with anger, after being presented with the knowledge that Mister Popular had stolen my rhymebooks. But I'm here to tell you that you made a mistake that night."

"Mistake? Only mistake is not background checking the hoodlums I allowed at my event. I am a businessman uhh, what do they call you...? *Eazy-E*? Do you know the type of discussions I still hear at summit meetings to this very day? What if you would have killed Mister Popular, at my showcase? That is why I can't do business with you. You are a liability, a risk. You may spaz out on the next man. I do not know and I'm not taking that chance. I do not care about your soap opera with these fucking rhymebooks. *Boo, hoo, hoo*. This rap shit is over for you, dude. Now if you will excuse me. It's button time!"

"You know what, go ahead and press that button. See, in your mind, you think you are taking something away from me that I never had. I am not losing anything from this little encounter right here. But about this rap shit, yeah, my passion and pride towards these lyrics is something internal. Regardless, I'm going to *blow* and I hope they sit us next to each other at the Grammy's. Oh yeah Yoo and about the rhymebooks, that's old news. Cannot get that back. Still, you would not understand why I did what I did at the showcase. You did not grow up like me. You do not come from the slums. You did not have to reach for the top starting from the very bottom. Anything that was ever taken from you, could have easily been bought back... Uhh, what is your real name? Billy Hill!"

"Watch it *young hopper*. You are treading into some quicksand now. I would stop while your ahead."

"Ayooo I'm not tripping on nothing, Duke. I am from the bottom and made it this far. Do you know what that means? Of course, you do not, *Mister Columbia University* graduate. Mother was a pediatrician and your *pops* had family roots connecting to two famous Canadian jazz singers," I laugh after witnessing Felix Stone's face. He did not know about the extensive research I did on him.

"All this 'hood shit you proclaim, but you do not know the first thing about the streets. Lesson number one, if you're going to do business with street niggas, at least know how the streets are operating. Then, you would have noticed that you had a fraud on your team and the realization is starting to seep out. I am glad that we had this meeting today, Billy. I learned something- the value of self-respect. Supreme Records is going down and I cannot be on your roster when it does. So, do me a favor and press that button!"

Felix Stone looked at me in a valiant way. Probably because I was the first person to overlook his status and *kick it to him real*. Silence and respect illuminated his cipher. He never laid a finger to press the button. It was as if he wanted a handshake from me. But I have made my peace and there was a city needing my guidance. Before leaving his office, a statement needed to be made.

"Oh yeah, I almost forgot. Here's a couple of my demos, so you can have something legit to listen to on your private jet. *Buster.* I am going back to my basement!"

Chapter 37

Ring… Ring… Ring…

"Hey baby. Swear I was just about to call you," I answered the phone after seeing Sidney was calling.

"Yeah, whatever Isaiah. So what took you so long?", she sarcastically responds.

"Guess you just 'beat me to the punch.' There is so much that I must talk to you about. I do not know where to start. But Sidney, about the other night…"

"Just chill Izzy, I understand. Besides, I have something particularly important to tell you. But I rather for us to speak in person. Where have you been staying at the past few days?," Sidney asks after interrupting my penitent speech.

"I had got a motel 'Ova West."

"What? Say it ain't so. You are staying on the Westside is a calculation even Einstein couldn't figure out. Let me find out you're trying to change."

"It's highly possible Sid. Especially when a man is trying to get his family back. Know what I mean…?"

"You're not trying to get your family back loser," Sidney playfully says.

"So, are you at the said motel right now?"

"No. I'm on my way back from New York right now."

"New York…? What the fuck?"

A verbal blackout occurred between us. I couldn't tell if she was pissed, sad or worried, beneath the curtain of strict stillness.

"Never mind Isaiah, I take that back. You're still the same."

"No baby, that's what I wanted to talk to you about. Everything happened so fast and I wanted to just give us some time to cool off. We never separated like this before. But I had to hit New York at such short notice. I went to see Felix Stone."

"Yeah, we definitely have a lot to talk about. Anyway, so how did that go babe? Did you *fuck him up*?"

"Oh, so I'm 'babe' again. Must be making progress."

Sidney smacks her lips. "Grrr, no Isaiah, shut up. Just tell me what happened before I get mad."

"Well, if you really want to know… In my opinion, everything went great. Better than what I had anticipated."

"That's good. Cannot wait to hear the specifics. So, are there any more surprises that you want to bestow upon me?," Sidney asks.

"For starters- I am really, really, really, really love you and I'm super, super, super, super sorry about the other day. Let me make it up to you. Know you are my queen and I'm nothing without you. *Fuck it*, let me put a ring on that finger. Are you going to let your man do that, right?," I told her. I can hear Sidney's smile through the phone.

"Nope, too late Isaiah. You should have put a ring on it when you had me. Now I am single and ready to mingle. Hey, can you watch Stacy tonight? I have a date," Sidney jokingly taunts.

"What? Ayooo do not play with me like that. Are you serious?"

"Isaiah, shut up. You know I am not serious. Does not matter how much you piss me off, my eyes are still only for you. Stop being a fucking cry baby all the time Yoo."

"Damn baby. You know that I get sensitive when it comes to you and Stacy," I explained.

Sidney starts making toddler noises. "Izzy, you know that we're not going anywhere. Jeez, stop crying. What is the new baby going to do, huh?"

"What new baby?," I asked dumbfounded.

"Oh shit. Nothing," Sidney reluctantly answers.

"Baby…? What are you talking about?"

"Nothing Isaiah, drop it. So, I am going to have Danielle watch Stacy tonight, so I could be with you. Cool? We need to talk."

"Sidney, I don't know if you want to come *stay* in this motel. It is not up to par with our normal living conditions. This is like the ignored stepchild of the *Marriott* or *Hilton*."

"So, I don't care Izzy. I am not sleeping another night without me in your arms. It has already been 3 days. There's a lot that we need to talk about and truthfully, *Wifey* wants some dick," Sidney boldly states.

"Ah, so the truth will set you free. Well, I'll be back in Baltimore within the hour."

"Okay baby. I have to go do Emily's hair, but afterwards, I have her drop me off. In the meantime, please do not do anything I wouldn't do, please!"

"Hmm. I'll try, how does that sound?"

"You better be good nigga. But hey, I must start getting ready, so I will see you soon," she tells me.

"All right. And hey, Sidney…?"

"I already know Isaiah and I love you too."

"How did you know what I was going to say?"

"Because I know my *man*, that's how."

"I'm the luckiest man in the world. I love you baby."

"I love you too Izzy," Sidney responded.

Chapter 38

It was barely 1:00 P.M. once I returned to my faded motel room. My life was in shambles when I disappeared from this vacancy only 36 hours ago; but now it seems as if I have secured the upper hand. I could not exactly pinpoint how things have changed, because quite frankly shit was still the same. Whatever the case, hopefully this prestigious feeling was not temporary.

How conclusive were my assertions towards Felix Stone? Was my confidence and morale attached to the core of our conversation? Growing up, every street rapper wanted to be with Supreme Records. My allegations would be misrepresenting if I stated otherwise. So why was I still jubilant, after my performance in his office, undoubtedly canceled any chance I had of being on his team?

I believed real talent could not be feigned. After listening to the monotony on the radio, then hearing my shit- the truth will always be the truth. Yes, absolutely, money is what makes money. But overall, in this rap game, talent plays a heavier role towards your success. Once all the money is gone, with no talent- you are just an *Average Joe*. But with talent and no money, you are an undiscovered beast.

Felix Stone will always remember the conversation we had in his office, yesterday. Even if I did not make it, I'll have the satisfaction of knowing that I gave him a premium outlook on character. Maybe I set the standard for artists he allows on his roster in the future. *Motherfuckers that would not kiss his ass for an advancement*. Why, because their talent trumped over any dollar amount that he could offer.

It did not matter to me anymore; I was in a league of my own. A League of extraordinary rappers and only a few resided there with me.

Besides my family, the only thing that carried substance in my life was, hip-hop. Any extra additions were antiquated. *I had done enough fucking up*. If I was going to make this rap dream a reality, I had to deceive my biggest fears. Suppress all my secluded anger. Welcome all embarrassment because that means a recognizable mistake has been made and I have the option of reformation.

That is why I respected my mother. After all her helpless moments, she still found the strength to correct herself. Even when her sickness brought her to the brink of extinction, she did not give up her crusaded battle. She fought to the end. It was in my blood to overcome the most unbearable obstacles.

Maybe that is what I needed. To talk to someone who overcame the streets and conquered success, but they are still labeled as being "broke." Someone who has been in the *hot seat* and escaped becoming a hostage of their own immorality. Someone sober-minded, who would not steer me in the wrong direction for a million dollars. My mother!

-#-

"Hey can Rashida Douglas get any visits right now? I'm her son and this is kind of important," I asked the same receptionist from The Water Shed. Nothing changed about her appearance, maybe except her perfumed fragrance. Guess it was mandatory to keep such a dull look in this institution. Who knows…? It was not my job to evaluate, I just needed my special clearance.

"Yes. I remember you, Mister Brown. Wait right here for me and I'll see if I can make that happen for you."

While waiting for the receptionist, whose name tag says "Serenity," I decided to browse through the assorted brochures that lined her working space. These were pamphlets, which characterized the hardships and successes of many drug-addicted women that have graduated from The Water Shed. One of the memoirs that caught my attention in particular was about a lady named Dionna. This was her story:

"As an adolescent young woman, moving from rural North Carolina to Baltimore's fast life; that

transition alone played a major role towards my development into adulthood. Compared to Baltimore, Rocky Mount did not have many temptations. I never did drugs in Rocky Mount. I never engaged in promiscuous behavior in Rocky Mount. I did not contract the HIV virus in Rocky Mount, and I didn't meet Gage in Rocky Mount, either.

I had moved to Baltimore during my junior year in high school and that is when me and Gage started dating. I had never met anyone like him. The way he moved, talked, and finessed his way out of situations was different from guys in North Carolina. I fell into the fairytale that we were going to be happily ever after. I thought I found my knight in shining armor.

The summer after graduation, me and Gage went to a party that was just supposed to be people from our class. Once we got there, I quickly realized that I only knew a handful of people that were in attendance. It was already too late though; I didn't know where I was, and my boyfriend was the transportation.

Throughout the night, Gage kept giving me drinks- which I later found out were laced with Extasy. He led me to a room upstairs, so we could have sex. I was fine with that because we had already been having sex for the past 2 years.

Halfway through our sexual acts, the door opened in and four men entered the room. The thought of having multiple sex partners at once would normally be disgusting to me. I was not raised as that type of girl. Guess the drug-induced coma I was in had allowed me to lower my guard and inhibitions. Once the four men finished, I saw them all give Gage an ample amount of money. When they left, I cried relentlessly in Gage's arms. He constantly assured me that we were just *having fun and that he loved me. Hearing the L-O-V-E word was the only thing needed for me to stay. Even after two more guys came into the room and the same process was repeated, I kept in mind that Gage would love me for this. Before drugs became my vice, Gage was my original addiction. Thinking back, I regret selling my purity for prostitution, all to be around someone who never truly loved me. A realization that took multiple rehab visits, prison stints, division from family and a fatal disease to altogether understand what was going on.*

It went from months to years of the same reckless acts. By age 21, I was an alcoholic, an avid cocaine/marijuana user and a woman who will perform oral for a few Xanax pills. This was the "life" though, according to Gage. Until his life was cut short by a lengthy prison sentence. Instead of discontinuing the life, I prolonged my dangerous behavior by finding various replacements. I had Gage number two, Gage number three, Gage number four and I could probably keep going to Gage number 15.

Somewhere around age 25 and Gage number 12, there were many nights that I thought about changing for the better. But once the fast life of the drug scene slyly entered the picture, those thoughts quickly subsided.

It was also around this time, one night, that I woke up in a pool full of blood. After going to the doctor, they informed me that I had been pregnant and had a miscarriage. A saddening disappointment.

This was also when the doctor did some blood tests and told me that I was HIV-positive.

It seemed as if my whole world started crashing down after hearing those results. I was in pure denial of how my life had enrolled into becoming a downward spiral. The blame was projected at everybody else except myself. It was Gage's fault for taking advantage of my gullibility and innocence. It my parents' fault for taking me out of my comfort zone and placing me in this jungle referred to as, Baltimore. It was the government's fault for allowing this disease to be coming up epidemic.

Even if these accusations were true, I was still the main person at fault. No one forced me to be responsible at the party that night. No one forced me to sell my body. No more force me to put cocaine in my nose.

That is when I realized that I couldn't reset the actions of my past. All I could do was move forward and *that is exactly the move I made. I placed my last $100 in a savings account and went to The Water Shed.*

The experiences I had throughout that three-year stay was immensely breathtaking. Not only did their medicine tame my virulent illness, but I was also reunited with my first love. Cooking. After the hospital appointed me a trustee over Food Services, my life began to take a turn towards the positive. The old Dionna, who could not discern left from right was gone and a responsible person took her place.

As a principal cook over the facility, I chose a healthy diet for the women in rehabilitation. Not bad for someone who has not enjoyed a home cook meal since high school.

One day in the kitchen, I was mixing ingredients and discovered a new food flavoring. This condiment was worth savoring, according to the recovering women. My sauce quickly became the norm in giving our food a distinguishable taste. One of the social workers advised me to make my new flavor, a trademarked item in grocery stores. I knew that I had to crawl before I walked though.

Upon my graduation from The Water Shed, Gage had found a way to contact me. He stated that his case was eligible for an appeal and he wanted me to write a support letter. He also said that we should reconnect and party like the 'old days'. Suddenly, all the memories started to surface in my mind, and it was clear that I never truly partied. All I did was destroy and I had a terminal disease as proof. I wrote him back and wished the best in his journey. I could not risk being driven back down the dark alley ways of my past life.

Closing that chapter of my life was empowering. It felt as if I could overcome any obstacle thrown at me. Even though I was HIV-positive and approaching 30 years of age, it was as if life had just started and the possibilities were endless.

I decided to live at the halfway house, provided by The Water Shed. They offered extensive help, even after the rehabilitation program. One of the main contributions that I took advantage of was the accessibility to using food stamps.

Instead of spending the funds on myself, I went to the meat market and bought poultry in abundance. The interest from my hundred dollars in the savings account, multiplied lucratively while I was in rehab. My plan was to provide a 'meals-on-wheels' service to construction workers, school kids and people attending city events. What separated my preparing's from other restaurants was the 'secret sauce' I invented at The Water Shed.

Those first few years sober and out of rehab, I managed to purchase a truck that helped me serve my products. I also met an investor who had fond feelings towards my life story. This is also the same invested who took a strong liking for my 'secret sauce.'

Fast forward a whole decade to where I am writing this autobiography... That same investor got my secret sauce patented and put it to every local grocery store. I now own four restaurants in the Baltimore/Washington DC area. That same investor accepted me for who I was and appreciated me who I am and is now my husband.

If I would have known success was this easy, I would not have ended up at that party with Gage. I would have created my own fun that revolved around productivity. Still, I have no regrets to the day. Life is about the experience we get from the mistakes we make.

My advice to women who are recovering addicts, is to take baby steps. Do not live a life of avoidance, but rather a life of acceptance. Accept yourself for the mistakes you have made. Love yourself for making the choice to go sober. Be willing to sacrifice anything to maintain your sobriety. And dream big, success is at your doorstep. I never once thought that I would be a wife, business owner and motivational speaker- when I was waking up from my drunken stupors, 15 years ago. All it took was a step in the right direction. All it took was a 'Hundred Dollars & A Dream!.'

-#-

What the fuck? Who would have thought that someone existing in the slums of "Rock Bottom," could overcome their misfortune and become a success? Being raised by a drug-addicted woman then hearing her story, almost brought a tear to my eye. All I ever did was steal, kill, and destroy; but something about Dionna really touched a soft spot in me. The part of her personal account that originally struck a chord was her last two sentences. How it only took a step in the right direction. It only took a *Hundred Dollars & A Dream!*

"Well Mister Brown, it looks as if your mother, Rashida Douglas, has actually checked out of the facility earlier today," Serenity explains to me after typing in some information on her desktop.

"Really? Are you sure? Has she finished the vitals of your program or something?," I asked.

"Nope. She was currently enrolled in the core part of our recovery curriculum. It says that the tempo of her progression was unfolding opulently. Oh, that's weird…"

"What? What's up?"

"The system shows that she had a special clearance visitor earlier and not even an hour later, she left. Administration says her behavior was irrational and unnerving."

"Who came to visit her?," I asked.

"Let's see," Serenity says while hitting a few buttons and tapping on her mouse. She has been extremely helpful.

"It wasn't anybody listed on her emergency contact list, but possibly still a family member. It shows a first name beginning with the letter E and the last name was Brown. Perhaps your father or another relative. Do you know him?"

"Hell no and my father died when I was a baby", I told her.

"I'm sorry to hear that Mister Brown. I wish I could be of more assistance to you, but that's all that the system is showing at the moment."

"It's all right ma'am. I graciously appreciate your help."

Any other words spoken to me would have become a victim of my inattentiveness. I was mentally confused. Distraught. Heartbroken. Thinking back to me and my mother's last conversation, her strange disappearance did not make any sense at all. *What made her discard all the growth that she has made and who the fuck was this E. Brown?*

Before walking off, I noticed this proverb that Serenity had commemorated on her wall. It was a saying that my mother used to recite to me when I was younger. I have not heard it in a while…

"God grant me the serenity to accept the things that I cannot change, courage to change the things I can and wisdom to know the difference."

Chapter 39

It smelt like sewage waste, outside of The Water Shed. Guess it was because of the proximity to multiple power plants and oil refineries. The bench that I was sitting on had a slogan written across it that said, *The Greatest City In America*. To make this type of assumption, I wondered what city council saw that was obviously always hidden from me.

Have they noticed the crater sized potholes on every street? Have they noticed that the homeless population was inclining at an alarmingly fast pace? What about all of the abandoned buildings, lots and dreams of the citizens? All of this fucking money that the government has, and it looks like I was raised in a third world country. I could suitably say if the government showed its presence more in Baltimore then we would have action at being "The Greatest City In America".

Why don't the other major cities in America look like this? New York, Dallas, Atlanta, Los Angeles, Seattle. Bet they had better representatives than us. *Not for long though.* Once I get *on* then I am going to *put on* for my city for sure. If I had 10 million dollars, I would unapologetically put nine million of it back into the streets of *Bmore*. That is how much love I have for every avenue, alleyway and project building that give Charm City its name. That is why in the end, I am going to be the face of Baltimore City!

While I was collecting my thoughts about the city, my mother, and this *dream*; a diplomatic figure came and sat on the bench next to me. He lit up a Newport

100. Ever since I was a shorty, buying a whole box of cigarettes was rarely my intentions. I would always buy some Lucy's (three for $1). Figured this was an effective method to still smoke cigarettes while reducing the risk of becoming a nicotine junkie.

A motherfucker who just bought a box of cigarettes were more liable to *down them bitches* in the same day versus someone who mentally limits themselves to three cigarettes a day. This was just a part of my twisted philosophy that tactfully worked for me. *Think about all the money I have saved throughout the years.* Priceless…

"Say my man? Do you have another bogey I can bum off you?," I asked the uninvited squatter. I have not been back to East Baltimore since the fight me and Sidney had three days ago. The cigarettes I have bought from Doc's were already in the air. With everything that has happened this weekend, I never found time nor a location to *cop* some more Lucy's. After the baffling news I just received, a Newport seemed like the route to mortal contentment.

"Yeah slick. Hold these down," my abnormal visitor says to me. He hands over a Newport box with two cigarettes in it.

"Appreciate that *G*," was my response to his generosity. After we caught eye contact, I knew something was wrong. His appearance was all too familiar and this potential problem did not seem like it would immediately perish. People are taken to jail all the time for coincidental happenings. It was just a mere coincidence that *Katy Perry* and *Katherine Hudson* had the same name. It could even be considered coincidental that someone was born on November 11th,

2011 at 11:11 PM. *But this shit, no deal.* This was almost as unpredictable as a meteor shower.

By the time reality hit me, I was already sealed to a petrified airspace. *This was the same motherfucker that…*

"You know I could have arrested you that day in the Somerset Homes?," the stranger sharply tells me.

This was an upscale version of random- the epitome of a 'blind side.' The same cop that witnessed my brutal execution, two months ago, in West Baltimore was the same motherfucker who just offered over the remains of his cigarettes. I had to stand stiff on the topic. I am still innocent until proven guilty, or guilty until proven innocent in the judicial systems' eye.

"So why didn't you then?," I sarcastically asked. Shoulders casually shrugged.

"For a lot of reasons. Mainly because of your mother though."

I snap, almost to the point where I would have whipped out my butterfly knife.

"Nigga fuck you! Fuck you mean, you did it for *Ma Dukez*? Nigga you do not know me, and I was never in the Somerset buildings. Fuck out of here!"

"Alright. Isaiah Malik Brown. Mother name is Rashida Douglas. You have an uncle named Leonard Gittens. Weren't you born on December 28th, 1987 at the Northeast Market? You have a birthmark on your left butt cheek. Anything else that you would like to know?"

"Nigga, what the fuck…? Are you the FEDS or something? Been watching me in the shower or something, *sissy*? You are tripping Yoo, fuck out my face! Keep your bogies, I'm gone," I say while proceeding to walk off.

"Isaiah, wait. I hate for us to meet under these conditions. But this is real. Look… I'm your father!"

I stopped in mid stride. Not because I believed him, but because I could not believe he had the audacity to say that aloud. After witnessing me *body* a nigga 'Ova West,' I could not believe he was brave enough to make that assertion.

"Ayooo I thought they give you all types of exams before you join the force. Are you sure that you passed the psychological test? You are tripping Duke, for real. My pops died when I was a shorty!"

"Look Isaiah. Just check this out," he says while showing me a wallet-size picture. This motherfucker was ancient. Had to be at least two decades old. I snatched the photo up to get an observation of where his delusions originated from. After taking one glimpse, I knew my whole existence was now in question.

In this snapshot- there was an infant, a woman and a man. From what I remembered about my baby pictures; this toddler could pass as being my identical twin. Off the top, I knew the lady was my mother. She still had the same youthful appearance now. And despite my opinionated reaction, the man was indeed the *Robocop* standing in front of me. So, what they looked like a happy family? Who cares that the picture said 1988 on it? What did this prove?

"Ayooo where did you get this picture from?"

"I've been holding on to it for the past 23 years. This is one of the last memories I had with you and your mother," he explains.

"Alright, alright. Not saying that I do believe you because this may just be some freakish coincidence. But everyone is positive that my real father is dead. So, if you are my real father, why aren't you dead?"

"Yeah Isaiah, I can understand why everyone thought that I'd died. It is a long story, but I promise you that I never stopped looking for y'all. I knew that I had gotten close to locating you when I *Google'd* your name and it said that you were property of the Maryland D.O.C. I was fucked up because my work assignment at the time had permitted me from contacting you. But I am telling you, God as my witness…"

"Whoa now, *TD Jakes*, I'm not trying to hear a sermon man. So, you say it is a long story huh? That is live," I tell him.

"Well 23 years is a long time, so I figure we have an hour to spare to hear your long story. If you are my real father, why did you disappear on your family? What happened?"

He pauses before answering. "Here, sit down with me Isaiah. Shoot me down on this cigarette."

"So, is this supposed to be our first bonding moment? Hope you don't expect me to call you *dad*," I said while lighting up the Newport.

"No, I don't expect you to call me dad. What I did was irresponsible and inconsiderate. I do not deserve to be called a father. If you ever have kids, no matter the situation… Don't put yourself in a predicament where you may have to leave their side!"

"Hmm. Thanks for the advice, I guess. But yeah, I do have a kid. A daughter and she is five. If you are wondering, no, I would not leave her side for 23 years while I'm physically free. Come on Money, you had a choice. Here, that is you," I say by giving him the leftovers of the cigarette. It was damn near at that point of no return. *The green line.*

"Go ahead and kill it. Damn Isaiah, I just wish you could put yourself in my shoes, 23 years ago!"

"Well sir, now is your chance to go ahead and enlighten me."

"23 years ago… Me and a buddy decided to take advantage of the emerging crack epidemic. We had two plugs- one here, in the city and one in Philly. I was getting the shit cheaper in Philly and bringing it down here. I told your mother that it was going to be my last trip. I had enough money saved up where we could have branched off and reached our full potential. *But this last trip ended up taking 23 years...*"

"Hold up Sun. You probably do not mind me calling you that. But I am about to *twist one*, you smoke?," I asked him while splitting my Dutch down the middle. I was lionhearted enough to roll up some weed in Downtown Baltimore, in public and in front of a rehabilitation center. Shit, my "popz" was a cop. How much trouble could I get into?

"No. I'm good," he timorously said.

"Alright, suit yourself. Keep going, what happened during this last trip? *Wish a nigga had some popcorn...*"

"I'm not trying to make an excuse Isaiah. But shit got real," he began.

"Once I had got back to Baltimore with the dope, me and my main man took it to our "drop off." The only people who knew the location of our meeting was your mother and the plug. We got set up. An ambush took place and we ended up getting robbed by like eight motherfuckers'. One of which was an undercover detective. *I had to go for what I know.* My partner got popped and I got shot for the second occurrence in my life. I survived after receiving four more bullet wounds. I could not go to the hospital because my face was on every city publication on the East Coast. I became extra paranoid that night after realizing I was set up and someone close had spilled out the information about my operation. I couldn't trust anybody, not even your mother."

"So, you think that my mother had set you up?"

"Thinking back on it, no, I don't believe she explicitly set me up. Could she have told somebody, who told somebody, who told somebody- it is possible.

But I was in my early twenties at the time with my life leaking out four different outlets. *I was not trying to hear shit*. Once I heard they put a $50,000 reward out for my arrest, I knew Baltimore was not the *wave* anymore. Had to go back to my comfort zone, Richmond."

"Whoa, hold up man, this shit is not making any sense. If you were wanted for multiple murders and one of them was a police officer, then how the fuck are you a police officer right now?," I asked after lighting up my *loud stick*.

"It's crazy how life works Isaiah. But understand, I was in these streets before you were even born. Let me hit that L," he says reaching for my Dutch that probably held at least two grams in it.

"About a year after the ambush, I was reading the Baltimore Sun and it stated that the cop killer was arrested. It was one of the niggas that tried to rob me. Among the deceased, my nickname was in there. That is how I knew your mother did not rat me out or sell my identity for a few dollars. Only one person in Baltimore knew my real name and that was your mother. Everyone knew me by 'Zeke.' But by the time I got back to the city, it was already too late. Your mother left no type of trail to find y'all. That's why I eventually joined the force."

"Guess I have no choice but to respect that. So, what's 'Zeke' short for?," I inquire in between breathing in the Kush smoke.

"Ezekiel. Ezekiel Brown."

"Wait, so you just got done talking to my mother then?"

"Yeah, but she acted like she had seen a ghost when she saw me. We didn't even get to talk because security was called."

I could not help but laugh. In a strange turn of events, somewhere deep inside formed a molecular feeling of sympathy for him. Principally, because I was a street nigga myself. Take what just happened with African Dee into extraction. What if, on my way to the Glover block, I gave Sidney the precisions of what was about to go down?

The same preliminaries took place; but come to find out African Dee and/or the police were three steps ahead of us. They knew the full details of our plan that I only explained to Sidney. Knowing that me and Byrd irrationally decided to rob African Dee and the only other person who knew the scoop was Sidney. Wouldn't I feel as if some deceptive acts were channeled from her cipher? It did not matter how much I loved her and Stacy because I honestly could not say that I would have ran immediately back into her arms. Instead, I would have *laid low* and did some thorough investigating. Especially after getting shot four times!

There was a lot to weigh on both sides of the fence. You had to take his mindset into account, plus the time period that they were in. There were no cell phones, Facebook, or FaceTime to help broaden the alleys of communication. I am in no way advocating the abandonment of your family. But coming from a street niggas' point of view, I had to have a very slight atom of empathy for his reasoning.

As I was terminating the remains of my blunt, Ezekiel pulls out something that looked like a checkbook. He begins filling it out.

"You know Isaiah, I've been absent from your life for the past 23 years and there's nothing I can do about that. I wish I could have been there for your first day of school, your first street fight and the first time you went to prison. I wish I could have shown you a better way out, a better route to the top. I wish I could have given you 'The Game' on *The Game* so you would not have had to hop out here headfirst. Man to man, I am sorry Isaiah. I really am. You could not estimate how many nights that I prayed to be reunited with you. How many nights I tried to picture what you looked like at age 5, 10, 15, 18..."

"I know an apology seems like the stereotypical thing to do, so here. This is for you and your family," he says giving me a check for $25,000.

Upfront, this is the most amount of money I have ever had. A roach would have labeled this opportunity as a lucky break. Good Fortune. But something did not feel right about his offer.

"You know, I appreciate this Zeke. More for what it symbolizes. But overall, I cannot accept this. I didn't earn it."

"This is a gift Isaiah. From me to you," he clarifies. "Think of it as compensation for all the birthdays and Christmases that I've missed."

"If you put it like that, guess I have no choice but to take it. So, where does this leave us now? What, are we supposed to go fishing on the weekend and you teach me about cuff links?," I asked.

"Whatever you want Isaiah! Whenever you need some advice or just want to talk, I am here for you. I know you are in these streets, so if you ever get into a jam; remember I am politically connected and can probably help you out. I have been around the block a few times, so what you do not know, I probably do know. Shit, whenever you just want to shoot some hoops or ready for me to meet my granddaughter, I am here. You are the only kid I have, and I wasn't there for you. But I still have action at being there for her. If you allow me to, I would like to spoil my granddaughter. I am not trying to put any pressure on you Isaiah, but here is my card. Whenever you are ready, feel free to hit me up. This is every way to contact me from cell phone, email to even *Twitter*."

While pocketing his business card, I wondered if there would ever be a day where I contacted him. Speculated if there would ever be a time where I addressed him as "Dad."

It was probably too late for the name calling, but somewhere down the line, I could see us having a friendship. The nigga seems like he could be trusted. He is a cop and I got him to hit the weed with me. He is a cop who visually observed me murder someone and the motherfucker still has not arrested me. Really, he joined the force to try and keep tabs on his long-lost *seed*. His tenacity deserved homage.

"Alright then, old man. I might just take you up on your offer- bust your ass up on the basketball court. But there's something I've been itching to ask you…"

He Chuckles. "What's up Isaiah?"

"You said that you researched me while I was in prison, but your job permitted you from reaching out to me. If we didn't know each other than where was the conflict of interest?"

"Well, remember when I told you how it's crazy how life works… You might want to brace yourself for this Isaiah. You see, we crossed paths way before that afternoon in the projects. Just neither of us utterly understood it at the time."

"Word! I don't recall seeing you before…"

"You have to think back Isaiah. Back to March 16th, 2008."

"Yeah. That is the day I went to jail. A white cop is who arrested me because I remember him helping me wash the mace out of my eyes," I told him.

"Yeah well, I was the security officer who pepper-sprayed you at the Supreme Records Talent Showcase!"

"What the fuck…? Hell no," I stated in disbelief.

"Yes Isaiah, before I became a peace officer, I was a bodyguard for many major industry figures. One of my main gigs was looking after Felix Stone' *sucker ass.* I have been his bloodhound since Supreme Records was nothing but a potentially dominant name. After that incident, three years ago, I decided that I was getting too old to be body slamming the up-and-coming 'hoppers. With all the money that I had saved up, I joined the force with my credentials to track you down. Not realizing you were the reason I quit on Felix!"

"Wait a minute Yoo, I'm still stuck on the fact that you used to babysit Felix Stone! This is some ironic shit Duke. Everything about you is limitless. Let me guess... You probably fucked Rosalyn, didn't you?," I asked not wanting to know the truth. If he fucked the Puerto Rican, gyro delivery *princess* than I might have become unresponsive to these interrelated similarities.

"Yeah man, these anomalies are strange and what's up with your boy, Mister Popular? Scary motherfucker. I probably would have died looking after him. When I saw what you did just because he won the showcase, I pictured what niggas would do if he won an MTV award. Didn't want any parts in that," he told me. We both roar in amusement like we were locked in a chamber, being suffocated by laughing gas. Maybe it was an effect of the weed. Or maybe this was genuine. My first "father-son" moment.

"But wait pause," he abruptly stops snickering. "What Rosalyn are you talking about?"

"This Puerto Rican from Brooklyn."

"Are you talking about the big titty bitch that delivers sandwiches? How do you know her?," he asked wide-eyed.

"I just left Felix Stone office not even 12 hours ago."

"Really, you were just in New York? What happened?"

"Well, obviously he didn't add me to the roster, if I'm sitting here talking to you," I expounded. "Our conversation was more me illustrating the picture that a gift, was a gift. Does not matter how much you try to subdue a gift; it will always remain a reward. After my natural talent for rapping was rewarded to me, it did not matter how much I tried to fight it; the cipher will always be my comfort zone. I will always have the power to produce captivating lyrics. I told Felix, it didn't matter if he fucked with me or not- I was going to *blow up* regardless."

"I like that Isaiah. You definitely inherited that game-winning drive from my genes."

"Yeah alright, old man. I heard about your boxing career. Where was the persistence in that? Got scared of *Mike Tyson*, *Lennox Lewis* and *Mayweather* coming to see if that shit was real huh…?," I began to ridicule.

"Oh shit, Isaiah. The 80's! We would have to get a bottle of 151, so I can take you back to the years of *Maurice King*."

"You knew *Peanut King*?"

"I know a lot of people Izzy. I can make a direct phone call to Felix Stone and have him appoint you as a priority artist, with a mandatory record contract that is escorted with a seven-digit minimum advancement. The nigga still owes me a couple favors. It would not be nothing to hang him off his 12th floor balcony, by his legs until he cooperates. You down?"

"No we are going to let him make it", I laugh after realizing that my biological father might actually be a gangster.

"How did you know that they call me Izzy B? From the showcase?"

"No, I thought you were just a pill-popping 'hopper at the showcase. But once I put the pieces together, I Google'd you. You are *mad* talented, for real man. You have skills. Hope you put that document I just signed over to good use," he tells me.

"Yeah, I have some new material in the *works* right now."

"Word up! I am going to be wearing my 'Fuck Mister Popular' shirt to all your shows. I bought them in three different colors."

Ring… Ring…Ring…

I looked at my screensaver to see that Sidney was calling. Must be almost time for our important "talk." Minutes turned into hours as I got carried away with meeting my father for the first time.

"Hold up right quick Zeke. This baby…"

"Do your thing *Young*."

"Yoo what's up Sid?"

I am not going to lie; having $25,000 in my pocket gave me a jolly feeling. I could not wait to edify my past 48 hours with her.

"Nothing… What are you doing baby?," she says sounding overly merry also. We are both full of surprises now.

"I'm talking with a good friend. I really want you to meet him someday."

"Uhh, okay then... So what motel are you staying at?," she asked getting straight to the point.

"The Westside Inn off Edmondson and Pulaski."

"Alright well I'm about to start heading that way. Are you going to be there when I get there?"

"Yeah, I'll be back at the room in about 20 minutes."

"Okay then baby. Guess I will see you soon. Love you *butthead*", she affectionately tells me.

"I love you too *babycakes*."

After hanging up the phone, I could tell Zeke was intrigued at the idea of having a daughter-in-law. *Honestly, I was intrigued at the thought of having a father.* I did a decent job raising myself, but still, there were so many unanswered questions. Besides Uncle Lenny, I did not have any male role models growing up.

The streets taught me about love and betrayal. Success and failures. Production and destruction. It will be nice to get someone else's outlook on these topics who are not from East Baltimore. Someone who has an approach on life that could be tested and potentially trusted, to be passed down to future generations. I did not know if I could fully trust Ezekiel Brown, but I was willing to give him a shot. I have met the source, now it was my job to uplift the family name.

"Well Zeke, I guess this is the cessation point for us..."

"No doubt Isaiah. I am comfortable with saying that this is not the last time. It has been a great pleasure to have finally met you. This is by far, the greatest day of my life. After 23 years of searching, I found something better. I found that my offspring has overcame the struggle and, in the process, became a mad. I am not religious, but after today, there is some type of God out there. If it is not inconveniencing you, do you mind if I had the privilege of shaking your hand?"

A truce had to be called with my pride. I could not veto his request. It did not matter how hardened the streets had conditioned my character; this was a tender occasion. When Zeke first paternally established our kinship, all types of "fuck you" … "I don't need you nigga" and "get lost" statements went through my head. But after understanding him, I concluded that there may be a time or two where I consider him a paradigm. Which normally is prohibited when your role model has always been the street signs.

We both stood up and faced each other; eye-to-eye, man-to-man. This was my father that I was looking at. This was the man my mother chose to go half towards my existence. Regardless of the circumstance of our reunion, this was still a powerful cipher. Father and son.

During our handshake, I noticed a tear roll down Zeke's face. This was not a teardrop of sadness nor sorrow; it was a teardrop that represented a fulfilling revelation for him. In his eyes, something was accomplished today that played a heavier significance than a *Superbowl* ring. In my eyes, I wanted this 'bromantic' embrace to cease. This was the first ever that I allowed a man-to-man hug to linger this long. The weight of our encounter has not fully hit me yet. Do not know when it will or if it will even happen at all. Only thing I know is that I met a pretty *cool cat* today. Someone who may gain access to my cipher in the future.

"Alright then Zeke. Until next time…"

"That's a bet Isaiah. Until next time. One love!"

Chapter 40

While waiting for wifey to arrive at the motel, I decided to do a little decorating to embellish the room. At least make it look like someone has slept here in the 21st century. Really, I was trying to set the mood so hopefully, we could kindle a greater understanding for each other. Apparently, there is a lot that needed to be addressed from both ends. So, I figured a desirable setting would make conversation hospitable.

I cleaned up and brushed the dust bunnies off the antique furniture. I bought a DVD player from the Westside Shopping Center as an attempt to form a familiar harmony. There was a peddler outside, selling bootleg CD's and it just so happened that he had a slow jam mixtape. No indication was needed to know that I added one of those *joints* to my collection. After pre-rolling four blunts and lighting the Leyland Cypress cinnamon apple candles, I knew it will be a memorable night.

Knock... Knock... Knock...

After every tap on the door, more blood flowed through my dick realizing who was at the other end. "All My Life" by *KC & JoJo* was playing in the background. I had two cheap bottles of *Barefoot Moscato* sitting in a bucket of ice. Ghetto Love.

Since the candles were lit, there was no need to turn on the flickering lights. Only thing missing from this festive scene was, Sidney.

Opening the door, it looked as if heaven were on the horizon and nightfall was approaching. Visibility was shattered by the celestial glow hovering around Sidney. After all the wrong I have done, God still blessed me. I could not believe my eyes; I was looking at an angel.

Sidney's attire was illustrious, grand in appearance. It was something about her voguish style that I have always loved. Her swag was pleasingly chic. She was wearing a crimson *Forever 21* tank top, with pink rhinestones assorted throughout the shirt. She had on some skin-tight *Derrion* sweatpants that were a mixture of royal red, hot pink, and light grey. She had on the crimson, pink and gray *Jordan 3's* for women. To top it off, she had an Ohio State Buckeyes snapback, turned to the back. *Nails done, hair done, everything did.* Plus, her scent was my favorite on women- Chanel Number 5.

"Baby," Sidney says exposing that *sweet* smile while jumping into my arms. I scooped her up and we instantly began an aggressive tongue-kissing match. With her arms around my neck and my hands gripping her derriere, I closed the motel room door by pinning her back against it. No escape!

Without stopping our make out session, I walked Sidney over to the bed and gently placed her down. Me in between her legs. I began to kiss and nibble around her neck and ear, while simultaneously unfastening her bra. That is when I stopped to look into her eyes…

"You know that I missed you right?"

"Well show me how bad you missed me," Sidney enticingly tells me.

"Shit say no more," was all that I could get out before my speech became muffled, by my *Polo* V-neck coming off. Sidney had done the works and afterwards, she unbuckled my *Versace* belt off my

Versace pants. Everything was all good until she stopped me from taking off her shirt…

"Hold on Izzy. I must tell you something first."

"Damn baby, you don't think it could wait until the end of *round one*? I just need a couple of minutes. Got to put this *motherfucker* out," I tell her Sidney.

"No baby it can't wait. Just chill, you are going to get this pussy. Here, take my shoes off!"

"Alright Sidney. So, what's up?," I asked while untying her left shoe.

"Well, you say that you really love me right?"

"Sid? I know you are not really asking me that like something has changed over the past nine years," I say matter-of-factly. Both of her shoes were now untied and off her feet.

"Yes Isaiah. Just answer the question…"

"Yes Sidney! I love you more than the street-level dealer who loves cheap prices. I want you more than a prisoner who wants parole. Anything else that you would like to know?"

"You still want me to be your wife one day…?"

"*Fuckin'* right and hopefully someday soon."

"Cross-your-heart-and-hope-to-die…?"

"If I'm telling a lie then there is a bullet in my right eye. Baby, where are you going with these rhetorical questions?," I asked.

"I was just making sure Izzy. Um, I do not know how to say this… But we are about to have another addition to our family!"

I could not believe my ears. "*Another addition to our family.*" This would be our second child together. I made a silent promise to myself, that by the end of her pregnancy we would have a house, car and for us to be financially stable.

Even though the thoughts of extra responsibilities emerged, I was extremely ecstatic at the news. I will probably be restless for the next nine months waiting for our unborn to drop. She had to be having a boy. Majority of the time that I was *nutting* in her, I was hitting it from the back- which is different from the sex positions that we favorably chose around the time that Stacy was conceived. Wonder how Stacy would take not being the center of attention anymore. Having to share her mother and father. *This shit was ill.*

"So, Isaiah? You don't have anything to say now?," Sidney asks after realizing that I haven't responded to her announcement. Thought that my ear-to-ear smile would have said it all.

"My bad baby! I was lost in deep abstraction. We must get you some prenatal vitamins tomorrow. But uhh, we also must get married before you drop my *second shorty.* That way, we would have the same last name on the birth certificate. You down?"

Nothing else needed to be said as Sidney pulled me back on top of her. She instinctively began to unbutton my pants and pull my zipper down; giving me the hint to take off my designer clothes. In less than ten seconds, all our clothes vanished besides her Victoria Secret Black Friday G-string and my Calvin Klein boxers. I even allowed my feet to become exposed. Had something different planned for tonight and it was called, lovemaking.

While we were erotically kissing, I moved her panties to the side and with two fingers and started to tamper with the *walls* of her pussy. Just as I expected, her shit was like Niagara Falls. I had nine months to cherish the sultry effects of pregnant pussy.

"Naked" by *Marques Houston* was playing when I plopped her left areola into my "suction cup." *Really, I 'tripped out' and forgot that she was pregnant because once I did that, the sour taste of breast milk attacked my tongue.* This was my future wife though, so I did not take offense to the startling realization. Instead, I gave the same attention to her right areola as well. Regardless, my taste buds were numb from the Moscato anyway.

After I noticed that Sidney was clearly ready to *take all of me*, I took my boxers and her lingerie off. Completely naked, body to body. My dick was rock hard as it brushed up against her clitoris. Just that slight touch alone relieved a lot of tension from Sidney's body. I could tell by the way she moaned and melted underneath my grasp. Still with no penetration, I bridged any remaining gap between me and Sidney. With her ankles wrapped around my lower back and my forearms positioned underneath her body; accepting my solid eight inches was mandatory when that time came. I was going to prolong that actual time though. True love caused me to just want to get lost in her sea green eyes.

"You know that I am in love with you, right?," I asked Sidney after giving her a peck on the lips. Our bodies still locked together, preparing for "take off."

"I love you too baby," Sidney says breathing heavily while biting her bottom lip.

"How much do you love me?"

"A lot. Isaiah, please! I need it now…"

"What do you need?"

"I need you inside of me," she says guiding my dick into her *sweet spot.* Sidney's face was invaluable as my head broke the surface. She managed to utter out the word "shit" as her pussy began to embrace me.

Sidney gripped my back even tighter as if she would lose me by letting go. She clinched her pussy even closer together as I slowly pierced my way towards her first orgasm. Her nails ventured even deeper into my back, the deeper that my shaft went exploring into her personal territory.

"*Ahhh* fuck baby. I love this shit," Sidney moans out in a pleasurable rant. I thought that she was going to bite her lip off.

"No baby look at me. I want to see your eyes while you take this dick," I aggressively told her. As she opened her eyes, I started to accelerate my strokes. Making sure that every nerve ending in her pussy had the chance to feel my thrust. As I increased my speed, Sidney went into a violent rapture of ecstasy.

"*Mmmm* baby, just take it. Please just take it," she euphorically yells.

"Open your eyes, Sid. This is what you asked for," I said as I began pounding away at an overpowering pace.

"Oh, I'm sorry baby. *Ahhh* yes, I am sorry. Shit," Sidney says as my dick started to reach spots she probably didn't even know were there.

"*Mhmm*. This is what you want, right? You have to take it like a "G" now!"

"I'm going to take it like a *G*, baby. I am...," she recites letting the inner white girl up out of her.

"Whose pussy is this huh?," I ask not letting up the force of my sexual invasion.

"It's yours, baby... It's all yours!"

"I cannot hear you..."

"*Fuck* Izzy, its yours. Damn baby, please do not stop. I want it just like this. *Ahh* shit Izzy... Fuck this feels so good. Yes baby, you are the best. Please do not stop, I am about to *nut... Oh my God, oh my God... Ahh*," she screams out from the results of a blissful climax.

As Sidney reached a point of no return, I slowed my strokes to truly capture this moment. Her face was flushed with different emotions such as excitement, trust, and love. Watching Sidney enjoy an orgasm made me feel welcomed. That no matter what my status was in this world, she would always be willing to receive me in this manner. She did not even know about the $25,000 check yet- so in her mind, she was basically fucking a *broke nigga*. Sidney was down for me and the cause. She was satisfied with knowing that I am the last person that she would ever have sex with. I could never grow weary of this shit.

"Knocking The Boots" by *H Town* was playing when I decided to change up the tempo. True indeed, Sidney has caught her *first one* of the night; but I still believed she cheated. She did not take this dick like a "G." Missionary position left too much breathing room. I was now in the business of making her tap out.

"Here, get up.," I tell Sidney as her pussy liberated my dick. She unhooks her legs from around me and watches in astonishment as to what I am going to do next. I climbed behind her in the spooning position, with my right hand massaging the *Izzy B* tattoo. My dick was alert and stiff, waiting at the entrance to her "great lake." I used my right knee to push her leg back as far as possible. There was no evading this gratifying pain.

"Baby! Please do not try to kill me," Sidney says slowly while easing my penis inside of her.

"Sid, it's already too late for that. Brace yourself…" was my advice so she could prepare herself. Taking it easy on her was a foreign thought in my mind. I leveled my pelvic region so there would not be any other detour to her pussy. In one swooping move, I shoved my whole eight inches towards her belly button. I was trying go harder than the velocity of my Glock 23.

Out of the corner of my eye, I noticed that Sidney was gripping the edge of the bed and trying to hide her face in a pillow. *Fucking cheater, knew she could not take the dick.* Bet she thinks twice before taking this pussy away from me again.

"Nope Sidney, give me that. Grab my hand," I told her after throwing the pillow towards the floor. I was now metaphorically acting a donkey in that pussy. Long stroke after long stroke, Sidney was getting closer to speaking another language.

"*Ahh* baby, I can't take all of it. Let me get on top," Sidney passionately pleads.

"Hell no. Thought this was my pussy…?"

"It's all yours Izzy, I'm sorry. Shit, you a fool in it. I love this dick Yoo… don't stop," she sensually tells me.

"This is all your dick, Sid. I am going to serve this motherfucker to you all night. Shit! You have that *A1*", I said trying my hardest not to nut yet. The more I avoided ejaculation, the deeper my thrusts had traveled. The deeper that my thrusts had traveled meant the more strenuous my grip on that ass was. Due to Sidney's skin tone, I knew that she would have noticeable bruises on her ass for the next few days. The cost of love, passion, and rough sex.

"You like the way that I throw this pussy back? Don't you, baby?," Sidney taunts after realizing the influence her *juices* were having on me. Every time that I dove in, she would clamp her pussy muscles tight around my dick- then, letting loose every time that I would retreat. Damn near sending me over the edge. Knowing that I was close to "retirement," I cranked up and let go of my inhibitions. I wrapped my arms around her waist and became a heartless murderer of her insides.

"*Ahh* damn baby, that's the spot right there. Please do not stop. I need it, I need it... Shit, that's number two for the night" was all Sidney needed to say for me to release my pressure at the same time. For a few seconds, we both drifted off on a stimulating excursion. Caught up in this trance so intense that we both could have forgotten our names and purpose. All I knew was that being in this sexual envelope with Sidney was the greatest place on earth!

Once we came back to our senses, a chemistry lesson was proposed. I never believed in having a soul mate, until now. Me and Sidney did not say anything to each other. Still in the spooning position, we kissed and upon opening our eyes; something caused us to ludicrously begin to laugh. We laugh at the assumption that high school sweethearts never last. We laugh at the roach, crawling on the wall of this motel room. We laugh at all the tests that our union has surmounted. We laugh at our undeniable love for each other.

Sidney grabs my hand and intertwines it with hers. Upon placing our hands by her heart, I scoot closer not allowing my dick to leave her. This was a perfect match from heaven. A moment that I would always treasure!

-#-

After me and Sydney finished another round of energetic sex, we laid stock-stilled just to simply talk. Nothing about our conversation was stodgy. We talked about everything under the sun. From the events of these past three days to us expecting our second child, Felix Stone, my junctional meeting with Zeke and the $25,000 check he gave me. Sydney also informed me that Emily said that we could tarry in her two unfurnished rooms, under 3 simple conditions: we would have to pay her $150 a month for room and board, Sydney agrees to do her hair twice out that month, plus I have to hook her up with one of my partners. That last request seemed the most complex out of all her stipulations. Emily was "greener" than Sydney was. Sydney had to adapt to fucking with a thoroughbred street nigga over the years. The only person I could see myself hooking her up with was, Lor Jeff. All of my niggas were either broke and in the streets, getting money and in the streets or writing letters trying to get back on the streets.

"Wow, that's crazy baby. I want to meet him," Sydney says in reference to Ezekiel Brown. She was analyzing the check to make sure it wasn't counterfeit.

"So, what are you going to do with the money?"

"Yeah, I have been thinking about how to utilize it so the family can reap full benefits. How do you feel about this…?," I asked Sydney anticipating her input. This put a smile on her face.

"In my opinion, our main necessities right now is a home and vehicle. We already have about 10 grand in your checking account, so after tomorrow, we would be looking at around 35 large. Shit, we can get a two-bedroom tenement and pay that motherfucker up for the next two years. I saw a dope ass 2000 Ford Explorer, Eddie Bauer edition for $7,500. With the last, let's say $15,000- we could furnish the spot and save the rest for my junior. We set after that… Nothing else we can ask for…"

"Yeah that's a good idea baby. I like the way you use the word 'we' at least five times. But I don't know, it was just something else that came to mind. I love your plan though Isaiah if that's what you want to do."

"Well what's up Sid? Speak your peace. I want to know your thoughts so we can produce a mutual agreement on things. Your opinion matters. You're the yin to my yang of our family," I explained.

"I don't know Izzy... Call me crazy, but I think you should invest the money into your rap career!"

What the fuck? I could not believe my ears. I thought every woman's fantasy was having a family, a home to manage that family and a reliable vehicle to transport that family. Here I am, trying to provide the essentials and she deemed that matter as being unnecessary. Hell, I didn't even think about investing in my own music.

"Sid, are you serious right now…? Technically we don't even have anywhere to live unless we are shacked up with someone. Why wouldn't we get our own shit? I want to be able to hop out the pussy and get a glass of Kool-Aid, with no drawers on…"

Sydney burst out in laughter. "Baby you *geeking* Yooo… Look I totally understand the issue of independence and I feel where you are coming from. We should definitely get a whip, so we don't have to catch the subway to my doctor's appointments, like last time. But you know, like I know, that we would never be truly homeless. I'm just saying, I believe this is your moment…"

"My moment…," I carefully deliberate.

"Here, you have the floor. Explain!"

"Izzy you know this is your moment better than I do. You do not feel the momentum? Ever since the Showcase… You getting locked up… Everything that has happened since you been out. You don't just randomly come up on $25,000 and it supposedly came from your biological father that you have never met. This is called your moment. The worldly energies working in your favor. You're supposed to take advantage of shit like this. Look baby, I don't care what you do with the money; I am going to ride with you regardless. If you want to donate it all to a Jewish charity, I'm still not going to leave your side. For better or worse, rich, or poor- I'm going to ride no matter what. Those are just my thoughts on the shit…"

"Word up! So you must really believe in a nigga then? Like I can turn this $25,000 into 25 million…"

"Baby I believe you can do whatever you put your mind to… I also believe that you won't be happy, settling for some project building on Broadway, as the location to raise our two kids. I can see you now, complaining about roaches, noise, and violence. Emily has a nice spot, 'Ova East' off York Road, where we can crash at until you get your shit shaking. Just trust me on this baby, I got you. Do your thing. Don't worry about the homefront, I'm going to hold this bitch down. But look nigga, you better not leave me for a white girl, like all the other rappers do when they reach Superstar status!"

After a period of me guffawing, I pulled Sydney close and gave her a loitering kiss on the lips. Still haven't replied to her ultimatum yet.

"Nigga don't kiss me. I'm serious," she protests.

"Alright baby. Well what if I left you for like a Korean bitch… Would it be as bad?", I jokingly asked her.

"Nigga get the fuck off of me", Sydney screams after lightly elbowing me in my stomach.

"Shut up Yoo, know that I'm just fucking with you. Hey, let me put this in you," I say signaling that my dick got hard after she striked me. We were still laying under the comforter, naked, so it was nothing for me to slide back into her "juice box."

"Hell no. Eat my pussy first."

"Shit alright. You said that like I wasn't trying to taste you tonight anyway."

Ring… Ring… Ring…

Looking at my screensaver, I see a number that was unprecedented. On top of that, it was after midnight and niggas I sold weed to knew that shop was closed after 10P.M. Anything after that was considered family time!

I saw that Sidney was getting impatient, waiting for my tongue; so, I ignored the caller and prepared to give her *sensitive spot* an I.C.U treatment.

Just as I propped my head between her legs, this *bitch ass* phone started going off again. The sounds of my "*Hundred Dollars & A Dream!*" verse, bounced around the room.

Ring… Ring… Ring…

"Fuck Izzy, who keeps calling you?," Sidney asks obviously annoyed at the interruption.

"You have your Korean girlfriend fiending for some dick this late Izzy. Wow!"

"Stop playing with me Sidney, I have never even seen this number before. The area code is 212… I don't even know where that is."

"Well damn, answer the phone and tell them to stop calling."

"Shit alright, hold on… Hello?," I reluctantly acknowledged the caller.

"Yeah man. Is this Izzy B?," a distinctive but rather familiar voice asks me.

"Uhh… Yeah!"

"Look here young hopper, you stormed into my playground demanding ten minutes of my time. Now I'm coming to your zone and I need ten minutes of your time."

"Wait a minute, wait a minute. Who the fuck is this?," I irritably inquire overdosed on hostility.

"Ha… Ha ha," he chuckles.

"This is the guy trying to make your dreams a reality. You should thank Rosalyn because now I am going to give you a shot. Say Izzy B, this is Felix. Felix Stone!"

Made in the USA
Columbia, SC
06 October 2022